THORN

THORN

INTISAR KHANANI

HOT
KEY
BOOKS

First published in Great Britain in 2020 by
HOT KEY BOOKS
80–81 Wimpole St, London W1G 9RE
www.hotkeybooks.com

A CIP catalogue record for this book is available from the British Library.

ISBN: 978-1-4714-0872-4
Also available as an ebook and in audio

1

Typography by Corina Lupp
Printed and bound in Great Britain by Clays Ltd, Elcograf S.p.A.

Hot Key Books is an imprint of Bonnier Books UK
www.bonnierbooks.co.uk

For every girl who has ever doubted she has what it takes.

THORN

CHAPTER
1

"Try not to embarrass us," my brother says. "If you can."

I look out at the empty courtyard and pretend not to notice Lord Daerilin smirking to my left. He has always enjoyed my brother's barbs, especially so these past three years. The other nobles around us shift, though I can't tell if they're amused or impatient. Mother frowns, gaze trained on the gates. Perhaps she's preparing herself for the king's visit, or perhaps she's only thinking that there's little hope I won't embarrass her.

The thud of approaching hooves grows louder. It sounds like a storm drawing near, a steady, dull rumble that warns of heavy rains and lashing winds. I clasp my hands together tightly and wish this moment over.

The party trots through the open gates, the wooden walls echoing back the clatter of hooves on cobblestones, the jingle of tack. The first riders pull to the side, allowing those behind through. And through. I glance worriedly toward Mother, then

1

back at the riders. I count a score of men, all in light armor, before I realize there must be at least double that. At their center ride five men, all dressed in similar finery.

With no audible command, the whole crowd of horses and men resolves into formation, the mounted guards lining up two deep to form an aisle between us and the five men at their center. The noblemen dismount in fluid leaps, as if they have no use for hands or stirrups. I catch a glimpse of our stable master waiting to arrange for the horses, his brows shooting up, eyes bright with admiration.

"His Majesty, the king of Menaiya," one of his men announces as the nobleman who must be their king steps forward from their midst and bows slightly. I ignore the rest of his introduction, long lists of titles, and genealogy. Instead, I study the king. Though he must be older than my mother, the years have treated him well. He is tall and slim. He wears the traditional summer cloak of his people: a flowing, unhooded affair with arms and an open front, silver embroidery cascading along the edges and accenting the midnight-blue cloth. Beneath, he wears a knee-length tunic lightly embroidered with silver and stones, and the curious loose pants of his people. His hair falls free to his shoulders, black laced with silver, setting off the gentle brown of his face and softening an otherwise hawklike countenance. A fine tracery of wrinkles gathers at the corners of his eyes. He glances over our little crowd of nobles and smiles and there is nothing, absolutely nothing, in that smile.

"Her Majesty, queen dowager and regent of the kingdom of Adania," Steward Jerash announces in turn. Mother offers her own curtsy to the king, and we follow her lead. Even though she wears her finest brocade dress—too warm for this early in the fall—she still possesses barely half the majesty the king projects. But then, our kingdom is nothing compared with theirs, a patch of forest fortuitously protected by encircling mountains. Menaiya is a land of sweeping plains, southern farms, and northern forests. And soldiers. I swallow hard, training my eyes on the ground. We only have fifty men in our whole hall. The king has brought enough seasoned warriors to take our hall and add our kingdom to his as easily as a spare coin to his purse.

Although, if the kitchen rumors are true, he isn't here for that at all. Or if he is, it's a longer game he's playing.

Jerash introduces my brother next, who bows a little lower than the king did. And then it is my turn. I curtsy, aware of the king's scrutiny, the way the whole of his entourage has turned their gaze on me. I keep my eyes lowered and my breathing steady. Let him be kind and gentle, as my father was—and let him have taught his son to be the same.

"Princess Alyrra," the king says. I rise and lift my eyes to his. He studies me as if I were a prize goat, his gaze sliding over me before returning to my face, as cold and calculating as a butcher. "We have heard tell of you before."

"My lord?" My voice is steady and calm, as I've learned to make it when I'm only half frightened. For all my prayers, there's no sign of softer traits in the man before me.

"It is said you are honest. An unusual trait, it would seem."

Dread curls tight in my belly. I force some semblance of a smile to my lips. There is no other answer I can give that my family will not despise me for. My brother has gone rigid, his hands pressed flat against his thighs.

3

"You are most kind," my mother says, stepping forward.

The king watches me a moment longer, leaving my mother waiting. Just when I thought I might finally escape my history, how my family sees me, I find I am mistaken. There is no better future to hope for now. The king has come for me, knowing full well I am nothing to my family.

He turns to my mother, offering her a courtly smile. At her invitation, he accompanies her up the three stairs and through the great wooden doors of our hall. My brother and I trail behind him, a mix of our nobles and the king's entourage on our heels.

"Honest Alyrra," my brother mocks, his voice loud enough for those nearest us to hear. "What a very clever, sophisticated princess you must be."

I continue on as if I did not hear. It is going to be a long week, watching my back and hiding around corners. With so many guests, the wine and ale will flow freely, which will only make things worse. Even so, it is not my brother's ire that fills my thoughts as I walk, but what the king intends in his visit, and why.

I manage to slip away when the king retires to his rooms to refresh himself after the ceremonial welcome gifts have been exchanged and light refreshments consumed. He will meet with my mother, brother, and their Council of Lords before dinner. Even though it's unlikely my brother will come after me at once, I take no chances, seeking out one of the few places he would never stoop to check.

The kitchen is caught firmly in the throes of preparation for tonight's feast. Cook shouts orders as she spices a pot. Dara,

Ketsy, and three other serving girls hustle to keep up with the chopping, slicing, and gutting. A soldier attempts to knead dough by squishing it between his fingers, and poor little Ano, who only gets pulled into the kitchen in dire emergencies, struggles valiantly to tie the roast to a spit.

"Give me that," I tell the soldier, rescuing the dough from him. "You help Ano with the goat."

He throws me a grateful glance and joins Ano by the fire. Ketsy perches on a bench beside me, peeling carrots.

"What are they like?" I ask, glancing at her.

She may be just barely out of her childhood, but she understands at once. "Polite. They aren't making trouble and haven't bothered the older serving girls as yet—not like *some* men who chase them whether they like it or not. But they've only been here a few hours. We'll see."

So we will. It's hard to say how far the Menaiyans' manners will stretch over the week. We'll get a full sense of them yet.

"Dara?" I ask, glancing at the older girl across the table from us.

"Oh, I'll be serving them dinner," she says with a half smile, her eyes on the peas she's shelling. "I'll tell you what I think after that. Anything in particular you want me to pay attention to?"

"How many speak our language," I say, flipping the dough over and starting to knead again. "If they say anything about their prince. What kind of man he is." If he is as shrewd and ruthless as his father, I add silently.

She nods. "I'll see what I can find out."

"What do you think you're doing?" Cook demands loudly.

I twist to find Cook regarding me darkly, hands on her hips.

Behind her, the roast is spitted and turning over the fire, the soldier nowhere to be seen.

"It's all right," I say. "I'm just kneading the dough."

"It most certainly *isn't* all right," she snaps, eyes narrowing. "I'll not have the king think we are in such desperate straits that our own princess must help in the kitchens. Dara can take the dough. You go sit in the gardens or do whatever it is that great ladies do."

"I've no idea what great ladies do," I say, pulling my bowl away from Dara as she comes around the table toward me. "I'm only a middling sort of lady, and our gardens are all herbs. They're hardly worth sitting in."

"Give it here," Dara says, making a swipe for the bowl.

"You'll give Dara that bowl or you'll not have breakfast tomorrow," Cook says with a glint in her eye. I hesitate, but she has made good on such threats before. "What if His Majesty gets word you're in here with us, hmm?"

"Oh, very well," I say, surrendering the bowl to a smirking Dara.

"Go on now," Cook admonishes me. "I'll let you help again after . . ." She trails off, as aware as I am that there may not be an after. "Go on now, child," Cook repeats, her voice gentling.

I choose my path carefully from the kitchens, giving a wide berth to the meeting rooms, as well as the main hall. This first day's discussion will likely center around the state of our two kingdoms and the relation between them. Each monarch will get a measure of the other. No doubt Mother and her council will harp on about the deplorable condition of the road through the high passes, and how it ought to be better shored up. But, while we rely on our trade with Menaiya, they have much more significant trading partners. I can't imagine the king worrying overmuch about the one road through the mountains to a tin-cup kingdom. He certainly won't obsess over it with the single-minded zeal of my mother and her council. Perhaps he'll be so disgusted with the discussion he'll shorten his visit and leave tomorrow.

One can hope.

Only I do not think he is used to giving up what he wants. If only I knew why he wants *me* for his son. Especially when he was so quick to mock me before our court.

I reach my room without mishap and bolt the door behind me. I would much rather go for a ride, but it is too close to evening and I don't dare arrive late to the feast. It will be hard enough to stay in Mother's good graces as it is. And anyhow, my brother may try looking for me at the stables.

So I dig out my two other best dresses, brush them off, and inspect them for signs of wear. I have three I keep for special occasions, and I've already worn the best for the king's arrival. After all, it's not as if that many foreign kings come visiting. Three dresses are enough for the yearly assemblies and the feasts when my mother's vassals visit, though I suspect the king and his court would expect more. I shrug and settle down to mend a fraying hem.

Jilna checks on me as the day fades. She has been in our employ as long as I can recall, her responsibilities shifting over the years. When my father died, it was she I went to for succor, and as I've grown, she's become the closest thing I have to a lady's maid.

"Cook is making an awful ruckus down there." She runs her hands over the repaired hem. "Did you fix this?"

"Just now. What's she upset about?"

"The dough didn't rise, so she had to start another batch, and the roast isn't cooked through yet, and any number of other things." Jilna straightens, her worn face easing into a smile. "I'm not sure if she just likes grumbling, or if it's her way of ensuring she gets complimented when everything turns out fine."

"A bit of both, I expect."

"Ha!" Jilna laughs and lays out the dress on my bed. "You'll need jewelry too."

"What for?"

"So you look more like a princess and less like a well-dressed scullery maid."

For all Jilna's efforts, I realize how shabby I must look in my old dress with my string of pearls and my three gold rings as I join my family in the small gathering room beside the hall, waiting for the king to enter. Mother still wears her brocade dress, a massive gold brooch pinned to her breast. My brother wears the long gold chains that were once our father's, his arms crossed over his broad chest, his boots planted firmly. And the king will wear his wealth not in gold but in the muted richness of the fabric of his clothes, the perfect finish of his boots. It is a much more subtle and certain majesty.

"He's coming," Mother says to my brother, voice sharp. "Smile."

They both do, bright and cheery and falsely welcoming. The king, entering with the two other men who are his vassals, glances at them with an answering curve of his lips. Then his gaze turns to me. I look back steadily, wondering what he expects, what he is looking for. His eyes, hard as onyx, give me no answer.

When he speaks, it is to Mother, a quiet greeting that allows us to move forward. I follow them into the hall for dinner and take my usual seat as the rest of our party settles.

"Trying to look your part?" The loud, contemptuous voice is unmistakable. Not that I could forget him. For three years now I have been forced to sit beside my mother's most highly ranked vassal, and the father of my own personal nemesis.

"Lord Daerilin," I say, risking a glance at him. "I see you are wearing your velvet doublet."

Daerilin turns a mottled pink but keeps going. "It's a pity you couldn't put on something finer for such a guest as this. Especially when he's come all this distance for you."

"Has he?" I ask, managing to let my tone betray only mild curiosity.

My chest feels hollow. I force myself to breathe, to keep my expression neutral. For all that I've discussed this with my friends from among the servants, hearing Daerilin say it aloud chills me. Once it seemed only half real, a strange and unlikely possibility, a fairy-tale escape from a family that bears me little affection. That was before. Now there is no arguing with the reality of the king, cunning and cold and here for me.

"I would have thought he'd bring the prince with him, then," I continue. It takes all my presence of mind to keep my fingers from clutching the stem of my goblet.

"And leave his court to play at politics on their own, when the Family is only just holding their nobles and mages in check? Hardly." Daerilin grimaces, reaching for his knife. "How you are related to your mother is beyond me." At his cue, a servant steps forward and carves three slices of roast goat. She places them on my plate before serving him, though I've made no move to lift my knife. It's been an unspoken rule, since that day three years ago, that the servants see to my needs first. A subtle but consistent statement of loyalty that never fails to irk Daerilin.

I glance toward the soldiers' tables surreptitiously. With their leather-and-bronze armor glinting in the firelight and ebony hair pulled up into tight knots, the foreign soldiers stand out like hawks among sparrows, the hilts of their weapons dark against their hips. Our own warriors and women look pale and washed-out beside them, our skin and hair so much lighter. And while our men wear their swords and daggers as well, with friendship bands binding hilt to scabbard, they have none of the practiced grace of the Menaiyans when they walk.

As I study them, I catch the eye of the foreign captain. Like the other soldiers, he wears his long hair in a smooth knot. Without a fall of hair to soften his features, he looks weathered and hard, his eyes flat, ungiving. I look away quickly, turning back to Daerilin. At least he might tell me what my mother hasn't deigned to share.

"We are hardly a strong ally for them," I observe as casually as I can. "I don't see why the king would come so far for me."

"Perhaps they're just looking for a mouse to snap up," he says. "Their royalty do seem to die with impressive frequency. They wouldn't want to upset their closer allies by accidentally killing off the bride." He lifts his goblet in a mock toast. "I daresay no one would raise an outcry if something were to happen to you."

I look down at my plate, the roast still untouched. Perhaps Daerilin is only baiting me. God knows he has enjoyed his taunts these last years. But the Menaiyan queen did die under mysterious circumstances a year ago, and there are precious few members of their royal family left now.

The servant at our back steps forward, refilling my goblet with juice for all that it's nearly full, and for just a moment I feel her touch my elbow, a reassurance that I'm not alone. I smile for her and force myself to take a bite of the roast.

"I hear," Daerilin says lightly, "that this Prince Kestrin is not one to be crossed. Quite a temper he has when he is displeased."

I wish that I could come up with a snide rejoinder, but my wits fail me. Better to remain silent than to continue opening myself to his jibes. When I make no further response, Daerilin turns to discuss a territorial dispute in the south with the lady to his left. The serving girl behind me slips me one of my favorite meat pies, and then, when I cannot manage much of that, a sweet pastry, her hand brushing my shoulder as she steps back.

My gaze returns to the foreign warriors. Their captain eats sparingly, one hand resting lightly on the hilt of his dagger. He watches me continually, unapologetically, as if he intends to take his full measure of me this night. No matter how long I look away, when I glance back I find his eyes on me. I doubt there is little he misses. Eventually I drop my hands to my lap and give up all pretense of eating.

CHAPTER

2

The following morning, I call on my mother as she dresses for a second day of meetings with the king. She waves her maids away at last and peers into the oval mirror that hangs on her wall. It is one of her prized possessions, framed in silver and polished to a shine, just large enough to show her face. She smooths her elaborately coiffed hair, her eyes finding mine through the glass.

"To what do I owe the honor of your presence?" she asks with cool amusement, as if just noticing me.

I gather my courage. "I wish to inquire as to the king's purpose in visiting us."

"Oh?" Mother smiles, her hazel eyes hooded. "Has it finally occurred to you to ask?"

"I've heard rumors," I say cautiously. And if I had any question about them, they were answered last night by Daerilin. Still,

I want to hear it from her. In truth, I wanted her to tell me before I had to ask, fool that I am.

She sighs. "Prince Kestrin is of an age to marry. His father has come to assess your worth as a bride."

"My worth," I repeat. "And what is that?"

"Not much," Mother says bluntly. "It is the only issue that gives me pause. We cannot be sure why he would settle for you." She must have discussed this in detail with her Council of Lords, and even they can find no reason for the king's interest. The thought raises the hair at the back of my neck.

"What has he said, though?" I ask as my mother turns away. "Surely you spoke of it yesterday?"

She pauses, her mouth pressed into an expression of distaste. "He gave only two reasons, neither of which I believe."

"What are they?"

"That he wished for an alliance outside of their own court, so Prince Kestrin chose you of his own accord. And"—Mother meets my gaze, her eyes darkening with anger—"that you are known to be honest."

"Oh." In an effort to deflect her fury, I ask, "Why would Prince Kestrin choose me?"

"He wouldn't."

I bow my head. Perhaps Daerilin is right: they seek a bride no one will miss should she die unexpectedly. My family has long considered me dispensable, my only use as a tool to secure a political alliance. In Menaiya, I will not even have that value.

"I hope we will reach an agreement by tomorrow," Mother says finally. She is beautiful in the morning sunlight, her hair glowing deep brown, her features smooth and her anger hidden. I can find nothing to say, looking at her and trying to understand. Tomorrow? Betrothed? When we still don't know why?

"Until then, stay out of the way." She turns back to her mirror. When I do not move, she gestures sharply to the door. "Go on, then. I've more than enough to worry about without you underfoot. And do not speak to the king if you can avoid him. There's no need for him to know any more clearly what a simpleton you are."

I leave in silence. For a moment, I stand in the hallway, considering another whole day closed up in my room, and then I turn my footsteps toward the stable. If my mother wants me out from underfoot, it is but my duty to obey.

Redna saddles Acorn for me at once. "Your brother was just here looking for you," she says softly, guarding her words from the Menaiyan soldiers tending to their horses farther down the main aisle of the stable. "Best ride out at once."

"I'll spend the day out," I assure her.

"There's dried fruit and a flask of water in your saddlebags."

I smile my thanks. Redna pats my arm and hands me the reins.

I take the path that cuts away from the village to the woods, keeping Acorn to a steady trot until we reach the forested paths. The trees stand spaced well apart from each other, the leaf-littered floor dappled with late summer sunlight. I guide Acorn to a dell we have often visited.

Leaving as I did, I have nothing with me to do today, no book to read nor embroidery to finish, nor do I seek any of the herbs that grow among the trees and in the clearings for our wise-woman's use. Instead, I sit on a sun-warmed stone, listening to the soft buzz of insects and the swish of Acorn's tail as he grazes, and think about the king, and his son, and my mother's words.

I cannot find out the king's motivations, and if neither my mother nor her lords can either, then it's unlikely I'll find an answer out here in the woods. But I do know that my mother fully expects the betrothal to go forward. What I must think on now is just how I intend to present myself to the king in order to escape his contempt as long as possible. He may speak of honesty as if it were a good thing, but his words were a political maneuver. He laid out my worth before the court with a few pleasant words, that he might watch their reaction. He'll find me to be as stupid as my family does soon enough, if he doesn't already. As will his son. And I do not know what I can do to protect myself.

As morning ebbs to noontime, a light breeze starts up.

"Old friend," I say, turning my head toward it. "Is that you?"

The Wind answers with a puff of summer. *Here.*

I smile. The Wind has visited me in this dell since I was a child. I learned quickly that it did not speak to anyone else, and over time it has become both my closest confidant and my biggest secret. It's hardly an appropriate thing to visit with woodland spirits—even if this one is nowhere near as capricious as the old tales would have me believe. Now, I say, "The king of Menaiya has come to visit."

The Wind ruffles my skirts. From my perch on a rock, I watch the few blades of grass bend beneath its gentle influence. *Visit?*

"Mother hopes he will betroth me to his son, Prince Kestrin." I think of Menaiya with its sweeping central plains and tongue-twisting language—a language of which I have only a rudimentary knowledge. I cannot imagine living there, in a city with no forests to wander and no one to speak with, no one but a prince I do not know. When I lift my hand to pat down a stray lock of hair, I realize my fingers are trembling. I clench my hands together tightly, pressing them into my lap.

The Wind lifts up and brushes back my hair. *Do not fear.*

I cock my head, considering. It is rare for the Wind to string words together, which means it must find this situation of grave importance. I smile. What could the Wind know of marriage?

"I've always expected that I'd have to marry eventually, to someone I didn't really know. But I—I'd hoped it would be someone who might come to care for me, someone with kindness in his heart." I think of the king's first mocking words to me, and his captain's cold assessment, and the distant court, and find it suddenly difficult to breathe. "I am afraid," I finally admit to the Wind, "of what will happen to me there. If I can even survive, as so many of their royal family have not." As none of their women have.

The Wind falls still. I wonder if it can understand, or if it too is lost for words.

I start back to the hall well before dinner, the Wind whispering through the woods with me, leaving me only as the path reaches the main road. Redna greets me with a nod as I enter the gates, deftly reaching for Acorn's bridle to help me dismount.

"They're still in the meeting rooms," she tells me. "But you'd best stay out of the halls."

This time, Cook does not send me away. Instead, she gestures to a stool beside one of the tables, informs me I'm not to work, and leaves me there. No one here will mention my presence outside of the kitchen, not with the king here and my brother on the prowl.

"Have you learned any more from them?" I ask Dara. "Have they mentioned their prince?"

"No, there's only a handful as speak our language, and they aren't given to gossip. Their captain, Sarkor's his name, keeps a keen watch on them."

I have no doubt of that.

"But they don't kick the dogs and they don't waste their food," she says. "I won't mind them staying here as long as they need, truth to tell."

And I wouldn't mind them leaving, if only they will leave me behind.

The next day, on my way to our hall's temple, I make a dire mistake. I assume the meetings will continue, that I can pass down that corridor without concern, but as I near the entrance to the meeting room, the door swings open. I step back, my stomach lurching as I meet my brother's eyes. He smiles.

"Alyrra, what a surprise." He crosses the hall and his hand closes tightly around my forearm. "Why don't we walk a little?"

I nod woodenly, aware that I don't dare pull away before the curious gazes of the other nobles leaving the meeting room. My brother leads me down the hall, the pressure of his grip a warning of what is to come.

"Princess Alyrra," an unfamiliar voice calls from behind us. My brother and I turn together to see the king striding toward us. "I see you wish to converse with your brother. I hope you will not mind my taking a few minutes of your time first?"

"Of course not, my lord," my brother says for me, releasing my arm. He turns to me, his smile a dark promise. "We can always speak later. I'll find you."

The king nods toward my brother and gestures me on. I fall into step with him.

"Do you have gardens here?" he asks. "Somewhere quiet to speak?"

"Only herb gardens, my lord."

"Good enough," he says, his teeth flashing between his lips. I lead him down to the back entrance to the gardens, and we walk along between plots of dill, thyme, and chives. I wait, knowing he will speak when he is ready.

"How much does your mother confide in you?" he asks as we near the middle of the gardens.

I slide a look at him from the corner of my eye. "Enough. My lord."

His lips quirk, the first true smile I have seen from him. "Is that honest?"

I pause beside a bed of borage. "How much do I need to know, my lord? You are here seeking a wife for your son."

"I am," he agrees. "How often do you participate in the discussions between your mother and the council?"

"I don't, my lord. You should know I am not . . ." I hesitate, aware that I have no place telling this king what he should or should not know. Or jeopardizing such an alliance for my land.

"Not what?"

I struggle to find an appropriate way to finish. "Not—it is not thought my place to attend such meetings."

"You would never inherit the throne?"

I could inherit, it is true, but I doubt the council would allow it given my history—and certainly not now that I might marry into another royal family, one that would be happy to add our lands to their own. Either way, should my brother die, the council would certainly pass over me in favor of our nearest cousin. "It is unlikely," I say finally.

"I doubt that," the king says. "It has been my experience that even young men die. What you mean to say is your council would not accept you should your brother die without issue and you were yet unwed. Why?"

If he knows all the answers, why is he asking? I look him in the eye and quip, "Perhaps I am too honest, my lord."

He laughs. "And too straightforward. You will have to learn to play with your words more." He reaches out, his fingertips brushing my arm where my brother held me. I flinch back reflexively, as if the bruises have already darkened—as if he could see them through my sleeve. He watches me, his eyes glinting in the sunlight. "Once you are Menaiya's," he says, "your brother will never hurt you again."

He dips his head in a bow and leaves me standing among the herbs.

I wait in my chamber all the following day, held in place by Mother's warning of the upcoming betrothal, the king's words my only company. I no longer know what to make of him. Was his promise of protection from my brother calculated to encourage me to overlook his first words to me? Does he think to win my gratitude now in order to use me for his own ends once I arrive in Menaiya? Or does he actually care that I not be harmed?

When the knock I've been expecting sounds, it is late afternoon. Steward Jerash waits to escort me down to the meeting rooms. It is the first time I've entered them since the king arrived.

Jerash announces my entrance to the room and bows low. I feel at once the sharpness of my mother's regard, the low-browed malice of my brother's. They sit with the king at the head of a great table. Before them, seated in chairs or standing respectfully, are arrayed my mother's closest vassals as well as the king's own retainers. I curtsy. When I rise, I meet my mother's gaze.

She smiles at me, the smile of a merchant having sold her wares. "Alyrra, the king of Menaiya has offered a match for you with his son. Will you accept?"

I have had time enough to find the words for my answer. They are as much for the king as for my family. "I will do only as you wish, Mother."

My brother, sitting beside her, frowns.

The corners of the king's eyes crinkle slightly, as if he is faintly amused. I will be loyal, my answer tells him. And the betrothal will transfer my allegiances to his family. Perhaps this will be enough to gain his protection in his own court.

"It is a good alliance, daughter," my mother replies smoothly.

"Then I accept." My words rustle through the room, carried by the shifting of nobles, the soft exhalations of satisfaction. There could be no other answer to give.

A court scribe lays a sheaf of papers on the table before me. I turn through the sheets quickly, noticing only that my mother has granted me some border estates in our kingdom for the duration of my life, something to still anchor me to Adania. The last page has a few lines of writing, leaving space for our signatures.

I sign carefully, pleased at how smoothly I write, at the way my hand does not tremble as I put down the quill and straighten.

The scribe places the papers before the king. As the king reaches for the quill, I see neither satisfaction nor sorrow in his expression. There is nothing to tell me his emotions; his composure is complete. He leans forward to sign his name in lieu of his son's, and then Lord Daerilin and another lord step forward to sign as witnesses, followed by the two lords accompanying the king. The scribe collects the papers and steps back, and the betrothal is complete.

The king turns to me once more and smiles, though I cannot tell whether it is a true smile or a courtly one. "I am pleased to have gained a daughter," he says, his words clear and carrying.

"I am honored to be welcomed to your family, my lord." Practiced words, dangerously empty sounding. I had not meant for them to carry so little weight.

I meet the king's gaze, willing him to see me as strong and capable and loyal. But he assessed what my family thought of me upon his arrival, and he has taken his own measure of me since then. The only thing that gives me hope is the promise he made in the herb gardens, and that may have been as much a battle strategy as a kindness. Yet it is all I have to rely on.

My mother speaks then, about the honor such an alliance brings to our land. A moment later, she dismisses me.

The rest of the evening blurs together. Jilna dresses me for dinner, adorning my neck and wrists with jewels from the treasury. Mother announces the betrothal to the hall as soldiers and servants alike cheer. Toasts are made to the new couple's good health. Even Lord Daerilin makes a speech on the long-standing friendship of our two kingdoms, yet I do not quite hear it as I sit beside him, cannot quite recall his words a moment later.

I leave the hall at the end of the meal, my head ringing with the din of so many people, my eyes tearing from exhaustion. I grow aware in a strange, detached way that there have been footsteps behind me for some time. It occurs to me to wonder who follows me, and then a hand closes on my arm and spins me around, shoving me against the wall.

"Think you're something special now, don't you?" My brother towers over me, his shoulders blocking out the light, his breath stinking of ale. His eyes are red-rimmed, narrowed with drink and anger.

"Brother," I say stupidly. His hands tighten on my arms, pressing me against the wall, his face hovering just above mine.

"Going to be queen, are you now? Think you're better than us?" His fingers dig into my flesh, nails pressing through the thin fabric of my sleeves to gouge my skin with bruising intensity.

"No," I waver, fear breaking through the bleakness that has gripped me. I need to get away from him. Now—before the Menaiyans see us, before he hurts me in a way that will be difficult to hide.

"Of course not." His hair falls over his forehead as he leans even closer, speaking into my ear. "You're only doing what you're told, aren't you?"

"It was never my choice," I say, trying desperately to pull out of his grip.

He laughs, tightening his hold on me until a soft cry breaks from my lips. "Oh no, I don't think you're going anywhere quite yet."

"Brother—"

"Do you know what a prince does when he marries a little witch like you?" He shoves me hard against the wall. Only the bulk of my hair bound up at the back of my head saves me from cracking my skull against the stone. "There are stories, lovely stories. The poor little princess is found floating in the well one morning, tripped and fell in quite by accident. Or they find her body beneath the palace walls—cast herself off in a fit of madness. These things happen, you see. Terribly sad. But the alliance stands strong, and the family mourns, and the prince remarries." He laughs, winding his hand into the hair at the base of my neck, forcing my head back so that I must meet his gaze.

"I expect he'll have his fun with you. Perhaps he'll throw you to his soldiers and let you choose your future: a brothel or a knife for your throat. You'd like that, wouldn't you?"

"He's not like that," I whisper, trembling. *Please, don't let him be like that.*

"Are you calling me a liar?"

I swallow a sob, shaking my head. His fingers yank at my hair; loose hairpins scrape my scalp.

"Do you think your betrothal will protect you from me, little sister? After what you did? You *dare* to insult me?" His voice rises as he speaks, spittle spraying my cheek.

"Is the princess unwell?"

My brother starts and twists to look over his shoulder at the speaker.

I sag against the wall as he drops his hand, the coiled weight of my hair dangling from what few pins still hold it.

"This doesn't concern you," he snarls.

"If the princess requires an escort to her room, I would be pleased to provide it," the unknown speaker says, his voice carrying the faint lilt of Menaiya.

I sidle past my brother and find myself facing the foreign captain, Sarkor, who watched me continually through that first dinner. His face is all planes and hard angles in the dimness of the hall. Is he actually challenging my brother?

"Do you require an escort?" Sarkor asks me with a slight dip of his head, as if he were my dancing partner. From his left ear a small silver hoop gleams in the darkness, set with an emerald.

It takes me two tries to get my words out. "N-no. Thank you." I take another step alongside the wall, then another, the captain watching me impassively, my brother tense with fury. I turn and begin walking, my feet uncertain beneath me. It is only a temporary escape. When my brother finds me again, he will be doubly angry. Ruthless.

Behind me, the captain begins to speak, his voice too low to pick out the words. I can barely keep from breaking into a run as I turn the corner to my room. What if my brother has gotten away from him already? And then I do run, pelting down the hall to my room. I slam the door shut and shoot the bolt home. My breath rattles in my chest. I lean my forehead against the door, half listening for the approach of booted feet.

When Jilna comes a half hour later, she knocks thrice, calling her name that I might know it is only her.

I sit hunched on my bed, listening, but I do not let her in, cannot bear to be touched, to be spoken to now, to have my brother's violence made real by her presence.

She is used to me, used to these things, and when I do not answer she leaves.

I undress slowly, awkwardly. I run my fingers over the bruises on my arms, then brush out my hair, careful of the tender spots where my scalp still aches. But I cannot wipe my brother's words from my memory, cannot escape the echoes of his voice.

It is long and long before I sleep.

CHAPTER
3

Four Menaiyan soldiers snap to attention as I leave my room the following morning. I stop short, my heart in my throat. They flank my door and the opposite wall, making a perfectly balanced quad. Each of them is easily as tall as my brother, and quite possibly more versed in violence. I do not know how long they have been waiting here.

But their captain defended me. I hold that thought as I watch them. Perhaps he sent them here as a further safety for me. They neither look at me nor speak, and after an uncertain breath I continue walking. They fall into step behind me.

I knew from my studies that all of the Menaiyan forces are broken down into quads: four men with a balance of skills among them. I knew this, but I had not thought of it when the king arrived with so many men. Nor had I thought of it when the king promised me his protection. Now there is no forgetting it.

Throughout the morning, they stay with me no matter where

I go. When I pass my brother in the hallway, the soldiers do not pause to bow to him, their steps behind me steady. The glance my brother gives me is filled with fury. If he finds a way past my guard, I don't doubt I will feel the full force of his wrath.

Only when I enter the hall for lunch do the soldiers leave me to sit on the dais by myself. Still, I can feel their eyes on me from where they sit at their table and I know that they will follow me out when I finish. Now that I am theirs, as the king said, they will guard me as one of their own. For all that I'm grateful, their silent presence leaves me on edge.

After lunch, the king goes out riding with my brother. In their absence, my mother calls me to her rooms to select fabric for my new wardrobe. She bides her time, waiting until the servants have been sent off on errands before she speaks to me.

"An interesting fact has come to my attention." She taps her finger against a length of rose-colored linen and frowns. "Linen may be too common a cloth to wear at court; we'll only have two traveling outfits made of it. Fetch a darker rose to match with this."

"Yes, Mother." I move to where the remaining linens are piled, my hand drawn to a gentle cream. It would look lovely paired with—

"Not the cream," Mother says irritably. "The darker rose."

I let go of the cream with a twinge of regret, and set aside the darker rose as commanded.

She gestures to the next batch of cloth, precious cotton brought up from the south, and says, as if to take me by surprise, "A quad of Menaiyan soldiers has been shadowing you."

I keep my head bent as I lift up the cottons. An interesting fact indeed. "They were outside my door this morning."

"Are they outside now?"

"They followed me here."

"Do they think I will attack you? Or that we cannot keep you safe ourselves?" Mother rises and reaches for the cottons, eyes flashing.

I let her take them, anger blossoming in my breast. Mother has never kept me safe from my brother. The only time I can remember not fearing him was before my father's death. "I expect so."

She stiffens, drops the cloth, and slaps me. The blow is not hard—at least it does not have half the force of my brother's blows. But still, it jerks my face to the side and brings tears to my eyes.

My mother stands before me, her face flushed and blotchy, nostrils flared in anger. She does not look beautiful at all. Now I see her as I never have before. She is no different from my brother. The same thoughts run through her, the same wishes propel her forward, the same passions guide her actions. She is as uncertain and insecure and small as he. I don't know why I never truly saw it before, or why the realization doesn't frighten me now. Instead I feel a strange mirth rising in me, in direct counterpoint to the pain from her blow. The sound bubbles up, bursting from my lips to fill the room.

"Mother," I say, my voice light with laughter. "You are not as wise as my brother. He is careful not to leave marks that others might see."

She lifts her chin, nostrils flared. "I will not be treated thus by my own kin."

"It is you who have struck me," I point out. "Not the other way around."

"You understand me perfectly."

"I do." I meet her gaze, aware that I have never fought her so before. I feel the same sweet rush as I did the first time I rode Acorn through the forests alone at the urging of my father. My father, who never struck me, who would sit with me and tell me stories, and spoke of honor as if it meant something more than protecting his pride through his politics.

Mother smiles suddenly, the cool beauty of her mask settling back into place. "I see there is more to you than I thought. Very good, Alyrra. You will need your wits about you to survive in Menaiya." She returns to her seat. "Pick up the cottons."

I bend to retrieve the cloth, the heady sense of success already fading as my thoughts center on Menaiya. "I'll need to take a maid with me, won't I?" I ask. Whatever support I can bring with me will be vital.

"A maid," Mother agrees. "And a companion for the trip. We cannot send you alone with an escort of men."

"I was thinking—"

"You will take Valka with you."

I stare at her, aghast. "Mother! Not *Valka*—"

"Enough. She will be your companion until you reach Tarinon, at which point you may do with her what you wish. But you are not to send her back."

"You know what lies between Valka and me. I can't have her as my companion." I would no more trust her than I would a cat with a mouse. I grapple for an argument against Valka. "How could Daerilin agree to let her go?"

Even I can hear the desperation in my voice. Valka is Lord Daerilin's only daughter, and the sole reason for his hatred of me. It's inconceivable he'd agree to such a scheme, unless he too finds his daughter utterly dispensable now that she has lost all worth in the court.

My mother closes her eyes in long-suffering frustration. "Find her a husband, Alyrra. She must marry among peers and you destroyed such hopes here. It is up to you to get rid of her."

"*I* did not destroy those hopes for her—she did. You know what she did," I say, working to keep my voice calm.

"I am well aware of what each of you did. Pocketing a trinket has no comparison to betraying one's vassal or peer in the manner you did. The Menaiyan king is a fool for speaking of your *honesty* when your actions speak to your disloyalty and stupidity."

I take a slow breath, knowing I need to change the course of this conversation. Mother will never forgive my actions on that day. I long ago gave up any such hope. I tried at first, spoke to her earnestly, explained how I had seen Valka with the stolen sapphire brooch before its owner even knew it was missing. When Valka blamed a serving girl for the crime, enjoining the guards to arrest her, I couldn't keep silent. But my mother has never forgiven me for publicly humiliating Valka.

"They would have hanged that servant for a *trinket*," I say now, because I cannot help myself.

"Do you truly think I care?" Mother demands. "After all this time, do you think I will trade the honor and dignity of my vassal for one useless servant?"

No. Perhaps even then, I'd known it. Perhaps that was why I'd ordered the guards to search Valka instead, and so all the nobles and servants gathered saw them pull the brooch from her pocket.

"It is because of you Valka has lived in disgrace these last three years, never leaving her father's lands," Mother says, her voice tight.

The serving girl left the hall as well, fleeing before anyone remembered her, but that doesn't bear mentioning.

"You know how your brother looked on her. You *know* what we hoped."

I know well, for the very next day my brother first pushed me down a flight of stairs. At least after that, the servants were always kind to me. With quick looks, flicks of their fingers, they warned me when my brother was near.

"I am sorry for it," I say now. "I wish she had not blamed the servant."

"*I* wish I had a daughter whom I could trust not to destroy this alliance with the Menaiyans. If you are sent home, for whatever reason, my *honest* daughter," Mother says, her voice soft, "know that I will have no further use for you."

I nod. It is no more than I expected, but it still hurts.

"Must I bring Valka? I cannot trust her not to betray me there," I say, making one last attempt. "She despises me enough to undermine the alliance."

"Then arrange a match between her and some Menaiyan noble who lives far from the court. It is your responsibility to see to her future, and you will." She turns her attention back to the cottons. "The blue," she says. "Pair it with white."

After my mother dismisses me, I visit the hall temple, my quad remaining on guard just outside the door, and then go to my room. I don't want to trail soldiers behind me everywhere I go. Will the quad stay on past the king's departure? I stand at my window, running through the possibilities, and just what my brother will do when he finally slips past their guard.

Jilna arrives as the evening deepens, come to hurry me into one of my better gowns for dinner. She gives my cheeks a good pinch to bring back their color.

"You look terrible," she admonishes me. "Like yesterday's porridge left out all night. You don't want the king to think you're unhappy with this, do you?"

I wince. "No."

"Good, then. Keep your chin up, smile, and get to the hall at once. They're holding the feast in your honor."

I follow Jilna's injunctions and take my seat at the high table with a smile that hurts my face. Tonight is the official betrothal celebration; the food and drink will last till the darkest hours of night. A troupe of performers makes a grand entrance, somersaulting and leaping down the hall to stand before the royal dais. They juggle apples and daggers in dizzying patterns, tell bawdy jokes, and engage in mock fights that show off their tumbling skills.

The Menaiyan warriors observe the performance with raised eyebrows and occasional glances at one another. When they do laugh, their faces are not kind. I watch them, wondering what amusements they are accustomed to, and wish that our old troubadour had offered the night's entertainment instead. Though his voice has begun to waver, his ballads are yet things of beauty.

By night's end, the watching and wondering has drained me, leaving me brittle, empty. As I leave the dais, the members of my quad slip away from their table to follow me back to my room.

Their faces are familiar now, though I have yet to learn their names.

A bulky package waits for me in my room, wrapped in velvet, resting innocently on my bed. I stand before it warily, not wanting to know its contents. Or who sent it.

"What's that?" Jilna asks when she sees it.

I shake my head.

"Open it, then," she says impatiently.

I unwrap the cloth to reveal a winter cloak. It is woven of wool softer than any I have felt before, embroidered in the same shadow-dark hue as the cloak itself, a blue so deep it might be made of the very night itself. The wool is lined with the dark fur of a creature I have no name for. It is no ordinary cloak but a work of art and time, something that would have taken months to complete. I run my fingers over the cloth, the fur. I have never received such a gift before.

"That'll be from the king," Jilna says with evident satisfaction. "And high time he gave you a gift. It ought to be jewelry, but no doubt there'll be plenty of that later. Perhaps they're keeping it for when you meet the prince."

"Have the servants heard anything more of him?" I ask. "The prince, I mean?"

She shakes her head. "Not really. Dara managed to tease a few words from one of the men—nothing much, but she thinks they hold him in high esteem."

It's something, at least. They respect him. I try not to dwell on the fact that our own guards respect my brother, lauding his hunting skills and swordplay. It hardly matters to them how he treats the women beneath him—not me, not the serving girls.

Please, I pray. *Please.* But I can still hear my brother's promise and Daerilin's words of what Kestrin is really like ringing in my ears, and I cannot find the words to finish the prayer.

I let Jilna pack up the cloak and hustle me into my nightdress. She blows out the lamp as she leaves. I curl up beneath the blanket, blocking out the world. Exhaustion tugs me down into sleep almost at once.

I wake suddenly, yanked back from a land of vague and unformed dreams by a sound that has no place in my room. I sit up with the shock of it, my breath quick and loud in my ears.

Silence.

I lie back down. Perhaps it was only a dream sound.

A man clears his throat.

I sit up again, half paralyzed with fear, as sluggish as if I moved underwater. Once more silence fills the room. But this time I know I am not alone, and my first, terrified thought is that my brother has come for his vengeance. I hold the covers up to my chest as if they might protect me.

"Who's there?"

Someone shifts with a faint whisper of cloth, but my eyes can make out nothing.

"Show yourself," I say, my voice high, pleading.

Another soft whisper—I turn my head sharply toward the sound—and a flame leaps to life behind a cupped hand. Yet there was no sound of flint and steel, no sound of anything but the movement of his clothes. *Magic.* There can be no other explanation.

The flame catches on the wick of a candle set on the mantel. The intruder steps back. It is not my brother at all, for this man has dark hair and soft brown skin. He dresses in the Menaiyan fashion, a long dark tunic belted at the waist and loose pants tucked into riding boots. The light glints off metal at his side—a sword—and gleams in his eyes. I have the uncanny feeling that he can see me perfectly well despite the darkness.

Fear tingles in my hands, but I'm not yet trembling. If I scream, will the Menaiyan quad be there to answer?

"What do you want?" I ask, too afraid to move.

"To speak with you." His voice has the same telltale lilt as the king's.

"Why?"

"You have changed your allegiances."

"I have gained new allegiances," I agree carefully. At least the man has made no move toward me yet.

He studies me a moment before asking, "What do you know of Menaiya?"

"Very little. There are the king, his son, and a third person—a nephew, I think. The queen died one year ago." I stop, wait for him to ask what he truly wishes to know.

But he only watches, expression unreadable in the shadows thrown by the single flame.

I press my hands flat against the sheets, wishing I could re-adjust them. "You have come a long way to test my knowledge."

He tilts his head, inviting me to continue.

"You were not among the king's soldiers. Indeed, you dress more carefully than any of them, except perhaps their captain. So you must have traveled here alone. It seems a great journey to undertake merely to speak with me." Though perhaps, for a mage, it is an easy thing. I have no way of knowing.

He makes no response.

I try another approach. "Will you not tell me your name? You know who I am."

"We will meet soon enough."

"In Menaiya," I hazard.

He nods.

"And you have given your allegiance to the king?"

"Yes." He smiles, one corner of his mouth rising higher than the other. A foolish question, then; he must be sworn to the king, here because of his oath.

"What do you seek now that cannot wait till my arrival?" Or even just till daylight, a place other than my darkened bedroom.

"I wished to see you myself," he explains. "To warn you." He crosses the room to the shuttered window, faces it silently before turning back to me. "Menaiya has many enemies, my lady. Now that you belong to Menaiya, those enemies are yours. You will need to be careful these next weeks. The king can offer you only so much protection until you reach his walls."

I swallow to ease the sudden dryness of my throat. "Menaiya is feared by its neighbors."

"Rightfully so," he agrees, and again amusement lightens his words. "But I do not speak of our neighbors."

"Then whom do you mean?"

He hesitates. "I cannot say—not here. Not now."

A shiver runs under my skin. How can I protect myself from a phantom?

"You must beware, lady," he continues, voice grim. "Do not put yourself in a vulnerable situation. Do not walk alone. Do not remain with anyone you do not trust."

And I am to trust him? Whom I do not know at all, and who

has put me in such a situation himself? Indeed. Tamping down on my disbelief, I say instead, "I don't even know who I will travel with to Menaiya." Except for Valka, whom I certainly don't trust. "How can I avoid them?"

"Be vigilant," he presses. I wonder if he even heard me. "Do you understand, my lady? You are in danger until you reach the city of Tarinon. Even there, you may not truly be safe."

No. I will have the prince to worry about, and a court more powerful and sophisticated than mine, and no one who speaks my language but the king, his captain, and a nameless man with veiled warnings. No wonder the king promised me safety from my brother but nothing else. My brother, it seems, will be the one thing that can't reach me in Menaiya.

Without warning, the shutters crash open, wood shrieking as they break, panels flying into the room. The man cries out, spinning toward the window, one hand rising, palm out. The splinters slam against the air before him as if into an invisible barrier, then ricochet toward the far wall. Light explodes through the gaping window, outlining the mage's profile in blazing white, momentarily blinding me.

I squeeze my eyes shut, huddled beneath the covers. When I open them again, the light has diminished to bright moonlight. Amid its pale rays stands a woman. Her skin is smooth and pale as milk, her hair shining and dark. But her eyes—they are cavities in her face, deep, bottomless pits. They hold me tightly in their grasp and I neither move nor look away. Then she turns her gaze from me, dismissing me.

I crouch on my mattress, gasping for breath, and try to get my bearings.

The man is still here, but he has backed up to the foot of my bed. He watches the woman steadily. I sidle to the edge of the bed, glancing sideways at the man, seeing him clearly for the first time. He seems almost familiar now in the cold wash of moonlight, for he at least is human. Long night-dark hair tied back, high cheekbones, defined jaw—his profile imprints itself on my mind in the moment that I see him. And then my eyes fly back to the woman as she raises her hand, snaps it through the air in a backhanded slap.

The man staggers sideways, toward me, as if her hand had connected with his face.

I scrabble to my feet, shocked by the line of blood that appears on his cheek.

His eyes pass mine, intense, and turn back to the woman.

"Leave," the lady says to him. Her voice is the murmur of water on rocks, of snow falling on oaks. "The girl is mine, as are you."

The man shakes his head. "No," he says, but the word is a little boy's plea. He falters under the woman's gaze.

Her eyes, I think, remembering the way their emptiness enfolded me. And then, *He is not my enemy.* It seems crystal clear to me with the moon shining in, lighting up the room with its strange whiteness.

"No," I agree, my voice strong and resonant in the stillness. "You are not welcome here," I say to the lady. "Leave us."

When I look into her eyes, I see my death looking back.

"I will teach you your place, girl." Her hand comes up and I see the glint of a gem on her finger, glittering with its own internal fire.

Beside me the man shifts, bracing himself as if expecting a blow—or perhaps expecting to catch me as I fall.

"No," I repeat, my voice wavering only slightly. I have granted her no hold over me, ceded her no right that will allow her magic to own me. She may hurt me, certainly, but I am not hers to be taught. I raise my chin. "You have no power over me."

For a moment that lasts a lifetime, she stands unmoving, hand raised. And then she smiles, a thin, cruel twist of her lips that turns my blood to ice in my veins. "No," she agrees, "over you I have no power. But do not think you are safe. You are mine as surely as if your mother swore you to me before your birth. But tonight, it is not you I am concerned with." She turns back to the man and her hand reaches out, gesturing elegantly toward him. "It is you."

He cries out, throwing his arm up to ward off her casual attack. But it is no use. Light envelops him: bright, blinding light that sears my vision, scorches my mind—a light that floods the room and takes all detail with it.

The lady, the mage, my room—all disappear, and I am falling through the shadows of my life, farther and farther away from the moon.

CHAPTER

4

T he window of my new room is crosscut by bars. I sit on the edge of my bed, under orders from my mother to get some sleep, while the striped early morning sunlight creeps across the wood floor and rumors fly through the hall.

It was my Menaiyan quad that raised the alarm. In their story, a soldier passing down the hall heard a strange sound, as of wood shattering. He knocked on my door to make sure all was well. When his hammering received no response, he tried the handle. By then his shouts had roused other guards—the rest of his quad standing beside him, I suspect—as well as those who slumbered in the rooms near mine. So a number of people saw the broken shutters and the princess lying senseless by her bed.

"A joke of your brother's, no doubt," Mother said to me once she had hustled me to my new room and dismissed everyone else. "You really should have had more sense than to faint over something so absurd as a rock hitting your shutters—or whatever it was."

I had merely nodded, still dazed. Mother informed me that the story would be that of a bird hitting my shutters, perhaps a large owl. When Jilna arrived with my breakfast some time later, she told me that the servants believe the Fair Folk had come for me; the soldier's knock and sudden entrance saved me from being carried off. The truth seems far less comprehensible to me than any of these possibilities—rock or owl or faeries.

I clasp my hands and sit there, rubbing my thumbs together as if that might allay the fear washing through me. A sorceress in the night. A Menaiyan mage who was powerless before her. A promise to destroy me for speaking up—*why* had I said anything? She wasn't my enemy until that moment, not truly.

I push myself up and cross to the door. At least at the temple I should find some peace, and it's not like anyone else uses it. I may as well be there as here.

I swing the door open to find my quad standing at attention. I hesitate, wishing I hadn't opened the door, wondering what story *they* told their king. But I'm not going to hide from them. I step out past them, walking briskly down the hall, taking the back stairs and servants' corridors to the temple, the sound of their boots a steady drumbeat behind me.

The temple is small but clean, lined with benches facing the front, a single window to the side letting in the bright autumn sunshine. A prayer book takes pride of place on a table at the front. I have used it on occasion, read through the ancient words of wisdom, the old stories of the blessed and the damned, the prayers still used from hundreds of years before. Today, though, I leave it alone and take a seat on one of the benches, let myself sink into the quiet of the room.

In this moment, I am safe. I can rest in that, even knowing that there will be more trouble to come, a danger I have no idea how to escape. So I sit, and when my mind keeps wheeling back to the night's events, I whisper soft prayers, the repetition calming me.

"Princess Alyrra."

I twist to see the king standing in the doorway, his expression grim.

"My lord." I rise and dip a small curtsy. The quad he assigned to me must have gotten him word, somehow, that I had left my room. Of course they did. How else would he have known where to find me?

He crosses the room, gesturing for me to sit as he takes a seat at the other end of the bench. "I am concerned by the stories I've heard. Are you well, child?"

I nod. "As you see, my lord."

He tilts his head, the telltale crinkle at the corners of his eyes showing his amusement. He knows that my answer means nothing.

"Your mother says an owl hit your shutters. I wondered—did you see what color it was?"

I blink at him. What *color*? "I—I assume brown."

"You did not see it yourself?"

He's come to find out the truth. Not of how I am, but of what happened last night. And perhaps he is the one person who might know enough to help me. "No," I tell him. "I don't recall the owl. I was having a—a dream, I think. One in which two mages argued. A woman who did not seem quite human, and a man who looked like he might be from Menaiya. The woman attacked, and then

I was suddenly waking up, your soldiers in my room and the shutters broken open."

The king has gone perfectly still, eyes so dark they seem carved of obsidian.

"Do you know what it means? The dream I had?"

He looks away. "Perhaps," he says softly, "that I have made a mistake."

My stomach twists. "My lord?" Does he mean that his enemies are more dangerous than he knew? Or that he should never have come for me?

He turns to me, his expression softening to show concern. It can only be a court expression, one he uses to hide his true thoughts. "Dreams can be portents of the future. I fear you will not be safe here over the winter, my child. I will speak with your mother. I suspect it would be best if you came to Menaiya as soon as possible."

He rises and moves to the door, then turns back. "Should you dream of the woman again, tread carefully. And come to me at once."

"My lord." I dip my head in acquiescence.

His boots tap softly as he departs. I hear him pause in the hallway, exchange a faint word with my quad, and then he is gone.

I turn to the front of the temple once more, wrap my arms across my chest. He knows the Lady, knows exactly what she is. Somehow, that doesn't comfort me at all.

The king leaves for his home three days later, on the assurance that I will be sent after him within a fortnight. By his agreement with my mother, I will winter in Tarinon, and in the spring be wed. He leaves me two quads as well as his captain, and promises to send an honor guard to meet me at the border.

The two weeks pass swiftly, filled with preparations for my departure, for there is my trousseau and jewelry to put in order, final feasts to attend, and farewell visits to receive from whichever court nobles wish to curry favor with my mother. It is late afternoon on my final day when I manage to slip off to make my own last farewells.

I have gotten to know the faces of the eight men who guard me, but they do not speak before me and rarely look at me directly. The one guard who speaks my language is Matsin en Korto. Like Sarkor, Matsin wears a silver earring, though his is set with a sapphire, a rank mark of a sort, I believe. As they have every day since they were assigned to me, my guard follows me through the halls now.

I stop in to the kitchens and Cook gives me a bright-eyed smile, promising to send my favorite meat pies with our party for our first meal on the road. They are all of them thrilled that I have escaped my brother, that I am going to a court they believe may finally value me. Dara and Ketsy catch my hands and dance me around the kitchen, the other maids giggling and the kitchen boys clapping. I finally break away from them, laughing despite my worries.

Still, Cook must sense my anxiety. She clasps my hand between hers, squeezing gently. "This new court, they'll only need to know you to love you. You'll win them over."

"Thank you," I say, because they believe this, and want it for me so much.

As I move to leave through the far door, my quad steps in

from the hall, following. The kitchen falls unnaturally quiet, the only sound their boots upon the stone floor. It is all I can do to cheerfully call my last goodbyes, darting out with my quad in my wake.

At the stables, Redna gives me a quick peck on the cheek. She smells of horse and leather. "We've gotten new tack for Acorn," she tells me. "Though your brother took the stable master to task for ordering it made."

"I'm sorry," I say, for all that I'm grateful for their care.

"We're going to miss you something awful, what with your brother's idea of kindness."

"You'll be fine," I say lamely. "Just stay away from him."

"And when he's king?"

"Maybe he'll fall off his horse and Cousin Derin will get the crown."

Redna snorts. "I'll wish the queen long life, and hope I'm married and gone when the crown passes." She squeezes my hand. "We'll all be praying for you. The Menaiyans that came here seemed to be kind men; they didn't flirt with the girls and they took good care of their horses. And they put a guard on you to keep your brother off—which is more'n your mother ever did. I think your prince will be a good man."

I nod, and Redna hugs me tightly. I carry her words with me as I leave, but I cannot take much heart from them. Not with the secrets the king is keeping, the sorceress he clearly fears, and the very real possibility that I was chosen because I am disposable— just as my brother and Daerilin warned, and even they did not know the half of it.

The rest of the day passes quietly enough, culminating in

a farewell feast that requires only my silent, smiling presence. When I am finally allowed to retire from the celebrations, I go straight to my room, my only thought that of bed. But sleep eludes me. Strange visions haunt my dreams, and twice I wake, expecting the Lady to have returned with her death-still eyes. Each time I find nothing but the darkness of my room, no sound but the creaking of old wood.

Jilna wakes me from a troubled doze at dawn, bringing with her a cup of warm milk and a tray of foods for which I have little appetite.

"Your mother has a new guest," Jilna tells me as she brushes out my hair. I twist to look at her, and she tugs me around straight again by my hair. "Do be still, child. He arrived late last night, and your mother went down to greet him, and he's been in to wait on her already this morning."

"Is he Menaiyan?" I ask, careful not to turn.

"No. From west of here, I think."

Then his arrival probably has no relation to me, regardless. I dress quickly, aware of how well Jilna knows me, how she holds out the sleeves of my dress just so. She brings me the cloak the king gave me, that our nobles might see me wearing it.

When she steps back, she looks at me almost hesitantly. "I've something for you—just a little thing to remember me by. I know you're going to a great court, and you won't have much use for the likes of this, but—"

"Jilna," I interrupt. "What is it?"

She presses a pouch into my palm, then clasps her hands together tightly, watching as I pour its contents into my palm. A small, worn silver oval disk on a thin chain tumbles out, shining in the lamplight. At the center of the pendant is an engraved many-petaled rose. As I swallow, my throat constricts. This is undoubtedly a family heirloom; a bit of wealth passed from mother to daughter through the generations. But Jilna has no daughter of her own to give it to.

"It's beautiful." I close my hand around the gift. "Thank you."

Jilna looks at me, her face alight, and then takes a quick step forward to wrap her arms around me. "Don't cry, dear heart."

Leaning into her, I take a few watery breaths, and then step back. She lets me go, watching as I fasten the chain around my neck. "I'll treasure it always."

"Aye, and if you lose it, I'll send my spirit to haunt you the rest of your days," Jilna warns. "That was my mother's 'fore it was mine."

"Bring her with you then," I say, grinning. "I'd like to meet her someday."

Jilna gives me a little shove. "Get on with you. Your mother's waiting for you."

My mother has prepared a different sort of farewell for me in her apartments. The curtains are still drawn across her shuttered windows, the single lamp doing little to brighten the room. She sits in a brocade armchair, a silk pouch, so much richer than the one Jilna gave me, clasped gently in one hand.

"So, you are off," she says lightly. "Is there anything you would ask of me before you leave?"

I consider her offer a long moment and then ask, "Who would have cause to hate the Menaiyan royal family?"

It's a question I've put to old tutors and servants alike, without success. No one has even alluded to a vengeful sorceress, though it certainly seems like the sort of thing that would bear mentioning.

My mother raises her brows. "More than a few people, I suspect, though the Family has no declared enemies. They haven't had a war in over a hundred years, not since this king's grandsire, I believe it was, took it into his head to cross the Winter Seas and loot the Far Steppes. Foolish of him."

"Why?"

"The war followed him home and killed off most of the royal family. The Family's dwindled since then. Strength gone out of the bloodline, though some call it a curse." Mother levels a hard look on me. "Don't be deceived. The king is neither weak nor easily fooled, and curses do not last generations."

"I know," I say, still no closer to the answer I am looking for. Despite her seemingly deathless eyes, the sorceress could hardly be so old.

"And do not assume that the soldiers who guard you are there for your protection alone. They will report all you do and say. Expect the same in Menaiya—if not with soldiers, then with whatever attendants they might assign you. And beware of being pulled into court intrigues. You are not so wise as to be able to play at such politics without bringing disaster down upon yourself."

"I understand," I say, my voice small.

"Do you? This alliance hinges on you. If you betray it, you betray our land and put us at risk of war. If Menaiya attacks"—Mother shrugs elegantly—"we have no hope of victory. You know that."

I nod.

"Good then; you will understand why I've decided to help you now."

"Help me?" I echo, bewildered.

She smiles, a slow cat smile. "Yes. It is vital that the prince takes to you and is willing to guide you through these first months. You are too stupid to manage it on your own. Therefore, I sent to our western neighbors seeking the help of a mage who lives in their lands. Last night, my messages were answered." She raises her voice, turning her head toward the connecting door. "Mage Efrin? If you would come in?"

The visitor is a *mage*? I take a step forward. "Mother, what is this about? What exactly have you asked him to do?" We have had a mage visit only once in my memory, in my childhood. He enchanted luminae stones for us that glowed with a steady light, and even, one morning, popped into the kitchen and laid an enchantment on the oven so that our bread did not burn for near on two years. But this—a mage visiting now, after my mother lectures me on my own stupidity—this is nothing so innocuous. My mother intends him to lay an enchantment upon me.

Mother sighs. "Do be quiet, child, or you'll embarrass yourself."

The next moment a tall, thin man with graying hair opens the connecting door. He wears the fine clothes of a nobleman: doublet and hose and polished boots. A pendant hangs from a chain about his neck, the ruby at its center gleaming with its own faint light. A mage's amulet, a reservoir of power to be drawn on when needed. Just like the one the sorceress wore on her finger, if much less fiery.

"My lady queen," the mage says, inclining his head. "Princess."

I dip my head to him, forcing myself not to look toward my mother again. She would ignore me regardless.

"I'm afraid we haven't much time, good sir," she says, offering the pouch she holds to him. "We would be most grateful if you could see to the spell at once."

"Of course," he says, accepting the pouch from her and turning to a nearby table.

"What spell is this?" I ask, keeping my voice low. "Mother?"

The mage glances once from me to my mother, his lips curled derisively, and then returns his attention to the pouch.

"Watch and see," Mother says, and rises to join the mage at the table. He has extracted a square of white silk no larger than a kerchief from the pouch. Now he lifts a needle that glints gold in the lamplight and takes my mother's hand in his. With a small, quick jab, he pricks her finger. As the first drop of blood wells up and falls to spread on the silk, he begins to chant:

"Heart's blood, ruby drop
Bind all love to you;
Mind's blood, dark drop,
Bind all knowledge to you;
Soul's blood, last drop,
Bind all strength to you."

A wave of dizziness passes over me. I stagger sideways, bumping into the edge of the chair my mother vacated. When I raise a hand to my face, it comes away damp with sweat.

"What have you done?" I demand, my voice shaking.

"Thank you, sir," Mother says, taking the folded silk from him. He dips his head, murmuring something, and departs without a glance toward me.

"Mother?"

She slips the kerchief back into the pouch. "I should think it abundantly clear, Alyrra. Mage Efrin has bound my knowledge and love of you to the blood. When you meet the prince, find a way to dip this in a drink of his—a goblet of wine should work well. I expect you will have to wait a few weeks. Make sure no one sees you, especially not him."

"What will it do?"

"Naught but make him aware of all that I know and what little I love of you."

I shake my head as if I could refuse her words, as if hearing what I already know about my mother's love for me shouldn't hurt me. It still does.

Mothers frowns and elaborates further, as if I am too stupid to have understood her. "It will make him more your ally than anything else I can do. If he loves you even a little, he will try to protect you. If he understands you, he will be able to plan for your shortcomings, insulate you from the court's politicking as much as possible." She hands the pouch to me. "Keep it safely. I shall meet you in the courtyard in a few minutes."

"Mother," I say, my voice rough.

"Leave be, child."

But it isn't her love I want to ask about. I raise my chin. "What did the last line mean—about strength?"

"What do you think? I've bound what strength you gain from me to it. That's why you mustn't lose it."

"But *why*? Won't I need all the strength I have for myself?"

Mother huffs contemptuously. "You are as weak as water. If your strength is bound to his, then you may be able to draw upon his own strength. You can only stand to gain from him. Now *go*."

CHAPTER

5

I stand beside my brother just within the great doors of the hall, my quad a ghostly presence at our backs. At least my early departure has offered me this: an escape from my brother before he managed to find a way past my guards.

We wait in silence for Mother to join us. My brother bends his head, his eyes slitted against the bright morning light, and makes no attempt to speak. For once, I am thankful for his penchant for drinking.

"Come along," Mother says, brushing past us. We follow her out to stand upon the steps, the courtyard filled with nobles and servants, the traveling party ready at their center. Mother wishes me health and happiness and begs me to write often in a voice that carries to the farthest servant in the crowd. I curtsy to her, and my brother leads me down the stairs to the carriage, pausing as a hostler brings forth a white stallion.

"My gift to you on your betrothal," he says, his voice rasping.

The horse stands tall, muscles tensed as it eyes me, its lead rope taut in the hostler's hands.

A gift? I glance past the horse to the traveling party, scanning the animals for Acorn. Surely he's been readied to come with me? But I can't see him anywhere.

My brother's hand squeezes mine painfully.

"A noble creature," I say quickly, "and a beautiful gift. I thank you."

We continue on, my brother muttering a few words about how well trained the horse is. I ignore him, still searching for Acorn. I spot Redna standing beside the stable door, her face grim. *I'm sorry*, she mouths. There, tethered to a ring just within, waits Acorn, a bucket of currycombs on the ground beside him.

I nod once to Redna, knowing she was ordered not to bring him out. His being visible at all is her attempt to assure me he's all right, even as I must leave him behind. I wish that I had known, or that I could make a scene now, before all the watching nobles and our guard. But I do not want such a story to be retold in Menaiya, and my brother knows it. Better to accept the horse he has given me as if it makes no difference than to let him know I care.

My brother hands me into the carriage and steps back. The veiled malice of his smile makes me stiffen even now, when I am finally out of his reach. I sit down gratefully, noting that Valka is already seated opposite me, her face turned to the windows. My greeting dies on my lips as I note her rigid posture, her hands clenched tight. Beside her sits the maid we are to share for the journey. I do not recognize her, but by her cool expression as she dips her head to me and her comfortable seat beside Valka, I surmise that however much this maid is meant to serve me, she is Valka's first.

The carriage starts forward with a jerk. Captain Sarkor and the Menaiyan quads lead the way, with Lieutenant Balin and our own guards bringing up the rear. Mother raises her hand in farewell, a show for the watching nobles. We turn out of the courtyard, the carriage rattling over the gravel, and as easily as that, my old life is gone.

I settle back in my seat, glancing covertly at Valka. It might not be possible to be friends, but perhaps we might be courteous with one another. I should at least make the attempt.

"How are you, Valka?"

She ignores me, not a flicker of her eyes suggesting she heard my words. I sigh and look out the windows to the passing trees. I wonder what I will miss from home. Mostly, I will miss Jilna. I will miss Cook, Redna, and the other servants, their smiles and small kindnesses. I will miss riding Acorn through the forest, and the little dell where the Wind visited me.

The Wind. I press my lips together. I have not spoken to it since my betrothal. When I tried two days ago, it did not answer. Its silence is just another goodbye, another friend I know I must leave behind. Yet I expected a clearer farewell. I expected to be the one to leave.

We pass the better part of the morning in silence, the only sound that of the carriage rattling along the road, the thud of horses' hooves. The forest changes from birch and elm to the occasional stand of pine or aspen as the day draws on. Sometimes the forest thins, giving way to grassy meadows and little herds of goats driven by village children who turn to watch us pass.

We break at midday, stopping at a clearing by the roadside. A brook burbles at its edge, separating us from the surrounding forest. The soldiers spread a rug on the grass for Valka and me, and bring out platters of food. I watch without enthusiasm, for all that Cook has indeed sent a full platter of meat pies for me. I would so much rather be sitting in my corner of the kitchen, laughing with the servants, than be here, surrounded by people yet still utterly alone.

"Come get some water with me," Valka says, appearing beside me with a goblet in her hand.

"Oh," I say, so surprised by her invitation that I accept the goblet. I follow her to the stream. She does not speak again, and I think better of addressing her, unsure if her words were a token of peace or only a momentary lapse. At least the stream is too shallow for her to drown me in.

I fill my goblet and drink, the forest water sweet on my tongue. Behind us, I can hear the Menaiyan soldiers speaking, their words mingling with the water's voice. Valka stands farther downstream, holding her own goblet. She looks at me strangely, anger and confusion playing over her features. I watch her uncertainly. With a huff of disgust, she whirls and stalks back to our meal, never having tasted the water herself.

We stop for the night at a small inn nestled at a crossroad. I am grateful for the tiny room I am given, separate from Valka, but tranquility eludes me. I lie still and think of the mage who visited me. There has been no sign of him since that night, confirming my initial surmise that he had not arrived with the Menaiyan party. Still, he claimed to serve the king. So why did he keep his name secret when he expected I would meet him in Tarinon? Will he be there when I arrive, or is he even now at the mercy of the Lady? And what if the Lady decides to make good on her threats to me before I reach Menaiya and whatever aid I might find there?

I do not remember falling asleep, but when I open my eyes, the shutters have been thrown wide. An owl, pearly white in the darkness, perches upon the sill, its great eyes watching me. I sit up and return its gaze. It leaps into the room, wings outstretched. My hands clutch the sheets, watching as the bird grows: its wings elongate into arms and its great luminous eyes shift in a blur of white to re-form as not-quite-human eyes in a fiercely beautiful face.

"Princess," the Lady says. She stands before the window, the bright downy white of her dress lighting the room.

I nod once, acceptance and acknowledgment wrapped up into one. I have run from my brother for years, and I know when I am caught. So I stay still in bed, my mouth dry and my fingers fisted into the sheets. I will have to get out of this myself, for the quad at my door may as well be stationed in the far plains of Menaiya. Last time, they did not come until the danger was past, whether by design or because the Lady kept them out. They will not come this time either.

"You have had time to consider your predicament," she says, her voice the pad of a predator circling. "I shall offer you one last chance. Will you give me what I require?"

I take a steadying breath. "W-what is that?"

"The prince."

"*Kestrin?*"

She dips her head, her eyes utterly dark. "Consider well, princess, whether you want me for an enemy."

That is not a question at all. Just the sight of her leaves me trembling. I cannot imagine what exactly the Lady wants with the prince, but if it were a good thing, she would not be here. Nor do I have any hold on the prince that I can transfer to her now— what she wants is a promise of treachery toward a man whose father pledged me protection. It takes all my courage to shake my head. "I cannot betray the man to whom I am betrothed."

"Is that your choice?"

My kingdom—and the safety of my people—depends on me not betraying my new family. One misstep and the king's soldiers could sweep down upon the hall, burn it to ashes while my dearest friends sleep within, and bring the rest of our land beneath a potentially unforgiving rule.

"Do you think I cannot gain him without you?" the Lady asks at my silence. "It will be done. You are merely a tool to that end. Tools can be replaced."

I have only and ever been a tool—something to be used or disregarded, my worth measured in my political acuity and marriage prospects. What the Lady wishes is a willing tool, and that I cannot grant her.

"I understand," I say quietly. "I wish you no enmity, but I am sworn to Prince Kestrin. I cannot betray his trust, nor the trust of his people."

"That is a choice you will regret," the Lady says, her voice cold, factual. "Good night, princess. Sleep well."

She turns, her dress whirling around her, and departs in a burst of feathers, wings outstretched.

With shaking fingers, I light the lamp next to me. I remain watching long after I have ascertained the Lady has truly left. Regardless, there will be no sleep for me tonight, not with such a farewell.

Eventually, I rise and dress myself, then splash water on my face from the basin. The cold of it makes my skin prickle. I tuck the pouch my mother gave me under the neck of my gown, beside Jilna's thin silver chain with its pendant. The one speaks of sorcery, the other of deep love. Neither, I think, should be worn by a princess going to meet her betrothed for the first time, for one is deception, and the other an almost childish hope of what is only a political match. Admittedly, it hardly matters what I wear if I cannot find a way to oppose the Lady. She has all but promised to destroy me—to replace me with a better tool. My hopes hinge on the sorcerer. I must find him as soon as I reach the king's city, find out what he knows of the Lady and how I might protect myself. If I can at all.

I rub my face, my thoughts turning to Valka. There is no way around the journey with her, but at least I might try riding the white horse rather than sitting across from her for hours on end. I step from my room with renewed focus, for this is one thing I *can* do something about.

A quad made up of a combination of my kingdom's guards and the Menaiyan soldiers trails me to the stables as the first light of dawn brightens the skies. The building is quiet, most of the hostlers gone off to eat their breakfast. The white stallion stands at the center of his stall, tail swishing, head turned toward me. The lone hostler left on duty approaches me deferentially.

"Is this horse in your charge?" I ask, recognizing him as Bol, one of our hostlers from home.

"Yes, Your Highness." Bol is small but sturdy, his face broad and weatherworn. There is gentleness written in the lines by his eyes.

I lean against the half door, looking in. "What breed is he?"

"He's from the southeast—a rare breed from the Fethering Plains. They've a fancy name, Highness, but I don't remember it. They're known for their strength." Bol hesitates, glances over his shoulder to where the guards wait at the door, and then whispers, "You won't want to ride him, Highness."

For just a moment, the world shrinks around me, pressing in. I turn to Bol slowly, forcing my shoulders to relax. "Why not?"

Bol meets my gaze worriedly. "He's wild-caught. He's not trained to take a rider."

Wild-caught . . . My brother chose a generous gift indeed. I should have demanded Acorn be brought along as well—it was my right. I stare at the white, wondering if I will ever truly escape my brother's ugliness, or if it will follow me wherever I go.

"I'm sorry, Highness," Bol says softly.

"Can he be broken?" I ask abruptly. The white is in the prime of life, with a high crest and proud bearing. He tilts his head, his ears swiveling to catch our conversation, his dark eyes bright with intelligence. But for all his power and grace, he's no more than a prisoner, a pawn in a vicious little game my brother will not let go.

Bol licks his lips. "He went wild when we tried to saddle him, and he isn't young. Even so, it might be possible."

Faintly, the sound of people crossing the yard to the stables reaches us. I am mildly gratified when my guards step out to stop whoever approaches. "Can you free him?" I ask quickly, while they are gone.

Bol stares. "Free him?"

"He's a wild creature—he deserves to go free." It will be something, to have given this horse back the life that was stolen from him rather than leave him to spend his days closed in a stall, or, at most, let out to graze the same pasture until he dies.

"I don't know." Bol glances toward the door, then to the horse.

"Try," I suggest. The king might grant me another horse should I ask for one, or lose this one, but he would hardly understand a request to free a horse.

"We are too closely guarded," Bol murmurs.

My quad steps back through the doorway, followed by a pair of the inn's stable hands.

I keep my eyes on Bol, but he will not meet my gaze. He is right; there is hardly a moment when the soldiers do not watch their charges. "Very well," I say softly.

I will just have to find another way, then.

CHAPTER
6

The day before we reach the border, we break for lunch in a wide mountain valley. As I step down from the carriage, Lieutenant Balin approaches me. "Your Highness, there is a creek running through the woods there, if you wish to refresh yourself before eating."

Unable to help myself, I turn to Valka and ask, "Are you going?"

"Yes," she says at once. "Here is your goblet next to mine." I take it with a half smile, knowing better than to read friendship into her words, and we start through the tall grasses toward the trees. She will never forgive me, that I know, but perhaps with enough moments like this, we might eventually establish a peace of sorts.

As we pass the soldiers, I watch Bol move to the back of our little caravan. He glances about once, nervously, and then lifts his hand to the white's halter and slips the buckle open. The white drops his head and steps back, pulling free. I look away as Bol walks off to help with the soldiers' horses. I hope the white makes his bid for freedom as softly as he can.

At the creek, I kneel to fill my goblet, my thoughts still with the white. The water is sweet and pure. Setting the goblet aside, I scoop up water to wash my face, the crisp coolness refreshing after the stuffiness of the carriage. Valka remains where we emerged along the bank. I can feel her eyes on my back.

"Won't you drink?" I ask. She frowns at me, almost angrily.

I sigh, turning back to scoop up more water, and then pause, staring. There is something odd about my reflection, but I cannot make out what, for the water does not run smoothly but in ripples and eddies. I dip my fingers into the creek, breaking the image. But it does not break.

Instead, a hand reaches up through the water and closes around my wrist. I choke on a cry of terror, jerking away, but the hand pulls down—hard. I lose my footing on the muddy bank and plunge headfirst into the swirling waters.

The world is strange, blunted, beneath the too-deep water. I twist and strike out, but cannot quite find my attacker. The hand still holds my wrist in an iron grip. I kick, desperately trying to tear myself away and push my way to the surface. How can the creek run so deep? The air burns in my lungs, spots dance before my eyes. Something touches my throat—a knife? I flail away from it, feel a slicing pain, and abruptly am released. I find myself on my hands and knees in the creek bed, coughing up water as gentle waves lap around my chest.

I look up in a panic, my hair sending an arc of droplets flying over the quiet waters, but there is no sign of my assailant. The creek runs clear, the water laughing and gurgling past. Only the birds are silent.

I struggle to my feet. On the bank, Valka smiles. For one sodden moment I think she smiles at me, but she is looking past me. A terrible fear settles in my stomach, as heavy and dark as lead. And even though I do not want to know, I turn.

The Lady stands in the water a few paces away. Her hair falls black as ink over her shoulders, framing pale skin, high cheekbones. Her dress seems made of water, her body beneath it as indistinguishable as a riverbed. It is her eyes I recognize, fathomless dark holes in her skull. She holds out her hand, a small, cruel smile flitting across her lips: the pouch my mother gave me swings over the water, the end of its severed cord caught between her fingers. It is all the power the Lady needs to work her magic over me.

When I finally raise my eyes to meet the Lady's, I recognize the look in her eyes.

"You have served me well," she says to Valka. Her voice has the whisper of daggers through night air. I raise my chin, refusing to look away from her.

"My lady, I have," Valka answers from the bank. "I have brought her not once but twice to water, as you asked."

"After your first attempt, I almost reconsidered our agreement," the Lady says with a hint of contempt.

Almost? My mind flits to the only other time Valka and I visited a stream together, some days ago. We remained in full view of our escort the whole time. Small wonder the Lady came to me with her final offer that night.

"It is well you did better this time."

"You promised me a reward," Valka says haughtily, furious at being reprimanded before me. I wait with her for the Lady's answer.

"You shall have your reward." The Lady's gaze remains on me. "You shall be princess."

"What?" I glance between them, bewildered. *Valka? Princess?*

"Be quiet," Valka snaps. "You've no say in this. The Lady has promised: I shall be princess in your stead and none will know the truth."

"No." I shake my head as if half-drunk. I cannot make sense of this. "No, you can't."

The Lady lets her hand fall to her side, and the pouch melts into her dress. When she raises a hand, I catch the gleam of the gemstone on her finger. She makes a quick sweeping motion, her fingers flicking out exactly as I remember that night in my room, and power washes over me.

I stumble back and fall against the low bank. I hear a faint cry behind me—Valka—and then my bones twist within their sockets, my muscles shriek, and fire spreads across my skin and fills my eyes with flames. I open my mouth to scream and my tongue shrivels at the touch of air. And then the pain vanishes, departing as swiftly as it came. For a moment longer, I remain unmoving, huddled against the bank, the current tugging at my legs; then I force myself to straighten, looking up to see Valka above me.

But it is not Valka. On the bank I see myself, straight brown hair braided back, small features pinched and tired, yet happy— happy because Valka is happy.

As if in a dream, I catch hold of my braid and pull it around: red and curly. My breath rasps loud in my lungs as I stare at my hair, and then at my fingers, long and slender and soft.

"What have you done?" I cry, staring at Valka-become-myself. Her lips turn back in a sneer.

I feel a strange emotion coming to life within me. I wheel to face the Lady, my face tight. "You cannot do this!" I cry, as if I might undo this travesty with my outrage.

The Lady smiles. "Indeed I can, and I have, little princess. What will you do?"

"She will be found out as a fraud. I have only to tell . . ." My words die in Valka's throat.

The Lady laughs, a fearful sound, pure and clear and cold. "You will never speak of this." A second time, her hand moves and sunlight glances off the gem.

A gold chain forms in the air and flies toward me, but I cannot move, rooted to the spot in an unfamiliar body. The chain wraps itself around my throat, tightening as if clasped.

"What?" I manage to gasp, and then it constricts, choking me as it sinks beneath my skin. I fall against the bank, clawing at the thing, unable to reach it, my vision filled with the dazzle of sunlight reflecting off water. Dimly, I hear my own laughter fall from Valka's mouth. I stiffen, my anger cooling, hardening into a lump beneath my breast. The chain loosens but I can still feel it hugging my throat beneath my skin, halfway up my neck.

"If ever you feel the urge to speak of this to another person," the Lady murmurs, "the choker shall convince you otherwise. Farewell, dear princess."

When I look up, one hand at my throat, fingers searching for a chain I cannot touch, the Lady is gone.

"Girl," Valka says.

I find I cannot meet her gaze, cannot bear to see her face, and so my eyes drop to her neck. A faint red mark shows bright against the paleness of her throat: it is where the Lady's knife sliced the pouch from my neck. The skin is sealed shut as if it had never been cut.

"You will call me 'Your Highness' and treat me with all due respect from now on," Valka says. "If you try anything, I shall have you executed for treason."

I do not really hear her, have no words for her. She turns to rejoin our escort, leaving me alone. A shudder runs through me, but it is a distant thing. I look around at the river, the sand showing clear through the water.

My eyes come to rest on a glint of silver. Dimly, I realize my teeth are chattering. I clench my jaw to stop them, staring down at the sparkle in the riverbed. Slowly, I bend, reach into the water, and close my fist over the glinting sand. When I open my palm, I find Jilna's silver necklace, the chain snapped but the rose pendant still there, caught in a loop. I grip it tightly and pull myself up the riverbank.

As I stand, the water drains from the dress I wear—Valka's dress—running in rivulets past my feet and back down into the river, leaving me bone dry. I shudder, close my eyes. *Not my eyes*, I think, and jerk them back open. Not my eyes. Not my sight or hearing or feeling. Not me.

I am shaking again. I wrap Valka's strange, soft arms around myself and breathe slowly, staring at the ground, thinking only of the path before me leading between the trees and out through the tall grasses. This is how you survive: one breath to the next, refusing each thought as it comes to you. This is how you get through the worst of things. With each step I take, a part of the clarity of what has happened slips away. I succumb to the enfolding grayness, letting myself drift up the path. It is a dream, a dream, naught but a nightmare.

I return to the clearing where our meal is set out. The soldiers treat me as they did Valka, calling me "my lady" when they speak, but mostly they are distant and unconcerned. They seem to dislike me; it is a hazy moment before I realize it is Valka they dislike and not me. I do not know how the meal passes. Each bite is a mechanical process of chewing and swallowing, and then the meal is done and I am stepping into the carriage. Valka remains outside, watching the men pack up.

Laina, the maid, enters the carriage and seats herself beside me. "My lady, are you feeling quite well?"

I shrug, the motion jerky. I need to focus, to start thinking in bigger pieces than each moment as it passes.

"Can I fetch you anything? A glass of wine, perhaps?" Laina watches me intently. She has shown more concern for me in these few moments than in all our trip. But then, she thinks me Valka, not myself.

"No," I force myself to say. "Thank you. It will pass." Even though it will not. The sorceress is hardly one to let her plans go awry, and she has caught me firmly in her net. It is the prince she wants, and if I will not be the tool she uses to get him, then Valka will. But what she wants with him, and why, I cannot surmise.

Laina, however, accepts my answer and asks nothing further.

Valka returns to the carriage when the soldiers are ready to move. She glances nonchalantly at me as she enters, but something in her stiffens. As she settles herself gingerly on the cushioned seat, I begin to understand. She too has lost her body. She feels the same strangeness, the same instinctual terror at the change of her hands, her hair.

The burning anger I felt growing in my breast when I faced the Lady reawakens. I will not let Valka see my fear, my discomfort. So, as I look at her, I smile.

She flinches, and I laugh, a high-pitched, quick sound that is not my laugh at all. It comes from some distant place I cannot name, and her face pales.

"Stop it!" My own voice raised in anger against me wrenches me to a halt. She raises her hand to her mouth, eyes bright and angry.

"Whatever happened to your voice?" My voice sounds smoother and sweeter to me than ever before, for it now has her honeyed tones.

Laina glances between us warily.

"Be silent! Or I shall . . ."

"What? What will you do?" I begin to feel a pressure around my neck, the golden chain—invisible, untouchable, yet there— pushes against my windpipe. I must not openly challenge her, not on this.

"I shall make you pay when we arrive in Tarinon." I see myself angry, eyes flashing, face pale. But the expression is strange. It is molded to Valka and not me.

"Perhaps," I say, not really hearing her anymore, for another thought has occurred to me: in Tarinon I might finally meet the mage, the Lady's enemy. Surely he will be able to help me.

We reach the Border House at sunset. Built at a rocky pass, it stands in mute testimony of the friendship (or simple indifference) of our two lands—rarely have we gone to war, never have we needed more than a stopping house here for patrols from either kingdom. Indeed, the Border House often stands empty through the winters, open for any who need shelter.

Now, the house overflows with light and waiting men. They pour out of the building and fill the road as we approach. From their midst, two men stride forward, their clothing and bearing marking them as nobles. I cannot see much of them past Valka, who moves at once to the door and waits impatiently to alight.

As she descends, Captain Sarkor addresses the princess with a bow. "Your Highness, may I present Lord Melkior, high marshal of Menaiya, and Lord Filadon of Barinol."

The two men bow deeply to her; she inclines her head in return.

The men could not be more different. One has the sense of great height when looking at Melkior, though not all of it physical. He bears himself proudly and his eyes hold definite authority; he is used to his power. So I understand at once why Filadon is mentioned second. He is slim and unassuming, his eyes gentle though shrewd and his lips used to smiling. He pauses to look past his new lady to where Laina and I still wait in the carriage, and nods to us while Melkior addresses the princess.

"It is our great honor and privilege to welcome Your Highness to the kingdom of Menaiya," Melkior says. "The prince himself wished to accompany us, but he has been taken ill of late and could not join us."

"I pray he recovers his spirits," Valka murmurs, all heartfelt concern.

Melkior smiles, revealing two lines of pearly white teeth. "By all reports, he is healing well."

Filadon gestures toward the house. "We have prepared a meal for you and your escort, Your Highness, if you will join us?"

"That was most thoughtful of you, Lord Filadon," Valka purrs. She starts forward and the two lords fall into step with her, accompanying her into the house. It is a strange thing to watch. In these few hours she has developed her own walk, nothing like my own gait. She moves with a certain confidence, her chin raised just high enough to require her to glance down as she reaches the threshold.

Laina clears her throat, and I realize I am still standing in the carriage door, staring. I jump down and hastily follow them inside. Laina scurries after me.

A rough table runs the width of the room, laden with silver platters of food and pitchers of both water and wine. I hesitate in the doorway as my eyes adjust to the lamplight. The princess sits at the head of the table, a lord on each side.

I must take my place now, I think with a sudden urgency, *or I shall lose even that.* I hurriedly seat myself next to Filadon, remembering his quiet smile.

Valka glares at me. I understand now more clearly than ever why neither my mother nor any of the courtiers took me seriously:

my body does not lend itself to grandness. Valka, trying to look proud and above me, appears only petty and cross, a mere child of fifteen years. Still, she must introduce me before she can snub me, else her companions may not know whether they dare join her. "My lords, allow me to introduce my companion, Lady—Valka." Her words are laden with contempt.

Melkior and Filadon bow from the neck.

I dip my head in return. "My lords."

"And my maid," Valka finishes, nodding to where Laina has taken up a station along the wall. So Valka has made me merely a lady-in-waiting, without known title or parentage, hardly worth mentioning before a maid.

I eat slowly, watching the lords, trying to work through how to reveal my new body's lineage as Lord Daerilin's daughter, how to create allies of these men when I have never been able to manage such a thing before. Neither lord addresses me other than to offer food or drink. Valka pointedly ignores me. By the end of the meal it is clear I will make no friends here.

The soldiers have prepared a back room for our use and Valka happily retires there after the meal, escorted as always by my quad, Matsin among them. Laina follows after her, as she would with me, to help the princess change with her usual brusque manner. And when I go in, she will flutter over me and grant me all the courtesies she usually showers on Valka. I do not want her mistaken kindnesses, or Valka's sneers. I do not want to watch Valka change, or fumble with the new shape of her body, or find the scars I've worked so hard to hide.

I rise and make my way outside, to follow the road to a stand of trees overlooking the pass. There, I find a seat on a stone. I wrap my arms around my knees and breathe in the clear mountain air. The last of the daylight slowly fades over the mountaintops. The soldiers at the house quiet, the sounds of conversation die away. Night spreads its mantle over the world. I look up through the branches at the canopy of stars. The air is cool, with a slight breeze blowing, and I left my traveling cloak in the carriage when I hurried after Valka to the Border House.

Valka. I close my eyes. The fragile peace the night has constructed around me begins to fray at the edges. That is my name now. And I must think of her as—what? Alyrra? No, but neither traitor nor princess seem right. She is Valka, whatever body she may wear, just as I am still the girl who was princess this morning. While I cannot claim the name Alyrra, I will not be Valka either.

I am not the princess. The thought whispers through me, raising the hair at the back of my neck. It means more than just that I have lost my body, lost the story of my life written upon it.

I am not the princess. I will not be queen. I will not marry a foreign prince, nor live in a court where my language is barely spoken. I will not have to learn to politick, to question my friendships, to trust no one. I need fear my brother no more, nor the cold contempt of my mother, nor the prince who awaits me. I have before me a new life now, if I choose to take it.

I have only to take this chance in my hands, let Valka take on the trappings of my old life, and—

I let out my breath in a sigh that drains all the sweet hope rushing through me. If the Lady wants some hold on Prince

Kestrin, just as she now has a hold on me through my mother's spell, then Valka will be the one to deliver that up. I may know nothing of the prince, but I do not wish such a betrayal upon him.

I must warn him, though how I might do so without losing the future that has just opened up to me, and while the Lady's choker binds my neck, I cannot fathom. Still, this I will fight for: a future free of fear and a life I wish to live, away from the court.

CHAPTER

7

Laina helps me dress in the morning, all smiles and curious looks while Valka sleeps on. No doubt she's wondering what could possibly have convinced me to rise so early when Valka usually sleeps as late as possible.

"Would you like me to walk with you, m'lady?" she asks, as she never asked when I was princess.

I shake my head, eager to step out on my own. I've hardly slept, kept awake equally by the hope of a new life thrilling through me and the unsettling truth that Valka will happily deliver Kestrin to the Lady once she has secured her own position—perhaps once they are wed and she is with child.

At least I have thought of one way to stop Valka: I will seek out the mage who came to my room and use him to deliver a warning to the prince regarding his betrothed. I may not know who the mage is, nor how to find him upon my arrival, but the morning brings with it the hope that I can sort out each trouble in its time. He serves the king, after all. Someone in the court will no doubt be able to point him out to me.

For now, I want to clear my thoughts, focus on how I can ensure a future I want. As Valka's companion, there will naturally be a place for me at court, but I would much rather leave politics behind altogether. How to accomplish that, I have yet to discover, but Valka should be more than happy to help me on my way out.

When I step from our room, I find the men have already risen and left the main room. Outside, I spy Melkior and Filadon standing together by the carriage, deep in discussion with Captain Sarkor, while the soldiers make ready to leave. As I reach the end of our little party, I stop in dismay. There, already tethered to the supply wagon, stands the white.

I go to him, stopping a few paces away as he swings his head around to watch me. "I'm sorry," I murmur. "I thought you escaped. I assumed you did—but you must never have gotten free of your halter."

He huffs softly, one ear swiveled toward the men loading the wagon. They hardly spare me a glance.

"I'm sorry," I say again before turning to resume my walk, but the pleasure of the morning has left me.

It will be up to me to try to free the white now. Free the white, warn the prince, and then find a way out of the court. Not one of them will be easy, nor do I know where I will go at the end of it all. Perhaps I can earn a place as a companion or tutor of some sort, though my limited grasp of Menay may make that difficult. I will have to work to learn the language as quickly as possible. I walk on, until the sun sends its first bright rays over the far mountains to light the sky, and still I have no real answers to the worries weighing upon me.

By the time I return to the Border House, all that remains within is a tray with breakfast foods. I sit down and help myself to the cold meats and bread laid out. Eventually, Valka emerges. Even though I have watched her all this last day and more, it is still a shock to see myself now, lips pursed, reaching for a piece of bread. I study her as she eats, intrigued by the way she chews, by the play of light on her forehead and cheeks. My own body, I note, lacks the softness of Valka's, the shapely form and unscarred flesh. As Valka reaches for more food, I touch the scar that curves across what were once my knuckles, my fingers pale against her skin. She jerks away from me.

"Do you know how you got that?" I ask, half amused.

"I don't know what you mean." Her voice is sharp.

"I was gathering rose hips to make a tisane for Jilna. I slipped at the top of a ravine and slid all the way down. There were brambles at the bottom and I sliced open my knuckles on them. Mother was furious." I rub my own knuckles, remembering the pain.

Valka stares at me silently; I cannot tell if she is frightened by my friendliness, or merely disgusted. Perhaps she is wondering if all my other scars have such innocuous explanations to them. Or why the choker hasn't silenced me. But it seems that, at least when I speak with Valka, I need not fear its effect. I rise and move to the door. Let her stew for a little on just how much she needs to know of my life to make her charade work.

Lieutenant Balin and his soldiers have gathered just outside, ready to take their leave of the princess. They do not give me more than a glance as I walk to the carriage.

Valka steps out soon after and smiles radiantly as she addresses our escort from home. "Lieutenant Balin, I thank you and your men for the service you have done me on this journey." She glances toward where I wait in the carriage. "I pray you will tell my mother you left me well."

"Your Highness." Balin bows deeply. "It has been the greatest honor to serve as your escort. I shall deliver your message to the queen myself."

Within a few minutes, the whole of our escort from home has mounted up and left, the horses' hooves raising a fine cloud of dust that drifts across the road.

Valka enters our carriage, looking about as if assessing it for the first time.

"I do wish you'd put your things away," she says, gesturing with disgust toward the bundles of fabric at the end of the bench where I sit.

I glance down in surprise: there is my traveling cloak, and beside it the cloak the king gifted me, which I wore on the very first day. Valka has no idea of its significance. I feel a surge of petty triumph and find myself smiling sweetly as I wrap up the king's gift within my own, humbler cloak. "Certainly."

Valka sniffs and sits down beside me, leaving the opposite bench empty.

"Where is Laina?" I ask in surprise as Melkior and Filadon climb up and settle themselves across from us.

Valka flicks her fingers contemptuously. "I sent her back. She has been rude and not particularly helpful. I saw no need to keep her."

Of course. I look out the window, making no further comment. Laina might have eventually realized something was amiss. Now Valka will be safe.

Valka and her two lords keep up a lively discussion through the morning, their conversation laced with allusions to Menaiyan politics.

"You mentioned Prince Kestrin was unwell," Valka observes in a break in the conversation.

"He took ill unexpectedly not quite a month ago," Filadon says. "While our king was with you."

"He went hunting one day and the next—" Melkior begins.

"The king's best healers have been attending him," Filadon continues, as if Melkior had not spoken. Strange that he should override Melkior so. "They assure us he will recover."

That is good, at least.

Melkior smiles amiably, but the press of his lips tells me that he is well aware of Filadon's slight. As if to spite his younger, lesser peer, he goes on. "Prince Kestrin's illness was not unlike what took the queen. We were worried at first that we would lose him as well."

"Then the queen died quite suddenly?" Valka asks.

Melkior nods. "Took ill one day, and the next day she'd gone, dear lady. She was as good a queen as we've ever had."

Filadon dips his head in agreement, but the tightness of his eyes betrays his contempt.

I wonder what Filadon's standing is in the court: he might snub Melkior in passing, but Melkior, rather than returning the snub, instead blathers on in concealed fury. As high marshal, surely Melkior holds the most powerful position among all his peers.

Who, then, is Filadon, and why was he chosen to meet us?

Later that day, as we wait for the soldiers to set out our meal at a makeshift table along the roadside, Filadon turns to me. "Lady Valka, you've been most quiet. I hope you are feeling quite well."

"Oh, quite well," I assure him, amused. I might have spoken more had anyone addressed me. But I've spent my hours of quiet in planning. I've no intention of wasting the opportunity now that he *has* deigned to speak to me. "Please, though, my lords, I beg you will not call me Lady Valka. It is too strange. My mother's name is also Valka—I have always been called Lady Thoreena instead."

"Why, of course," Filadon says, with a slight bow.

Melkior echoes his bow, his expression one of polite boredom.

Valka glares at me, her cheeks paling in anger.

"I thank you, my lords." I smile at Valka. A new name for a new life. She may be princess, but I will be able to let her identity go while she must ever live with mine.

I remain quiet through the rest of our meal, smiling and nodding when addressed, and enjoying the simple but hearty fare of breads, cheeses, fruits, and cold meats.

Soon enough, we climb back into the carriage and continue on. The rocky pass gives way to sparsely forested mountains, and more and more we see open slopes with lush grasses and the last wildflowers of the season stretching between the thinning stands of pines and oaks. We should descend to the plains within a day or two.

We reach our night's destination of a small roadside inn with good time, the sun still a handbreadth above the horizon. After washing up in my room, I make my way around to the corral that holds the bulk of our horses, looking for the white. The hostlers have gone in for dinner, leaving the horses unattended, though visible from the kitchen door. At the far end of the corral I spot the white. He watches me, head raised, bright eyes alert. My heart aches for him.

"I don't know how I'm going to free you," I say, resting my hand on the wooden rail. Tonight there'll be a guard posted, and even now the kitchen staff pass the door at intervals, just enough of a presence that I dare not let him out. "Valka's the sort that will send you to the knacker when she realizes she can't ride you. I wish you'd gotten away when you could."

"I chose to stay, princess," he replies, his voice deep and gentle.

My mouth drops open. What? "Did you—did you just *speak*?"

The horse seems mildly gratified by my shock. "Yes," he says.

I can see his mouth move, though his lips don't quite shape the word that rings in my ears. He's speaking, out loud, shaping sounds a horse's mouth has no ability to make.

"But *how*?"

"I expect that should be obvious."

I press my hand against the top of my head, as if I might thereby straighten my thoughts. Nothing makes any sense at all, except, perhaps: "Magic?"

He dips his head, for all the world as if he were a courtier.

"Are you cursed?" I demand, letting go of my head to catch the rail between us.

"No," he says, his voice lightening with amusement. "Not at

all. It is my nature to be able to speak. I merely prefer not to flaunt it before your kind."

"How did you—end up here?" And why wouldn't such a creature have used his voice to gain his freedom?

"I was caught in a moment of distractedness," the white says. "Your brother merely traded for me, after hearing that I wouldn't take a rider." He continues conversationally, "Your brother is quite the fool, by the by. I'd lost almost all hope for humanity until you came along."

A giggle escapes me, and then another, edged with hysteria. It is all I can do to swallow down my laughter before I draw the kitchen staff's attention. My brother called a fool by a talking horse, and I the hope for humanity? Perhaps I'm losing my sanity. Perhaps this is the Lady's revenge, to tease away my grasp on reality, until I'm chattering away at butterflies and no danger to anyone but myself. And no help to anyone either.

"You should have left," I say softly, because mad or no, he is still here, and Valka will not value a horse she cannot ride.

"I stayed because I like you. You have something of justice and mercy in you."

"That's not a good reason. Whatever I may or may not have in me, I haven't much power to protect you. And the princess will surely . . ." I gape at him, stunned. *Princess*, he called me when he first spoke. *Your brother*, he said.

"I know what happened to you. I left your party and was in the woods farther down the river when your life was taken from you and given to her. I had not the power to intervene, but I could act as witness."

His voice is deep and steady and true in my ears. This is no hallucination, just a reality I had not imagined.

"And so you stayed with us," I finish softly. "But tell me, how can you speak? What are you really?"

"I am a Horse, one of the old race, as different from your beasts of burden as you are. Your hostler was not too far off when he claimed I came from the Fethering Plains, for I was born not much farther south than that. That was long ago, even as humans measure time."

He shakes his mane, glancing toward the kitchen door, but all lies quiet there. "Have you thought on how to undo the spell?"

"Undo it?"

"Of course! You wish to undo it, don't you?"

I gather myself. "I did initially, but—but I have had time to think about it, and I don't want to anymore."

"You don't want to anymore." He repeats the words carefully, as if they might change their meaning as he speaks.

"No."

"Why?" If a horse could look flabbergasted, I imagine it would look much like the white before me.

"I don't have to be what I was. Don't you see? I never was very good at it, and I hate the court, and this is my chance to leave it all. I can choose my life now."

The white studies me, and when he speaks next, it is with certain accents of disappointment. "You feel no duty toward your people?"

A slight flush warms my cheeks. "I have left my people behind. No matter my rank, I can't help them from Menaiya."

"The Menaiyans *are* your people. They have chosen you. Would you send them a viper in your place?"

I pause, thinking about Valka, about court life. "She could only do as much harm as the royal family permits. If they allow her anything, then they are probably just as bad. I wouldn't know how to counter them. Besides, she will do much better there than I. She understands politics."

"It is rare for someone who wants power to truly deserve it. She will bring unhappiness to this land. You would do your best not to." He is trying to be patient with me.

I shake my head. "Va—"

I break off as the choker snaps tight around my neck, cutting off my breath and blood with it. I stumble forward into the fence, one hand at my throat as my mouth gapes open. And then my breath rushes back in with a wheeze.

"Princess?" the horse asks softly.

I straighten, drop my hand, and try again, as if nothing were amiss. My voice comes out rough and uneven. "She is not innately evil. She is simply unfeeling and petty. She will care more for her dresses and jewels than anything. As princess, she will have everything at her disposal. There are much worse things in a ruler than a love of trinkets."

If I could only be certain that Valka won't betray the prince, I'd have no concern at all. But she will, for the Lady holds Valka in her hand now, too. I may not be able to stop either the Lady or Valka, but I can warn the prince. And surely I can do so without reclaiming my old life.

"Do you care nothing for your own name and position?"

"There is more to life than names and positions." Frustration gives my voice an edge. "I have never truly been a princess." At least the choker allows me to claim that.

"Yes," he agrees after a short pause. "You have never wanted your power. That only makes you a better princess than most."

A contrary talking horse—who would have thought it possible? "Why do you care what position I hold?"

"I thought you would care. I think you still might, given time. And it seems that you will have as much of it as you wish." He turns away and steps past the other horses. "Come visit me again, princess."

I watch him, watch the way the other horses take no notice of him at all: a talking horse with a sense of honor. I do not know what to make of that.

I return to the inn and spend dinner mulling over our conversation. If I barely notice Valka and her lords, I doubt they realize it. Even lying in bed, I cannot comprehend why the white would care when he had his own freedom at hand. Or hoof, as the case may be.

Eventually, I fall into an uneasy sleep and dream of the plains. It is a moonless night, the land brightened only by starlight. The grasses seem deceptively short at first, but as I walk they rise up to brush my shoulders. It is hard walking and, while I travel a straight and purposeful path, I do not know where I go, for I can barely see over the tops of the waving grasses.

I come to the ravine so suddenly that I fall, sliding down its steep sides in a shower of shale. It is barely a dozen paces wide, the rocky sides so sheer they tower like stone walls above me. I pick myself up gingerly, rub the grit from my hands. My eyes are drawn to a faint light glowing farther along the rift; when I reach it, I find the opening of a tunnel.

The tunnel continues straight for a few paces with the light remaining steady. Then I turn a corner and step into bright lamplight. A spacious room has been hollowed out of the rock. It lies completely empty but for a great, carved stone pedestal that stands at the center. Above it hangs a lamp that shines bright and steady, lit by a luminae stone rather than fire. I approach cautiously, but I am alone, the entrance I came through the only one.

A shallow pan filled with sparkling water rests upon the pedestal. I peer into the water uncertainly, remembering the last time I looked for my reflection. But I see nothing strange, nothing but myself.

Myself. My breath escapes me with a grunt, as if I have been struck. The face looking back is the face I have always worn. As I stare, the image shifts, my features blurring as they change, hair darkening to black. A pair of brown eyes blink up at me from a man's face.

With a sickening lurch I recognize him as the mage from my chamber. His brow creases, shadows flicker across his face, and his lips move, shaping my name: *Alyrra*.

I shake my head, my fingers curled tight around the edge of the pedestal. He leans closer, confusion etched in the lines of his face, and again I see my name on his lips.

No. I push away from the pedestal, stumbling over my own feet in my haste to reach the door. When I step through it, I fall into a smothering darkness. I reach out desperately as inky blackness fills my sight, pools in my mouth. My fingers, curled into claws, catch on the edge of *something*, and then I am tearing away my bedsheets, moonlight filtering in through the shutters and my lungs filling once more with the sweet night air.

CHAPTER

8

The following day, we descend from the foothills. The plains stretch out as far as the eye can see, vast and waving, the grasses golden with the late summer heat. I note with relief that they are not as tall as I'd dreamed, barely reaching the horses' knees.

The villages we pass are spread out, the land surrounding them planted with crops, wheat and corn, as well as lower-growing vegetables and small orchards of fruit-bearing trees. Sometimes we pass great areas fenced all around, within which horses roam. These, Melkior tells the princess, are the ranches upon which some of Menaiya's finest horses are bred.

After dinner at this night's inn, I visit the stables. The hostlers have yet to return from their meal, though a soldier stands guard outside the building. As I reach the stall door, the white sticks his head out to bump my shoulder with his nose. I brace my feet so he doesn't knock me over.

"Have you thought further on your future?" he asks, keeping his voice low.

The only thing that has changed is that I am no longer quite so eager to meet the mage—what if he sees through the enchantment that holds me, as he did in my dream? I don't want him to force me back into the role of princess, but I have no other way to deliver a warning to the prince.

I answer the white with a question of my own. "What makes you think either of us can do anything?"

He sighs, a great whoosh of air beside my ear. "I can't. Only you can undo the Lady's spell."

"Me?"

"You must either cast a counter-spell of equal strength or you must convince her to lift it."

I almost laugh. One is as impossible as the other. "I am no sorceress," I say dryly.

"Then you must find out what she meant to gain by attacking you."

She wants Prince Kestrin—who was laid low by an unnamed illness the last anyone of our party knew of him. "Perhaps she has already gained it," I mutter. But no, she would not have switched Valka and me had she already achieved her aim.

"You have met her before," he says.

"Yes."

He waits, ears swiveled toward me.

"It's the prince," I admit. The words are loud and ugly in the space between us. I wish I did not have to say them. "She came to me twice. The second time she said it herself: it's Prince Kestrin she wants."

"So the impostor will deliver him to her," he says quietly. "And you will stand by and watch?"

"No—no, I won't." I shake my head, my hands clenched tight. "I'll warn him. And then I'll get away from the court. I don't have to *be* princess to warn him. It's just . . ." I trail off, shake my head. There are still pieces that don't fit together.

"What?"

"The Lady's so powerful. I don't understand why she would need . . ." I swallow past the slight tightening of the choker, and try to keep my words vague. "Why she would need either of us to—to take him."

The white tilts his head, thinking. "You're sure she could overpower him?"

"I think so." The mage fell easily enough before her. I am still only hoping that he survived the encounter. What likelihood is there that a magic-less prince would do better?

"Then there is more at play than just brute power. Perhaps she wants him to capitulate, to surrender himself to her. If he cedes his will to her, she'll have a hold on him that nothing can break."

I look away. For that, she would need a bait he would give himself up for. *This is why the Family wanted me, a princess whose death no one will mourn.* I close my eyes, but I cannot hide from the truth before me. When the time comes, the prince intends to give up his bride to save himself. Only it will be Valka he betrays, who intends to repay him equally.

"Princess?" the white queries.

I open my eyes, swallow to ease the ache in my throat. "I'll warn him," I say, because I must. Because I have only guesses about the prince right now, none of them good, and none of them certain.

The white sighs. I lean against the stall door, trace the lines of his neck and back with my eyes. He's a great creature, strong and noble, but there's a weariness to his stance I can't place. Nor can I understand why he gave up his freedom to come back and speak with me, hope for humanity or not.

In the quiet, I ask, "Will you tell me your name?"

He considers me and then huffs softly. "Falada."

A faint step sounds from outside. He turns away to nose at his hay. A moment later, a lone hostler enters the stable, pausing to bow when he sees me. "My lady, can I help you?"

I shake my head, happy to hear him speak my language. "No, thank you." I leave the hostler to his work and return to the inn for the night.

The next morning begins as any other. I do not suspect trouble until I catch Valka's self-satisfied smile as she steps out of the carriage to stretch her legs at midmorning.

"Have my horse saddled," she orders Captain Sarkor. "I am tired of the carriage."

"Your Highness," Sarkor replies curtly. He walks down the road to the end of our party, where the white is tied to the supply wagon. I watch after him surreptitiously.

"You will join me, my lords?" Valka turns a sunny smile on our companions.

"With pleasure," Melkior says. Immediately a second soldier is dispatched for the lords' mounts. I sense Filadon's quick glance, but there is no fourth horse for me. Had there been, I would have opted to ride long before this to escape Valka's company.

I move away from their little group, watching as the hostlers unload the requisite saddles from the wagon. Daerilin did not give his daughter a horse to take with her. Did he refuse her one? Or did Valka refuse it herself, already expecting to replace me and knowing I would miss having a horse? It would be a petty sort of revenge, just the sort of thing she might do.

Only now she has a horse she cannot ride. I don't imagine this ending well.

I watch as a hostler approaches the white and places a saddle blanket across his back. Falada snorts and steps away, his head snaking around, teeth bared. The hostler stumbles back with a yelp and the white rears in response, the blanket flying off his back like chaff, the whole wagon jerking as his lead snaps tight.

"Easy," I cry, running toward them. The soldiers form a ring around Falada at once, though they stay well back. The white snorts and pulls at his lead, the muscles of his neck bulging.

"Easy," I say again, darting between two soldiers to get to the white.

"Veria—*lady*, get back," Sarkor orders.

I hold out my hand to the white, willing him to listen to me. "Easy," I repeat.

He drops down to look at me.

"Gently now."

Falada stands perfectly still.

"No one's going to ride you," I tell him.

His ears flick toward Sarkor, who has begun to walk toward me. With two quick steps, the white reaches me and drops his nose into my hand.

"There," I say, patting his cheek with my other hand.

Sarkor's hand closes on my elbow and pulls me back.

"He just spooked," I say, trying to pull out of the tight grip.

"Indeed," Sarkor replies. "That is why I ordered you back."

"They shouldn't try to saddle him." I let Sarkor guide me out of the ring, for his grip is like my brother's and will brook no argument. Surely he will not strike me?

"They won't," he says, and fires off a string of commands to his men in Menay. I don't recognize all the words, but *princess* and *horse* and *later* all stand out.

I glance over my shoulder. The men keep their distance from the horse, moving off to go about their duties.

Sarkor walks me away from the road. My skirts snag on the grasses, tugging back as he hauls me forward. I am grateful when we come to a stop. We are no longer within easy earshot of our traveling party. We are still perfectly visible to them, but I am not sure enough of Sarkor to take comfort from that. His grip is tight, unyielding, but not painful. Yet.

"You *fool*," he says, swinging around to face me. He releases my elbow and his hands settle in fists at his waist. "What were you doing?"

"He wouldn't hurt me."

"You've seen less of that horse than the princess has," Sarkor snaps. "He went wild and you *approached* him. Against my orders." Orders he'd snapped out in two different languages, trying to stop me. He'd been frightened, and that has only angered him more.

"I didn't mean—"

"Don't lie to me," he growls.

I stand completely still, my eyes on his chest barely two hand spans before me. I wish he would step back; I dare not move.

"You heard me and you did as you wished. Had you been harmed, I would have been called to account."

"I'm sorry," I whisper.

"As long as you ride with me, you ride under my command. Do you understand?"

"Yes."

"I have sworn to deliver your princess and all who travel with her to Tarinon in safety. If you endanger your lady or any of my men again, I will see that the king deals with you. He will not be pleased."

"I'm sorry," I repeat, my voice wavering. "I didn't mean to endanger anyone. But . . ."

"*But?*" he echoes, half incredulous.

I don't look at him. "The white—she shouldn't ride it. Not now and not later."

A pause. "Stallions can be chancy, but there's no reason why she can't control it."

I shake my head. Perhaps he's heard that I rode often, but Valka is not half the horsewoman I am, and in any case, Falada is clearly not about to let her sit him.

Sarkor studies me a long moment. "What do you know of it?"

I take a careful breath. He's clever, and he knows that Valka—the Valka I am pretending to be—has rarely been near the white. "It's a gift from her brother," I say. "He gave it to her at the last moment, to replace her own mount."

Sarkor looks past me toward the line of horses and wagons. "What exactly are you saying?"

"You've taken a measure of the prince."

"Have I?"

That's not something Valka would have known—no one but my brother and I know of Sarkor's intervention in the hallway. For a moment, I flounder for an answer. When I find it, I speak as if coming up for air. "You set quads to guard the princess these last two weeks."

"You think you know the reason why?"

I look up without thinking. Displeasure deepens the faint lines around his mouth.

"N-no," I stammer. "No. But, but you must have guessed—her brother was not kind to her. It would be a jest on his part, to gift her a horse that can't be ridden." Especially when the Menaiyans are renowned riders.

Sarkor knows it. I can see it in the tightening of his jaw, the flicker of his eyes back toward the white. But he won't admit such a thing out loud to me. His honor demands that he protect my family's integrity in public, regardless of what my brother is truly like. Sarkor looks down at me, his face hard as stone. There is a threat that I recognize in the line of his shoulders. "We have great respect for Princess Alyrra's family," he says, his voice soft with menace. "Understand that."

I nod jerkily.

"If I hear you spreading such rumors, here or in the palace, rest assured the Family will know where they began."

I nod once more and drop my gaze to the grass.

"I expect there will be no further cause for us to speak," Sarkor says. It is more an order than anything. I shake my head, but he's already gone, striding back to the road. I wait until my hands stop trembling before I follow.

"How could you bring such a mount?" Valka demands that evening as we prepare for bed. It is the first time she has addressed me of her own accord when we are alone together. "It's useless. I'll have it sent to the knacker!"

I stiffen, fighting back a wave of dread. She mustn't see that I care. I force a soft laugh. "It was a gift from my brother. You cannot truly be surprised that it can't be ridden."

She pauses, one corner of her mouth lifting in a smirk. His cruelty was never aimed at her, and even now, she only finds it amusing. "Was it?"

I may have only this one opportunity to speak for the white's life. I nod, watching her carefully. "Now that he is your brother, you had better be careful of the games he plays. If you have the horse killed, that will be a victory for him. He'll use it to point out your ignorance in killing a perfectly good breeding animal, and no doubt do more when he comes for the wedding. It will cut you down before the rest of the court. If you act as if it makes no difference to you, that will aggravate him, and you will have won."

Valka frowns. "What? Shall I take advice from *you*?"

I've gone too far. "I hardly care what you do," I say, turning away.

Valka makes no response, though I can feel her watching me angrily. I can only hope she'll reflect on my words before making her decision.

Valka does not attempt to ride again. Both Filadon and Melkior proffer her their mounts. She declines their offers with flashing eyes, furious to have become an object of pity. If I did not care for the white's future, I would be amused by how well my brother's ploy has played out: Melkior's offer to Valka is all wide smiles and condescension for this poor girl who could not even bring a worthy mount with her.

Filadon, however, surprises me. There is nothing of arrogance or judgment in his offer to Valka, or even in any of his actions toward me. Indeed, whenever he and I find ourselves alone together for a few moments—waiting in the inn yard before a departure or arriving at breakfast before the others—he speaks to me kindly.

He does not ask about the princess, or our relationship, or give any indication that he has a motive in befriending me. Nor does he dismiss me as Melkior has; even in company with the princess, he has a smile for me, and will offer me food or drink before I ask. Valka has had to bite her lip more than once, for how can she be angry with Filadon for such small attentions when he has tendered her no insult? I wonder if this was why Filadon was chosen to meet me: because, at heart, he is a kind man.

Perhaps I can ask for his help in finding a new position, away from court. At least I might rely on his small kindnesses as I settle in at court under Valka in these first weeks, and try to envision a future I might actually want. For all the quiet hours I've had in the carriage and alone in my room at night, trying to imagine a life of work that I might enjoy and am qualified enough to do, I have come up with very little.

Now, as the king's city grows from a smudge on the horizon to a great stone wall cutting through the plains, I have no better plan than what I started with. I sit across from Valka, watching as we roll through the massive gates and into another world. The whole of the city of Tarinon lies crowded within these walls, built up into many-floored buildings of yellow brick. People fill the streets, overflowing into alleys and hanging off stairwells to watch our party arrive. Children perch on lower rooftops, barefoot and laughing. I stare out, amazed at the size of this city, at the height of the buildings and the flashes of wealth I glimpse through the sheer mass of humanity. The people are all here to see me—or what I once was. Looking out at them, I am desperately grateful to have escaped the court of a king who rules so easily over so much.

The crowds end abruptly at the palace gates. We clatter into a gleaming courtyard, the horses' hooves ringing on the cobble-stones. Valka rises as we roll to a stop, stepping to the carriage door even as the footman moves to open it. I look out, searching the gathered nobles for a glimpse of the man I would have married, the man I now need to warn. Here is the life I am bidding goodbye. Here is the life I will not have to take.

Valka descends as the door swings open, eagerness written in every move.

"Your Majesty, the princess Alyrra ka Rosen," Melkior intones, having dismounted from his horse a bare moment before; the nobles nearest the king shift back, giving me a clear view of the young man who remains at his shoulder.

My breath stills in my lungs. I know this man who stands beside the king, have seen this prince before. He is as tall as his father, with the same dark hair as all their people, but where the king has curved, hawklike features, his son has more feminine high cheekbones. Still, they share the same defined jaw, the same air of natural authority.

"Alyrra, may I introduce my son, Prince Kestrin," the king says, and the sorcerer from my chamber bows in return to Valka's curtsy.

My hands clutch at the window frame, as if I might anchor myself against this reality, as if I might somehow catch myself before the world tilts any further off balance. The mage *is* Prince Kestrin.

Valka looks away from him coyly. The prince stands stiffly, as if he yet battles some illness and fears to let slip any sign of weakness. His eyes flicker once to the carriage, skimming over me as if I were no more remarkable than a shadow, and then return to Valka. I cannot say whether her behavior strikes him as strange—coyness when she should be struggling with the realization that she has met him before.

I want desperately to step forward, to tell him: do not trust her. He came to warn me, prince and sorcerer though he may be, and so I should return the warning. I *must*. But even as the words form in my mind, the chain the Lady placed around my neck tightens.

My breath comes fast and hard, my thoughts slowing as I watch Valka step forward to take the prince's arm. I must step down now, join them before I am left behind and forgotten. But my fingers still grasp the window frame, and I cannot make myself follow.

The prince leads his lady toward a huge set of doors intricately carved and elaborately inlaid with bronze-work. I stare at them numbly, remembering the big double doors to our hall at home with their iron bands and blue-and-white paint. They would look like a piece from a child's playhouse here, small and ridiculously simple.

At the king's nod, the doors are thrown open in welcome. Instead of entering, he pauses on the threshold, then turns around. Melkior and Filadon step back so as not to crowd their king, as do the other nobles around them. The king's eyes come to rest on me from across the courtyard, cold and sure. He knew I was here, knew that my companions were leaving me behind, and he chose to play along and then stop them. Nodding toward me, he says something to Valka where she stands with the prince.

I force myself to unclench my fingers, push myself to my feet and move to the door, my legs creaking, as if I had turned old in the time since we arrived. I step down, watching Valka's smile, thin and pleased and cutting as a knife. It is too late to join my party now, too late to hold on to what position I had. She has already cast me off; this is all she needed to show the court that I have no place with her. I am just as foolish and stupid as my mother always said, and I do not know what it will cost me.

Valka says something to the king, one hand gesturing dismissively, and then they continue into the hall.

I am lost in a sea of sound and movement. Our horses are led away, their hooves clattering over stone. The soldiers call greetings across the courtyard, servants bustle past, and the remaining nobles retreat to the hall. Everywhere there is the sound of talking: laughing, shouting, swearing, every last word in Menay. And the one ally I thought I had, the one man whose enemy I share, is no ally at all but my betrothed.

I wrap my arms around myself. Now that I've let myself fall behind and be forgotten, there will be no easy place for me in the court, nor anyone to help me find some other position. I feel as if at any moment parts of me will start breaking away, my soul splintering beneath the sudden onslaught of knowledge.

"Lady?" A short, severe-looking man stands at my elbow. I

turn to him as one drowning reaches for aid. He eyes me dubiously. "Follow me."

His voice is deep, his accent so thick it nearly obscures his words, but he speaks my language nonetheless. I latch on to his face, well shaved yet dark with bushy eyebrows and sharp brown eyes. His hair, unlike the soldiers', is cropped short. I follow him across the courtyard to a side door, and then down hallway after hallway. I follow blindly, not caring where I walk. Finally, the man stops, opens a door, and gestures for me to enter.

I step into a small bedchamber. Behind me, the door clicks shut. The man's tread fades into silence. After a time, I walk to the small chair set beside the window and sit down. I smooth the fabric of my skirts over my lap, arrange my hands carefully. I know Falada will be well cared for, that my trunks will not be lost, that the only thing, truly, that may be lost is the prince, and of him I will not think.

CHAPTER
9

Evening gathers in the corners of the courtyard below, soft blue shadows spreading their wings over the mosaic-tiled floor. This one courtyard alone, with its tapestry of flowers and circles interwoven and spread across the ground, tucked away and barely used, tells me how motivated the king was to find a princess no one would mourn should she fall prey to the Lady. What other reason could he have for staying longer than the moment it took to glance over our roughly cobbled yard? We are not their equal, my family a troupe of commoners in comparison to the residents of so opulent a palace.

The numbness has faded, as it always does, leaving me wound tight with a panic I won't admit to. I've lost my place at court before I ever had it, and with it any chance of using the court to find a way to a new life. If Valka casts me off, where will I go? I do not know this city, barely understand the language, and while Filadon was kind to me, I doubt he would help me in the full face of Valka's displeasure. But far worse than my fate is the knowledge that I have no easy way to warn the mage to beware of Valka—the mage who is my betrothed. To warn Prince Kestrin now would be to risk his learning my true identity, and yet I cannot stand by and let Valka betray him.

A knock comes at my door: a confident tap-tap-tap that breaks through my thoughts. I turn toward it, gazing through the half-remembered scape of my darkened room. The knock comes again. I rise and move to the door, open it hesitantly.

Captain Sarkor stands in the brightly lit hall, accompanied only by Matsin en Korto. Sarkor sketches a slight bow, his eyes grim, his lips straight. His is a face of strength and intellect. I wish suddenly that I had not angered him the day Valka wished to ride the white. Had I not, I might be able to speak to him now, might ask him what has passed while I have waited alone in my room.

"Lady, the king requests your presence."

I nod, step out to follow them. Valka has cast me off so completely she will not even see me. Why the king would interest himself on my behalf, I cannot guess. I must tread this path carefully, that he not decide I am a threat to the princess.

The hallways we walk are lit by sconces set in the walls, evenly spaced. At first the halls strike me as rich, with wood floors and a band of mosaic tile toward the ceiling, but as we continue, the corridors grow richer, more exquisite, with woodwork and carvings, meeting with mosaics at shoulder level that rise to the ceiling. I can hear the quiet rumble of many people, distant laughter and music drifting toward us. The lamps are replaced by luminae stones, their magical golden glow gentle and steady. I count a dozen before I give up counting at all. We had only four at home, and placed them all in the king's room for his visit. Though perhaps now that Mother has managed to bring a mage to our hall, he will enchant a few more for her.

My fingers fist around the fabric of the skirts as I think of Mother and Mage Efrin casting their spell, dismissing whatever opinion I might have had. What a stupid way to tie up such power over me, in a *handkerchief* that could be so easily stolen. Without it, the Lady would not have had any hold on me, to take my body from me or silence me. I doubt my mother believed I would lose it, or that it could be used so terribly against me. But then it has also been the vehicle of my freedom, so perhaps I should be grateful for my mother's shortsightedness.

The soldiers stop before a door of carved and inlaid wood. At Sarkor's knock, a voice answers in a short, distinct command. He opens the door, stepping in to bow. "Your Majesty, may I present the lady Valka, called Thoreena, companion to the princess Alyrra."

I enter and drop into a curtsy. Sarkor bows once more and departs, and still I wait.

"Lady Thoreena," the king finally says, and I rise from my curtsy. He is dressed in a cream tunic trimmed with beige and gold, his sword belt replaced by a gold embroidered sash. He does not need a weapon at hand here. Instead, he holds a goblet, fingers curling gently around the slender gold stem.

I lower my gaze to his feet and see that he wears slender leather slippers, embroidered, with a long, curled toe. I stare at his shoes, mortified. He must have thought our hall filthy—from the cobbled yard to the scuffed floors to the rushes and dogs in the hall itself. He must have. He never wore anything but boots during his visit.

"I hope you have been made comfortable here."

"Quite," I say, and then catch myself. "Your Majesty."

The liquid in his goblet twirls as he considers me. I have not changed or washed since my arrival. His gaze lingers on me, but he lets my words pass. "You are aware that you have displeased the princess."

"Your Majesty," I agree.

"She has asked me to find you some work, to make use of you." He pauses, but I make no reply.

I watch his fingers on the goblet. The fragile glass cup cradled by its gold stem seems as delicate as this moment, the possibilities I dare not hope for: that the king himself might find me a post, a future from which I might build a new life. I stay still, my expression empty, that he not guess at the hope flickering in my breast.

"Can you tell me what has so displeased her?" he asks.

"She has said nothing?" I ask, looking up slowly. Valka is not the type to pass up a chance to express displeasure. The king is playing a game, then, with my future hanging in the balance.

"She has said very little," the king replies. "I would hear more."

I consider him. In the half-lit room, my thoughts are more lucid to me than the dream of this conversation. He is trying to bluff me into speaking the truth, hoping I will believe that Valka has already spoken half of it. But he has no idea of the truth, any more than Sarkor, who watched the princess's every move but one.

"I would not say more than the princess herself wishes to tell." For all his questions, I doubt the king would reward me for betraying the princess. To him, I am just a tool to be used and tossed aside. There is no sign of the man who spoke of protecting me from my brother. His protection is no longer for me.

"I have discussed what posts we have open with Steward Helántor." He smiles a lovely, empty smile. "All we have to offer is the job of goose girl. I assume you will accept it." He lifts the goblet to his mouth, takes a sip, waiting.

He expects me to cry out in protest, beg a reprieve of some sort. But I can only think of Redna and her horses, and of Dara and Ketsy—now I will be among their number. I dip my head so he does not see the smile I cannot quite banish. I *will* be free, away from the court—

"Unless you are able to provide an escort for yourself," the king adds casually.

"An escort?"

"You cannot make the return journey to Adania alone. While I might offer you a mounted guard, I would need to know more regarding your falling-out with the princess before I did so."

"Your Majesty." There is nothing for me at home, that much I know. But here—here I might have a new life, if only I can act as if I do not care for it. The king waits, watching me. I am aware of the hardness of his gaze. I wonder what he sees in me, what it was that Valka said.

He turns, sets his goblet down on a small table. "Helántor will come for you in the morning." His words are cold, half bored.

I curtsy and turn to leave.

His voice stops me. "If you decide you would like to speak with me again, he will arrange it."

I nod in acknowledgment and slip out the door, holding close the hope of the new life the king has granted me.

Early the following morning, Steward Helántor escorts me through the palace to a small side courtyard. I recognize him as the same distantly polite man who approached me in the courtyard yesterday. Now we take a carriage down one of the main roads away from the palace, turning off just before the city gates. We roll right past an immense stable, and stop in front of a *second* stable, set back behind the first.

I follow Helántor inside curiously, for there are clearly no geese here. He leads me up a dim stairwell by the door to a stuffy little landing. There, he opens a door to reveal a small, bare room: mine. The second door on the landing remains closed. "Here, the key," he says, holding out an iron key. I take it, the metal warm in my hand, and follow him back downstairs and on to a third building, the goose barn.

"Corbé!" calls Helántor as we reach the open doors. A low gate keeps a milling, honking flock of geese contained within. A figure makes its way toward us from the depths of the building, shooing geese out of his way with a staff. The floor, where it is visible, is covered with straw and feathers and goose droppings. I've worn the sturdiest traveling clothes I could find in Valka's trunk, including her most thick-soled slippers, but I'm still not dressed for this role.

"Aye?" Corbé's voice is abrupt, harsh.

Helántor replies in Menay.

They talk for a few minutes, but my coming is clearly no surprise. Corbé is well built, with stocky shoulders and big hands. He must be a few years older than I, and a head taller to boot. He looks at me once, a long, unhurried assessment. I do not like his eyes, though I am not sure why.

Helántor turns to me. "First, you and Corbé take these geese to pasture. Then you return and clean. Corbé will show you. Then you will go to pasture, help bring geese back at night."

I nod. It seems straightforward enough.

"Good," Helántor says, and without a backward glance, he leaves.

I watch him go, my stomach tightening. He's leaving me here—of course he is. This is the life I wanted, isn't it? Freedom from the court, a way to earn an honest living . . . so what if I don't know what I'm doing? I'll learn.

Corbé opens the gate for me. I step in and follow him across the enclosure, my slippers squelching in the filth hidden beneath the straw. The barn itself smells so strongly of both geese and droppings I have to hold my breath to keep my stomach settled.

In a series of gestures, Corbé mimes my duties: rake the droppings, shovel them into a barrel by the door, and throw down more straw from the loft overhead. Then he takes a staff from among the tools leaning against the back wall, shoves it into my hands, and turns away.

With a shout he rouses the flock and drives them toward the gate. The geese pour out the door into the yard. With another shout and a few expertly thrown pebbles, Corbé herds the geese around the corner of the stable opposite and on toward the city gates, gesturing for me to follow behind.

I do, hesitantly using my staff to hurry along the stragglers. A few of the geese try to nip me, turning and jabbing their beaks at me when my staff comes too close to them. I have to push them with it harder than I like in order to get them to follow after their brethren.

It's a long walk around the two stables, through the city gates, and on down the road to their pasture. The land here lies untilled, maintained as meadowland for the king's geese and other livestock, sheep or goats. Meat and eggs and milk for the palace kitchens, no doubt.

The same low stone walls run along the road, occasionally dividing one pasture from the other. By the time we finally leave the road for a narrow path between two short stone walls, and from there turn through a break to a pasture, I have been pecked a half dozen times and am heartily sick of the geese. As soon as they spread out in the pasture, some going to drink from the stream while others pause to tear at the grass, I turn back.

The goose barn lies empty, the straw underfoot matted with droppings. By the time I am done raking and am ready to shovel the mess into the barrel, I am drenched with sweat. It is noon before I have thrown down more straw from the loft overhead and raked it out evenly. My arms and back ache with the unaccustomed lifting. I push a tendril of red hair behind my ear, the feeling of wrongness so slight now that my hand hardly wavers as I tuck it back.

Before I leave for the pasture, I return to the second stables hoping to find a common room like the one I remember from home.

A pair of hostlers stand in the hall, talking together as they look in at a horse. They glance curiously at me as I pass, and a moment later the elder of the two—a man built as big and burly as a bear—sticks his head into the common room to check on me.

I freeze as if caught stealing, but he takes one look at the small piece of flatbread I have found and nods with understanding. He produces a burlap shoulder sack from a cabinet, as well as some cheese wrapped in a cloth and two apples. He adds a tin cup and hands the sack to me with a smile. I carry his kindness with me on the long walk to the pasture, my steps light.

Corbé glances toward me with a scowl as I cross the pasture to the stream. He's angry, though I can't say why. Perhaps he does not like the idea of sharing the pasture with someone else. Well, I'm more than happy to give him his space.

I go to sit halfway across the pasture. I am not about to let one unfriendly man rob me of my chance at happiness. Instead, I let myself sink into the quiet, thinking of my work, and of Valka. I do not necessarily care for the prince, but Falada was right: rather than endanger herself, Valka will use Kestrin to establish herself and betray him when the Lady requires it. I can think of only two ways to stop Valka. I can warn the prince, though how I can do that directly without appearing to betray the princess, or reveal my own identity, I don't know. Or I can find some hold on Valka herself—a hold she will understand. But no matter how long I worry at it, I can't discover what that might be.

I close my eyes and think of other things: of the forests, the dell, my old friend the Wind. It is too much to hope that a little forest wind sprite would follow me over the mountains to the plains, and yet I *had* hoped, just a little. But there's been no sign of the Wind since I left home.

Sometime later, I rouse from a light doze to the sound of Corbé shouting to bring the geese together. Our return is slow going; Corbé ignores the flock near me and I must constantly turn aside for rebel geese. It is only once we pass the city gates that Corbé takes full control of the flock, gesturing for me to go ahead to the barn before turning them into the yard. I hurry past the stables to open the gate and let the feathery crowds in.

Corbé considers my morning's work while I put away my staff. He nods once, almost sullenly, and turns his back on me.

I open my mouth to speak and then close it. None of my language lessons ever included the words to ask a goose boy why he dislikes me, or whether I have not done a good job cleaning a barn.

I return to the second stable, my feet dragging. The sounds of voices raised in conversation carry down the hall from the common room. I stand a long moment by the stairwell to my room, but I cannot expect dinner to be delivered to me on a tray. Steeling myself, I start forward. At least the man this morning seemed kind.

I peek in from the doorway. A group of men and women sit together over their dinner. They laugh as they converse, their manner easy and assured. One of the women glances up as I waver on the threshold. Her eyes are a gentle brown, laughter lines softening them just as age has softened the skin of her cheeks, left her fingers gnarled and calloused. She raises her hand in greeting, and at once the attention of the room turns to me.

I grip a fold of my skirt and rub it with my thumb. They bob their heads and then wait, watching me. I feel as out of place among them as one of my charges might among theirs. They are all of them certain in themselves, strong and purposeful, their movements sure.

The gentle-eyed woman stands up and pulls a stool to the table, speaking words that shuffle across the distance between us and slip out the door behind me. She gestures to the stool, then places her hand on her breast and says her name, another twist of syllables I can't quite follow.

I smile hesitantly, point to myself. At least this much I can manage in Menay. "My name is A—" The choker snaps tight around my neck, and I break off, shocked at the pain, at the way the walls spin. That I should so easily have given this woman my name. That I should have forgotten the threat of the choker simply because I cannot see it.

A hand closes over my elbow, and as I begin to cough, regaining my breath, I find that I have been hustled to the stool. The woman pushes a cup of water into my hands. I smile painfully, sip the water as I recover myself. The hostlers eye me cautiously, as if I might fall over before them, the big, burly man who helped me earlier today watching me worriedly from the corner.

I set the cup down on the table and point to myself again. "Thoreena."

Reassured by my ability to speak, the hostlers introduce themselves in a quick round of pattering, singsong names I cannot catch. They ladle out a bowl of stew for me, hand me a flatbread, and wait patiently as I eat, only occasionally murmuring a comment to each other.

I leave as soon as I am done, smiling and nodding to them,

as glad to escape, no doubt, as they are to have their common room returned to them. It will get better, I promise myself as I let myself into my room. I will learn how to clean the barn properly, and Corbé will not mind me then. And as I learn Menay, perhaps I may even make friends among the hostlers.

I hold that hope close as I drift off to sleep.

CHAPTER 10

Corbé gives me no greeting when I arrive at the goose barn the following morning. He opens the gate for the geese without a glance at me, his mouth twisted in distaste. I keep my attention on our charges and follow after him without a word.

After we take the flock to today's pasture, I return to spend the cool fall morning cleaning out the barn. That is the hardest part of the day; the best is my afternoon in the pasture. There is a particular tranquility to the land, a calm that the honking of geese and flapping of wings only enhances. There is no fear here, no threat of my brother nor sneering contempt of a peer, nor any prospect more grim than the visage of my fellow goose boy, and there's always hope he will improve. There is peace in this pasture, and quiet in my evenings alone in my little room above the stables, and the possibility of friendship with the hostlers of my stable to bear me up.

I eat dinner with the stable hands again come evening. They

speak more among themselves, welcoming me and then forgetting me except to make sure I have what food and drink I wish. I watch them covertly, studying the three men, all within a few years of each other, and whose features carry a certain resemblance mirrored by the younger woman at the table. I wonder if they are siblings, and if so, if the older, gentle-eyed woman is any relation of theirs as well. I listen to the patter of their conversation. Their words are quick, accompanied by frequent laughs and lasting smiles. It is enough to make me want to shout—what use was my studying courtly phrases? Why couldn't my tutors teach me the language of living and laughing? *I will have to learn*, I think wearily. Somehow, I will have to teach myself.

Before I leave, I touch the older woman's sleeve and show her a small wild rose I found beside the goose pasture, one of the last of the season. "Thoreena."

She looks at it. "Thorn." She points to the thorny stem, nodding, and turns to her companions before I can stop her, speaking quickly.

"Thorn," they say, pointing from the rose to me.

"No, no," I say quickly. I have to resort to my own tongue, explaining uselessly, "Rose and thorns together—the whole plant—thoreena."

But they do not understand, and when I leave a few minutes later I am known only as a highly accented "Thorn."

I venture forth from the stables, twirling the rose between my fingers, unsure whether I should laugh at myself or snarl with frustration. What coincidence of usages has allowed these two words to be shared between our tongues, when so much else is different?

Outside, the night air is chilly. I leave the rose by one of the drinking troughs and cross the empty yard to the first stables. Curiosity and a nagging sense of worry carry me through the still-open doors to walk past the stalls in the hopes that, perhaps . . . yes, there.

Falada turns his head to watch my approach, ears pricked forward, his face faintly luminescent in the half-light.

"Well, it's about time," he grumbles as I reach him.

I swallow a laugh.

He eyes me narrowly. "What do you find so amusing?"

"Did you miss me?"

"No," he replies immediately. If he were human he might have blushed. "Do you realize I've been locked in this stall since we arrived?"

"They didn't take you out to the practice ring?"

Falada snorts in disgust. "They tried to saddle me. Can you imagine? A hostler riding a true Horse? Unheard of!"

"I suppose you didn't let them, then?"

"Of course not," he snaps. "Would you?"

I blink, try to imagine myself being taken as a beast of burden. "I don't know," I say, wondering if I have always been that, if I have only just now escaped it, or embraced it. He glares at me, and I say quickly, "I hope not."

"Well, then." He looks at me expectantly. When I hesitate, he lifts his head and orders, "Let me out, princess."

I wince. "Softly! And I can, but I'll have to put a halter on you, for form's sake."

He acquiesces, and with a minimum amount of fumbling

with tack on my part, we walk out to the ring together. As I unbuckle his halter, the ring's gate closed and latched behind us, I ask, "Have you ever let anyone ride you?"

He shakes his head free and then pauses, dark eyes meeting mine. "Never." He takes off, galloping at breakneck speed around the edge of the ring. I climb up to the top of the fence and sit there to wait.

It is not even a quarter of an hour before a hostler comes sprinting out of the stable. He glances around, spots the halter hanging over the gate, and the next moment has climbed into the ring with it in hand.

"It's all right," I say, the foreign words awkward on my tongue, but I don't think the hostler hears me at all. I watch as he tries to corner Falada, but the white will have none of it, prancing away, then breaking into a gallop and swerving around the poor man.

I jump down from my perch. "Falada!"

He comes to me at once, the hostler watching grimly. I turn to him with a forced smile and hold out my hand for the halter. He studies me carefully as he hands it to me. He is as old as the hostler woman in the second stable, tall and sinewy. He watches me as I slide the halter on Falada. I hope I have not angered this man as I did Sarkor.

Falada cooperatively lowers his head to me, and a moment later I hand the hostler the lead. Falada promptly plants his feet apart and refuses to move.

"Falada," I say again, gently, reaching to just touch the man's sleeve with my fingertips. "For God's sake, don't be an ass; go with this man."

Falada snorts and glares at me, but when the hostler tries to lead him out of the ring again, Falada follows.

In the stables, the hostler ties the lead to a ring and leaves, returning with a bin of brushes and hoof picks. Recognizing disaster when I see it, I take the bin from the man, gesturing to Falada and then myself: I will care for him. The hostler looks at me again, and I wonder what he has heard about me, what the rumors say of the princess's cast-off companion. What he thinks of a woman who would take off a horse's halter to let it run free in a practice ring.

He steps back, tilting his head.

Only after I have vigorously brushed out clouds of white hair and picked clean all of Falada's hooves does the hostler seem satisfied that I know what I'm doing. I am grateful to Redna for humoring me many an afternoon, teaching me how to help her with Acorn. I murmur a soft prayer for her as I work. Still, the hostler relaxes only once Falada is back inside his stall, his halter hanging from the hook by his door.

I turn to the man before he can leave, pointing to myself. "Thoreena."

"Thoriné," he echoes, the last part blending away so that it sounds almost as if he too has said "thorn." He introduces himself as Joa, and with a nod departs.

"A fine fellow, that Joa," Falada mutters darkly once the hall lies empty again.

Chuckling, I turn back to him. "I'll try to take you with me to watch the geese tomorrow. Would you like that?"

"It will be good to be out on the plains again."

"All right." I turn to leave.

"Before you go, princess, there's something you might want to consider."

I pause. "What's that?"

"Won't your mother notice if you don't write to her, or if, when you do, your script has changed?"

"She might," I concede. My mother's voice, directing me to write often, echoes in my ears. Perhaps this is the hold I need on Valka. . . .

"You'd better figure out what to do, then, hadn't you?" Falada watches me intently.

I almost smile. "Yes. I will."

"When?"

"Tonight. I'll go up to the palace and talk to—her." As much as I've been thinking about dealing with Valka, I don't want to go there at all. Even armed with this.

"You'll tell me about it in the morning."

"All right."

The walk to the palace takes me half an hour. I see no one but a few drunkards. I hurry past, head bent, and though one or two call out, no one follows after me. Here and there an inn door stands open, light pouring out with the sound of voices.

The palace guards eye me curiously. I've changed into a fresh set of clothes, replaced my slippers with clean ones, and scrubbed the dirt from my hands, making myself more or less presentable, but I still hardly look the part of a Menaiyan noblewoman. After a stammered explanation, though, the guards wave me on through the gates.

The great hall's doors stand open. The palace still feasts at long tables set out across the hall, stretching down the corridors created by the rows of pillars. The floor shines in the light of the luminae stones, for there are neither rushes nor dogs here. Instead, tiled mosaics spread across the floor in a crisscrossing geometric pattern that draws the eye on. Far away, across the hall, the royal family and highest nobles sit at their table on the dais, framed by ornate arches carved into the wall. Even from this distance, the brown of Valka's hair—mine—stands out amid the darker hair of the Menaiyans.

A doorman steps forward and clears his throat. I drag my eyes away from the hall. He speaks, but the words are in Menay and I can only shake my head in frustration.

"I am Veria Thoreena," I say carefully in Menay, naming myself as a lady. At least I have this much. "I must see the—zayyida. Zayyida Alyrra."

His brow creases as he deciphers what must, no doubt, be an atrocious accent, but then he nods, waving over a page. I follow the boy out of the great hall, through hallway after hallway, coming finally to a sweeping marble staircase that takes us up to a carpeted hall of deep red, lit by small lamps set in carved niches along the wall.

The sitting room the page shows me into is lavishly decorated. The floor is spread with a silk carpet depicting songbirds hiding among flowers and vines. Low couches line the wall, a series of ornate tables arranged at intervals before them. A chandelier lit by luminae stones draws the eye to the center of the room, where a low, many-sided table stands bearing an exquisitely engraved, inset silver tray.

I stand gazing at the room as the page calls a greeting,

wondering if I should feel regret. I feel a twinge of envy—how different is this room from my own in the stable! But I would not want to be princess. Not for all the pretty things in the world.

A woman answers the page's call, entering from a connecting room. She looks like a lady of import herself, but she's holding a folded tunic in her hand. A highly valued attendant of some sort, perhaps. The page tells her who I am as well as that I seek an audience with the princess. She considers me shrewdly, dismisses the page, and leads me across the room toward a window. A small chair has been set in the far corner, half hidden behind a folding silk screen of mountains and snow. I thank her, sinking into the chair. She shrugs one shoulder, her expression a mix of contempt and amusement, and returns to her duties. I lean back, grateful. At least this way I have the chance to organize my thoughts while Valka finishes her meal below.

A half hour stretches into an hour, and then two, the evening growing late. Eventually, I hear voices from the hallway, muffled by the door but vaguely recognizable. Then the door opens and closes, and I hear Valka snap, "Mina! Zaria! Where are you both?"

My mouth drops open in surprise. Surely her attendants are higher born than common maids? I would have expected some semblance of respect for them from Valka. They hurry into the room with a rustle of skirts and murmured apologies, the words foreign but the sound familiar. Valka snaps at them again, her voice growing fainter as she moves into the other room. Still, I can hear her railing against the uselessness of attendants who hardly know her language.

Eventually, the attendants emerge once more. I listen

to their fluid voices, the whisper of their skirts as they walk. I wonder if they have forgotten me, but then the woman who showed me in appears before me. With her is another woman, tall and elegantly dressed, her eyes bright and hard.

"You are here to see Princess Alyrra, yes?" the second woman asks in my own tongue.

"Yes," I say, rising.

"You are the one who came with her?"

"I am."

"Ah. Well, we cannot stand in your way, then. Go in." She smiles coolly as she gestures toward the door to the next room. Her companion, glancing between us, grins as well, her teeth flashing white.

I take the luminae lamp they offer me and enter the connecting room. The attendants leave without another word, but I hear their muffled voices as the door closes. This second room is another sitting room, smaller, simpler, and yet even more elegant. I pass through it to a third room: Valka's bedchamber.

As the door swings open, my lamp lighting the room within, Valka grumbles a question. She lies on a low divan that serves as a bed, the covers pulled up over her shoulders, face turned to the opposite wall.

"I said, what do you want?" she demands, her voice loud and jarring.

"What do you think I want, Valka?" I ask lightly, setting the lamp on a slim table beside the door. My choker presses against my throat, but there is no one here to overhear us, and her true name comes easily enough from my lips.

She well near flies out of bed to face me, her back pressed

against the opposite wall, one hand clutching her neck. Brown hair, straight as always, falls over thin arms poking out of the sleeveless nightgown.

"I'll scream! Don't you come near me!"

I almost laugh at that. "I've only come to talk to you. After all, I've no interest in being hanged for a traitor."

Her fear gives way to fury. "I shall have you thrown out of the city! You forget that if it weren't for me, you would have nothing now."

Does she think I have a great deal with my sleeping mat and stool? I meet her glare, knowing I have only a few more moments in which to make this conversation mine. "Only a fool would send me away. Or have you not figured it out yet?" At her silence, I give her my most condescending smile. "You need me for my knowledge."

"Oh, indeed?" she asks, her voice sweetly venomous. "What could you possibly know that would be of any use to me here?"

That her betrothed is a mage, that the king has spoken to me privately both before and after Valka's betrayal, that he knows the Lady has visited me at least once, even if I spoke of it as a dream? But I say only, "I know what my family expects of me, and what will raise their suspicions. My mother will expect you to write regularly."

Valka rolls her eyes, the picture of a petulant young girl. "If that's all, I'll write her in the morning. I don't need *you* for that."

I raise my brows. "You may have my body, but you do not have my script."

"Then you shall write what I tell you, or I shall have you thrown out!"

"You've already had me thrown out," I observe.

"I'll—I'll—"

"I will write the letters," I say, cutting her off. "On one condition."

Valka glares at me from across the divan, brown eyes glittering with malevolence. "You lay conditions on me? Do you think I don't know you won't try to take back my place?"

Her place? I grit my teeth, make myself take a calming breath. "I do not want your life. Here is my condition: lead your life well, and it's yours. Don't, and I will finish you."

"Finish me?" Valka laughs. "You are nothing compared to me. I will do as I wish—"

"If you betray the family you are marrying into, I will expose you. I will expose you by the letters that will be found written in your script, describing your treachery, and by the things you should know that you have no concept of. I will expose you a dozen different ways. If you think your humiliation over a stolen brooch was painful, consider what you will face then." The choker may silence my voice, but I expect I could write the truth. Even if I can't, Valka doesn't know that.

"You *dare* to threaten me? Do you think I fear you?"

I shrug, as if it hardly matters. "Perhaps not, but you need me for these letters, or your little ruse will fail. And I will make sure it fails if you betray the oaths of allegiance you took on when you stole my skin." I wait, watching her, assessing just how much of what I'm saying is actually getting through to her. Humiliation is the only thing Valka understands; it is the one thing I can imagine binding her by—that or death.

Valka bristles. "I made no such oaths. I have become a

princess, and I will be queen—and you will not steal that from me again."

"It is you who have stolen my life," I say softly, "and you are welcome to it. You know my terms. Do we have an agreement?"

She glares at me, thinking through my offer, and then a smile lights her face—it is unnerving to see those features so transformed by greed and happiness. Her answer is laughably conservative in comparison. "Very well."

She walks to a writing table and gathers up a sheaf of papers for me. "You are content to be a servant, then? You are more the fool than I thought."

I let her words slide past me. They are no different than what I heard every day of my life at home. With a faint smile, I take the papers from her. "How will I get the letter to you?"

"I will send a servant."

"It will be ready in the morning." I pause in the doorway. "And Valka? If you betray the prince to the Lady, I will kill you, cost me what it may."

CHAPTER

11

I take a few minutes early the next morning to go through Valka's trunks, delivered to my room last night while I was up at the palace. The first trunk contains the clothes and belongings Valka brought with her, including a small box of jewelry; the second contains her trousseau. I sit back on my heels. Daerilin truly did not wish to see Valka again. She had been sent here, to Menaiya, to marry where she might and be forgotten by those she left behind. A sadness wells up inside of me for the future Valka faced. Almost, I pity her.

I look through her belongings hesitantly. I do not want to take anything of hers, but my old slippers, caked in goose dung and sagging at the seams, will hardly last another day. I also want gloves for my hands, rubbed raw by the shoveling and raking. I've been wrapping handkerchiefs around my palms to protect the blisters there from bursting, but gloves would do a much better job. Thankfully, I find a pair of riding boots that fit perfectly. But the gloves are all silk and utterly useless. I will have to make do with the handkerchiefs.

As I shift Valka's fancier clothes from the traveling trunk to make space for what I can use, I uncover a corner of the deep blue cloak the king gave me—the cloak Valka adjured me to put away when she saw it in the carriage. My fingers trace a line of embroidery, the fabric thick and warm beneath my touch. I can never wear this cloak, not now that I am no longer princess. Best to hide it away. I move it to Valka's trousseau, layering it beneath a stack of brightly colored silks, and close up the trunks.

Then I sit down to write my letter, using one of the thick beeswax candles from Valka's trousseau to light my work. It seems a fitting use. I doubt she'd argue with it.

A page knocks at my door just as I fold the letter into an empty sheet of paper and seal it with a few drops of wax. Valka will read it and then place it in a proper envelope with her own seal. The one my mother sent with me.

I open the door and the servant bobs his head and says, "Letter, veria." He wears a different version of the hostlers' outfit: where they sport olive tunics and tan trousers, with a dark green sash at the waist, he is all blues and whites. I hand him the letter and he departs with a quick bow.

Once I've helped take the flock out to pasture and cleaned the barn, I seek out Joa. It takes a few broken phrases and plenty of gesturing before he understands my request to take Falada with me to the goose pasture, for I have no wish to be mistaken for a thief. Eventually, he assents and Falada, thankfully, consents to being put on a lead. Once we make it through the city gates,

I unbuckle his halter and he takes off, racing down the road and then trotting sedately back to walk with me.

"Feeling a little cooped up, were you?"

"Of all human inventions, stalls are by *far* the worst."

I grin and shrug noncommittally. "You could always leave."

"I could," he agrees, his tone making it abundantly clear that he doesn't intend to. "Did you meet with that Valka woman?"

"We came to an agreement." I am suddenly loath to tell him more.

"Yes?" he prods.

"I'll write those letters home for her. In return, she'll keep the oaths she inherited from me."

Falada's tail swishes once. "Will she?"

"I told her I'd kill her if she betrays the prince."

Falada jerks to a stop. I don't look at him, continuing steadily down the road. After a moment, he follows. "Would you?" His voice holds the first twinge of uncertainty I have ever heard from him.

I sigh. "If she betrays the royal family, I will expose her, including who she really is, and then she will be charged with treason. It amounts to the same thing." And then I will have destroyed Valka finally, and will be princess again, pushed back into a betrothal I want no part of and walking among those who had come to like her—or possibly even love her. All while the Lady looks on, planning some new way to teach me my place and take Kestrin. That's not something I want, even if Valka's actions call for it.

Falada makes a slight sound of consideration—a *hmm* of horse-ly sorts. "You said this sorceress is after the prince?"

I nod, feeling a tightness begin around my neck.

"And you also said you would warn him."

I did, but that was before I knew that the mage who came to my room was the prince himself. "He knows enough to be careful."

"How would he?"

"Because the first time the sorceress came to my room . . ." I glance around, wishing something would interrupt me. Falada watches me patiently. I sigh. "That first time, the prince was there too."

"He was *there*?" Falada lifts his head, neck arched, to stare at me.

"He came to my room. I thought he was a mage who served Menaiya, but when we arrived at the palace and I saw the prince—it was him."

"Then your prince is a sorcerer. No doubt the king is as well. There is no other way Kestrin could have reached you." He shakes his head. "They must have fallen out with this sorceress and she is looking for revenge."

I flush. "I *did* say that. And since the prince is a sorcerer, and knows quite well who is after him, I'm sure he can take care of himself. As long as I can keep Va—" My breath stops in my throat with a jerk.

I grab a handful of Falada's mane as pain slices through my neck. The world sways around me. I close my eyes, clinging desperately to Falada, my lungs burning. And then the chain loosens. I take a long, faltering breath, then another. Falada stands stone still beside me. I force myself to step away from him and smooth down his mane with shaking fingers.

"My apologies," I rasp. Stupid of me to nearly say her name again. I need to be more careful.

"Let's keep walking," Falada murmurs. "If you are able." I shuffle along beside him. I see the reason for Falada's concern a moment later: a wagon approaches. The driver—a farmer with a load of crates filled to the brim with apples—watches us intently as we pass. We must make an odd picture together, a small foreign woman carrying a halter and a staff, accompanied by a white stallion wearing not a single piece of tack. The crunch of gravel beneath wagon wheels steadily dies away, leaving only the faint whistling moan of the wind over the plains.

"Alyrra," Falada says, breaking our silence. "Why do you think the king and his son chose you?"

I shrug. I intervened to help Kestrin against the Lady, or at least tried to, but the prince could not have foreseen that; that encounter came after the betrothal was announced.

"What makes you a better choice than a princess from a richer nation, a princess raised to be a queen? One who could never learn to be a goose girl?"

"Thank you," I say, glaring at him. "No, I don't know why they wanted a clumsy, incoherent princess from a tin-cup kingdom like ours. Even Mother couldn't figure it out." I cannot quite bring myself to share the one possibility I do understand.

"Then how did you convince them you were the right person?"

"They were already convinced when they came."

"In that case, they could have sealed the betrothal by letter. They wanted to meet you. Or at least, the king did, and I have no doubt that he told the prince what he thought of you. *Before* the contracts were signed."

I look up, taken aback. I had not thought of that. But . . . "Just because the prince dabbles in magic doesn't mean his father does too." I wipe my palms on my skirts; they are sweaty despite the cool day. "Does it?"

"You don't have any sense of magic, do you?" Falada asks. "Transporting yourself to another kingdom—which is to say across a mountain range as well as over plains and forests—is no easy task. To do it with enough precision to arrive in a particular person's bedroom, when you have neither met the person nor seen the room, requires mastery."

"And he could not have become a master without the king's knowledge," I finish.

"The king's knowledge, yes," Falada agrees, "but also his help in training, and in keeping it secret. Mastery at such a young age as his is unusual. He would have had to devote much time and energy to it."

"Why do you think it's a secret? Wouldn't the court know—and the—the Circle of Mages?" I stumble, trying to dredge up what memories I have of the regulation of magic in Menaiya. I can't recall much. Magic-working hardly seems like something that would be easy to conceal, though.

"If the court knew, then everyone would know. Even the hostlers in the stable would mention their sorcerer king, but I've heard no word of it," Falada points out. "*Why* the Family would want it secret is easy enough to guess. The Circle can't control what they don't know. It's a question of power."

"You understand Menay?" I ask in surprise.

"Of course," Falada says, not to be deterred. "But consider this, Alyrra: you have a family of sorcerers with a great and potent enemy. They must have seen something in you to make them choose you. What did you do?"

"I exchanged less than a dozen sentences with the king up until the betrothal. I was put under guard for my own protection in my own home. And I stayed out of the way."

Falada considers this for a moment. "You showed yourself to be without pretensions, undervalued by your family . . ."

"And vulnerable and biddable," I finish. We are nearing the flock now, having already left the road.

"Perhaps," Falada muses. "Perhaps they were looking for someone whom they could trust, someone who would accept their authority and be grateful for their continued protection."

"Maybe they wanted a princess whom no one would miss if she were to get killed," I say, the words breaking from me on a tide of bitterness.

Falada does not respond immediately. When he does, it is to ask, "What would you have given to be valued and protected?"

I pause, staring at the ground. I wish that I could lie to him. "A lot," I say roughly.

"Your loyalty?" I don't look up, but I know he is right. Perhaps Falada can see the truth of it written on my face, for he says gently, "Ah, child, I begin to see why you prefer the life you are making for yourself."

Somehow, that only makes me feel worse. "Come on, then," I say, moving ahead. And even though there's no reason to rush to the geese, Falada follows after me without comment.

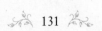

131

The day passes quietly. Falada wanders about, grazing among the high grasses but always coming back to me. The geese splash along the edges of the water and pick through the surrounding plants, searching for tasty morsels. A goose opens her clipped wings and flaps them in vain, beating at the air, managing only to ripple the water around her. My fingers graze a bruise on my thigh from a peck this morning. Still, looking at the geese now, I pity them.

Corbé watches us darkly from his seat across the meadow. I can almost feel his anger in the air. Even Falada, as he pauses next to me in the early afternoon, softly asks, "Your fellow goose boy doesn't always look that black, does he?"

"No." I reach up to scratch Falada behind his ears. "I don't quite understand him."

"Jealousy," he says, and steps away, leaving me to worry at that one word for the rest of the day.

Falada helps drive the geese back to the barn, prancing along near me, chasing feathery rebels back to the flock. He seems to take a sheepish pleasure in such work—as if he would have thought it beneath him to drive geese and is somewhat embarrassed to find that he enjoys it.

When we reach the stable, I rub him down and brush out the grasses caught in his tail. Falada waits patiently, eyeing the serving of oats and grains awaiting him in his stall.

"You can't possibly be hungry. You've been eating all day!" I say as he goes straight to his food.

He throws me an amused glance. "Think of it as dessert," he suggests.

In the common room, I tear into my own dinner in a way that would have made Mother purse her lips and glare icily. My meal is a steaming bowl of vegetable stew seasoned with spices I have no name for, served up with flatbread. I doubt any meal has ever tasted half so delicious as this. The other hostlers glance at me, grinning, and bend over their bowls as well.

When I am finished, I push my bowl back, ready to leave. The older hostler woman reaches out and sets before me a trio of green leaves. I glance from it to her; she points to herself, saying her name slowly. I pick up the leaves; they are long and slightly rough-edged, with a peculiar texture to them. I rub the edge of one to release its aroma, lift it to my nose, and am rewarded with a familiar scent as cooling as it is sharp. A smile breaks across my face. I know this herb well, though I've only ever seen it dried before. The hostler's name is Sage.

When I look up, the second woman presents me with a dried violet, perhaps from an apothecary's shop. She is young and pretty, a few years older than I am, her eyes bright and merry. Her brothers grin and hold up their names—the youngest a rowan branch, the second the leaves of an ash tree, and the eldest an oak leaf. They teach me their names in Menay, and I laughingly repeat them, commit them to memory: Sage, Violet, Rowan, Ash, and Oak.

I carry the warmth of their kindness with me to bed and wake in the morning still smiling.

CHAPTER
12

"You're not wearing—" Sage begins, staring as I step into the common room.

I glance down, as if Valka's red linen traveling outfit I've put on might have turned into a dress fit for a palace feast on my way downstairs. It's relatively new, which is to say I haven't exposed it to the geese yet, but I ripped a seam in my green skirt yesterday when I stepped on the hem trying to avoid being pecked, and there's nothing else that will serve.

"Violet," Sage says, and delivers a short command in an undertone, the words a staccato beat I can't quite follow.

"No," Violet says cheerfully enough that I think she's actually agreeing with Sage. "Come along, Thorn."

Grinning, Violet turns me around and summarily bundles me back upstairs and into the room she and Sage share. She takes a skirt and tunic off a hook on the wall and presses them into my arms. "Change," she says, enunciating the word carefully so I'll understand.

I stare at the clothes. I hold a pale yellow tunic paired with a burnt-orange skirt, perhaps the only set of clothes she owns that aren't the tan and olive uniform worn by all the hostlers. The fabric feels strong enough to withstand a great deal more wear than anything I have.

"Change," Violet repeats, plucking at the clothes and miming taking off my tunic.

"Yes, yes," I say quickly, before she actually does help me. She turns around, grinning, while I shimmy out of my clothes. Violet is slightly taller than I am, but she and Valka have similar figures. The skirt and tunic fit surprisingly comfortably.

"Thank you," I say as Violet presses my discarded clothes back into my hands in a well-folded stack. She waves a hand, dismissing my thanks. I glance around the room again, see the two sets of hooks, one by each sleeping mat. Violet's has only her spare work clothes now. "I will—give?" How does one say return? I touch the front of my tunic and mime handing it back to her.

"No, no, for you!" she insists. "You need good clothes for work. What do you think Sage will—" And again I lose her words in a flurry of syllables. Well, Sage would likely be displeased if Violet took back her clothes at the end of the day and I wore my red dress tomorrow anyhow. But I can't very well steal her only set of nice clothes.

"For you," I say firmly, pressing my own stack of clothes into her hands.

She pulls her hands free. "Don't be a goose!"

A goose? I blink at her, and she laughs. I find myself grinning back at her. I listen to her bright-voiced chatter as she leads me to my room to set down my own clothes, and then takes me down-stairs again for a belated breakfast. Sage, when she sees us, gives us a wide smile and joins Violet's talk, filling the room with the sound of friendship.

That evening, a quick, hard knock sounds on my chamber door. I look up from combing my hair and grin. It is probably Violet, come to call me a goose again for leaving my outfit on her sleep-ing mat. But really, she can't expect me to just take her clothes and give nothing in return.

The knock sounds again. I wind my hair up into a messy bun and open the door. Matsin en Korto stands in the shadowy hall. I blink, as if he might disappear if I only clear my vision, but he's still there, the silver ring in his left ear glinting in the dark. He makes a cursory bow and says, "Veria Thoreena will come with me."

I follow him down uncertainly. As evening has deepened, the stables have grown quiet, the horses all resting in their stalls. The faint sound of conversation drifts down the hall from the common room.

Outside, Matsin hands me up into the waiting carriage and shuts the door, the rest of his quad already in their places. With the crack of a whip, the carriage turns out, rattling up West Road toward the palace. I wonder if the king intends to question me again, and if so, why he has sent for me in such a manner. Perhaps the carriage is meant to remind me of what I have lost, or perhaps the soldiers are meant to intimidate me.

But it is not the king that the quad takes me to, conducting me down quiet hallways. When Matsin opens the door to a small evening room, nodding for me to enter, I find the prince instead.

The room is well lit, showing two low armchairs tilted toward each other in front of a small fire, the floor spread with a plush, knotted carpet, a writing table and chair set against the wall. The prince stands silently at the center.

I curtsy at once, keeping my head bent to hide my confusion. What would Kestrin want with me, thinking me nothing more than Valka's cast-off companion? Behind me, Matsin closes the door, leaving us alone.

"Rise," the prince says, his voice already familiar to me. I straighten, raising my gaze to meet his. He is exactly as I remember him, dark eyes glinting in the lamplight. Only his face seems more drawn and weary than before.

"I apologize for bringing you here in such an abrupt fashion— I am afraid there are few who speak your language in the palace. I hope you have taken no offense." His voice is gentle, even sweet, and utterly lacking real emotion. I remember hearing Matsin speak my language to my own escort on our journey to the border. He spoke well enough; he might have offered an explanation tonight had he been so instructed.

"None at all, Your Highness," I reply on cue. Any thought I might have entertained of warning Kestrin directly stills at this little deceit of his. He is shrewd, and has called me here for his own reasons. That is what I must concern myself with right now.

"I am glad," Kestrin says, stepping toward me. "I have a small favor to ask. I need a letter written to your queen. While I pride myself on speaking your language, I have not yet mastered its written form. You will help me?"

"Of course, Your Highness." My heart beats painfully loudly in my ears. What could he possibly want from my mother that Valka couldn't ask for herself?

He gestures to the writing table. "I will dictate the words," he explains as I sit down. He takes up a station at the corner of the table, watching as I ready myself for the task.

Kestrin dictates a simple formal letter, beginning with the usual "To Her Majesty the Queen," proceeding through to "the delivery of a particular cloak, gift from His Majesty the King of Menaiya, which Her Highness left behind," and ending with "sincere gratitude." By the time I am done, my palms are sweaty, my stomach knotted. And all the while he has watched me as I wrote.

I lay down the quill and hand the letter to the prince. He takes it from me and then, to my surprise, he moves to the small table between the two chairs and picks up another paper. He stands, his back toward me, and studies the papers. I rise and wipe my palms on my skirts. I cannot see what the other paper is, nor do I want to know. I would much rather leave now, and never come back.

"Your Highness," I finally venture, throat dry. He turns to look at me. "May I return to my room?"

He lowers the papers. "Your letter has raised some interesting questions for me."

"Your Highness?" I pray he does not hear the slight wavering of my voice. His story is beginning to unravel in my mind—there must surely be court scribes who could easily have written such a note to my mother. Why did he not ask them?

"Come sit with me." He takes one of the chairs, the papers still in his hand. I move with leaden feet to the other.

"You seem to have displeased the princess Alyrra during your journey," the prince observes. I dip my head in assent. It certainly seems so. "Tell me, then, how did you come to write a letter from her to her mother?"

"Your Highness?" My words are hardly more than a whisper. As I meet his gaze, he smiles. There is nothing good in that smile.

"Perhaps you have forgotten. I traced a copy to be sure you would not. Listen:

"'Dear Mother:

"'It has been two full days since we arrived in Tarinon. I hope you will forgive my tardiness in beginning this letter, but I have been kept very busy. As I am sure Lieutenant Balin gave you a favorable report of my well-being at the time that he left, I hope you have not worried.

"'We were met at the border by two of the king's lords, Filadon and Melkior by name—'

"Shall I go on? Or is it starting to sound more familiar now?" the prince asks amiably.

"It is familiar," I say hoarsely.

"Why is that?"

I shake my head. I can think of no explanation but the truth, and that I cannot tell him even if I wished to.

He drops the letter on the table between us. "I do not believe Alyrra cares for you enough, or trusts you sufficiently, to have you write a letter for her. Certainly she would not request a letter of such an intimate nature. How, then, did you come to write this?"

I train my gaze on my hands. They are clasped just so on my

lap, the fingers of one hand cradling the other. I should speak, I know it. But even so, I let myself slip deeper into the detachment that has always protected me before, if not from pain, then at least from my own fears.

"And how came you to sign it for her?" His voice is rich and low, and laden with distrust. "Not only is your hand the same, but you have the exact same signature as the princess; I compared yours to the signature on the betrothal papers and could hardly note a difference."

Still, I study the way shadows gather in the hollows of my palms, the contours of my hands.

"*Look at me.*"

My eyes snap to his, for his voice is that of my brother. But he does not raise his hand, does not lean forward to reach me. Instead he speaks, his voice as cold and hard as iron. "How do you write her script and sign her name?"

I study his features—the high cheekbones, the sable hair, the tightness around his eyes, his lips. Hiding within myself will not save me, or him. Whatever small trickeries he may use now, I still owe him something for the trust I have betrayed in accepting the life of a goose girl.

But when I open my mouth, different words slip out. "Let me go."

Kestrin arches an eyebrow, but I see something in his eyes shift. *Pity?* "My father offered you a chance to return to your home," he says, willfully misunderstanding me.

I shake my head, make myself answer. "There is nothing for me there. My—family would be upset if I returned." At least my voice is stronger now.

"Lord Daerilin doted upon his daughter."

For a moment I am at a loss, and then I almost laugh. "Perhaps at court. Every person is different alone with their family." It is a truth I have long known.

Kestrin leans back in his chair, his arms crossed over his chest. In the lamplight he cuts a dark and imposing figure. "Tell me how you wrote that letter."

The words settle around me. I know he will not let me leave until he is satisfied with my answer, an answer I would not give him even if I could. But there is a way, I think, to explain the letter without telling the full truth. He meets my gaze, waiting, and into the silence I begin to speak.

"There was a time, Your Highness, when you might have considered the princess and I inseparable. We grew up together, took our lessons together. We learned to write similarly, and I often wrote letters for Her Highness, only bothering to show them to her before sending them. I learned her signature to simplify matters. Despite our disagreements before and during the journey, I still owed her a favor. I agreed to write the letter for her, since she felt unable to write it herself. That is all."

For the space of a breath, I think he believes me.

"You are lying."

My heart jumps a beat.

He continues, "The princess had few friends growing up. She never had a longtime friend, as you claim to be."

His words are accurate—but they do not sound like Valka's. She was never lonely. Friends and family always surrounded her, both at my family's hall and her own home. No doubt that is the truth she would have spoken of.

"Did she tell you that?" I ask.

"No," he admits.

"Then how do you know?"

"I have my sources," he responds enigmatically. The words make me want to laugh. They remind me of children keeping secrets from each other: *I know something you don't know.*

"Perhaps your sources erred," I say, amusement lightening my voice.

He looks at me sharply. "They could not have."

"Your Highness, you have seen enough of the world to know that there is never only one truth, one side of a story. Perhaps your sources are true; I do not doubt they faithfully reported what they understood. But perhaps I am also telling you some part of the truth. To say that your sources lied, or that I do now, is to claim knowledge of the unknown.

"The princess and I spent our childhood together at the hall. Your sources can verify that. We shared our tutor. How your sources have interpreted our friendship beyond that I cannot guess, but you must remember it is only their interpretation. That we had a disagreement no one will deny; perhaps you will understand that we have now made a certain peace between ourselves."

"After she banished you to a life of hard labor."

I wince and then catch myself.

Kestrin gives me a sad smile. "There is another thing I do not understand," he says.

I wait.

"Why did you use her script just now?"

 142

For a long moment I can only stare, like a hare watching the falcon's descent. Then I stammer, "I—I did not think."

He turns his gaze away, quiet. "Be more careful in the future, lady," he says softly. "I doubt the princess will like how lightly you use her script."

I feel myself hunch down, afraid suddenly that he might tell Valka himself. Afraid that he will ask other questions of me, keep asking until I have tied my story in knots.

"Go," he says with a wave of his hand. "My quad will see you home."

I leave before he changes his mind.

CHAPTER
13

My interview with Kestrin leaves me shaken and uncertain. I did not imagine he would send for me, that he would be watching Valka quite so carefully. Are there other mistakes I have made, or a thoughtless word Valka might let slip, that could bring his attention back to me? It seems terribly possible. But as one day flows into the next and he does not send for me again, I begin to find my balance once more.

Each day I learn a little more of Menaiya: that the quads stationed at the city gates never grow lax, continuously drilling and practicing; that the bakers' boys bring their goods out into the street and cry their wares as they walk beneath buildings; that the children are often playing, but their clothes are ragged and they seldom wear shoes.

I also begin to learn the words of our meals from Sage and Violet: bread, porridge, cinnamon, nutmeg, water. From Joa, who sometimes meets me when I bring Falada in, I learn the language of the stables: harness, lead rope, saddle. The hostlers listen to me patiently when I ask, pointing to different objects, and they speak carefully that I might hear each inflection, each accent. I am surprised at the time they take, even Ash and Oak, listening to me, making me repeat a word until I have it right. In truth, my days are filled with a quiet grace the likes of which I have never known.

I practice my new words during the day as I watch the geese; Falada murmuring corrections and helping me with phrases I do not know how to ask for from the hostlers. It is a welcome reprieve from thinking of my interview with Kestrin, of the cloak now hidden away deep inside my trunks, and how finely balanced this life is upon the whim of others.

"They like you," Falada notes one evening after Joa has stopped by.

I pause, currycomb in hand. "Why would they?"

"Same reason I do." I have begun to recognize certain expressions in his eyes when the set of his ears or the arch of his neck tell me nothing—now humor shines bright in his eye.

"They see me as the last hope for humanity?" I quip, sliding the comb over his coat.

He gives a soft huff, a horse laugh, and returns, "Perhaps not that. But you are quiet and easy to get along with, and you do not shirk your duties."

"Being a goose girl is not all that rigorous."

"You carry it off with great aplomb. Not every highborn lady would sing ballads while raking goose dung."

"Hmm." I return the currycomb to the bucket, twisting to hide my blush. It did not occur to me that anyone would hear my singing, or that it might be discussed to the point that Falada should catch wind of it in the stables. It seemed only natural, after a few days, to sing as I worked.

After a moment or two of rooting around in the bucket, I come up with a hoof pick. Falada cooperatively lifts a hoof, and I start working out the day's rocks and muck.

"I want to walk around the city," I tell him. "At home there was only the village below the hall. There must be so much more to see here." I set his hoof down and straighten, stretching my back. "Would you like to come with me? I'm not sure I want to go alone."

"Certainly," Falada says.

I kneel, reaching for the next hoof. "After dinner?"

"I don't believe I have any other pressing engagements," he says wryly. I rest my head against his leg and laugh.

Barely an hour later, with my dinner comfortably filling my belly, we start up West Road toward the palace. I haven't much interest in walking the same—the only—road I know, though, and we strike off on a side road almost at once. To my surprise, the streets are full of life despite the nearing dusk. Children shout and chase each other, women meet in doorways and on corners, men shoulder their way into taverns and teahouses. The alleys we follow break off the main road to run between ancient stone and brick buildings crowded close together. Wide doorways glowing with lantern light invite customers into shops selling everything from baskets to knives to cloth. The roads meet at central squares and circles, then branch off again in what feels like a never-ending labyrinth of buildings and sheer humanity.

Eventually, we turn back, making our way out again before darkness fully descends. Just off West Road, facing into a narrow alley, I find what I did not realize I was seeking: a temple. It is a quaint thing, no larger than my room in the stables, without a single piece of furniture. There are woven grass mats spread across the floor, and upon one wall, an inscription in Menay that I have not the knowledge to read. A simple arch in the wall acts as a doorway, with a mat beside it for worshippers to leave their shoes.

I peel off my boots and step inside, breathing in the faint, dry-dusty smell, the darkness here as gentle as an embrace. When I exhale, the lingering tension of the last weeks slips away. As different as it may be from our temple at home, there is still something profound in its simplicity. Here is peace and quiet, a safety from waiting responsibilities and remembered oaths, a place in which to simply be.

It is too dark to stay long tonight, but I already know I will be back.

"Come sit with us," Violet says the following evening as I rise to leave the dinner table, my thoughts already on returning to the temple.

"Sit?" I echo.

Sage smiles. "Not at the table, of course."

They pull out the boys' sleeping mats—rolled and stored away in a cabinet—throw down a few cushions, and settle on the floor. There's a practiced ease to their actions. This is what they must do every night after I take myself away thinking the evening over.

"Can you sew?" Violet asks, patting the cushion beside her. She reaches for a work basket and, at my hesitant nod, puts a saddle blanket with an unraveling hem in my hands for repair. The others all settle with their own small tasks, and take up their conversation once more.

Oak, shyest of all of the hostlers, sits in the farthest corner of the room bent over his work and offers only occasional tidbits to the conversation, his deep voice rumbling forth from the darkness. Ash, tall and lithe to his elder brother's barrel chest, does everything with quick, sure strokes; his laughter flashes through the room, his words nimble and often too quick for me to follow. Rowan is the youngest of the brothers, still in his final growth, his elbows sharp and likely to knock against things, his crow's nest hair throwing a tangle of shadows over his earnest face.

In comparison, Violet is both bright laughter and quiet caring; her gentle brown eyes, clear and untroubled, glow with a light that softens her features. Sage, I have deduced, is also a relation of sorts, their aunt by a degree or two of separation. She watches over them as a mother eagle over her nestlings. She rarely flexes her wings: a sharp look serves well enough to quell Ash's protestations or Oak's hesitant suggestion of an idea she disapproves of.

So, the evenings pass, and over the polishing and repairing of tack, I listen to the discussion of each day's events, the newest rumors, the happenings in the city and the court. Only sometimes do I excuse myself early to return to the temple with Falada and sink into the quiet there. And every night as I lie in my room, I think through what I have heard and understood. Day by day, night by night, I begin to understand more, begin to piece together Menay, begin to build my life here more completely.

And yet I cannot quite escape my old life, the knowledge I bear.

"Did you hear?" Oak asks us one evening. "The Circle of Mages has petitioned the king to appoint a third heir."

I look up sharply, wondering if I misheard. *Petition, king, appoint, heir*—these are all words I learned from my tutors.

"A third heir?" I repeat. "Why? There are two heirs, yes?" If the Circle is pushing for a third heir, they are quite possibly jockeying to put their own in power. I wonder if they know enough of the Lady to expect, or perhaps be planning on, the death of the king and the existing heirs.

"Aye, the prince and his cousin," Rowan agrees.

And then they are quiet.

I look from face to face, and find Ash watching me, his gaze steady, almost encouraging. Does he want me to ask more? Why doesn't he speak up himself? But more than that, I want to know how much my friends suspect—whether the common folk have any idea of the Lady's existence, or know better than I why she has set herself against the royal family. And if the Circle is planning on their demise.

"Why?" I say again, wishing I had greater dexterity with Menay. I understand a great deal more than I can cobble together myself. "Is there . . . trouble for the royal family?"

Ash lets out a soft, humorless laugh. "Trouble. Yes, Thorn, there is trouble."

"Rumors, only," Oak rumbles.

"Rumors or no, the family has chirana since the Fae Attack," Ash says.

Chirana—grown weak? Or perhaps just dwindled. My mother told me the same thing before I ever left home, citing the war that followed the Menaiyans home a hundred years ago, the so-called

Fae Attack. I didn't believe at the time that the Lady could be so old; now I no longer know what to believe. "Is it—bad magic?"

"A curse?" Ash shakes his head. "Perhaps. But curses do not last generations, or so our mages tell us. And they cannot seem to stop it. Even the delegation here from the Far Steppes could not save the queen."

"Delegation—of *Fae*?" I demand.

"Yes," Sage says. "If the 'curse' is Fae in origin, then it would take the Fae to break it, or so the reasoning goes."

"Why?"

"The Fae claim to be formed of fire," Violet says. "It is said they can see the play of light and shadow around us in a way we cannot begin to understand, and so they can touch the lifesong of everything about them to weave what we call magic."

It takes me an extra moment or two to follow her words, and then I understand. This is why, even if the prince has studied magic all his life, he doesn't stand a chance against the Lady.

"So," Oak says, as if he heard my unspoken thoughts, "if even they cannot stop what haunts the Family, then there is not much to be done. Our queen still died. No one knows, truly, what happened to her."

I stare unseeing at my hands. No hope. Not for Kestrin, not for his family. What could I possibly do, returning to the palace as princess? If even these Fae mages could not save the queen, what chance do I stand? None. None at all.

"No one ever sees our royalty after they die," Rowan says softly.

I look up at him, chilled.

"We see the funerals," Violet argues. "The bodies are shrouded, of course."

"You know the rumors, though—that the Family themselves disappear."

Falada *said* the Lady did not wish to simply kill Kestrin. That she wanted him to submit—but what then? What does she do then? I cross my arms, holding myself tight.

Oak sighs. "All we *have* are rumors. There's no good that comes from speculation. God grant the Family long life."

My friends murmur their agreement, a patter of sound as much reflex as prayer. Sage sets her bridle aside and stretches, one hand at her back. "The king should appoint a third heir, regardless. It will give the people some surety."

"Aye, well, the Circle should keep their noses out. Could be Zayyid Kestrin's new wife will bear him an heir as soon as they wed. No need to push for one now," Rowan says.

I stare at the mending in my hands. An heir. Yes, of course. That's what marriage is for: alliances and heirs. And I've thought of the likelihood that Valka won't betray Kestrin until she's settled, with child and sure of her future. But somehow, hearing Rowan now shakes me. The prince will wed her, will be hoping for a child from her to secure his family's power, and she will use that to destroy him.

"No one wants a mage-king next," Oak says. "Too much power in one person if that happens. The king's too wise to allow it."

No, he's just too wise to let anyone know that's exactly what they have. I force myself to bend over my mending once more, letting the conversation move on to other topics.

But the memory of my friends' words lingers, following me through my days, casting a pall over the quiet rhythms I have grown used to. Valka's betrayal seems as pernicious and terrible in its small way as the threat of the Lady, and I have no answer for either. What I have is a home that grows steadily more comfortable, like a skin I have settled into and made my own, and I do not want to give it up to face the impossible.

Valka sends a page for me late one evening, the boy stepping into the common room and bringing our conversation to a sudden halt. All the peace of my days drains away as I follow him up to the palace. Mother will have sent a letter, and Valka will need me to answer it. Will it mention the cloak? As much as I wish I could bundle up the stupid thing and deliver it to Valka, I don't trust her not to charge me with stealing it. Nor do I have any way to dispose of it myself, and so it remains, hidden deep within her trunks.

Her attendant, an altogether different woman from the two I met before, shows me in with a polite if distant smile before departing herself. Valka waits in the second sitting room, eyeing me with disdain as I enter. The past month has worked wonders for her appearance. Her hair shines a deeper, more lustrous brown than I remember, her skin cream and rose in contrast. Her figure has begun to fill out, developing curves I never had the appetite to sustain. She has begun to look the part of princess.

"Here," she says, thrusting the letter at me. I cross the room to take it, read it over with interest. It is short but surprisingly kind in tone, at least for my mother:

Alyrra,

I am pleased to hear you are settling in. You must establish yourself well. Your behavior now will decide how your family will treat you in the future. I always considered you rather weak and stupid in politics, but perhaps you will prove me wrong.

I will expect another letter from you shortly. Describe your acquaintances as well as you can; I shall advise you as I am able. For now, keep your relations with Melkior and Filadon. Do not offend but do not strive to please.

Mother

At least there is no mention of the cloak—though perhaps the answer to that request has yet to come. At least I expect Kestrin had a scribe write to my mother for it regardless of what he did with my letter. When I look up, Valka rests her hands on her hips as if I were a naughty child. "When will you have the reply ready?"

I raise my eyebrows in exaggerated surprise. "How can I? I have no idea what you've been doing. You'll have to tell me yourself."

Valka purses her lips, eyes narrowed. "All right."

I seat myself at her writing table and straighten the papers there. "We'll start with Filadon and Melkior," I tell her as I dip the quill. "What have you seen of them this past month?"

It seems that both the lords have distanced themselves, Filadon receding to a bowing acquaintance while Melkior might pause to greet her before moving on. Their replacements I do not like the sound of: younger men and women who dance attendance upon her. The ladies join her most mornings to embroider—the princess is making a tunic for her betrothed—but from Valka's description they are all gossipmongers vying with each other for her favor. She has accordingly used them to gather information on each person she meets, though most of it I distrust. How can one trust informants who care only for their own good graces? Surely they would not hesitate to blacken a rival's reputation. But Valka seems oblivious to such possibilities, happily describing each of her companions as I listen and then laboriously write out the letter in my own words but without my perspective. It is a strange thing. I feel slightly ill by the end of her tale.

I make Valka seal the papers, her crest pressed into the wax. I pray the prince cannot replicate the seal and so will not read the letter. Valka leaves it on the table and rises to retire to her room. She makes no provision for the possibility that her attendants may report on her to others, or that her belongings may not be inviolate. I watch her, thinking perhaps my mother's letter to her was more applicable than one might have thought.

Valka pauses at the entrance to her bedchamber. "Are you content, then?"

I consider her, nod. "I will hold to our agreement if you will."

She smiles, a sneering little curl of her lips, and I know that she has thought up some response for me. "I am not yet convinced you will behave, though. Here is a word of warning for you, goose girl. If you should come sticking your nose in where it doesn't belong—if you even consider trying to sneak your way back here—I will see you hanged as a traitor. And—" She holds up a hand, as if I would argue that she still needs me when she already knows she does. "*And* I will see that the white stallion you've grown so fond of is done away with as well, your brother and his insults be damned. Do you understand?"

My stomach clenches tight. It is all I can do to meet her gaze steadily. "Do that, and you will have little chance indeed of fooling my mother when she arrives for the wedding. I have no interest in the prince, so long as you do not betray him. There's no need for such threats." I rise and brush out my skirts. "Good night, Valka."

Her face twists into a snarl as I turn away. Even though I know I should not have taunted her with her own name, I cannot help the smile that touches my lips.

CHAPTER

14

The following morning, a thin layer of ice carpets the ground, crunching beneath the horses' hooves and leaving behind a faint powdery white. The trees at home would be bare now, and the frost would have traced out the fine veins of the leaves underfoot and coated the pine needles with fairy dust. I know these things, and yet I cannot quite remember the sight of the forest from the road, the trees of my little dell.

As we near the boundary wall, the flock within sight, I force out the words I know I must say, the words that have haunted me since my conversation with Valka last night. "I think it would be best for you to leave."

Falada stops to look at me. "Why?"

I turn to meet his gaze. "The princess said . . ."

"Yes?"

"If I—if she hears that I've sought out the prince, she'll have you killed. I've no interest in speaking with him, but he's already sent for me once. And I can't ignore his orders. What if she finds out? Falada, I *can't* let you die because of me."

He considers me a long moment as I stand there, my hands shaking and fisted into my skirts. "It's all right, Alyrra," he says softly. "Valka will not endanger herself so. She needs you too much right now to risk losing your help in maintaining her act."

"You don't know that for sure," I say roughly. "She's petty and mean. She *could.*"

He dips his head. "It is a risk I am willing to take."

"Falada—"

"I also prefer not to travel so far through the winter," he says, as if the snows have already come. "I'll leave you in spring."

After the wedding. I shrug, turn away. I do not want to think that far. And part of me is desperately grateful that Falada will stay with me. "Where will you go?" I ask instead.

"South of the Fethering Plains."

I glance at him askance. When he says nothing more, I ask, "Do you miss your home?"

He tilts his head curiously. "My home?"

"South of the Fethering Plains?"

"My home," he murmurs softly. "We Horses do not have a particular home: every open space is ours. But I miss certain places. Certain other Horses."

"You have a family," I say disbelievingly.

"Of course; is that not how most creatures come into the world?"

I snort. "I don't mean parents."

 157

"No," he agrees, amused. "I have two children, both grown."

"And a wife?"

He looks out over the plains, and there is that weariness in his eyes again. "Yes."

"What is she like?"

"Selarina was hot-tempered and brilliant and more stubborn than anyone I have ever met." He looks back at me. "Even you."

"Was?" I echo softly.

"It has been a year, but the ache does not get any easier. When I was caught, I considered giving up altogether. And then you ordered me to be freed and were caught yourself. So, I will see you through this."

I nod, careful not to press him further. We all need our quiet. We all have our unspoken sorrows, hopes we cannot mention, choices we may yet regret.

When we reach the pasture, I turn toward my regular tree, Falada beside me. There, in the half-bare branches of the oak, perches an owl, its snowy-white feathers bright against the dark. I stare at it, the breath caught in my lungs. It returns my gaze, yellow-gold eyes bright and knowing. Then, with a great flap of its wings, it departs.

"Just an owl," Falada murmurs beside me.

I nod, knowing full well he's wrong, that the Lady is watching me, reminding me she is still here.

I find a different tree to sit beneath.

Two nights later when I return to my room from my day in the pastures, I find it empty, my belongings gone. All that remains is the small stool and the rolled sleeping mat. I stand a long moment, remembering how foolishly I looked down on Valka for assuming the sanctity of her belongings. When I turn back to the door, I find Matsin en Korto waiting for me.

"Veria," he says, gesturing toward the stairs, as if he does not speak my tongue at all. I dip my head and follow him down to the carriage I passed on my way in. He must have watched me go by, and given me the time to discover my trunks were gone. I wonder if it was by his own choice or on Kestrin's orders.

All the way up West Road, and then through the halls of the palace, I try to think what I will do, what I can possibly say to the prince. For it will be him, no doubt, and he will have found the cloak hidden within the trunks. Why else would he have ordered them taken, and then sent for me, if not to search for the cloak and now charge me with its theft? But even when I step into the room where he waits, dip into a curtsy as my guards depart, I still have no idea how to save myself.

"Come sit with me." Kestrin lazes in his chair at the table, before him a silver platter heaped with fruit. I have become so used to hearing Menay, the words of my own tongue sound faintly strange to me. I move to join him in silence.

Kestrin picks out a peach and cuts it with a small jeweled knife. He sets down each curving, golden slice on a plate before him. "Are you hungry?"

"I am well, Your Highness." I drop my eyes from the peach to the tabletop. My stomach tightens as I think of Sage and the other hostlers sharing their dinner, then of the peach. It must have come from afar, for here the trees have all shed their leaves already.

He sets down the last slice on the plate before him, glances at me inquiringly. "Surely you miss such treats now?"

"I am grateful for what I have, Your Highness."

"Hmm." He spears a peach slice with the tip of his knife and lifts it up, meeting my gaze as he bites into it. I blink—when did I shift my gaze to him? I turn my face back to the table, waiting as he watches me.

"Yet you seem to have taken more than your share."

"Your Highness." It is not so much a question as an acknowledgment.

With studied casualness he says, "Explain how you neglected to mention you had the princess's cloak in your keeping when last we spoke."

I consider the angles. There are not many. With a small smile I reply, "Your Highness did not ask."

"A clear failing on my part." My eyes dart to him, catch the faint curl of amusement at the corners of his mouth.

"It is not the cloak that concerns you," I hazard.

"It is not *only* the cloak that concerns me," he corrects me. "I have taken the liberty of looking through your trunks."

"Indeed," I say, my voice flat. What else has he found that he intends to hold against me? There were only my clothes, the jewelry, my small clothes. I can feel myself flushing at that.

"Are you upset?" His voice is almost teasing, as if this were all a good joke among friends. But I do not count him a friend. Like my brother, he will either laugh at my anger or hold my impudence against me. I dare not answer him.

"Come now, lady. I thought we had gotten past the part where you sit still as stone and refuse to speak. Or have you actually turned to stone?"

"Your Highness?" I ask, unsure what he might say next if I don't answer.

"Ah, good; you have found your voice." He taps the butt of his knife against the table. He is growing irritated with me. I swallow hard, a bitter taste on my tongue.

"I was surprised to find you have a trousseau."

"Yes."

"Lord Daerilin expected you to marry?"

"Yes."

"Yet he knew your prospects were not good. Your strained relationship with the princess would not have placed you well. Even we have heard of your reputation here."

"Of course," I manage, my voice strained. I watch his fingers turn the jeweled hilt of his knife, his thumb rubbing against the precious stones.

Abruptly, he sets it down on the table. "Why did you not return the cloak?"

"I would have been charged with stealing it," I admit, looking up.

"And now that you have been found with it?" His eyes are dark, intent and ungiving.

I try not to think about what exactly the punishment for stealing from a princess might be. It is likely not so different from the punishment for stealing from a noble lady back home. Now that I am a servant—and have Valka's reputation of thievery already attached to me—the consequences could be dire.

"I didn't steal it," I say, my voice growing whispery with fear. I clear my throat, press my lips together to keep from speaking.

He doesn't believe me. Or maybe he does. Either way, this won't be easy.

"How did it come into your keeping?"

"It was given to me."

"By whom?"

I don't want to lie to him. It surprises me, actually, to find that I don't. Not when a lie could save me from his suspicions. Now, instead of answering directly, I ask, "Who do you think would give it to me, Your Highness?"

Kestrin watches me shrewdly. "Alyrra had no cause to give you a gift meant for her."

I shrug.

"Lady, I cannot help you out of this if you will not help me. Tell me how you came to have the cloak."

"It was given to me," I repeat.

"When you were yet called Lady Valka."

Why is it that everything I say must be a lie? "As you wish," I murmur.

"It is not as I wish. You puzzle me exceedingly, lady."

"I do not mean to cause trouble," I tell him.

"I almost believe you," he says so quietly I wonder if he speaks to himself. Raising his voice, he goes on, "Here are the puzzles I will unravel: the cloak, which passed from the princess to you without her remembering. Your name, for you told Lords Filadon and Melkior that you preferred Thoreena to Valka, that being your mother's name. Yet your mother died many years ago, and was named Temira. Then there are your trunks, trunks containing marriage gifts that a father you claim has no love for you would not have given you.

"Your character is also an enigma. Spoiled, pampered child that you were, you now labor uncomplainingly, one might even say happily." He laces his fingers together. "Your conversion mirrors that of the princess, who turned from a shadow into a conceited, pompous young woman in a matter of days."

I flinch—torn between pleasure that he sees Valka for what she is and humiliation that he meant to marry a *shadow*. Is that what people thought of me? Kestrin tilts his head at me as if in understanding. I cannot say what he thinks he has seen in my face.

"Will you explain these things?" he asks.

I force myself to answer him, starting with the easiest mystery first. "It is true I changed my name. I saw that in coming here I would begin a new life. I wished to leave behind my past, start anew."

"A simple explanation," Kestrin agrees readily, his smile the bared teeth of a predator scenting blood. "Believable, even. And yet it does not seem likely."

I shouldn't have tried to explain. "It is what it is," I say, striving to sound slightly irritated.

He leans back in his chair. "The matter of the cloak yet remains." His words are heavy with warning.

"I leave it to your discretion." I let my eyes drop back to the tabletop. It is a golden wood, the surface as smooth as water. I wonder what he will do to me.

"You are too trusting, lady."

I incline my head.

"What does your new name mean—Thoreena?"

"I-it is thoreena," I stutter to hide my initial confusion. "A small rose that grows wild in the mountains. It has only a few flowers; mostly it is leaves and thorns."

"Why did you choose such a name?"

"I have always loved the plant." Even as I say the words, I realize my mistake. Once more, I have painted for myself a history that is not Valka's. With each detail, I convince him further that I am not the person I claim to be. "Your Highness must understand, I have spent the last few years in the south, on my father's lands. I have changed much since I left our queen's hall. Your reports will have told you only of the girl I was—not of who I am now." I speak a little too fast, even to my own ears. Yet truth bleeds into fiction, and fiction into fact, and I am beginning to lose hold of the threads of my own reality.

"You care for thornbushes where you once cared for jewels?" he asks lightly.

"Your Highness mocks me."

"You must admit it is a strange thing to claim, lady."

I hesitate, searching for an argument. "I could not name myself Ruby or Diamond, could I?"

He smiles, and I know that the silence between his demand and my answer has told him what I wished to hide. "No," he agrees. "But let us consider your story. The pampered aristocrat, having turned into a rather charming goose girl in the course of a month or two, shows herself to have that which does not belong to her, coupled with riches enough to buy her a station well above that of a goose girl."

I feel my jaw loosen in shock. Is Valka's little store of jewelry really worth so much? Or is it just that the post of goose girl is so very low?

"Well?"

"I had not thought to sell anything."

He appears truly amazed by the simplicity of such a statement. "You had not thought?"

I spread my hands before me. "I can hardly speak Menay, Your Highness. Who would I go to? How would I explain myself to avoid suspicion of thievery?"

"You are already under suspicion of thievery," he observes.

"Precisely."

"Why did you not seek help?"

Did he honestly expect me to petition him for help? As cold and calculating and dangerous as he has presented himself? I'd sooner trust my fate to the Lady. I do not actually mean to laugh, but the sound comes bubbling up before I can help myself, as it did long ago when I spoke with my mother. I press my hand to my mouth, force myself to breathe. "Forgive me, Your Highness," I say, "but who should I have asked? Should I have begged your father's help when he has made me a servant? Should I have asked for your help?"

He surges to his feet, his chair scraping against the stone floor. "How dare you speak so to me?" he growls.

I flinch, the hand covering my mouth tightening into a claw so that I gouge my own cheeks with my nails.

He leans over the table, palms pressed flat against the wood, eyes boring into me. "Do you disdain our kindness in keeping you when the princess wished you cast off? Dare you suggest that we would not have helped you in so simple a matter as this?"

"Yes." My voice is hoarse with fear, and even as the word leaves my tongue, I brace myself for the blow that is sure to come. But it does not.

He straightens and turns away, stalks to the window.

I consider his back, the rigid line of his shoulders. I think that I am already lost, for he will neither forgive this incident nor forget the matter of the cloak. So I speak.

"Your father offered me passage home if I informed him of certain matters concerning the princess. When I refused, he sent me to my new duties assuring me that, should I wish to betray her, there would always be a willing ear.

"As for Your Highness, you care for me only for the knowledge you believe I have. Each time we speak, it is only so that you may try to pull some fact from me you are convinced I know. You would not help me to better my situation any more than your father, for you need me to feel that I need you, that I will be in your debt for your help. Is this not the game you play? Or have I—have I mistaken you?" I end uncertainly, wishing desperately that my diatribe were wholly undeserved.

But the prince makes no sound, and the silence grows between us.

When he turns back to me, his face is closed, expressionless. I cannot read the look in his eyes. I think that he will beat me for the satisfaction of hearing me scream.

He crosses the room slowly, deliberately. I stand up as he nears. I know that I am trembling, but I cannot hide it any more than I can hide the fact that I draw breath. He stops a handbreadth away. His eyes are sharpened onyx, glinting in the lamplight. I think the force of his wrath will put my brother to shame. But even now he stands still, gazing down at me.

"You fear me."

It is a statement requiring no agreement. I look away, turning my head to stare at the wall. Will he play another game, then? Is he worse than my brother?

"Sit," he says, surprising me, one hand waving toward the chair by my side.

I slide into it, my hands curling around its edge as he takes his own seat. I focus on the table, trying not to think.

"That white stallion you take out to the fields with you every day—what breed is he?" Kestrin asks, as if he had just met me outside the stables.

It takes me a moment to reply. "I do not know, Your Highness. I was told . . . he comes from the Fethering Plains."

"A beautiful specimen. The master of horses is considering breeding him."

"Breeding him," I repeat idiotically, unable to follow this new thread of conversation.

"The horse has a good build. He is strong and fast," he explains, the epitome of a casual conversationalist.

"I expect—I expect that is true. I just don't know that— Falada will breed. He hasn't yet." At least, I can't imagine Falada agreeing to any part of such a scheme.

"You seem to know more of the horse than the princess does," Kestrin notes. "How did you learn its breeding history?"

Damn his word games. I dare not remain silent, and yet I dare not speak. I do not understand Kestrin. Were he my brother, or like him, by now he would have finished his game. I do not know why he drags it out, or why, having drawn me into the open, he does not attack.

"Tell me, Thoreena, your father's southern estate that you have lived on these past few years, what is it like?"

"Your Highness?"

"Has Daerilin a hall or a manor house? What are the grounds like? I have heard much of them, but would know your opinion."

I stare blankly at the table. I do not know. I never listened to what little talk there was of the estate, for such talk invariably involved Valka. I have no answer to give him.

"I think you have never been there, little thorn," Kestrin says, his voice almost gentle in the silence.

I do not think it strange that he no longer calls me lady. I bite my lip, then take a breath to answer, but he cuts me off.

"Remember that it is a crime to lie to one of the royal family, a crime punishable by death, for it is considered a betrayal."

"Your Highness, tell me what you want of me," I plead.

"The truth. Who are you?"

"I am the goose girl. There is nothing more I can tell Your Highness." The chain presses gently against my throat.

"If you were not the lady Valka before you reached the border, then what happened to Lady Valka?"

"I cannot say, Your Highness." His face has lost its frozen aspect, his eyes glinting in the lamplight. He is closing in on the kill.

"And the princess?" he demands, surprising me. His voice is sharp as cut glass. "What happened to *her*?" He's afraid. The moment I see it, he realizes his mistake. His features twist and then smooth out. "Do you know, Thorn, what changed in the princess you served?"

I shake my head, not daring to speak—not to him, and not when the choker still presses against my throat.

"Then you admit to having lived a lie among us, you who were never Lady Valka?" He raises an eyebrow, half grinning, and though he has just warned me of the dangers of lying, his demeanor now invites confession.

I find myself hating him for it—for the ability to play with me so easily.

"I admit only to wishing to live in peace," I say, my voice not quite steady.

He considers me. "Tell me why you fear me, lady."

I try not to flinch, but his damned eyes see everything.

"At least twice I have seen you look at me with such fear as I have seen only in the eyes of hunted deer."

I let my gaze wander across the table, pause over the plate of fruit, and finally come to rest on the small jeweled knife. "I have only ever known one other prince, Your Highness."

He stills. "You judge me by his standard?"

"I am not in a position to judge princes."

"Yet you expect the same from me, don't you? He would hurt a woman for the sake of inflicting pain. He has hurt you before."

I swallow, refusing to meet his gaze. My brother hurt me, true, but I wasn't his only target, just his favorite.

"Your fear is a strange thing. You fear brutality from me more than you fear punishment within the law—and yet you are guilty of breaking the law. Why?"

I cannot imagine that he does not know. How can he be so

169

quick to grasp what I wish to hide and yet not see this? Or perhaps he only wishes to make me speak.

"Thorn?"

I glance up at him. "You and your father *are* the law. Should I not fear you before I fear it?"

"Perhaps." We sit in silence. He reaches out to play with the jeweled knife absentmindedly, then sets it down, raising his gaze to me. "This has been a most educational evening. I thank you for it."

I stand, one hand gripping the table edge. I cannot quite believe he is letting me go.

"Tell me one more thing before you leave: Shall I trust you?"

He is the one who urged vigilance on my journey. How could he ask me this now? Unless it is a trap of words—for how can I say no and not meet a punishment, or say yes and not be called to account for failing to answer him earlier?

But then his words echo back to me from our conversation, offering me a way out. "Your Highness has long known of my reputation for dishonesty," I say, my voice small with shame. "I cannot counsel you on this."

He does not answer me.

CHAPTER
15

I seek out the temple the following night, as if I might shelter there from the prince's words. I sit cross-legged on a woven grass mat, the stone floor hard and cold beneath it, and listen to the sounds of the city going to sleep. Falada waits patiently in the alleyway, his breath occasionally misting past the door.

I close my eyes and sink into the quiet, seeking the tranquility I've always found here before. Tonight, it eludes me. I wanted so much to get away from the court. In the month or two I've lived as a goose girl, I've found contentment and friendship and hope. In one night, Kestrin has shown me just how fragile my new life is. Did I really expect it would be so easy to leave my old life behind—that if I did not reach for it, it would let me go?

Pressing my fists against my thighs, I focus my gaze on the old grass mats. What is it I truly wish for? I think of the books I used to read, and while I miss them, I now have the time to think back over them, consider their arguments and opinions as I watch the flock; this I would not change. My life has the necessary comforts—food daily, work to keep me busy, time to reflect, and some small company to share it all with. While a hot bath might be nice, it is too small and irrelevant a thing to pray for. This is the life I've made for myself, and I want it in a way I haven't wanted anything else I can remember. It is a wanting that is quiet, and steady, and deep as the beat of my heart.

I rub my face, and open myself to my fears. I see Corbé, his lips curling back as he meets my glance every morning at the barn door, and I want safety from that look and its attendant meanings. I wish safety for Kestrin from the Lady who threatens him, as little as I understand him—safety for him and from him. I wish Valka might be kept in check, her interests bound to the court and affecting the common people not at all. I wish the Lady might leave me where I am and never look at me again. And I wish Falada safe from Valka, that she forget him completely.

The faint sound of shouts echoes from afar. I look up with a jerk, listening. Silence, and then another shout, loud and harsh, not quite so distant.

"Alyrra! Quickly," Falada says, his voice sharp with apprehension.

"What is it?" I start to my feet.

"Trouble," comes the succinct reply as I reach the doorway. "We need to leave."

I struggle to pull on my boots, stamping to get my right foot the rest of the way in—and then it is too late to run. A tall boy hurtles around the corner, the bright fabric of his cloak flapping behind him. The alley here is so narrow that he slams into Falada's bulk before he can stop. He falls back, gasping a curse.

I freeze, staring at him. Shouts echo from the street behind him, his pursuers closing in. The boy struggles to his feet awkwardly, cradling his arm. Falada snorts and presses toward me to give the boy space to pass. But the boy will never make it now, wounded and unsteady as he is. He will be caught no matter what he does.

I know what it is to run without hope of escape.

"Let him into the temple," I order, sidestepping Falada before he can hem me into the doorway.

The shouting is nearly upon us.

The boy whips his head to the side to look at me, the motion making him stagger as if drunk.

"There," I snap, pointing to the shadowed interior. "Quickly. Rah!" *Go!*

He bolts through the darkened doorway.

"Falada, stand here beside me," I hiss.

He does, blocking the doorway with his flank. When I lift my hand to his neck, the muscles there are rock hard.

A quad of soldiers barrels around the corner. If I'd thought at all about who might be chasing the boy, I would have guessed they were other boys, young men protecting their territory or bullying an outsider. But in the faint light of the alley, I can see the sheen of the well-oiled leather armor they wear, catch the glint of swords held at the ready. The soldiers skid to a halt, doubt in their eyes as they look at me.

"There," I say in Menay, pointing to where the alley opens out into another street. My hand is remarkably steady. "There!"

For a moment longer they pause, and I know that they will remember me. I only hope they will not blame me for having lost their prey.

"Niroh," the first soldier shouts, and they are off once more, boots pounding the hard-packed earth.

I watch them go. I could leave the boy now—I've given him the chance he needs to escape. But, as I duck my head into the temple, I remember the way he staggered as he turned to look at me, the way he cradled his arm. "Niroh," I say softly, echoing the soldier. *Let's go.*

The boy approaches the door warily, turning his head first toward me, then Falada.

I unfasten my old traveling cloak, my gaze focused on my hands. Strange how they've begun to tremble only now. I hand the boy the cloak. "Wear this."

He understands at once, clumsily slinging it around his shoulder to mask the brightness of his own cloak.

"What's wrong with your hand?" I say sharply, reaching out to touch his wrist.

He pulls back, his breath hissing between his teeth.

My fingers come away wet with blood. I cast Falada a worried look.

He watches me mutely. Belligerently.

I sigh. I have gotten myself into this, and I must get myself out—but not without helping this boy. I will not have more on my conscience than I do already. And Falada will help me, despite himself.

"We need somewhere quiet so I can see to his wound," I say in my own tongue, careful not to look toward Falada.

He snorts and starts toward the street.

I hustle the boy along beside me as fast as possible. If the soldiers return, they will certainly recognize Falada and me. To be caught helping their fugitive escape would be no small offense.

Falada leads us from the street down another tight passageway and into a back alley behind a row of dilapidated buildings.

"Show me your arm," I say in Menay when we come to a stop.

The boy stands unmoving, the cloak wrapped around him and the hood pulled up. He is taller than I am, and I realize as I look at the shadows of his face that I have no idea as to his actual age. I'd thought him a boy only because he was slim and quick.

"Your arm," I repeat, pointing in case I have used the word for knee or toe instead.

He complies, holding out his arm, the cloak falling back. His sleeve is soaked in blood.

The boy inhales sharply as I push the tattered fabric up to reveal the cut. In the stark moonlight, the wound is terribly clear—a deep gash almost the length of his forearm, from the back of his wrist to his elbow. It bleeds freely; he must have great restraint not to pull away from me.

I release his arm, my thoughts racing. I must stanch the bleeding. But how? The boy squats down, his back against the wall, head bent, one hand pressing on the wound, but that will hardly be enough. I need something to bind it—anything. I glance around, then down at myself. My sash. I yank at it, fingers sticky with his blood.

The boy makes no sound as I kneel beside him and wind the sash around his wound, a makeshift bandage. Immediately, the blood flow lessens. He cradles his arm against his chest as I move away.

"Shurminan," he murmurs in thanks. I cannot make out the age of his voice either.

"Ifnaal." I lean against the wall, my legs weak beneath me. The cold of the bricks seeps into my shoulder and a shiver runs through me. I miss the warmth of my cloak.

The boy stands and then staggers sideways, unbalanced. It is only Falada's quick step up to him that prevents his falling. He hangs on to Falada, one hand thrown over his neck, gasping for breath. He will not be able to make his way to safety alone, nor can he walk hanging on to Falada, for Falada's back is too high for comfort.

So it must fall to me. As it should; it is only right that I finish what I started. When the boy raises his head to get his bearings once more, I take his arm from Falada's neck and hang it over my shoulders. Wrapping my arm around his waist, I ask, "Where?"

He nods his head toward the end of the alley, and we begin to walk. It is a slow and awkward passage, with Falada following us like a phantom.

I lose track of our path before long. With the weight of the boy bearing me down, I can only look up when he does, pausing at cross streets and the mouths of alleys. The wind cuts through my clothes, numbing my cheeks. Soon, the only warmth I can feel is that of the boy against my side.

Twice I stop, depositing the boy on the ground beside me before sinking down to rest. My legs and back ache fiercely with the strain of supporting him, as do my fingers when I uncurl them from their grip about his clothing. It is later now than I've ever been out before. If it weren't for Falada pacing beside me, watching the streets, I would be terrified of getting lost, or of meeting with trouble and not making it home at all. But with Falada by my side, I keep my focus on getting the boy home, or wherever it is he considers safe.

Finally, we come to a small wooden staircase running up to the second floor of a building. We shuffle to a halt, and a moment later my legs give out. I fall forward with the weight of the boy, slamming into the stairs. My head bounces off the wooden steps with a sharp crack of pain, my arms too numb, too slow to break our fall. I blink my eyes to clear my vision, wavering for a breath, two, and then lever myself up painfully.

The boy lies perfectly still.

My heart fails me. What if he—what if I've—

"Alyrra," Falada murmurs behind me.

"I'm fine," I whisper. "But he's . . ."

"Check."

I roll the boy onto his back, clumsily trying to shield his wounded arm. At least he doesn't suffer the pain of it. I lay my hand uncertainly against his chest and feel it rise gently and fall back.

"Unconscious."

"Get your cloak."

I pull the edges of my cloak out from under the boy, unwrapping it.

"Come," Falada says as I swing the cloak around my own shoulders. The edge of it flaps against my arm, soaked with blood. Falada turns back up the alley.

"We can't leave him out here." I hang on to the wooden rail, the pain in my head leaving me slightly off balance. The boy lies at my feet, silent and still as the dead.

"He'll be fine. In a little while it will be dawn, and whoever lives up there will find him. Come."

"No." It is hours till dawn, the cold a creature that gnaws at me.

"Alyrra, this is no safe place for you."

"You need to stop calling me that." My breath comes in short, hard gasps as I stare at Falada.

He watches me in return, waiting.

I pivot, gritting my teeth as the world swings with me, and start up the stairs.

"Child," he hisses after me.

I ignore him and concentrate on making my legs move forward and up. He's more than capable of defending himself if a passerby comes along and thinks they've found a horse free for the taking. It's the boy who's in danger, unconscious and bleeding.

The staircase ends at a small wooden platform. From the crack beneath the door comes the shine of lamplight.

I rap twice on the door and step back.

There is the muffled sound of movement on the other side of the door, and a voice calls out sharply with words I do not know.

I glance down to where Falada stands beside the boy.

Again, the voice orders an answer from me. The speaker has come up to the door.

"I don't know," I say in Menay, hearing the high-pitched waver to my voice.

The door crashes open and a hand flashes out. In that hand is a sword.

I stand perfectly still, my blood thundering through my veins, echoing in my ears.

The blade wavers in the air a handbreadth from my throat.

I follow the shining length of metal down to the gloved hand that wraps around its hilt and up the man's arm to his face. It is a strange thing, all hard angles with a straight scar running from one corner of his mouth down his chin. His hair is cut short, lying gently against a high forehead.

"Your friend," I rasp in Menay, and move one hand to point down the stairs.

"Yendro," the man says.

I blink at him—is that a word I should know?

Another man steps up beside him to look at where I point. This second man says something I do not quite catch, his voice a steady tenor, calming. The sword wavers before me. I watch it, half hypnotized by the play of light upon it. Then it is lowered and the second man descends the stairs.

The scar-faced man watches me while we wait, his gaze keen. My paler skin and scruffy appearance will not be lost on him, I realize unhappily. He might easily find out who I am if he cares to inquire.

The second man calls out, his voice sharp with concern. With a muttered word, the scar-faced man sheathes his sword and starts down the stairs.

I back into the corner made by the railings as he passes me. I can see into the room now; three more men stand around a table, their chairs hastily pushed back, hoods pulled up to hide their faces. They too wear swords. I wonder uneasily exactly who the boy is to have such friends. But I've made my decision to help, and it is done. Now I need only get away safely.

The two men lift the boy and maneuver him up the stairs, their faces grim. As soon as they pass me, I start down.

A voice calls after me. I glance back to see one of the hooded men behind me, sword in hand.

"Stop," he says, voice low and harsh.

I race down the stairs. Falada waits, turned so that his side blocks the bottom of the stairs. It is an offer I don't second-guess. I throw myself at his back, scrabbling for a hold on his mane as I heave one leg over. He springs into a trot, then a gallop, nearly knocking me off. With each pounding step, pain jolts through my skull, bringing tears to my eyes.

Behind me, I hear the man cursing, but his voice fades quickly beneath the beat of Falada's hooves. We fall into a walk within a block or two, the road behind us quiet. I breathe a prayer of thanks and turn to slither from Falada's back.

He sidesteps up against a wall, stopping me. "Stay," he says. "You are tired, and we will make better time this way."

"But . . ."

"Quiet," Falada says, and starts off once more, his gait gentle, smooth.

Long before we reach the stables, I fall into a doze, waking only to open the doors and let us into Falada's stall.

CHAPTER
16

"What's wrong with your head?"

"Nothing," I say a little too quickly.

Violet reaches over the table to catch my hand before I can hide the bump on my forehead. "Nothing?" She peers at the bruised skin, breakfast forgotten. "Dear Lord—what did you do? What *happened*?"

"I fell."

She mutters something in Menay.

"What is it?" Ash asks from the door as he sets down a bucket of water. "Something wrong?"

Violet gestures angrily at my head and launches into a tirade of unknown words, and a few known but strung together so quickly that I cannot quite catch them.

Ash walks over, his eyes on the long lump at my hairline. "Who did it?" he asks me so quietly that at first Violet doesn't realize he's spoken.

I shake my head. "I fell."

"That's what she says," Violet says. "Does that look—" She launches into another whirl of unknown words, turning to glare at Ash.

"On stairs," I explain, wishing for the umpteenth time that I had greater dexterity with Menay.

Ash reaches out and touches the tender skin around the hard central lump. I stiffen and pull back, unnerved. He drops his hand.

"All right, you fell," he concedes. "Who pushed you?"

It takes me a moment to answer, my throat strangely tight. "No one."

He looks skeptical.

"I fell," I repeat, my voice soft. "Truly."

"Well." He fetches the bucket and takes it to the counter.

"Ash." Violet stands with hands on her hips.

He shakes his head, speaking quickly, and she replies on the heels of his words, their sentences overlapping and cutting through each other. I slip out unnoticed, hurrying to the goose barn.

"You're happy this morning," Falada observes as we walk down West Road once the barn is clean.

I break off humming to grin at him. "I—well, yes, I am." Deep inside, I hear Ash ask, *Who pushed you?* It is a question I have waited half a lifetime to hear. I am amazed the sun does not shine.

"I wouldn't have thought a bump on the head would improve you so. The next time you walk around looking like a rainy day, I'm taking you to find another youth to save. Or is it the actual bump you require?"

I laugh, and immediately regret it as pain laces across my forehead. "Was I that bad?"

"Worse," Falada tells me, sidestepping my shove. "Will you tell me why you were so unhappy all yesterday?"

I take a breath, let it out, and find myself saying the most irrelevant thing first. "The hostlers are thinking to breed you."

"Are they? I shall be sorry to disappoint them. And how did you, with your limited vocabulary, learn of this new plan?"

I grip my staff, my knuckles whitening. "The prince told me."

"Kestrin? Indeed." And then, gently, "What else did you learn from him?"

"He knows I am a fraud. He considers me a puzzle of sorts, not particularly important, perhaps entertaining enough to keep for a winter evening's amusement. I don't doubt he'll send for me again."

Falada's breath makes dragon smoke before us.

I make myself go on. "He had my belongings brought to him, and he found the cloak the king gave me. He knows I was never Valka."

"You do not wish him to find you out."

"No," I agree quietly.

Kestrin is both sorcerer and prince. He frightens me more than my own brother. I would never want my husband to have that sort of power over me.

"What do you think Kestrin will do when he does discover who you really are?"

"I can't say. Perhaps if he hasn't guessed yet, he won't."

Falada eyes me askance. "He knows you have the princess's signature."

I swallow a curse, furious with myself. Of course he knows I have her script. My own script. Who could do that? Certainly not an ordinary lady's maid. If I'm not Valka, and I'm not a maid, that leaves only one other person: the princess herself. I shake my head in denial. I wish I had thought through my words to Kestrin. I wish I had been able to think at all. If I hadn't been so afraid of him, I would have realized what I was doing. But—why did he let me go, then?

"What will you do when he comes to you with the truth?"

"I don't know." I glance up at Falada, but all he does is watch me. "What would I do as princess?" I demand. "I've listened to Valka's account of the court—I would no more fit there than a goose girl born and bred would. I do this post more honor than I ever could that of princess."

Falada huffs softly. "Every post is what you make of it. Valka may adorn the title of princess better, but you will put it to better use, if you wish to." He nudges my shoulder gently with his nose. "But it is not the post that concerns you, is it?"

I rub my arm, where a scar once showed beneath my sleeve—a scar Valka now wears. I have never spoken of my brother's abuse to Falada, or to anyone really. But this, the fear that closes up my throat, this is his legacy that I carry with me. Kestrin has not struck me—yet. But I would not put myself in his power any more than I would go home to my brother.

"Alyrra?"

"I'm afraid of Kestrin," I admit finally, head bent. "I'm afraid of what he might do to me."

"Do you think he would harm you?"

I remember the force of Kestrin's restrained anger. He was close to violence, but even so, fists aren't his only weapon. "There are more ways than one to hurt. Falada, he's threatened me with execution for lying to him. I don't think he would actually carry it out, but I don't *know*. He has made the threat, and if he is capable of that . . ." I shake my head. "I am no princess. I don't know how to play at politics, or protect myself from him, especially if we were wed. And he is not even the worst of it. There is still the Lady to consider. She would not forgive me if—"

"If you fought back against her?"

"Yes. I don't know how you expect me to help Kestrin. I'm no sorceress, nor have I any talent for magic. I don't see what I could possibly do."

"I don't know," Falada admits. "The question is, what will you be able to live with when this is all done? Can you live with the choices you are making now? Or will they end up destroying you?"

"Going back will accomplish nothing," I respond savagely. "Kestrin will die one way or the other, and I will be used as a pawn again if I am not sent home—or punished here by his family."

Falada studies me a moment, and in the silence I hear how clearly I've failed to answer his questions. But he does not demand I respond; instead he asks, "And when the time comes for the Lady to take Kestrin, what will Valka do?"

I stand completely still at that, listening to the whisper of his words fade away. It is easy for me to suggest that the prince might die, but to hear Falada so bluntly refer to Kestrin's imminent murder brings me back to myself.

"What will Valka do?" Falada prods.

"She will give him up," I reply, hating her, hating myself.

"When?"

"Once she is well settled. Married, perhaps with child."

"So she would not allow herself to be a pawn."

"No."

"And what will you choose to do, Alyrra?"

"I don't *know*. I'm a goose girl, Falada. I'm dispensable, a pawn by definition."

"That is your choice."

"You are impossible," I snap.

Falada sighs and continues on toward the goose pasture.

As we draw within sight of the flock, I hold out my hand to him, touch a wisp of his mane. "I can't make the rules, Falada. This isn't my game."

"Whose game is it, then?"

I shake my head. "I can't learn magic. I can't hope to fight the Lady when no one else here can."

Falada looks at me curiously. "No one has asked you to do either of those things."

"No," I mutter.

We walk the rest of the way in silence, Falada throwing me the occasional unreadable glance.

CHAPTER
17

The following days dawn in shades of gray, layers of clouds obscuring the sun from sight. A frigid wind blows from the mountains, rustling across the plains and whistling through the walls of the city. For a little more than a week, the clouds withhold their promise of rain or snow. I miss the crisp coldness of the forest winters I have known. I daydream of warm bread and mittens and the weight of snow on pine trees. The winter here is a different creature altogether, lying heavily over my shoulders and stealing into my bones.

This morning, a hunting party rides out, perhaps the last before full winter arrives. Well-nigh forty horses wait, tethered to the practice ring fence; they are outfitted with sleek hunting saddles, or else richly caparisoned in gold and silver for the ladies who will accompany the hunt. Young men in palace uniforms rush in and out of the stables, pestering the hostlers and checking the horses' gear.

Sighing, I enter the stables and slip into Falada's stall, going to stand by his head. "It's too busy to take you out," I whisper.

"You do not want to attract undue attention from Valka's quarter," Falada agrees. "The hunt might pass the pasture." A point we have discussed before. Unsaddled, unbridled, and in the company of a servant, Falada would attract as much attention from the palace folk as a gryphon strolling through the city gates.

"We'll go for a walk together tonight," I promise. Falada only nudges me on my way out the door to my duties.

Once I finish the barn, I make my way back out to the geese. The flock is settled into the low pasture today, set back from West Road. I cast a quick glance at our charges to ascertain none are in danger of casually wandering off, select a stone seat some distance from Corbé, and unbraid the first short span of my hair. It is still wet from last night's washing, and the curls have tangled abominably despite the braid, or perhaps because of it. Even as cold as the day is, my hair could do with a good airing out. I spread each lock to work the comb through it a handbreadth at a time.

I think of a hundred things as I brush: that the hem of my skirt will require mending; that I need better gloves if I can find a way to get them; that, although my trunks have reappeared, the cloak remains with the prince, who might at any moment work out my identity. Pressing my lips together, I yank the comb through a knot and think of the injured boy instead, hoping he survived the night, that his friends will forget me. Because, however loyal they may be to him, I can still remember the flicker of light on the blade held before me.

It takes a moment for the crunch of pebbles beneath booted

feet to make its way to my ears. I turn to see Corbé advancing toward me. I grab my staff and stumble to my feet as he closes the distance between us. He smiles, and it is a smile that turns my stomach to ice.

I glance around in panic for Falada, for anyone, but there is no one here.

"You're a pretty thing," Corbé says, his voice low and gravelly. "I've been wanting to get ahold of that hair."

"No." I back away. I do not know the right words, can't think of how to tell him to stay back.

He lunges forward to catch hold of my braid where it's still plaited together, hauling me toward him. For a moment it is not him I see but my brother, eyes glittering, lips drawn back in sneering enjoyment. *No.* I don't even realize I'm moving until I feel the whistle of my staff through the air and then the satisfying jolt of wood in my hand, hard against my palms.

Corbé roars, his face twisting in pain.

I raise the staff and bring it back again, watch the way the dark pole meets his cheek. Blood spurts from his nose, droplets spattering my face as his head snaps to the side. He shouts words I have not yet learned and releases my braid to clutch his face.

Only once I'm free do I realize what I've done, feel the shape of my mouth as I gaze at him. I run. I gain the crest ringing the meadow in moments, throwing all my mind and energy into this one thing: to run. If all that I am and have been and can be is focused into this one reality of running, perhaps I can escape all that I may be. It is the only thought I will allow myself.

I run until the plains are strange to my eyes. Though I cast my gaze back, I cannot see how far I have come, for there are no landmarks but the city itself, a dark blot on the plains. Still, should I run so far that I reach the sea, I should not have run far enough, for the thing I run from rides on my back and in my blood, and will not be shaken.

Finally, exhaustion overtakes my limbs and I drop into a shuffling walk, my mind still caught up in what has already passed. Once more I feel the grain of the wooden staff in my hands, the way it swings so easily—as if I had practiced such a move in such close quarters more often than I have drawn breath. Blood lifts in the air, arcing away, taking my breath with it. My lips twist, my brother's smile stretching across my face. Again and again.

My feet find a worn path, and I follow it blindly. I cannot see past the darkness clouding my vision, and so, though the world is still bright with light, I do not see the chasm until I step forward from the path into thin air.

I swallow my cry as I fall, rolling and skidding to the bottom of a rocky ravine. A shower of pebbles comes loose and pelts me from above. I huddle there, pressing myself into a ball, and concentrate on the pain of my hands rubbed raw by the fall, my scraped knees, and the cut across my shins. These things are real, their pain deserved. I realize dimly that someone is sobbing: the sound comes from far away, echoing through my mind as if down dark stone corridors.

I lie there long enough for my ragged weeping to still, long enough for the scratch on my shin to cease its bleeding. Finally, I sit up, prop myself on my hands using my tattered cloak as a cushion for my bloodied palms. The rocky sides of the ravine rise around me, twice as tall as a man, sheer enough that only a few grasses cling to the cracks and crevasses.

A gust of wind sends a single pale feather from some unseen bird spinning past me. The first drops of rain from the clouds overhead spot the ground. I doubt I will be able to claw my way back up now, certainly not if the rocks grow slippery.

I will walk, then, until I find a way out.

The going is slow. I dropped my staff in the first frantic moments of flight, and even now when it might have helped me, I am no longer sure I want it. The rain falls steadily. It weighs down my cloak and skirt, wet folds sticking to my legs. Cracks in the stone begin to appear, shallow fissures barely an arm's length deep. A breeze whips through the ravine, cutting through my clothes. When I look at my fingers, they are white with cold. My teeth chatter uncontrollably. Yet I do not think it can really be that cold. There is no sleet, no ice.

I slow to a stop. Perhaps I should have walked the other direction. Perhaps—

A burst of wing and feather rises up from a great dark fissure tucked between two slabs of rock. I stare after the snowy-white owl, knowing I should be afraid, that it might have been the Lady herself, but I cannot summon the emotion. The owl disappears into the rain, but the fissure remains, and even though I do not want to see it, I find myself taking one staggering step forward, and then another, until I stand before the dark opening. It has the vague comfort of a half-remembered haunt, and seems deep enough to offer some shelter, though why the Lady would show me such a thing, I cannot fathom. Perhaps she does not want me dead yet, the lesson she wished to teach me not quite taught.

When I stoop to enter, I realize that the fissure has been hollowed out, the tunnel carved into it cutting up through the rock so that I can move without bending over. I stand for a moment in the twilight of the tunnel, listening to the moan of the wind, the patter of raindrops on stone. The air lies still here. I rub my hands over my face as if I could wake myself from yet another nightmare—one I have dreamed before. But the tunnel remains, neutral in its reality, and behind me the rift.

I make myself follow the tunnel, one hand trailing along the rock wall. It makes a single turn and ends at a slab of rock smooth as the fine silks Mother packed in my trousseau a lifetime ago, but for a single fold of stone at the tips of my fingers. A handle.

I rest my forehead against the stone slab and wrap my arms across my chest. Darkness surrounds me, leaching away detail, leaving only the slightest trace of reality. I know already what I will find beyond. I do not need to push open this door, peer into the darkness within. My dream-memory serves me well enough: it will be a round room, the curving walls smooth and unmarked. At the center will be a stone pedestal, an ornate lamp hanging from the ceiling above it.

I swallow down a wave of nausea. Kestrin called me here through my dreams, meaning to call the princess—I remember the confusion in his eyes when he looked at me from the basin of water. This is his room the Lady has led me to, using wind and rain and a flicker of feathers to bring me here.

I want nothing more than to flee this place.

I clasp my hands together to ease their trembling, take a deep breath, and turn away from the closed door. I shuffle doggedly toward the mouth of the tunnel. I will find some other place to shelter, and, when the rain has eased, make my way home.

I am but a pace away from the opening when I hear

voices—men's voices, the words unintelligible, thrown about by the wind. Instinctively I back away.

Where to hide? I dare not return to the room. The tunnel itself offers perilously little cover. Still, there is a slight outcropping of stone between the mouth of the fissure and the turning point in the tunnel. I seat myself in the fold created by the stone, push myself back as far as I can go with my knees to my chest, and spread the dark folds of my cloak over my skirt and boots. It is not much of a hiding place.

The voices echo into the tunnel with the tramp of boots. I tuck my hands behind my knees, holding myself still. A few more words, the sound of boots approaching on the stone floor, and then a cloaked figure passes me. He walks confidently, looking neither to the right nor the left. Moments after he disappears around the corner, a golden light flowers, filtering into the tunnel, then narrowing to a sliver as he shuts the door.

I venture only one look toward the tunnel mouth—a figure sits on guard, blocking the entry.

So I wait. The cold of the stone climbs up through my legs from the ground and wraps around my chest, sliding like a knife between my ribs. I think my blood must freeze in my veins. I cross my arms over my knees and rest my head on them, partly for the comfort of moving my back away from the stone, and partly to muffle the sound of my teeth chattering. Eventually, though, they stop of their own accord. I think that I have been waiting a hundred years; almost I cannot remember what for or why. I let my eyelids fall shut and listen to the half-heard sound of my heart.

"Veriana."

The word makes its persistent way through the foggy tunnels of my mind. How strange that someone would call me "my lady."

"Veriana, wake up. Wake up."

I have the distinct feeling of being shaken—a disjointed, unreal sensation, for I cannot quite remember the way of my body.

"Thorn."

I force my eyes open, focus on a pair of dark eyes. They are the gentle brown of a forest streambed, dappled with sunlight. I wonder if I am home again; if the darkness I have surfaced from has carried me to another time and place so that, when I step forth fully from the depths, I will find myself in my own woods once more.

"Here now, drink this." A liquid pours into my mouth.

I swallow reflexively. Water, deliciously warm, flows through my chest, cascading over my ribs to settle in a warm pool in my belly. When I look up again, I do not see his eyes anymore—I see him.

"More?" Kestrin asks.

I nod wordlessly. It was the luminae stones' light in his eyes that glittered gold. He moves away, going to a small brazier of coals with a pot over it. A second man kneels by it, dressed in hunting clothes much like the prince. He looks vaguely familiar, but I cannot place his name, staring blearily at his fine features, the dark hair curling around his collar.

I don't know how long I remain there, sipping water. The prince wraps my hands around the warmth of the mug and helps me to drink at intervals. I realize gradually that I am nearly dry, that I am wrapped in various layers—blankets as well as cloaks. I have begun to shake again as my body regains sensation, numbness burned away by an aching pain.

"She is too weak to leave on her own." The prince kneels beside his companion, though I do not recall him leaving me.

"It is not cold enough for her to have frozen," the man says, his voice stirring echoes. Where do I know him from?

"No," Kestrin agrees.

The man looks toward me. His face is too bright to focus on, for the light from the luminae lamp falls directly on him. "She has had a shock."

Kestrin nods, dropping his voice as he answers.

I look around, the light showing me what I already knew I'd see: smooth stone walls and a stone pedestal at the center, though the bookshelves and sheaves of scrolls, the tables pushed against the walls, seem strangely out of place. The room looks used now, has the feel of a study rather than an ancient, forgotten sorcerer's room.

Sorcerer.

The word resounds in my mind, as if I had spoken it aloud. I close my eyes against it.

"Thorn." Kestrin touches my hand.

I start.

"We must get you to the city. Can you stand?"

I nod uncertainly, and Kestrin holds my arm to help me up. The other I use to push off the stone wall. It is an awkward process, but finally I gain my feet. The room twists around me, light streaked with darkness. I gasp, stumbling sideways against the wall.

At that, Kestrin is done with courtesies. He kneels and orders me to clasp his neck, and lifts me up on his back as he might a child. I rest my head on his shoulder as he carries me out and up a thin winding path to where a pair of horses wait.

There, I am boosted up before a rider, a flurry of words whipping past me. I do not realize that the rain has touched me until I feel a cloth dabbing my face dry. I look up to find that I sit sideways, and that the man who holds me before him is not the prince at all. It takes me a moment longer to finally place his name: Lord Filadon.

At least now I understand why he was chosen to meet me at the border. He may not have great holdings or a fine title, but he has the confidence and trust of the Family.

"Where?" I ask, voice rasping.

"Easy," Filadon says soothingly.

I look around dazedly, but there's no sign of Kestrin. We ride alone through the plains.

"The prince returned to the hunt," Filadon explains. "I am taking you to the palace."

"But I live—in the stables."

"There are no fires in the stable to warm you. Softly now."

I close my eyes, too tired to argue, and sink into oblivion.

CHAPTER 18

"Are you awake, then?" A gray-haired woman leans toward me from her seat on a carved wooden chair.

I blink at her, bewildered, then glance about. I lie nestled among blankets on a low divan in a room I don't recognize. The palace. I'm in the palace.

"Good," she says, getting to her feet. "The prince wants to see you. Let's get you dressed."

She steps to the door to speak with someone outside while I struggle to sit up, my mind trying to grasp the implications of a dream room turned real, one that the Lady led me to and left me there to be found in.

The next moment, the woman is beside me, pulling free the blankets. "Move along," she says, and then I've no time to worry as she whisks me out of bed and into my clothes. They have all been washed, fraying hems darned and wrinkles pressed out. There is a new sash as well, replacing the one I used to bind the wounded boy's arm all those nights ago. Even my boots have been repaired and polished.

"How long did I sleep?" I ask as she surveys me critically. It has taken me that long to remember my Menay.

"A day or so," she says absently. "You'll do. Come along."

She sets a brisk pace from the room. My body aches, and I feel more tired than I would have thought possible. Have I really slept so long? What must Falada think? And Sage and the other hostlers—have they been worried?

The woman ushers me through a narrow door at the end of the hall and down a servants' corridor to a private library. Kestrin sits alone at a table, intent on the book before him, three more piled beside him. I pause on the threshold, and the woman gives me a little shove forward before closing the door behind me with a click.

He looks up, blinking as he focuses on me, and smiles. There is neither mockery nor flattery nor cruelty in it. It is the quick, instinctive smile of a man whose gaze alights on something he likes.

It shocks me to my core.

"Thorn," he says, rising. "You are feeling better?"

I nod mutely, still unnerved by that look. At least he has elected to address me in my own tongue, that I might not miss his meaning.

"I was . . . surprised to find you where you were. Were you running from something?" he asks. "On the plains?"

I open my mouth and then close it again, unsure what to tell him. Would he punish Corbé, or bring the blame back to me? I cannot let myself trust his smiles or the tenor of his voice. I know he can play games.

"Or were you running *to* something?"

"No," I say quickly. "Away."

"I see. Will you return to the stables?"

"Yes, Your Highness." Where else would I go?

He hesitates. "I thought you might consider a position here, in the palace."

He knows. I feel the blood drain from my face and it is all I can do not to flee. Panic churns in my stomach. I won't. I won't.

"Lady?"

"No." I clench my jaw to keep the other words in: *Please. I don't want this. Leave me alone.*

A silence draws out between us. I train my gaze on the table, afraid of what I might see if I look in his eyes. Perhaps I am wrong. Perhaps he means only to offer a distressed servant a change in employment. Or perhaps he knows exactly what he's offering.

"You might be safer in the palace." He says it lightly, as if it were a casual observation.

I risk a glance at him. He watches me, dark eyes shrewd. If he knows, wouldn't he force the issue? But there is no if—the evidence is piling up against me. He must know—he called me *veriana* when he spoke to me in his secret study, a study he led me to once before in a dream. The question is only what he will do about it, and what the Lady will do in return.

"I would prefer to return to the stables," I say, my voice not quite steady.

Another silence, in which I can feel him watching me, weighing my answer.

"As you wish," he says finally. "If you need anything, you will let me know."

Relief makes me light-headed. I bob an awkward curtsy and retreat to the servants' door, stumbling in my rush to get away—to have him let me go. It hardly seems possible, and I don't quite trust it.

The same elderly serving woman waits outside to usher me back to my room. When I tell her haltingly that I wish to return to the stables, she raises her eyebrows and then acquiesces, as if I requested a great favor. But I cannot risk staying here longer than I must, cannot risk Valka learning of my presence. The woman leaves me at a servants' exit onto the side road skirting the palace, nodding toward the gates before striding off to other duties.

The walk to the stables is longer than I remember. I stop at intervals to rest against buildings, my legs still weak beneath me. By the time I reach the temple, I have neither breath nor balance to take me farther. I stagger through the door and sink down to sit on the grass mats, the stone wall cold against my back. I'll let myself rest a little and then go on.

A faint scuffle in the alleyway disturbs the quiet. I look up to see a young boy peering in at me, hesitating just within the temple door. He is a slight, bony creature with great brown eyes and stringy hair.

I blink and he disappears, leaving me unsure if I saw him at all.

I pull my knees up, wrap my arms around them. The temple slowly fills with evening gloom. I need to get up, but I can't quite find the energy. I rest my head on my knees, drained by the knowledge that Kestrin has found me out, that the game we play has changed. All I want is to go *home*, to the stables, and stay there.

Abruptly, the temple darkens further. I look up to see a man filling the doorway, cloak swaying. He looks in at me silently. I watch him, and some part of me cries out that I should run, that this man might be like Corbé, but I have not the strength to fight this.

"Are you well, kelari?" The man's voice rumbles through the room.

I take heart from the fact that he has addressed me as *mistress*. The respect of it suggests he won't bring me harm—a slim hope, but something. I push myself to my feet. The temple tilts as I move. I take a gasping breath, one hand reaching out to steady myself against the wall.

He moves, a fluid rippling of cloak and shadow as he crosses the temple to me. "I'll escort you home," he tells me, putting a hand under my elbow.

Home. I look up at the hooded face of my helper and recognize the scar that runs from lip to chin. This is the man who met me with a sword the night I walked the wounded boy home. I nod.

We leave the temple together, my companion guiding me back to West Road. I lean heavily on his arm, keeping my gaze on the cobblestones as we follow the road, block after block.

He stops at the edge of the turn-in to the stables. "Can you go the rest of the way on your own?"

I consider the distance. I will have to walk the length of two practice rings and the first stable between them to reach my room. Falada's stall is much closer. And as much as my companion may not want to set foot in the king's stables, with the soldiers that pass through here on a regular basis, I do not want him to see precisely where I live either. He already seems to know more than enough.

I take a shaky breath, nod. "I will be fine," I assure him. "Thank you, kel."

"You are welcome."

I start forward, striving to walk steadily. By the time I reach Falada I have only the strength to pull the stall door closed before I sink into the straw in the corner.

"Alyrra, are you well?" A great brown eye regards me from barely two hand spans away. I reach up to rest my hand against his cheek.

"Fine, Falada. Just tired."

"Where have you been?" His voice is gruff with worry.

"Is it safe to talk?"

"You may speak with impunity," he replies. "Only I must beware."

"Yes." I lean my head against the wooden wall, breathing in the smell of horse and sweat and sun-sweetened hay. "I went out to watch the geese as usual," I tell him. "Corbé took them to the lower pasture. When I got there, he came over to me and—I spooked, as a colt might, I suppose. I hit him with my staff. And then I ran and lost myself and part of the hunting party found me and brought me back." I gasp as I finish, as if I have not breath enough left in my life for this short story with its shadow truths.

Falada sighs, and in that simple exhalation I hear the rest of my story. "Child," he says softly, and that is all.

I wake the following morning to a grim realization: the scarred man is having me watched. I scrub my face wearily. There is no other explanation, unless it is the boy I helped himself, which seems unlikely considering his youth. Either way, there's no question that the street child I glimpsed at the temple went to fetch the scarred man.

I stare across the stall to where Falada drowses, one leg slack. Whoever the boy may be, and whatever his crimes, there's no use worrying over it now. I force myself up. My chest aches and my throat feels raw; thrice during the night I woke coughing. But I had better not miss any more work.

Sage embraces me tightly when she sees me standing in the common room doorway. I stand stiffly, surprise making me slow, and she releases me with a soft half laugh. "I'm glad you're back safe," she says, and ushers me to the table, where a bowl of porridge waits.

I sit before the bowl and watch her pretend not to watch me. Her brow is furrowed, and her eyes when they meet mine are anxious.

"Where were you?" Her voice is quiet, gentle.

"I—" I stop, not sure how much to tell her, if I even have the right words.

"Corbé came back alone with the geese. We ilakina."

I shake my head, and she tries again.

"We were scared for you. Ash and Rowan went to the pasture to look for you. Then we heard from the palace that you were ill and would return later."

I nod. "I was ill."

"Corbé would not tell us anything, only that he fell and hurt himself."

"He does not . . . like me," I say, aware of how terrible an understatement this is, that it does not begin to catch the darkness that lies between him and me. I try again. "I am afraid."

Sage's eyes narrow. "Did he hurt you?"

Yes. No. I didn't really wait for him to do very much before I hit him.

"Tell me," Sage says, just as Ash once asked, *Who pushed you?*

I stare at her, and a part of me wants to weep for these words, for the care behind them. "Corbé," I say, my voice faltering, "he grabbed me by my hair. I did not know what he would do. So I hit him with my staff and ran."

"I see," she says, her voice soft with anger. "I will have Oak and Ash speak with Corbé."

I flinch. "But—"

"No, Thorn, they must." She reaches across the table and closes her hand over mine, squeezing gently. "Corbé thinks you are alone here, without protection. An easy target. He is wrong, and he needs someone to tell him so. This will not come back to hurt you, I promise."

"Thank you," I whisper.

"Is there anything else?" she asks. "Anything I should know?"

I shake my head. "No. Only I don't understand—Corbé has always hated me. I don't know why."

Sage frowns. "Corbé's father is a verin, but his mother is a servant—like you and me. He hates his father because his father left him here. Perhaps he does not like you because you are a veria. You had what he could not."

"His father is a *verin*?" I repeat, shocked that he should have a lord as a father.

"Yes."

I look down at Sage's strong, calloused palm cupped around my own newly work-roughened hands. "But I work too. I am a servant now."

"Hate is a strange thing, Thorn. We do not always understand it. You are here, but you are still a veria, and the people of the palace still ask about you."

I look at her sharply.

"They ask. We"—she tips her head to indicate the common room—"we do not talk about you. We say only that you do good work, and that you are learning Menay. But others watch you and report what you do. You should know that."

"Who?" I ask tightly. "Who asks?"

"I believe both the prince and the princess."

I nod. That much, at least, should not surprise me. At least the king is not watching me too.

"Thank you." My words are so quiet I think that they could hardly have reached her, but she gives my hands one last squeeze and stands up.

"I'm going to speak with Oak and Ash. Make sure to eat your breakfast."

"I will," I promise, and force myself to finish off my meal.

I take Falada with me to the goose barn when I am done, standing by his side while Corbé drives the geese out. Corbé seems no different to me than before, but for a scabbed cut and a fading bruise below his eye. It is only when he looks at me that I see my brother in his eyes. It is a look that takes the breath from my lungs and leaves my throat so dry I cannot find my voice.

I think of Sage's revelation, but I find that my fear overpowers my pity. I do not want to care about Corbé's past, his half-noble lineage. I do not want him near me.

As the last of the geese leave the barn, Corbé strides ahead to direct them. Falada nudges my shoulder, nods toward the staffs that lean against the back wall. I walk over to them slowly. It seems to me that they are bars stolen from a prison, that I have seen their smaller brothers strung across the window of my room back home.

"Take one," Falada tells me; it is not strange to me that his voice is both sad and stern. The wood grain is familiar to my hand, the roughness of it sliding easily against my calloused palm and sending a shudder through me.

Falada watches me covertly, staying by my side as we follow the geese, catching up before they reach the road. He steps away only a few times to usher back geese to the flock that have slipped my notice. I nod to him gratefully but do not call out; my throat aches fiercely, and I wonder if I will yet catch my death of cold.

On the way back from the pasture, Falada says, "Have I told you the history of my kind?"

I glance at him curiously. He has never mentioned anything of the sort. "No."

"I want you to hear it." Falada lifts his head, looking out over the plains, and when he speaks again, his voice is deep and fluid. "There was a time when all the thinking creatures lived in harmony. Men and Horses shared an equal space as companions and caretakers of the earth, for neither race yet called themselves rulers, nor cared for power."

Falada's words paint a history so long past no human has recorded it. I sink into the comfort of his knowledge, the depth of his voice.

"Then Men began to take a different course from Horses, using our lesser cousins, the unspeaking horses, as beasts of burden. Where the Horses had once taught humans how to venerate God and laud the world about them, the humans now used those songs to glorify themselves. Corrupted by greed and wishing for glory, the humans grew power-hungry. They thirsted to be remembered by future generations, to gain a measure of immortality. They became warlords and princes, calling others to fight for them, continually killing for a piece of land over which they might have absolute control for a little time. These humans drove the Horses from their lands, wanting neither their honor nor their peaceful example.

"It was this discord with the Horses that pushed humans to develop writing, for writing allowed humans to politick and communicate without our knowledge. Here humans could exemplify their superiority without question, proving once and for all their right to master the earth.

"In the end," Falada tells me ruefully, "it came down to our hooves versus your fingers. Not to mention your opposable thumbs."

I look down at my hands.

"If one of my kind was caught, they were put to death. We became hunted, a danger to society, for we created an imbalance in a world where only Men were to rule. We were the seed of revolt, the possibility of another option. That is why you had never heard of us; we have learned to keep away, to stay out on the empty plains or wander only those lands left untouched by Men."

"I am sorry," I whisper.

"It is no fault of your own."

"Hmm." I stamp my feet against the cold, not sure why I still feel guilty. We have come to a stop some distance from the city gates. I look up at them, still far enough away that I cannot make out the separate figures of the guards. With a sigh, I turn and sit on the stone wall running alongside the road.

"That," Falada says, as if I had posed him a question, "is why I cannot teach you how to read Menay. We Horses are illiterate."

"Fingers," I muse.

"And thumbs."

"Do you think I should learn to read Menay?"

"Perhaps. You will need to eventually," he says.

Because Kestrin has already found me out. But he let me go, and I don't want to think about being made to return. Instead, I say, "I am learning to speak it. You know how hard I've been working at it."

"You have learned the words. Now you must use them. Language is a weapon, Alyrra. You must defend yourself with what you can."

I wrap my arms around myself, cocooning myself in my cloak. "I don't think any words would have helped me—with Corbé."

"Perhaps not just then, but before, and now after, there are chances."

True enough. I wonder if I could have trusted Kestrin with what happened. But I have told Sage, and that is more than I have done before. With a sigh, I look up at Falada. In the dim morning light, his coat shines white, his eyes dark and kind.

"We should keep going," Falada says gently. "It is cold, and you are not yet strong."

We walk back to the city in silence. It takes me longer than usual to clean the barn, my back and legs aching.

Falada gives a warning huff, and I turn to find Ash and Oak approaching the barn doors. The expression on Oak's face is hard in a way I haven't seen before. Ash has a sharpness to him that glitters in his eyes.

"We just went up to the goose pasture and had a chat with Corbé," Ash tells me. "He won't bother you again."

"He shouldn't," Oak says. "But if he does, you tell us. He knows what will happen in return."

I nod, disquieted by their expressions.

"It's going to be all right," Oak says, his features softening. "You'll be all right now."

"Thank you," I say, and find that I mean it with all my heart.

When Falada and I reach the goose pasture, Corbé does not look at me. Nor does he glance at me again through the afternoon, keeping his face turned away. Only as we drive the geese home do I realize why: his lip is swollen and newly scabbed. For all that I do not like the idea of violence, I am grateful that he has not dared to look at me all day.

That night I take the blankets from my room and move them to Falada's stall. As the days pass, Sage brings me an herb to steep in hot water to soothe my cough. And Violet brews the tisane in the morning and leaves it out for me to drink before I leave for the goose barn. Yet both, when I thank them, shake their heads as if they have done nothing at all, as if it is silly of me to mention so small a thing.

And every night Falada stands by the stall door, raising his head to watch me when I cough, and nudging me awake when my dreams wrap me too tightly in the panic of memories I do not want.

CHAPTER 19

My days pass in a haze of work and tiredness. I go to the palace only once, at Valka's request, and sit with her to compose another letter to my mother. Valka sneers at me, but she cannot hide her discomfort with the contempt of my mother's words in her latest letter. As I listen to Valka's accounts of court life, though, I find myself agreeing with my mother for once: Valka is only weakening her position with all her games and politicking.

But Valka isn't hearing any of it. "Useless advice," she says, flicking my mother's letter away. "At least she managed to return that cloak to me. I cannot believe you left it behind."

"Did I?" I ask, feigning disinterest. "How very irksome for you. Now, how shall we begin?"

The letter is not ready until late, Valka cross with having to devote such time to it, but I am grateful to leave it signed and sealed on her desk.

As I rise to leave, she says, "Remember to stay in your place, goose girl."

She doesn't know—can't have found out about my night here, my interview with the prince in his library. "I have not forgotten our agreement," I say evenly. "So long as you honor it, I will stand by it."

"Oh, indeed." She sneers. "If you don't, I will see you regret it."

I let myself out, hurrying down the now familiar hallways. I have met no one else while at the palace tonight—even Valka's attendants are absent—yet I know that means nothing: the prince will know of my visit. I wonder what he will make of it. Or rather, I fear I know exactly what he will make of it.

I wake the next morning to find the world buried beneath great white drifts, the usual sounds of the stables strangely muffled. Horses stand patiently outside, each in their own woolly blanket, their breath puffing forth in swirling clouds.

When Falada and I reach the goose barn, I learn what I have occasionally wondered: that the geese will no longer be taken out now that the snows have come. Instead, Falada watches from the gate as Corbé and I rake up around the flock. After we lay down fresh straw, we haul in buckets of grain to pour into the feeding troughs and then part ways, silent as always.

Falada and I walk out to the snow-buried meadows together; there is something in that part of my day I do not want lost, even if I no longer must walk to the pastures. The road has been traversed by both horses and wagons, the snow churned to mud by their passing. It is the plains that steal my breath.

Here is the reality of a sweeping white prairie running out

till it blends with the gray horizon. The wind whistles in my ears, catching at the hood of my battered cloak and slicing through me to numb my bones. Only a few trees grow here, small copses at the corners of meadows, or gathered along an ice-rimed stream, rubbing bare shoulders together. They greet me like old friends returned after a long absence, their branches laden with snowscapes and icicles. I find my eyes growing blurry, tears running in icy tracks down my cheeks.

We return from our walk just past noon. I rub Falada down, the work bringing warmth back to me, needling my fingers and toes. I am unspeakably grateful that he is still safe, that Valka seems not to have heard of my stay at the palace. Hooves picked and horse blanket draped, Falada follows me into his stall. I settle on the straw as he watches me, and can't think what to do.

"Bored?"

I throw a handful of straw at him. "It isn't funny. I've a whole winter ahead of me."

"Then you'd better find something to do."

"Yes, well," I grumble and trail off, having nothing else to say. Falada huffs softly and turns to put his head over the door, his ears swiveling to catch the sound of a conversation from the common room.

I look at him, then at the opposite wall, then at my stained and ragged skirt. What was it I used to do every day for the first fifteen years of my life? I loved to go for walks or rides, but it is too cold for that. I used to read what books I could find, but here I have none. What else? Surely I did more than read and walk?

I close my eyes and breathe in the damp horse smell of the

barn. I suppose I used to watch people—during receptions and hearings and meals, and in the laundry room and kitchen, and even in the village. Read and walk and watch. It is not even enough to count off on one hand.

Falada's ears flick toward the hallway. I hear footsteps and then Joa steps up to the door, offering his hand, slightly cupped, to Falada. Joa, I have learned, is not just another hostler but the master of horses himself, in charge of both stables.

Falada considers Joa carefully before reaching out and blowing lightly into the cupped hand.

From where I sit, I can see the smile that touches Joa's lips.

"He likes you," I observe.

Joa blinks once into the darkness of the stall before he sees me. "He's a hard one to win."

"You're winning him." The words are slightly awkward on my tongue, but I'm confident I've at least used the right ones.

"I've a long way to go to get where you are. How are the geese?"

"Fine. We aren't taking them out anymore. It's just the cleaning in the morning and an extra feeding at night now."

"Why don't you help out around here in the afternoons?" Joa suggests casually.

Help out? With the horses? I feel a grin spread across my face. "All right," I say, beaming so wide Joa chuckles.

"We're short a hostler," he explains, swinging the door open and stepping back to wait for me. "It'll be good to have an extra set of hands in the afternoon."

I scramble to my feet and follow after Joa as he explains

just what I have gotten myself into.

I learn very quickly that working in the stables is not all that different from my work with the geese: I am only mucking out stalls. It is backbreaking, palm-blistering work, except that now, having been broken and blistered by the geese, I find I am only achy, calloused, and inordinately proud of myself.

"One would think you'd discovered how to turn lead into gold, the way you strut around grinning," Falada comments a few days later as we walk out past the gates, frozen gravel crunching beneath our feet. Joa and I have struck a bargain. Between cleaning the goose barn and lunch, I have my own time. After lunch, I become a full-time mucker.

"I have found my calling in life," I explain with mock seriousness. "I have finally discovered the one thing I excel at—"

"Shoveling horse dung?"

"Quite," I say loftily. "I cannot expect you, as a Horse, to understand."

"Mmm."

"In the first place, horse dung is far superior to goose dung, being of larger size. In the second, it is of greater import, being of significantly magnified stench. In the third—" I break off as Falada butts me with his head. "Hey!"

"Spare me, O Lady of the Shovel."

"Don't forget the pitchfork," I reply tartly.

Falada snorts. "Really, though, I am amazed."

I kick a clump of snow, remembering the little dell where the Wind would visit, and then think of Redna and the many afternoons I spent with her. "Some of my happiest moments at home were when I was out riding Acorn. I used to envy his hostler for the time she had with him and the other horses. Now I'm in her place, doing the work I've always only watched."

"If there were no Lady, you would be content with this life, wouldn't you?" he asks.

I glance at him askance. He looks somber, saddened. "Yes," I admit.

He dips his head in acknowledgment.

"At least I still have my shovel for now," I quip with forced lightness. "I can take on any amount of manure with that."

He huffs softly. "Let us hope so."

With the change in weather, I spend significantly more time lingering over my meals with my friends and sitting with them in the evenings. I join in the conversation with renewed determination, asking questions and making comments. While Rowan might sometimes duck his head to hide his amusement, or Violet might discreetly rub the smile from her mouth when I say something particularly confused, mostly they listen thoughtfully and phrase their replies so that I may catch their meaning.

And each night, as I lie on my patch of straw, Falada a pale white presence beside me, I review these conversations and kindnesses. I worry away at the importance of writing and the use of speech, the creation of Horses and Fair Folk. But then, when I can find no other distraction, the darkness begins to fill with shadows I can no longer keep at bay. I lie on my back, staring open-eyed at the stall, and I cannot calm the beating of my heart, cannot blot out the words and cruelties of my brother, the daily memories of Corbé, the feel of wood in my hands. Whichever way I turn, there is the threat of the Lady, her chain still wrapped around my neck, the net she has cast still waiting to ensnare Kestrin. When sleep comes, it is fraught with darkness, echoing with the beat of wings against air.

One crisp, clear morning, I venture back to the temple in the company of Falada, in the hope I might find tranquility there. I scan the streets as we walk, wondering if I will see the large-eyed urchin who found me when I was ill.

Near the temple, a trio of boys plays in a rectangle of bright morning sunshine between two buildings. One of them spots me and nudges his friend; he looks up and I recognize him at once. He stares, then scrabbles to his feet and sprints down a narrow passage between buildings, his friends at his heels. I watch them go, quite certain that my prayers will be more social than expected.

In the temple, I let myself sink into the stillness. I have prayed often in the quiet moments of my days, sitting with Falada, and in the warm darkness of the stable at night, when I wake from liquid dreams that shift and swirl and lose their form but hold always within them the glint of eyes and the gleam of teeth in a smiling mouth.

I wrap my cloak around myself and breathe in the sweet, cool air, my eyes tracing the words upon the opposite wall, a prayer I still do not know how to read. I remember how I prayed the night the boy was chased by the soldiers. I wonder if he was sent to me, if I was given the chance to help him—or the chance to choose between helping him or the soldiers. I wonder why he is having me watched so closely.

I let these thoughts fade away, listening to the sounds of the city around me. Kneeling on the stiff grass mats, I let myself sink into prayer. I pray for all the things I have known and learned and felt: for the look in Corbé's eyes and the fears that rule me, for the prince and his hopeless struggle against the Lady, and for the Lady herself and the hold she has upon me, and again and again for myself, and for the feel of wood in my hands, and the vicious stretch of a smile across my face as Corbé bled.

Outside, Falada gives a warning snort. One hoof scrapes against the temple wall as he shifts.

I rouse myself from my prayers and go to the doorway, knowing whom I will find. The scar-faced man watches Falada from a few paces away.

He inclines his head to me. "Peace, veria."

Ah, so he has found me out to be a lady, then.

"Peace, kel." I stand by Falada's head. I doubt he recognizes the man, for Falada did not come up the stairs with me that night.

"A friend of ours has asked that you meet him. He waits for you at the Clever Fox."

I glance at Falada. He swishes his tail once, as if to warn me off such an invitation. He *wouldn't* like the sound of this, of course, but I can't help wanting to know how the boy made out—and why, precisely, he is having me watched.

"There is a stable for your horse," the man says, following my gaze.

"Where?"

He approaches, kneels to pull off his boots. Speaking quietly, he describes precisely which turns I must make to reach the Clever Fox. I pull on my own boots, listening.

When he is done, he steps past me into the temple. Only then does he look at me again. "Will you remember the way?"

"Yes."

"He is waiting."

I follow the alley toward the backstreets, Falada at my side. Tension radiates from him like heat.

"Remember the boy we helped?" I ask, stepping over a discolored puddle edged with ice, my boots sliding in the mud. "That was his friend who opened the door to me. He, um, helped me home from the palace after I ended up there."

Falada lets out his breath with a huff, unappeased.

"I know," I say softly. "But I want to know why they're watching me. And I don't think they'll harm me. The scarred man could have done anything he liked when he found me in the temple before. Instead he walked me home. I—I'd like to know what they're about."

Falada tosses his head in disagreement.

"I'll try to be careful," I say, and leave it at that.

The stable hands clearly expect us, waving me over and pointing out an empty stall. "You'll want to take that back stairway up, kelari," one of them tells me as I swing Falada's stall door shut.

Upstairs, a serving boy scrubs the floor. He backs out of the way, watching as I walk to the third door on the right and knock.

A man opens the door, his beard and hooked nose visible even in the shadow of his hood.

I step back in confusion, but he gives me a slight bow.

"Please come in, veria." He opens the door wider, gesturing for me to enter.

I cross the threshold hesitantly, wondering if I've made a

mistake. I wish desperately that Falada had been able to accompany me—and then the man leaves, shutting the door behind him.

I glance around uncertainly. To one side of the room, a pair of wooden benches flanks a stone fireplace; toward the middle, a collection of mismatched seats faces each other. It is an odd attempt at a sitting room, perhaps only cobbled together for the occasion.

A man sits motionless in one of the high-backed chairs. I blink at him, taken aback at his presence, his stillness. Like his friend, he wears his hood up. The light from the window behind him makes it hard to discern the details of his face. He does not speak.

I swallow, wishing again for Falada, but I have gotten myself into this, and I must get myself out. I cross the room, coming to a stop before the nearest chair. "What do you wish of me?"

"Two things," the man replies. "First, I would settle my debt with you." He gestures to a pouch that sits on the little table beside the chair.

I glance down at it. "What debt?"

The man draws up his right sleeve, letting his cloak fall away from his arm. A still-new scar runs the length of his forearm, the skin stretched pink and tight over the closed wound.

"Oh," I say stupidly, staring. The wound looks even more wicked in the light of day. The sight of the arcing gash not yet fully healed steals my presence of mind. I should have suspected it was him, only I had thought him a boy before.

"I would thank you for your help," he reiterates, straightening his sleeve.

"I don't want money." I might like a pair of gloves, but I'm not going to ask this man for them—certainly not when he would equate his life to their worth.

"I have nothing else to give you," he tells me. "And I would not be in your debt."

I peer at the shadowed planes of his face beneath the hood. "You have already repaid me. Your friend helped me home from the temple when I was ill."

The man inclines his head. "That is the second matter I would speak with you about." He leans back, tilting his face to watch me. The light from the window outlines the barest details of his features: a smooth-shaved chin, slender nose, deep-set eyes. A young man, not yet in his prime but certainly no longer a boy. "It is not wise for you to walk alone at night. Even during the day, you must be aware of where you are."

"I was ill," I repeat, flushing.

"All the more reason to be careful," he observes. "Your horse is a peculiar protection to you; I have seen dogs trained to guard, but not horses. He has a mystery about him that keeps you safe when you are with him. Alone, it will only take one drunk, one lout, to destroy your honor. And that is not the only danger here."

"What do you mean?"

"Have you not yet learned that our great land has fallen prey to slavers?"

I stare at him. His voice is light, mocking, but his gaze on mine burns bright. "Slavers?" I echo uncertainly.

"They are generally referred to as snatchers," he explains, as if that would help me. "And by and large, they only snatch children—usually under the age of thirteen or fourteen—just old enough to bring in a good price, I suspect, leaving behind those in their prime who would be missed from their work. Perhaps that is why you have not heard of them."

There is some puzzle here I don't understand, and it has nothing to do with my not working with children. "Does the king—the lord high marshal, even, do nothing?"

"They do a great many things," he says. "But little of it affects the snatchers. You are just young enough that you, too, should be wary when you are on the streets."

I nod mutely.

"Good. Do you understand further you were a fool to come here today? You do not know me, do not know what I might do to you."

Fear makes my palms damp. I glance toward the door: solid oak, thick and ungiving. The window is the only other escape route, and I would have to pass the man to reach it.

"You see the danger," he observes, satisfaction warming his voice. "You are safe here, but do not be so reckless in the future."

Relief gives my tongue courage. "I recognized the man, and the boy in the street. I knew they were friends of yours."

"You caught sight of Tarkit?"

"Perhaps? A young boy saw me earlier. He came into the temple the day I was ill, as well. He must be eight or nine years."

"He is eleven. Children who are not fed well do not grow well."

I clasp my hands before me, aware that they are just barely trembling.

If he notices, the man gives no indication. He stretches out his legs, his eyes on my face. "Tarkit is useful but too honest for the streets. He also lacks the necessary discretion. He was not to let you see him."

"Why were you having me watched to begin with?" I ask.

"As I said, I owe you a debt. I also considered it likely that you would need protection given the circumstances under which you helped me."

"And as I said, I did not help you for a reward," I repeat, grateful to shift the conversation.

"Yes." He pauses. "Why did you help me?"

I walk around the grouping of chairs to sit next to the man so that we face the room together. At least this way it is harder for him to read my face. My eyes wander over the scuffed wood floor, the worn furniture. "I don't know," I tell him finally. "You were slowed by us; I couldn't let that mean your capture."

"You could have misdirected the soldiers and left me."

True. I lean my head back against the chair, look up at the ceiling. Soot darkens the beams, masking detail. In the far corner, a dusty spiderweb hangs abandoned. "You needed help."

"I see," he says.

After a breath, I ask, "What will you do with Tarkit?"

"He should be apprenticed to an honest trade, but he can hardly afford it, nor am I in the business of apprenticing my errand boys to others. I will see about him."

"What does he want to do?"

"He wants to be a baker. I believe he thinks that then he'll never go hungry." I hear the amusement in the man's voice, and a hint of sadness.

I consider this, remember the boy's angular face. "How much does an apprenticeship cost?"

"Ten silvers a year; he will need two years before he will be offered wages."

I think of Valka's trunks, of the wealth within, and feel a curious sense of lightness as I say, "I will pay for it."

The man tilts his head as if in thought. "You are very idealistic for a servant. You will end up hungry and on the street—or worse—if you are not careful."

"When I do, it will be my idealism that will send an escort to walk me to safety." Just as this man did.

He chuckles softly. I smile, turning toward the sound. He leans forward, elbows on his knees, eyes studying the ground.

"And when I am cold and hungry, I will remember that I have helped a young man learn a trade that will keep him well the rest of his life."

He turns his head to look at me. The very keenness of his regard frightens me. "You are not what any of us thought," he murmurs.

"What do you mean?"

"You are neither goose girl nor veria, but something better than them both."

"You are mistaken," I say, the words bitter on my tongue. "I am nothing."

He considers me. "I hope you do not believe that."

I study my hands, the dry and cracking skin, the ragged nails. They are working hands now. He was right the first time around; I am nothing more than a naive fool of a serving girl. I shake my head. "How will I get the payment to you?"

"I will send Tarkit to your temple in two weeks' time, once I've made the necessary arrangements. He'll tell you where to meet one of my men. I am afraid it would not be wise for me to meet with you again."

I nod. From elsewhere in the inn, the sound of laughter drifts up to us. I wonder what I have done in helping a man who has others he can order to guard or meet me, who is informed by a network of street children and beggars. Did I obstruct the path of the king's justice? And what am I risking in dealing with him further?

I moisten my lips. "Will you tell me who you are?"

He does not answer at once. When he speaks, his voice is quiet, emotionless. "Go back to the stables and ask the hostlers there who Red Hawk is; they will tell you. As for the debt I owe you, I will clear it with you soon, in a way you'll accept. Until then"—he dips his head toward the door—"I wish you well."

CHAPTER
20

As has become our habit, Falada and I walk out to the pastures. The wind lies quiet, making the day seem almost warm, though the clouds hang low and foreboding as always. We walk on in silence, turn off the road to follow one of a myriad of ragged paths. The grass here is bent and broken, clumps sticking up through the ice-rimed snow. White with a lacing of brown, like the feathers of a great snowy owl.

I shudder. "Falada?"

"Yes?"

I open my mouth to speak and then close it again, look out over the snow-swept plains. Falada waits, as he always has. Is it too cowardly to suggest we both leave—he flee the threat of Valka, who may yet decide to punish me through his death, and I a future as princess that, if I choose to pursue, I doubt I will survive long in?

"Alyrra?" he asks, and in that name I hear my answer.

"Nothing."

He nudges my shoulder with his nose. I turn and take a step to rest my head against his neck, and wish my story were already told.

A quad of soldiers enters the first stable early the next morning, just as I am stepping from Falada's stall. They glance toward me as they near, and then the lead soldier's eyes narrow as he looks past me, to Falada.

"That's the one. Keep an eye on it while I talk to the master of horses."

I stand rooted to the ground as the remaining three soldiers slow to a stop a few paces away. They say nothing, but their eyes glance off me as they look around, keeping an eye on the rest of the stable. Behind me, Falada snorts softly.

That's the one.

"Kel," I say, taking a small step toward the nearest soldier. "Are you—did you say you are here for this horse?"

"We're here for it," he agrees, and now they are all watching me keenly.

"What do you need him for?"

The soldier flicks a single glance to where his quad leader has disappeared. "It's the zayyida's orders," he says finally. "Damn waste if you ask me."

Valka's orders. I shake my head. "She's—you mean . . ."

"He's being sent to the knacker for dog meat," one of the other soldiers says, his voice flat.

I take a step back, and then another, until my back is pressed against the stall door. It's been nearly a month since the hunt, a month since I've seen Kestrin at all. I've done nothing since . . . I even wrote another letter for her since then! But perhaps she has only just learned of my stay at the palace, my interview with the prince. But why hasn't she called me in, why hasn't she—

"Thorn."

I turn, aware of Falada watching me from just within the stall.

Joa strides down the hall, the quad leader at his side. "These soldiers are here for the white," he says as he reaches me.

I shake my head desperately. "No. Falada isn't hers. She *can't* kill him." It's a stupid argument, and I know it even as the words leave my mouth, because Falada *is* hers so far as anyone at the stable knows. I should have made him leave. I *knew* the danger. Why didn't I push him away when I had the chance?

"I am sorry," Joa says quietly.

There is no arguing here, no matter how little the soldiers themselves want to carry out this order. It has been commanded, and it will be done. I cannot run to the palace fast enough to stop it, that I know. Nor will Valka change her mind. "At least allow me to say goodbye," I tell Joa.

"I can grant you a few minutes," he says, and motions the quad leader forward. The man glances askance at Joa, but doesn't argue. They walk toward the great double doors, the rest of the quad falling in behind them.

I slip back into the stall. "Falada," I whisper. "If I ride you, they won't dare hurt you. We can get away—both of us together—the city gates are right here."

"No, child."

"No? What do you mean, *no*?" Desperation claws at my throat.

"They will shoot me and arrest you. We would be hunted even if we escaped the gates."

How can he give up without a fight? "You cannot let them kill you!"

"If I struggle, they will know I am a thinking creature and I will endanger my people. If you struggle for this, you will endanger all that now hangs in the balance."

He is right. I feel perilously close to tears. "I will kill her."

"*No.* You will not attempt to avenge me. Do you understand?"

How can I understand?

"Alyrra," he repeats softly, urgently. "Do you *understand*?"

I cannot escape his gaze. "Yes."

"One more thing. Have my head hung in the city gates that I might see you."

"What?" I stare at him, appalled.

"Do it."

"As you wish." I hear the sound of approaching boots. "Oh, Falada," I whisper, and step forward. He lowers his head to rest his chin on my shoulder. I throw my arms around his neck and bury my face in his mane. The boots stop outside our stall, silence rolling out to smother every other sound.

Falada lifts his head, disengaging himself, but as he does, he brings his mouth to my ear and breathes softly, "Stay."

I nod, touching his cheek, then turn toward the men. Joa stands at their front, and it is to him I speak. "I want his head mounted and placed in the gates, that I might remember him."

"His head—the *gates*?"

"There are other things hung there," I say, as if I ask only a little thing. At least this much is true: there is a wooden cage hung high up, for what purpose I do not know, and sometimes there are ribbons or garlands strung up, or prayer flags. None of them, though, involve the dead.

"What you ask will cost money," Joa says uneasily.

"I will pay." One of the soldiers reaches out, unlatches the door, and swings it open. Another throws a harness to me. I catch it clumsily. "Joa, see that the blade is sharp, and it is done well. Gently."

"I will," he promises.

I turn to Falada, holding the harness.

He watches me, unmoving.

I toss it into the back of the stall. "He has followed you once before and he will follow you now. He will not require a harness."

Joa nods.

"Even there—keep a hand on his crest, and he will do as you ask."

"Very well," Joa says. "Let's get this done." He starts toward the stable doors, the two soldiers holding back for us to pass. Falada walks in step with me. When we reach the doors, I put a hand on his crest. He looks down at me, his eyes old and weary and so very sad, and then he steps out, following Joa around the practice ring and out of sight, toward the knacker and his death.

CHAPTER
21

I stay in Falada's stall until I hear Joa return, the sound of hostlers calling greetings to him. He stops at the stall door. I do not think I have ever seen him so grim before. He studies me in turn, though I cannot say what he sees. At length he says, "It was done well. He had an easy death. I am sorry for this, Thorn. He was a good horse."

"Yes," I say softly.

"His head will be hung as you ask. If you give me the money, I will see to it."

"Yes."

"Are you well?" His eyes flicker over my face uncertainly. I nod once, step out of the stall, and close the door.

In my room, I throw open the traveling trunk. Wrapped in a kerchief at the top are the paltry few copper coins I have earned working here. I push them to the side, knowing they are not enough, and search through the clothes. I know that I could take

Valka's jewelry, that I have only to open the larger trunks and I will find more than enough for what I've promised Red Hawk as well as this—but I do not want anything of hers to touch Falada's memory.

Instead I find the pouch with the gift Jilna gave me many months ago. I tip the necklace into my hand, the silver chain and pendant shining in the dim light.

I lift the chain, barely believing my eyes. It has been repaired, the chain mended as if it had never broken during the Lady's attack. Why? Why would he have gotten it fixed? For surely only Kestrin had the opportunity to go through my trunks, in his search for the cloak. Did he hope I would find it soon after he returned the trunks? That I would take it as a sign of the kindness I insisted he lacked? Or was it merely a token action, something to assuage a guilty conscience?

I am grateful, suddenly and fiercely, that I did not find the necklace until now, did not have the chance to choose to wear it. I think of Jilna, with her tired face and her thin arms holding me tight, and I do not want that memory tainted. I clench the necklace in my fist and go down to find Joa, hoping it will be enough.

Night enters the temple long before it settles upon the rest of the city, filling its alley with deep shadows while the sun still lights the sky. I sit hunched in the corner, my arms hugging my knees, and fill my mind with the things around me: the faint sound of people on West Road, rustling in the stillness and then fading to nothing; the dirt that has accumulated on the mats so that, when I press my forehead to the floor in prayer, the grains stick to my skin; the way the wind whips into the little room at intervals, slapping my cheeks and snatching away what warmth I gain between gusts.

Wherever Red Hawk's watchers are, they have missed me today. Tarkit is nowhere to be seen and no one but strangers stop in to pray. They offer me a nod or smile before going about their devotions, then depart as quietly as they came, and I sink ever deeper into the silence of my soul.

The hours have slipped away like this. Now, with night approaching, I can no longer focus my thoughts on my surroundings. They fall away from me, sinking into darkness, and I am left holding tight to myself. I thought I would have cried, would have mourned my friend with a river of tears, but I cannot. My throat aches so that it is difficult to swallow, my chest is tight, but my eyes are dry as bone. I wonder what Falada would tell me now, if he were suddenly returned to me. As if he stood beside me, I hear his voice: *What will you do?*

What can I do? I bite my lip, holding it between my teeth and concentrating on the pinprick of pain.

I can imagine Falada turning his head toward me, eyes sparking. *Will you leave her to practice her mercy on the prince and all Menaiya?*

I can't face the Lady now. I don't know what to do.

With a half-gasped laugh, I realize Falada's response: *I did not suggest you face the Lady.*

I push myself to my feet, my joints creaking and popping. As I promised Falada, I will not avenge him, but that does not mean I shouldn't face Valka. Outside, the sky still shows a hint of light above the walls of the surrounding buildings. West Road bustles with end-of-day business, lantern light pouring out of open shops, the scent of food on the air. With so much activity, at least I need not fear for my safety.

I pass through the palace gates without glancing at the soldiers. The main doors are closed against the cold, but they are hardly the only entrance. I follow the wall until I come to a servants' entrance, the door propped open. I pass down strange corridors with quick steps, making my way in the general direction of the Receiving Hall. Once I reach familiar halls, I continue on to Valka's apartments. Twice I pause before I turn a corner, waiting for those already there to move on, their voices fading.

I drift to a stop when I reach the sweeping staircase up to the royal suites. I have not decided what I will say, only that I must address her. Now, standing before the stairs, I try to order my thoughts.

"Veria."

I jump, twisting to face the prince. It would be him, of course. There is no one else I could possibly meet in this godforsaken place but him.

"Forgive me. I did not mean to startle you."

"No," I agree.

He looks at me sharply, but I have nothing else for him.

"If you would accompany me, veria."

He holds out his hand and I place my own in it without thinking. He tucks my hand into the crook of his arm and leads me up the stairs. We pass Valka's apartment without a word. He releases my hand only so that he may open a door, and nods for me to enter.

I hesitate on the threshold. These are his rooms. I should not be here.

"Go in," he says from behind me. I do not know where to go, pausing in the middle of the sitting room before I move toward the fire.

Kestrin does not speak at once. I hear him walk to a side table, then cross to me. He holds a goblet out. I take it, my half-numb fingers clumsy, and bring it to my lips, then stop. The heady, fruity scent assaults my nose. I do not need to look down to see what I hold.

"Drink it," he says.

I remain unmoving, the goblet nearly touching my lips, and I think of my brother, his breath sickly sweet as he towers over me. I step back and hurl the wine into the fire. It spits and smokes before flaring up brighter than before.

Kestrin stands perfectly still.

I hold the goblet out to him, my eyes trained on the fire. When he does not take it, I lift it up and set it on the mantel.

"You needed that," he tells me.

"No."

"Come sit down, veriana."

My lady. I take a half step back, my eyes snapping to him.

His brow creases in the beginning of a frown.

It is only courtly manners, to refer to a lady as "my lady"—so why should his use of it make me want to run away? It takes all my will not to retreat further. "I would rather go."

He laughs harshly. "I am sure you would. I am always forcing you to speak with me." He shakes his head. "Please, veria, sit."

For a long moment I consider him, the fact that he is asking, not commanding. Then I drop my gaze and move to a chair.

The prince takes a seat beside me and watches the flames.

A silence grows between us, allowing his words to dig their poisoned talons into me, injecting a bitterness into my blood that I can well-nigh taste on my tongue.

"You did not force me to take shelter in the entrance to your hidden study," I tell him, my words so soft they seem to get lost even as they leave my lips. I wonder if they reach him, for he makes no sign of having heard. I turn back to the fire. "That was my own stupidity."

"You might not have survived had you not," he says.

I shake my head. I could have gone back to the city, and if I had, Falada would still be alive. There can be no other explanation for Valka ordering Falada's death—not when I have done nothing else that might anger her. She must not have heard at once; it would have taken some time for the story to slip out, considering how few people Kestrin involved in my stay in the palace.

"Why are you here?" Kestrin asks abruptly.

I look at him sharply, and for the first time tonight actually see him. He is dressed for an evening banquet, his tunic topped by a long, open-fronted velvet jacket, exquisitely embroidered, his hair falling loose about his shoulders. It changes his aspect, makes him look both younger and gentler. I clear my throat, unnerved. "I would speak with the princess."

"I suspected you were not seeking me."

It is almost a joke, but I cannot summon even a flicker of amusement. "No."

"No," he echoes. "What do you need of her?"

I shake my head.

He tries again. "Will you tell me what has happened?"

I do not look at him. I would not know how to explain what Falada was to me without letting slip his secret.

"Something has happened, I can see that. It has leached the color from your face." He purses his lips. "First I find you half-frozen on the plains. Now you appear in the palace like a ghost, with nothing to say but that you would see the princess. What has she done?" He half smiles. "Or has someone died?"

I start and turn away quickly. "Nothing. It's nothing."

"Who's dead?" His voice is hard, the question commanding an answer.

"No one—just a horse—that is all." A log cracks on the fire, sending a small shower of sparks across the grate. My eyes sting when I close them, but still I have no tears.

"The white? Who used to go everywhere with you?"

I nod.

"When?"

I grip my hands together in my lap. "This morning."

"I see. You are sure the princess issued the orders?"

"Joa said so."

"He could not have been mistaken?"

"I don't know. I intend to speak with her."

He studies me. "What will you say?"

I shake my head, say again, "I don't know."

Kestrin shifts, watching me keenly. "She is expecting you."

I meet his gaze in surprise.

"She has ordered her attendants to sleep in her antechamber tonight and requested a guard by her door. You won't be able to pass through to see her in private."

I close my eyes, remembering my first visit to Valka, her terror at finding me in her bedchamber with her. Yes, she expected me tonight. For all her tricks and power, she fears what I might do in private. I feel a smile twist my lips, and then I press my hand to my mouth, forcing the smile away. I swallow, opening my eyes to stare ahead of me.

This is why, I think. This is why Falada told me not to avenge his death.

I stand up. "I'm going."

Kestrin raises his eyes to mine. "Are you sure that is wise?"

"I won't speak to her. Not now." I shake my head slowly, my heart sickened. If I go to Valka tonight, I will have only a wish of violence against her—she will have made me come to her, and the power will still rest with her. I need to wait until Valka needs something from me, as she will. And I must think on what I want from her in return. In this moment, it is abundantly clear that my threats will not hold her. She will simply plan to eliminate me before she betrays Kestrin, rather than risk her agreement with the Lady.

Kestrin rises to face me. "Did you walk here alone from the stables?"

"I—yes."

"I will arrange for a quad to escort you back down."

And chance such a story reaching Valka, after this latest display of her kindness? I think not. "I can walk myself home." I cross the room to the door.

"Thorn." I look back at him, my fingers curling around the door handle. He stands with his back to the fire, woodland eyes shadowed. "I do not doubt your ability. It is only that you are a woman alone in the city, and it is dark." He closes the distance between us. "Let me call my quad for you."

I think of Red Hawk, and of Corbé, and know Kestrin speaks truth. "I thank you," I say wearily.

Kestrin pulls an elegant, braided rope that hangs beside the door. I listen for the sound of a bell, but hear nothing. He reaches out and takes my hand. I look down, frozen in surprise as he cradles my hand in his own, traces the calluses on my fingers, my palm. A shiver runs up my arm, curling in my belly, but I cannot move to pull my hand away. No one has touched me so before, as if I were precious.

"I cannot protect you when you are so far from the court," he says softly.

His words release me from the spell of his touch. I pull my hand free.

"I have not asked for your protection," I say, my voice shaking.

The words hang in the air between us. Kestrin does not answer, the silence growing long between us, until finally a knock at the door heralds my escort home. But even after I have left the palace behind, I can still feel his touch upon my palm.

CHAPTER
22

I spend the night in my upstairs room, alternately pacing a tight circuit and stretching out wide-eyed and exhausted on the sleeping mat. I have not slept here since that first night that I returned still weak from the palace and slept in Falada's stall instead. The room feels empty and cold now, the four walls bearing down on me through the darkness. I doze fitfully and finally fall asleep near dawn.

When I go down to the common room for breakfast, Sage has already set bread and cheese on a plate for me. Violet sits at the table, pressing her thumb against the crumbs on her own plate and licking them off. They both look up as I enter.

"You look terrible," Violet says without preamble.

"Violet!" Sage chides.

"Well, she does." Violet turns back to me. "You'd better start eating regular again. You didn't eat at all yesterday, and with this cold weather you'll be sick as Moonflower is if you aren't careful."

"Moonflower's sick?" I ask, without much hope of distracting her. I recognize the name only as one of the many horses stabled here.

"Like to die," Violet informs me. "And you look like death waking up. When I saw you come in last night, I thought it was just a trick of the darkness, but it's not. You look dreadful." She grins as she speaks, but the gravity of her words won't be undone.

"Thanks."

"Violet," Sage explains, sitting down next to me at the table, "is worried about you."

"And Sage," Violet responds, "sat up half the night listening to you stomp circles in your room, not because she was worried about you but because she prefers to sleep sitting up with her eyes open."

"I didn't mean to wake you," I say guiltily. "I didn't realize I was that loud."

"You weren't. We just sleep in the room next to yours," Sage tells me.

"And the floorboards creak." Violet points at my plate. "Eat your bread."

I take a bite to humor her, glancing at Sage for help.

"We both agreed it wouldn't do to speak to you in front of the boys," Sage says.

Violet nods. "That's right."

"But we know you had a close bond with that horse, and word is he was killed because of that." Sage tips her head toward the palace. "If anything like that is liable to happen again, you tell us and we'll keep you and yours safe."

I stare at her.

"Even," Violet adds, "if that means making someone up there cross."

"*Especially* if that means making someone up there cross," Sage says.

"Eat your cheese," Violet finishes, smiling.

I obediently take a bite of cheese. With my mouth full, I protest, "But that could be dangerous for you. And—"

"Dangerous? *Dangerous?* Did she say dangerous?" Violet cries.

Sage nods somberly, her eyes crinkled with amusement.

Violet raises her eyes heavenward. "Thorn, let me tell you about dangerous. Dangerous is cutting your finger on a rusty nail. Dangerous is walking too close behind a skittish horse. Dangerous is going anywhere in this city at night. Dangerous is *not* helping someone stay safe."

I shake my head, thinking of helping Red Hawk, then of Valka's vengeance. "If they're willing to kill a horse like Falada, they won't worry about hurting a servant as well."

Violet lets out her breath in a gust of frustration. "Thorn. Of all the ways I could die that I meet with every day, I would much rather die from helping someone. Weigh it," she says, holding up her hands to form an imaginary scale. "Die helping someone, die getting kicked against a wall. Hmm, what would you prefer?"

I rub my hands over my face. "I don't want any of you to get hurt helping me."

Violet throws her hands up in disbelief. "So you *want* Sage to die of lockjaw?"

I laugh despite myself. "You know I don't! I don't want you taking risks for me."

"Very noble," Sage observes. "But we're family here—we *are*. Your name fits right in with ours, so don't doubt it for a minute—and family looks out for each other."

Her words warm me like the glow of a friendly fire. *Family*. This is what I have missed all my life: Sage's motherly touch, the boys' brotherly concern, Violet's sisterly love. They are everything I have ever wanted, and nothing like my own family. I can only grin foolishly in response.

"Well, I'm glad that's settled," Violet says, jumping up and heading for the door. "I've got to check on Moonflower again."

Sage smiles as I look after Violet. "No more putting yourself in harm's way, Thorn. You have trouble, you tell us." She reaches over and squeezes my hand. "We mean it."

She shoos me off to the goose barn a few minutes later. Corbé has not yet arrived, so I open the doors and begin raking. I am grateful for his absence, working as fast as I can in hopes of missing him entirely, but just as I shovel the last of the dung into the barrel, he stumps through the gate.

I turn to him. "I didn't come yesterday, so let me finish our work today. Then we'll be even."

He stands at the gate with his back to the light, making it difficult to read his expression. I think perhaps he is surprised, but the emotion is fleeting. His face becomes hard and displeased as always. "I do not leave my duties undone."

I flush and shrug, turning away from him to stow the shovel. I hear him start toward me and instinctively I pivot back, holding the shovel ready.

He pauses, then continues walking, passing me to climb up the ladder nailed to the back wall. He forks down straw from the loft while I replenish the food and water for the geese. Neither of us speaks again.

Joa comes by to check on me as I muck out stalls in the afternoon, but after a quiet hello and how-are-you, there is nothing left to say. I feel his eyes on me more than once as I move between stalls, but he does not approach me.

After I finish, I find I have nowhere to go, no one to spend this time with. I leave the stables slowly, moving toward West Road. I can feel the old numbness calling me, and I know I could sink into it again, let the very deadness of my emotions protect me. The hours are easily lost that way. I could go to the temple, sit there in the silence, away from the horses and the watching eyes of the palace.

But, somehow, my feet turn toward the city gates. There, within the great stone passage, hangs Falada's head. It has been mounted on a wooden board and nailed up, hanging an arm's length above my head, if not more. I stare up at it and my stomach tightens painfully. His eyes and mouth have been sewn shut with great, ghastly stitches. The silken hair of his face shows gray with damp, dull and lifeless.

I do not know why I came here. My grief flows as heavy as lead in my veins, my body slow and unwieldy. I turn away, back toward the stables.

Princess.

I twist, my gaze flying up to Falada's head. It hangs unmoving, as dead as if it had been carved from stone. And yet—surely I heard the echo of a voice?

"Falada," I whisper.

"Princess." This time there is no mistaking it—Falada's

voice, deep and resonant and utterly impossible.

How can the dead speak? They can't. It is my own mind playing tricks on me.

"Is there a problem?" I whirl to find a guard walking toward me, squinting to see me through the shadows.

I force a smile and lift my hand as if all were well in the world, as if I could refute the strange unreal reality of a dead voice ringing out secrets into the dank air. Perhaps he can see the panic in my eyes, for he comes to a stop, hand on his sword. I turn, set one foot after the other in the hope he will let me go. Whatever he might have seen in me, he does not call out again. Instead, he watches me through the gates and back toward the stables.

Even though I have left him behind, stepping into the stables themselves, I can still feel the force of his gaze on my back.

"Thorn?"

I jerk to a stop, one hand reaching to grasp a wooden stall door.

"Careful—that's Moonflower's stall!" Violet says.

I snatch my hand away just as the mare within turns with a snort, teeth bared.

"Oh," I say, staring at the horse. She's pure black but for a white marking on her forehead, her coat damp with sweat. A slimy green substance leaks out the corner of one sunken-looking eye. I suspect the other looks just as bad. She's certainly ill, but she seems far more concerned with keeping me out.

"She's as pretty as her namesake," Violet says, taking my elbow and guiding me back, "and her manners are just as poisonous."

How curious. Violet's usually much more forgiving. "Did she hurt you?" I ask.

Violet grins, half shrugging as she walks me along. "She stepped on my foot and I'm still a bit grieved. I keep hoping she'll decide I'm hers, but for now, she doesn't like a one of us."

I rub my face. Violet has brought me to the common room.

"Sit down," she says, giving me a nudge toward the table. "I'd like to ask a favor."

"A favor?" I echo, sitting down while Violet puts together a plate of bread and cheese.

"Whenever you're passing through, give Moonflower a smile, a gentle word, and a carrot or an apple, would you?"

I squeeze my eyes shut, try to commit this to memory. Smile, word, treat. "I can do that."

"Good," Violet says, setting the plate down and sitting across from me.

"Will she be all right?" I ask, voice quiet.

Violet smiles. "She will. I've been exaggerating a bit. Joa's watching her as carefully as I am, and we're relatively certain she'll pull through just fine."

I nod, comforted.

"Don't go feeling all soft over her now," Violet says with a grin. She nudges the plate of bread and cheese a little closer to me. "You'll never *guess* what that demon of a horse did last week."

I look from the plate to Violet, and the kindness in her eyes, and find that I actually am hungry. So I pick up a slice of bread and cheese and listen as Violet regales me with stories of Moonflower's evil cunning.

That evening we have a guest for dinner. When I enter the common room alongside the boys, I find Sage chatting with a young man of no more than twenty. Like the other hostlers, his hair is cut short, falling in a fringe by his chin. It sets off the sharpness of his jaw, the fine line of his nose. He does not wear the hostlers' uniform, though, but his own carefully mended clothes. From the way he embraces Ash and ruffles Rowan's hair as they greet him, it is clear they are old friends, his appearance no great surprise. When Violet enters, just behind us, her quiet greeting seems to brighten his whole being. He dips his head, flushing slightly as he answers.

Ash and Oak exchange a knowing look and firmly maneuver the young man to sit between them.

Rowan, seated beside me, leans in and murmurs, "Ash thinks he's a bit sweet on Violet. What do you think?"

I shrug uncertainly.

With a grin, Rowan says, "Massenso, this is Thorn. She works the geese and has started helping out in the stables as well."

"Happy to meet you," the young man says politely, and turns his eyes to Violet and keeps them there.

Rowan smothers a laugh.

Massenso brings more news of the city. I listen quietly, trying to fill the hollow place in my chest with the sound of voices, but my thoughts keep drifting back to Falada as he walked to his death.

"They've backed off on their demands for a third heir," Massenso says.

I look up, blinking as if to better focus on him. What? Does he mean the Circle of Mages?

Ash snorts softly. "Of course they have. It was just a ploy to put the thought in people's heads. They'll wait a few months, and if the prince and his new wife don't immediately announce a child to be born, they'll make a second push."

"Just an opening gambit, then?" Violet asks with a frown. "Is the Circle so sure the princess won't bear the Family an heir?"

"Perhaps they know something the rest of us don't," Oak rumbles.

"About the princess?" Sage asks.

"Or about why our Family keeps dying," Massenso murmurs.

I go still at that. How well does the Circle know what hunts the Family? Are they planning on Kestrin's betrayal as certainly as the Lady is?

Sage shoots Massenso a warning look. "No one knows anything about that. Now, what about Verin Melkior? You've heard he's ordered a crackdown on thieves in the city."

"Of course," Massenso says. "The king thinks they are a danger, but they're only thieves." He lifts his chin in challenge. "It will be news when they crack down on the snatchers."

No one answers.

"Snatchers?" I repeat, remembering Red Hawk's words. I have not yet asked them about either Red Hawk or the snatchers. I meant to, and then Falada was killed and I forgot myself.

"They snatch our young women and children," Rowan says, not a trace of laughter left in him now. "From the street, from their beds, from wherever. A score or more every month just from this city, I would guess. Perhaps more."

Ash grimaces. "Melkior would do better to track them than worry about thieves."

"Thieves are also a danger," Oak rumbles. "Perhaps not as

much as the snatchers, but the feuds between the thieving rings must be stopped or there will be blood on the streets."

"I would take Red Hawk any day over the snatchers," Violet says lightly. "They say he's not all bad."

I nearly choke on my bread.

"That's right," Ash agrees, pouring water into my cup. I drink it thankfully. "A good man with a bounty of a thousand gold coins for his head."

"A thousand—?" I echo, nearly dropping my cup. In all the time I have worked, I have not yet earned a silver. The king must want Red Hawk dead very much.

Violet nods. "He's the leader of the ring of thieves based in the west side."

"Not like Bardok Three-Fingers on the east side or the Black Scholar on the south. They've only got five hundred a piece." Rowan winks at me.

"It will be the death of him one of these days. Greed's a powerful thing. One of his men will take the gold, hand him over to the king, and retire into the country on his own private estate," Sage says.

"What has he done?" I ask, painfully certain that I do not want to know.

"He's stolen from half the nobles and our wealthiest merchants, not to mention the king himself. A good number of them have pledged to pay the reward in return for his death," Massenso tells me.

"Why?"

"Because he stole from them," Ash repeats. "Just last month

he and his men robbed a bride and groom on their way to the groom's estate south of the city. Cleaned out all the wedding jewelry and took the groom's shoes to boot."

I shake my head, barely knowing what to think. "But . . . why does he steal? Where does the money go?"

Massenso shrugs. "To hear the king's men, Red Hawk's a power-hungry bully, buying his way into every dark business there is. Though no one believes he deals with the snatchers."

"He takes care of his own," Ash agrees. "He hires poor folk who have nothing to live on and gives them enough to get by. There're probably a hundred street urchins who would give their lives for him, for the coppers he tosses their way to keep their eyes open for him. But he's playing his own games too, setting by a store for himself. If he's wise, he'll know that he can't keep on thieving without getting caught."

A hundred street urchins. Thinking of the children I've seen, I can believe it, and also understand why Red Hawk had not yet arranged for Tarkit's apprenticeship. It's not something he could offer all the children he pays, nor would he want them all to hope for such from him. And then, he's a thief.

"I've heard enough of Red Hawk to hope he doesn't get caught," Rowan says bluntly. "Better him than the Black Scholar."

The others shoot him warning glances, but none contradict him. Violet turns the conversation away altogether to the possible change in smiths the stables currently rely on.

I listen quietly, thinking of whole networks of thieves on the brink of murdering each other, and the very real possibility that the Circle of Mages plans to profit from the Family's demise.

CHAPTER 23

Rowan looks up from currying a horse as I enter the second stable, my morning cleaning done. He grins mischievously. "I hear there's a package for you in the common room."

"A package?"

"Aye, a lad dropped it off earlier this morning. Seems Violet's not the only one with an admirer."

"It must be something else," I protest, flushing. "I don't have anyone like that."

He nods sagely. "Go see what it is, and then we'll argue."

"I will," I say, relieved.

I hurry straight to the common room, grateful to find it empty save for a package that sits on the table, a burlap-wrapped bundle tied with a bit of cord. I unwrap it to find more cloth inside—a heavy, dark green wool. I lift it up and its folds fall open. It is a cloak.

"Isn't that pretty?" Violet says from the doorway, startling me. "Put it on, then. Let's see."

I unfasten my old cloak, dump it over the bench, and swing the new cloak over my shoulders. Violet helps settle it on my shoulders, tugging the folds into place. "That green sets off your eyes. And it's a good warm cloak for this weather."

"There's a brooch too," I say, spotting the feather-shaped bronze pin.

"Isn't that fitting," Violet says, grinning, and pins it on.

"Thorn has a lover!" Rowan shouts from the hallway.

I swing around, scrabbling to open the brooch. "I don't!"

Violet giggles. "She's turning redder than her hair, Rowan! Let her be."

The next moment, Ash joins Rowan, and they jostle each other into the room. "What's this? Who's the man?"

"It isn't anyone!"

"Well then, who sent it to you?" Violet asks practically.

"I don't know," I admit.

"There's something still left in that package," she observes. "Take a look."

Violet is right. At the bottom of the cloth wrapping lie a pair of leather gloves and a small square envelope.

"Mighty suspicious-looking," Ash says, peering over my shoulder.

"Can you read it?" Violet asks, eyeing the script narrowly. It's written in my own language. At my nod, she says, "Well then, see who it's from."

I open the envelope slowly, wishing I were alone, and pull out a square of paper. It says only, *Warm days, peaceful nights. K.*

"Not what you expected, then," Ash observes.

I look up at him.

"You went all still and serious," he elaborates, "so I'm guessing it isn't an admirer."

Rowan sighs. "And I was so hopeful."

"I don't think I should wear it," I say, putting down the envelope and making to take off the cloak.

"Don't, Thorn." Violet catches my hand. "You need that cloak. Whoever sent it to you knew your old cloak wasn't half as good as a threadbare horse blanket. And you could do with a pair of gloves to warm your hands. God knows we could all use gloves."

"I'm not sure if I should."

"Can you return them?" Ash asks.

Without insulting him? "No."

"Would you be in their debt if you used them?"

I hesitate, considering the angles. Are they a peace offering? A token of friendship? Perhaps, but not a debt. "No," I say again.

"Then use them," Ash says simply, and the others nod their agreement.

Violet bundles up my old cloak in the wrapping cloth and hands it to me. "Keep this for the spring when you'll want something light."

Valka finally sends a page for me one afternoon a week later. I follow him up to the palace, grateful for the warmth of my new cloak, the gloves that protect my hands from the biting cold. The page leaves me to wait in Valka's empty apartments.

Alone, I walk through the rooms, taking my time, observing the changes. The first sitting room has been rearranged to allow for larger parties, with fewer tables and more couches. In the second, there are new baubles on the side tables: priceless glass globes, little golden boxes, ornately painted vases.

I walk to the desk, stand a moment before it. Valka will be here shortly. If I am to face her with Falada's death, then I need all the power over her I can muster. That includes knowing just what my mother has written her—now, before she arrives. I take a deep breath and open the compartment.

Inside I find the letters I have already answered from my mother, with a new one topmost. I unfold it, perusing it quickly. It is dated nearly a month ago. Valka has had this letter a little while at least and has been putting off its answer. The letter itself runs long, containing strict admonishments for my foolish behavior in growing distant from Melkior and his ilk, recommendations on how to draw them back into my circle, a concise analysis of how my politicking may influence my future power, and suggestions on how to dress and act to keep Kestrin's interest alive. It ends with an injunction to send more news at once, and mentions the preparations being made for the queen and prince to attend the wedding in the spring.

Mother is growing anxious with Valka, anxious that the alliance this marriage is meant to secure will be undermined by the princess's politicking. I weigh the letter in my hand, then reach out to rifle through the remaining letters. There aren't any other new letters from my mother, are there?

But no, there are just the few I've already seen. Below them lies an artist's sketch of Valka, posed for her portrait. I examine it, but the girl drawn there with her pitiless gaze and a touch of arrogance to her smile looks no more familiar to me than the face of any other court noble. I hesitate, my fingers on the edge of the paper. The outer room lies silent, and I want to know what else she keeps here, this woman who pretends to be me.

Beneath the sketch lie two notes from Kestrin, hardly more than a line in length. I run my fingertips over his script, familiar as it is from the note he sent with my new cloak. These notes came attached to some gift, for they do little more than address the princess, suggest she might find pleasure in the contents of an unknown package, and end with his signature.

I had not thought how Kestrin would handle his relationship with Valka, whether he would woo her or dismiss her. These two notes tell a tale I had not envisioned: Kestrin as the courtly lover, sending his betrothed trinkets. Even when he knows her to be false.

A shiver runs through me, and I remember him in that first conversation after I arrived in Menaiya, when he sent for me to write a letter for him, and then again after he found the cloak. How changeable he seemed, how easily capable of sliding between friend and foe, his true thoughts almost indiscernible. He had been terrifying, and I see a hint of that same man in the notes before me, purporting care where he has none.

I shove his notes back under the artist's sketch with shaking fingers. Beneath them lie a few sheets of unused parchment. I lift these up, uncovering letters from home I have not seen before, letters from Daerilin. I pause, listening again, but there is still no sound of Valka. I open the first of these letters, and the next, and the third after that, skimming them quickly before returning them to the compartment. From Daerilin's words to his daughter, it is clear he believes her part of the court, enjoying her time in Menaiya. Each gives some news of her family and some token pieces of advice regarding her position, followed by a fatherly adieu. There is little of substance in them. He thinks his daughter well placed for marriage; that is the only news he wishes to hear from her.

Kestrin has read them as well, I am sure, just as he read that first letter I wrote for Valka. Anything that passes through these rooms no doubt passes by him. I wonder what he thought of Daerilin's letters, how far they helped him to unveil Valka's true identity. I smile thinly, thinking that my first statement to him—that my family expected my marriage and would not wish for my return home—might have been neatly corroborated by the letters. If only they were not in Valka's keeping. She should have burned them rather than kept them as her own.

I hear a step in the other room and drop into the nearest seat. Valka enters, sweeping in with her chin tilted up. It seems an uncomfortable way to walk.

"I see you have forgotten your court manners," she says.

"Perhaps." Did she expect me to curtsy?

"How are the stables treating you? Still shoveling dung?"

"An honest living often involves dealing with others' filth."

She arches an eyebrow. "Indeed." She walks over to her writing desk and fishes out the newest letter from my mother. "This came some days ago. You'll write the response now. My attendants will be here shortly and I want you gone by then."

"If that's all," I say, rising from the couch. Then I turn on my heel and start for the door.

"You're angry about the horse, aren't you?" she calls after me, her voice light and mocking.

I grit my teeth and turn to face her. "The horse?"

"The white. The master of horses said it couldn't be saddled. It was hardly fit for the dogs. I should have had it killed when we first arrived, considering how it went wild on the journey."

"It's a pity you didn't," I say coldly. "Then I might have excused you."

"Excused me? Since when do I answer to a servant for my actions?"

I shrug. "I might ask the same. But it doesn't matter, does it? The horse is dead, our agreement is finished, and I am going."

"You'll write these letters, or you'll be sorry," she snarls.

"You'll find a better reason for me to write them, or I'll disappear. There are other places I can work. What will you do then?"

She pales. "No one would take you."

"Oh, I disagree," I say easily, for all that I have no idea. "But that's hardly your greatest concern, is it? When my family comes for the wedding, do you think you'll be able to fool them? They'll want to know why you haven't written. They'll be watching very carefully because they'll know something is wrong—they already know you've been politicking like a fool. And not at all as I would. Only if you keep up the pretense now can you hope to slip past them then; they'll think your change due to living here, not something that has been done to you. Think hard on that, *princess*."

I watch the emotions slide through her eyes: anger, fear, hate. There will be no place for me in the stables and goose barn once she weds, that I know.

"What do you want?" Valka demands, haughty as ever.

"I wanted you to keep your word and leave me alone."

"You dared to throw yourself at my prince as if you were some maiden in distress, and he kept you *here*—and you charge me with breaking my word? What of you? Did you think I wouldn't find out? That horse was mine—I had every right to kill it. You're lucky I didn't have you whipped."

If only she had struck out at me directly, instead of murdering Falada. I press my hands flat against my skirts. "I was *ill*. It was Filadon who brought me here, not Prince Kestrin. And as soon as I was well enough to leave, I did."

Perhaps Valka knows that Kestrin called me in to speak with him—but then she ought to know that I could not have refused such an interview.

"You were to stay in your place!" she snarls.

Nothing I've said matters to her, that much is clear. I take a deep breath. "My place? What is that exactly, Valka? What am I?"

Valka glares at me, cheeks blotchy with anger. Looking at her, I can no longer deceive myself that she won't always put herself before anyone else. "You are nothing," she says, enunciating each word carefully.

"Then you will not need me."

I turn on my heel and stride through the outer sitting room. I hear the ink pot shatter against the wall as I close the door behind me.

I take a moment to gather myself, knowing Valka will not act against me quite yet. She still believes I have a price. She will bide her time. When she cannot put off an answer to my family any longer, she will call me in one last time. I will have to have a plan by then.

Outside, the wind whips through the courtyard. I wrap my cloak around me, grateful for its warmth, and start toward the gates. As I reach them, a riding party trots in. I step back against the stone wall, watching the front mounted guards swing past, followed by Kestrin and the king, and behind them the rest of the guard.

Kestrin catches sight of me at once. Even with his face shadowed by his cloak's hood, I see the gleam of his eyes as they fasten on me. He nods once in greeting. I shrug deeper into the cloak he gave me, dropping my head to stare at the cobblestones underfoot until his party rides past. I can only hope Kestrin did not watch me all the way through, that his father did not take notice. I set off once more, hurrying down West Road as if I might so easily leave him behind.

CHAPTER
24

A few nights later, I let myself into my room to find a small white envelope waiting on the threshold. Inside is a short message written in my language: an invitation to a private dinner being held in two days' time. It takes a moment for the signature to sink in: Verin Melkior.

I stare down at the bright envelope with its elegant script. Melkior may be the lord high marshal of the realm, but he showed little to no interest in me when we traveled together. This invitation can really only be from the prince.

I think of Kestrin, of his discreet greeting as he rode through the palace gates. The way he cradled my hand in his own after Falada's death. Something changed in that meeting, and now he doesn't intend to let me go. First the cloak, now this invitation. It couldn't be any more clear.

I take a breath, let it out slowly. Whatever Kestrin's motivations,

I don't want to see him again. And regardless, Valka will lash out at me anew if she learns of this. I am already balanced on the knife's edge with her, her hatred just barely outweighed by her need of me. If only I could speak with Falada—though I expect he would only ask me what I think I should do. The thought of him stabs at me. I miss little things, the way he used to nudge my shoulder with his nose—and bigger things, the constancy of his friendship. His death leaves an emptiness in my life I can't seem to fill.

I look back down at the invitation, as if I'll find my answers there. I run my finger over the dark ink, turn the envelope over, touch the broken wax seal. I've still two days to decide. Two days to find a way to refuse a lord his invitation.

Sleep is slow to come, and broken. When I wake, I open up Valka's trunks and look through her jewelry. Today will make it two weeks since I spoke with Red Hawk, though it might feel like a lifetime. Tarkit will be waiting for me. I am only helping a boy gain an apprenticeship he cannot otherwise achieve, I tell myself as I ready myself for the day. It doesn't mean that I approve of thieves, per se. Or of Red Hawk in particular. In truth, I don't know anymore what to think of him.

Once my morning duties are completed, I follow West Road up to the temple, trudging past the shops. As I turn into the now-familiar alley, I spot Tarkit. He huddles in the doorway, as sallow and scrawny as ever, dark hair hanging in rattails over his eyes. His two friends pocket whatever treasures they were looking at when I turned the corner.

The boy jumps to his feet. "Kelari!"

"Tarkit," I say, smiling.

"You didn't bring your horse!" cries the older of Tarkit's friends.

"No," I manage, grief clawing at my throat.

"That's all right," Tarkit says with a little shrug. "But did you really see me those times? Before?"

I press my grief down, away, so that I can speak past it again. "Yes, I did."

"Oh." He looks down glumly.

"But I had to look for you," I amend.

He brightens at this. "Really?"

I nod, the weight in my chest easing as I watch him.

"Well, my mother wants to meet you. Would you like to come visit?"

"Your *mother*?" This cannot possibly be another code name for Red Hawk.

"She can't walk much," Tarkit explains. "Or she would have come herself."

"I would be honored," I say, recovering myself.

"Come on, then," Tarkit chirps, and sets off at once.

I follow after him, his companions hurrying to keep pace with us. "Who are your friends?" I ask.

"I'm Torto!" the first boy pipes up. "I'm ten, and my baba's gonna apprentice me to a carpenter." He gives me a proud, gap-toothed grin. It takes me a moment to realize the gap will be with him the rest of his life; he is long past the age of losing a front tooth to make way for a new one.

"That's nothing," Tarkit says. "I'm gonna be a baker. I start next week!"

"Who is your master?" My question unleashes a flood of information, including the size of the shop, the number of apprentices, the new set of shoes he will be given, and how his first task will be to draw water for all the baking. When he pauses for breath, and perhaps to dredge up any additional details he has somehow left out, I turn to the third boy. "And what's your name?"

The boy, by far the youngest and the dirtiest of the three, shrugs and looks to Torto.

"That's my brother," Torto explains. "His name is Fen but he doesn't talk at all."

I nod knowingly. "He's shy."

"No, he stopped talking. He doesn't talk to anyone now, not even our mama."

"Why?"

"He got snatched," Tarkit whispers. "He managed to escape and get back home to us, but he didn't ever talk again after that."

Fen glances at Tarkit, then up at me, his small body tense.

"I'm sorry," I say without thinking.

Tarkit looks at me curiously. "It's not your fault."

Isn't it? As princess, wouldn't it be my responsibility to consider their safety—if not now, then within a few months of my marriage?

"Anyhow, he doesn't remember it," Tarkit says.

"What?" I ask, taken aback.

"Being snatched," Torto pipes up. "Whenever we get back one of the snatched, they have to be blessed. The snatchers put the Darkness on them, but the blessing makes it okay."

"What's the Darkness?"

The boys look at me in surprise.

"It's just the Darkness," Tarkit says. "Their minds go dark. But the blessing saves them from that."

"By taking their memories?"

"Just of the snatching, sometimes a little more than that. And who would want to remember that anyway?"

I frown, fighting a niggling sense of wrongness over a "blessing" that takes your memories whether you want to keep them or not. Clearly this is something the boys accept, though. Just as they must accept the reality of people being snatched off the street. I shiver, cross my arms to hold myself in.

The boys lead me into a wide cobbled square. A set of gallows has been erected here, and while they are empty, their solid, enduring presence brings a dark gloom to the square. A beggar sleeps curled up against the platform, shielded from the wind.

"What is this place?" I ask as we start across the square.

"Hanging Square," Tarkit says as indifferently as if we were passing through his kitchen.

Torto, noting my stare, expands on this. "It's where all the bad people are killed. Sometimes they chop off their heads instead of hanging them." He then proceeds to describe a particularly gruesome execution where a murderer made an ill-fated attempt to escape with his head attached, only to be mobbed and torn to pieces. I try not to listen, letting his story patter past me, and take the first opportunity to ask more about the boys' apprenticeships. So, between tales of carpentry and baking, we arrive at Tarkit's home.

Tarkit lives in a run-down yellow-brick building. While the streets are littered with refuse, inside, the stained halls have been swept clean. We descend to the basement and duck through a low, cloth-covered doorway into a dark room.

"Is that Kelari Thorn, Tarkit?" a woman asks, her voice gravelly.

"Yes, Mama. I brought her to see you like I said."

"Light us a candle and go play out front. Stay near, hear me? You'll walk her back."

"Yes, Mama." Tarkit lights a stubby candle that throws a wavering yellow light over a woman lying huddled in blankets on her sleeping mat, a stool beside her. He leaves the candle on the stool and departs, Torto and Fen right behind him.

"Good evening," I say, dipping my head to the woman.

"Come closer, kelari. I want to see your face."

I kneel beside the sleeping mat, meeting the woman's gaze. Her features, ravaged by illness and hard living, still show traces of youth. While her hair has a sprinkling of gray, her cheeks are yet smooth; while her brow is furrowed with wrinkles, her lips are still firm and pretty. I would guess her to be no more than ten years older than I.

"You're a lovely girl," she says, smiling. I almost shake my head, deny Valka's beauty as having anything to do with me, and just catch myself.

"Tarkit told me about you, and then we learned he'd been given an apprenticeship. People don't do that, you know, pay for a whole apprenticeship just like that. I asked Artemian and he wouldn't say at first who it was, but then he told me."

Artemian? Is that another name for Red Hawk, or just one of his men? Despite my curiosity, I bite down on the question, listening as the woman goes on.

"I wanted to thank you, kelari. You've given my Tarkit what I always wished for him. I gave up hope of getting him a place after his father died." She reaches out and grasps my hand, her own hard and knobby, her fingers stiff as claws. I wonder if her feet are equally disfigured, bent by illness and cold, leaving her bed-bound. "Thank you," she says.

"I didn't—" I hesitate, clear my throat, start over. "Tarkit's a good boy. He helped me. I'm glad I could help him back."

"No," she says. "You weren't paying a debt. You know that. I just wanted to see your face and thank you myself. That's all."

I nod, at a loss for words. She pats my hand and asks me what I do, and we talk for a few minutes about the geese and the stables. Then I say goodbye and walk back outside.

Tarkit greets me with a shout, and Torto and Fen race up alongside him. "We'll show you the city now, aye?"

I hesitate, but it isn't even midday yet. There's plenty of time before I must return. "All right."

"We'll start with the well," Torto says imperiously. "The others will be there."

The well lies only a short walk away, a small stone circle at the center of a square, a bucket lying beside it attached to an iron ring by rope. A group of children play around the well. As we near them, my escort breaks into a run, shouting names. They are swallowed immediately by the group, disappearing into a dizzying swarm of arms, legs, and heads.

"Who's that?" one voice cries. The little figures turn to look at me as one.

"Yeah, Tarkit, who's that came with you?"

"Oh, that's Thorn."

"Yeah?" says one of the boys. He stands about a head taller than Tarkit, his face long and his ears protruding like the two handles of a jug. "Where'd she come from?"

"She works down in the king's stables," Tarkit explains. "But she used to live in the mountains, and now she's the friend of a friend." The way he says that last phrase, I've the feeling it means something to the children that I don't yet know.

They look me over with bright eyes.

"There aren't any foreign women that work in the stables," says one of the girls.

"That's right," I agree. "I've only been staying in the stables. I'm actually a goose girl."

"Goose girl!" cries one of the boys. "Honk! Honk!" He is joined at once by the rest of the group, who honk and scronk in a most un-goose-like manner, milling around me and yanking at my cloak and skirts.

I stare down at them, momentarily speechless, then burst into laughter. "You'd better be grateful I don't mistake you for my geese. I've got a staff I keep just for them!"

I catch hold of the nearest girl and give her a good tickle. She shrieks and breaks free at the same time two boys jump on me, holding on tight as leeches. I stagger to the side, tickling one while I try to escape from the other. Just as I get free of him, two girls reach up to tickle me as well. With a cry, I go down in a mass of arms and legs, tickling as fiercely as I can amid shouts and howls of laughter.

"All right!" I cry as three more children throw themselves on top of me. "Mercy! Mercy!"

The children take a few more minutes to calm down, but as I offer no further resistance, they eventually allow me to sit up.

"She's all right," says the jug-eared boy.

"Yeah," Tarkit says as he picks himself up off the ground.

I look around at them, their thin faces and sharp elbows, their ragged clothing and unkempt hair. Their breath makes puffs of smoke before them so that I look through a mist at them, their features first focused and then hazy, ghostlike. "What's your name?" I say to the boy.

"I'm Lakmino," he says, raising his chin proudly.

I dip my head in solemn greeting. "And what are the rest of your names?"

They introduce themselves in what amounts to a shouting match, jumping up and down and shoving each other. While I manage to catch at least three names, within a moment I have lost which little person each name belongs to.

I push myself to my feet. "Since I'm new to the city, why don't you tell me what I should know about it?"

The children glance at each other, then to Lakmino.

"Well," he says importantly, "we know everything that happens here."

The other children nod in agreement.

"The first thing you should know," Lakmino continues, "is that there are good thieves and bad thieves, and the bad ones sometimes steal people."

I flinch, even though I should have been prepared for this between all I've heard, and now having met Fen.

"It's true," says one of the boys from the back. "They snatched my sister last year, and we didn't never find her."

"Yeah," Tarkit says. "And they snatch young women too. So you better be careful."

"Tell her about the guards," whispers a girl.

Lakmino takes the cue. "Don't go to the guards if you need help. They'll only laugh at you unless you have money. You can come find us, and we'll get you help. My brother's big and strong, and so are Gira and Moté's brothers."

The other children nod and mutter their agreement.

"Thank you," I say soberly. "I'll remember that."

"Come on, then," Tarkit shouts, and grasping my hand, he tugs me along. "We'll show you around!"

We spend the next hour or so together, the children taking me to all their favorite spots, vying with each other to be the first to explain. In addition to the well, I walk past the healer's home, look down from the roof where the children normally pelt people with snowballs, and see the back of the local butcher's shop where wormy meat can often be gotten for free.

The city streets feel different here from those I once walked with Falada. Here, people move slowly, as if walking were only marginally easier than standing still. Some carry sacks of coal or bundles of wood; others pass with the whiff of food; most merely wrap their clothes tightly about them. Many have upon them the look of hard work, their naturally brown faces sallow and thin, their eyes shadowed. Occasionally, a man or woman huddles at a corner, bundled in ragged blankets and cloaks and scarves. They hold out empty tin cups and shake them at me, but I have left my purse at the stables and have nothing to give but what I have brought for Tarkit.

The only place I see that speaks of plenty lies just past the boundary of the children's domain: they take me to the riverbank to stare across at a great temple built on a cobbled plaza below East Road. The building is magnificent, with carvings cascading up the marble facade and decorating the arched doorways. In between flows the sparkling expanse of river, a few wide-bottom boats filled with cargo just visible.

"That's Speakers' Hall," Lakmino says, his voice hushed with longing. "They have a free school, if you can pass the test for it. Anyone who studies there never goes hungry again."

The other children are still for once, and in their eyes I see the reflection of unspoken, unattainable dreams. Despite the beauty of the building across the river, I am glad when we turn back into the narrow alleys and the children begin to jostle and laugh again.

By the time we part ways with Tarkit's friends and head home, it is just past noon and time for me to return to the stables and my afternoon duties. Tarkit's face is pale with cold, his shoulders hunched. He walks quickly, his head darting back and forth.

"What are you looking for?" I ask, half teasing.

"You should always be careful," he says. "Torto's cousin got beat up by robbers last month in the middle of the day. It's okay when there's a bunch of us, but now there's only you and me. And the snatchers don't always care what time of day it is. Usually it's at night, but sometimes they just sneak up on you and—wham!— you're gone."

Red Hawk, among others, warned me of this, yet somehow I ascribed the danger to midnight streets, dark alleyways, not a brightly lit afternoon. I keep watch after that, scanning the alleys and doorways for men or groups of boys. I follow Tarkit as he crosses streets or turns down different alleys to avoid others, his route no longer seeming quite so erratic or whimsical.

"This isn't the way to the stables," I say, recognizing the streets from my walks with Falada.

"No," he agrees quietly. "I'm taking you to meet Artemian."

It's the same name his mother mentioned. "Who's that?"

He puts his finger to his lips to hush me.

I keep my peace and watch the streets carefully for landmarks. Finally, down a narrow back alley, we enter a brick building. A shadowy set of stairs delivers us to a landing with two doors, one of them boarded up. Tarkit knocks on the other, calling out his name.

I hear a step from the other side and the door swings open. "Come in."

Tarkit leads the way into the lamplit room. My old friend, the scar-faced man, closes the door behind us. "Wait by the door, boy. I'll speak with the lady in the next room."

I follow him, studying his long stride, his broad shoulders and wiry build. A swordsman, I think. There is more gray than black in his short-cropped hair and I realize with shock that he must easily be twice my age, perhaps three times that.

"Artemian," he says, closing the door behind us. I *had* guessed that.

"Thorn."

"Do you have the money for the boy's apprenticeship, veria?"

I slide my fingers under the sash at my waist and pull out the pouch I took from Valka's trunk, handing it to the man. He opens it and tips its contents into his palm: a delicate gold pendant adorned with pearls. Wordlessly, he drops the pendant into the pouch, closing his fingers around it. I watch him, wondering if I have misjudged it.

"You haven't much experience with valuing jewelry, have you?"

I flush. "Is it too little?"

"No, veria. This little trinket of yours will pay for ten boys, not one."

I let out my breath in relief. "Then use it for ten."

He pockets the pouch silently, his brow furrowed.

I lick my lips and say, "Thank you for helping me that day when I was ill."

Artemian shrugs. "Our friend asked that we keep an eye on you. I myself am grateful for the service you did him." His fingers flick to his pocket. "You've got this pendant here, enough to keep you for years, and yet you're willing to work at the stables for a pittance. Why? Why not use a portion for the boy, and keep the rest for yourself?"

"I don't need it," I say. "Not the way he does, or the other children I see on the street."

I am aware of the man's eyes on me, aware of my cracked and calloused hands, the sores at the corners of my mouth. But every day I have three meals, every night I have a place to sleep. *And it isn't mine to take.* I stare at the ground, wondering what I have become, if I have turned into a Red Hawk myself, stealing Valka's jewels. But she took mine in turn, all the jewelry I brought for my wedding. Would it be such a terrible thing if I put her own wealth to good use?

"I see." He rubs his arm with his hand, as if his muscles ache. "I want you to remember this place. If you need something more from our friend, come find me. If I'm not here, leave a lock of your hair and I'll find you."

"My hair?"

"It's an uncommon color. I'll know it's yours."

"Oh."

"Go in peace, veria." Artemian opens the door, waving me out to rejoin Tarkit.

Alone in my room later that night, I throw open Valka's traveling trunks and search out something to wear to Melkior's dinner.

CHAPTER
25

I perch on the small stool in my room, trying to sit straight as Sage pulls and tugs at my hair, forcing it to do her bidding. I have washed myself clean, scrubbed the grime from my hands, and donned an embroidered silk skirt and tunic I half like, unearthed from among Valka's trunks. I have even dabbed a bit of lilac water on to hide the scent of the stables that yet lingers.

"You're sure about this?" Sage asks.

No. Only, why is it that the children must rely on thieves, when the royal family might so easily improve their lot—when ten apprenticeships might be bought for the price of a single pendant? And why is it that the thieves are the Family's target, when it is the snatchers the people fear?

"I think I need to go. I just don't . . ." I pause, clear my throat. "I don't know what will happen if the princess hears of it. I suspect she'll lash out at me directly, something small but ugly. But

274

if she decides to hurt me through my friends—that's you and your family."

Sage's hands are steady, never faltering in their work. "We'll beware, then. I'm glad you told me."

I turn my head, trying to see her face.

"Hold still," she says, pulling my head straight by my hair. It is so much like how Jilna used to treat me I almost laugh. But my worry for my friends bleeds the laughter from me before it ever reaches my lips.

"You could lose your jobs," I say.

"It would be a loss," she agrees. "The boys and Violet can go back to their parents' farm, though, if they wish. And I've good enough references I can easily find another stable to work at. If this is something you need to do, we'll stand by you." She gives my head a pat and steps back. "There now."

I reach up a hand to check my hair. Sage has braided it up and around my head, a simple but elegant style, but I suddenly wish it didn't form a crown.

"All right?" Sage asks.

"Thank you," I say, smiling. "It feels perfect." And it does— balanced and smooth and snugly pinned.

"Off you go, then," Sage says.

Downstairs, the carriage driver hands me into a plush interior of velvet cushions and gilded metalwork. For all my efforts, I feel like nothing more than a servant playing at dress-up, riding in a carriage meant for greater people.

The carriage takes me from one world and delivers me through the palace gates to another. I sit in the darkness of the carriage looking out at the private courtyard we've come to a stop in, the marble pillars and mosaic-tiled walls. I feel as I did when I first arrived in Tarinon, Valka across from me and the tastes of uncertainty and fear mingling on my tongue.

I cannot remember much of Melkior. He is tall, with a wide smile and shrewd eyes. I search my memory for any other bits or images that might offer further insight, but come up empty-handed.

The footman standing at the door clears his throat. I rouse myself with a faint smile—it seems I will always be slow to step out. The footman helps me down, and I cross to the main door. A young man in courtly clothes opens it and ushers me through a small foyer richly adorned in mosaics. He does not introduce himself, nor speak, only bows me through the far door, remaining behind as I enter a plush sitting room.

Here I detect the hand of a woman; no doubt Melkior is married. It is surprising, then, that his wife did not address the card to me herself. The room is carefully laid out, with low gold-and-maroon couches lining the walls, interspersed with small gilt tables of various shapes and sizes that are set with silver trays filled with delicacies.

Kestrin lounges on one of the couches. He is dressed elegantly in a dark green tunic and cream sash. Both are lightly embroidered, with a touch of cream at the cuffs of his tunic, and green chasing its way along his sash. He wears calf-length boots, and I can just make out cream pants tucked into them.

I curtsy as he looks up at me. Him I expected to find; what is strange is Melkior's absence.

Kestrin rises at once, offering me a courtly bow. "Veriana, may I welcome you? Our hosts will join us shortly."

"I thank you, zayyid. I hope I have not inconvenienced his lordship."

Kestrin spreads his hands, smiling. "Verin Melkior did not expect you quite so soon. We are notorious for starting our functions long after the appointed time."

"I see," I say sweetly. He planned this little tête-à-tête; I'm not about to take the blame for it. "It is not my habit to keep a carriage waiting. I suppose in the future I should, that I not abuse my hosts' hospitality."

I startle a genuine laugh from him. He gestures to the sofas, still grinning. "Won't you join me?"

"Who will make our party tonight?" I ask as I seat myself. "Will your lady be in attendance?"

He moves to a side table bearing a variety of drinks and a tray of goblets. "The princess and her closest friends have traveled a few days' journey south for the purpose of an outing."

"I am not much of a replacement, zayyid, though I may speak the same language."

"Oh, I wouldn't worry about that," he says, setting down a goblet of juice on the table beside me before he seats himself. "As for the rest of the party, Verin Melkior and Veria Dinari are our hosts, though their two daughters and son are dining elsewhere tonight. My cousin, Verin Garrin, will also attend. He is usually as prompt as yourself."

I vaguely remember being told about him—the only other member of the royal family. It had not occurred to me until now to wonder what became of his parents. "I do not believe I have met him before."

"He was in his lands to the west when you arrived. He has come to the palace for the winter, but there have been few opportunities for an introduction."

"No," I agree, striving for a light tone. "I tend to avoid the court unless I have an errand, and apparently he has a similar contempt for goose barns."

"Though your errands have proved most intriguing," Kestrin observes.

"My errands or my property, zayyid?"

"Both, I must admit. You've given me mysteries enough to occupy my idle hours these past few months."

Oh, indeed. "Is that why I have been invited here, that you may allay your boredom on a winter's evening?"

"I thought it might not be a bad thing for you to have allies among the court," Kestrin says, voice softening.

Allies? When these people all believe me the cast-off companion to a scheming little princess? "I doubt I could command any true friendships here, considering my position."

"I think you underrate yourself, veriana."

"Am I a lady again, then?" I ask. If he thinks me foolish enough to forget the danger the court poses to a serving girl, I have no qualms with reminding him of what he himself has called me before. "Pray when was I restored to such a title from that of 'thorn'?"

He laughs a court laugh, but his features grow still, his expression bland. I have turned his mood. "You have by your own admission always been a thorn."

"No, zayyid, not always. Just upon my arrival here. It is a distinction of a sort, you know, to be a bother to a prince."

"I believe you have likewise always been a lady of high distinction."

I bite my lip. I had forgotten the barbed sting of the language of the court, and now my mind stumbles over its dusty store of half-meant responses and finds nothing fitting. "I did not think I was so very early," I finally say, abandoning the subject entirely.

"Our hosts should be in momentarily."

I smooth a fold from my skirt, look up. "Zayyid, why have you invited me here, truly?"

"Melkior—" the prince begins.

"—invited me here on your bidding," I finish for him.

Kestrin nods once. "He too may be a friend to you."

"He too?" I echo.

Kestrin's eyes flicker earth and gold in the lamplight.

"Have I another friend in the court?" I ask.

"Are you so surprised?"

I look away. I don't want to play this game with him. "I do not seek friends in the court," I say, my voice tight.

Kestrin hesitates, eyes fastened on me. It's only when I turn my head to return his gaze that he answers. "I owe you an apology for how I have treated you. I misunderstood the situation, and believed you were not to be trusted. I was wrong, and I am sorry for it." He pauses and then says, "I trust you."

I flinch, though he has made no move toward me. "You shouldn't," I tell him abruptly.

"Why?"

Because I have already betrayed you once. I shake my head, for even the thought of the words brings the familiar pressure to my throat.

"Why?" he says again, his voice gentle.

"It is unwise to put your trust in someone with a reputation for dishonesty," I say. But my argument is flawed, and he knows it as well as I. My true reputation is the opposite of Valka's.

"Would you betray me?"

"I hold no allegiance to you," I say stiffly. Surely he understands the Lady will use me against him? That she already has?

"Would you betray me?" he repeats, his voice even and measured.

"I am—easily manipulated."

"Then I will not trust your enemies or mine."

Readily said, but his enemy is far too cunning to dismiss so lightly.

Before I can formulate a response, the prince shifts in his seat and tilts his chin slightly as he listens. A faint step sounds from the hallway. "I expect the evening shall begin shortly," he says. The court has returned once more to his voice. "I hope you will enjoy it."

I incline my head and clasp my hands lightly in my lap.

A young man enters, dressed much like Kestrin, but where the prince tends toward darker clothes, his cousin prefers the light. His tunic shines a sky blue edged with silver and tan embroidery. The cousins share the same sculpted features and shrewd eyes, though Garrin has an easy smile and a casual bow that are more lighthearted than anything I have seen of Kestrin. Though perhaps that is not a fair comparison.

I rise to curtsy.

"Garrin," Kestrin says quietly from his seat, "allow me to introduce Veria Thoreena. Veria, my cousin, Verin Garrin of Cenatil."

"I am honored to make your acquaintance, veriana," Garrin says, dipping his head. He is just as practiced at hiding his emotion as his uncle, the king, though his demeanor is more pleasing.

"The honor is mine, verayn." I nod, aware of Kestrin's gaze, that I have never called *him* "my lord." But that would mean something, and with Garrin, it's just a courtly phrase.

I sit down again, settling my skirts around me while Garrin finds a seat. Just as he leans back and looks toward me, Lord and Lady Melkior make their entrance, inciting another round of bowing and scraping.

Dinari immediately draws me into conversation. She is exquisite in appearance, her form petite, her fingers delicate, her hair smooth and lustrous. Dangling earrings accentuate the line of her neck, and gems hung on gold threads sparkle over her hair. It is difficult to tell whether she is meant to adorn the jewels, or the jewels to adorn her. I think she must be twice my age at least; her face, while showing maturity in the fine touch of wrinkles by her eyes, yet displays the youth of her manners. Her voice when she speaks is light and feathery, her manners impeccable, and yet I do not trust her as I suspect Kestrin wishes I would. When I meet her gaze as we discourse on the weather, I find it to be half veiled, her emotions no easier to read than the king's.

We proceed to a magnificent dining room where we are served course upon course of curried meats, creamy soups, and spiced vegetables. There are only two men to wait upon us, and neither are dressed as servants—from their fine clothes in differing colors to the way they both seem attuned to the prince, I suspect they may actually be his own attendants. I recognize one of them as the man who showed me in to the prince.

Partway through the second course, Dinari draws Kestrin into an animated conversation with Melkior, leaving me with little to do but listen.

Garrin, seated beside me, takes advantage of their distraction. Smiling, he leans toward me and speaks in an undertone. "I understand you had a falling-out with the princess on your journey here."

I blink at him in surprise. Has Kestrin told him nothing? Or is this cousin of the prince merely testing me? "We have had more than a few disagreements," I say with an attempt at gentle amusement. "Is there one in particular you wish to inquire about?"

His eyes flash. He is unaccustomed to being taken so lightly, or made to look impolite. "Oh no," he says, as if I have misread him completely. "I only wondered that you have not attempted to set things to rights. Surely your actions could not be so reprehensible as to be unforgivable. Have you not begged pardon of the princess?"

Begged pardon?

His eyes brighten with laughter as he watches me.

I force myself to unclench my jaw. "I am quite certain," I say softly, "that how I have chosen to handle our disagreements is no concern of yours. Though I must ask, since you seem so convinced of the princess's magnanimity, have *you* begged her pardon on some offense of your own?"

"Certainly not," he says with ill-concealed mirth. "You see that I am still a lord in my own right."

"Garrin, my dear boy," Dinari says, turning toward us and

saving me from any further response. "Whatever are you talking about?"

I wait, watching to see if he will admit our conversation to the now-attentive Kestrin.

"We were merely reflecting on the nature of forgiveness," Garrin says genially. "And how to ask for it."

"Ah," Dinari says, and a moment later turns the conversation to the new improvements being considered for Speakers' Hall.

Thankfully, Garrin does not single me out again. After dinner, we withdraw to an evening room. Dinari seems well versed in how to maintain a flow of conversation, even in such a small party as ours. It is just as well—left to myself, I would run out of topics long before the evening finished. Eventually, the men rise and Kestrin and Garrin make their adieus. I curtsy, and once Melkior has seen them out, he returns to escort me to my carriage.

As we leave the evening room, I realize that I have an unexpected opportunity in his escort. Slowing my pace, I turn to him. "Do you spend the rest of the winter at court, verayn?"

"There is much to keep us busy this winter. We will stay on till spring."

"I understand that there has been some trouble in the city," I say, hoping to draw him out.

"The thieves are a plague this year," he replies darkly.

"I mean specifically those thieves who snatch people as well."

Melkior glances at me from the corner of his eye. "Oh, I do not think that happens very much. The threat of slavers is greatly blown out of proportion. It is the thieving rings we are concerned with—the Black Scholar, Red Hawk, and their ilk. It is my work to track them down."

I have to bite my tongue to keep from arguing about the snatchers. I am unlikely to convince Melkior to act upon the snatchers in the few moments of our walk to the carriage, not when the noble families clearly care more for their purses than the poor of their city. I can at least learn more of Red Hawk. "What then?" I ask. "What is the punishment for thievery?"

"For simple thievery—very little. A flogging and a day in the stocks will do. But for such men as these, the king has decreed the punishment as death."

"Death, verayn?"

"A lady might not understand the gravity of the offense," Melkior says, all condescension. The door to the foyer has been closed, and he reaches to open it.

"Is it so grave a thing to steal when given no other choice?" I ask quickly.

"It is not simple thievery that we discuss, but organized rings. They make their own laws and demand their own allegiances, flouting the king's authority. Judge for yourself, veriana." Melkior opens the door, standing back to allow me through.

"Your arguments are strong," I agree reluctantly; as a threat to order and society, the rings of thieves might appear dangerous. I do not yet know enough to argue the point, only that Red Hawk takes care of his own, and is inarguably a thief.

I step through the doorway to find Kestrin waiting for me.

"Peace, veriana," Melkior says from behind me, and shuts the door.

"Zayyid," I say to Kestrin, taken aback, "I did not expect to see you again tonight."

"I am glad I can occasionally surpass your expectations," he says, grinning, and offers me his arm. "I wish only to learn how you enjoyed your evening."

"It has been most interesting," I hedge. We enter the courtyard where the carriage waits.

"I thought as much. How did you like my cousin?"

I cast about for something nice to say. "He is very different from yourself, zayyid."

Kestrin hands me up into the waiting carriage, then pauses, retaining my hand in his. I take my seat, my outstretched hand still caught in his, and wait.

He smiles crookedly. "You have a way of not answering questions that I am coming to enjoy."

I feel myself flush, but it is not all embarrassment. "I thank you," I mutter.

"I hope you will join us again."

"I would not intrude more than I have already."

"It is no intrusion, veriana, but a pleasure."

I meet his gaze. "While you may find me an interesting topic to fill your idle hours, zayyid, I pray you will pity a poor goose girl and let her be."

My words sink into the quiet. A horse shifts, its hooves scraping the cobblestones. Kestrin stands still, my hand caught in his, his eyes darkening with an emotion I cannot name. It is neither anger nor sorrow.

Finally, he says, "There will be another dinner in three weeks' time. Will you not come?"

"Zayyid." I look away, knowing how it must go. I am, after all, a servant. "I can only obey."

He releases my hand as if I had burned him. "No. I would not rob you of your choice. But if you change your mind, I hope you will tell me."

Is he truly letting me go? I dip my head uncertainly. "Zayyid."

"I thank you for this evening, veriana." He swings the door shut and calls up to the driver.

I fall back against the cushions and close my eyes, but the whole drive to the stables I see the prince as he stood in the court-yard, telling me of the next invitation, listening to my response, face drawn and woodland eyes shadowed. The expression lingering about his mouth and lurking behind his eyes haunts me, but I still cannot put a name to it. It is only once I have returned home, changed my clothes, and curled up under the covers on my sleeping mat that the right word comes to me: despair.

CHAPTER
26

"You're still not sleeping well, are you?" Violet asks, intercepting me as I deliver my morning apple to Moonflower.

I shake my head, watching the black nab the apple with her teeth. She lifts it from the stall door and turns away to enjoy it. Not only does she appear much recovered from her illness, but she doesn't snort at me anymore. "I'm trying not to stomp around as much now," I tell Violet.

"Why don't you share our room?"

"What?" I say, not sure I heard her right.

Violet shrugs. "You might sleep easier with other folk around you."

"I might." I have never shared a room before, other than my nights in Falada's stall. There was a comfort in that, which I miss dearly.

"I can't imagine sleeping alone," Violet goes on. "I'm so used to the sound of other people, I think it would be too quiet. Sage says I laugh in my sleep, but I'll tell you what I know for sure: Sage snores." With a wink, Violet skips down the hall, her laughter drowning out Sage's protestations of innocence from the next stall over. I can't help chuckling at them both.

Moonflower pokes her head out again and eyes me thoughtfully. I am beginning to think we are almost becoming friends. Her prickly personality joined with her obvious delight with the treats I bring her never fail to make me smile.

"No more apples," I tell her now, showing her my empty hands.

She huffs.

Grinning, I continue on to the goose barn. All morning, as I shovel and rake and haul water, I mull over Violet's offer, wondering what it would be like to sleep in the same room as someone else. It must, I think, take a deep trust, an unshakable certainty in the goodness of others.

In the afternoon, Joa stops by to check on my work as I muck out a stall.

"I've a mare that's getting old and needs to be exercised every day to keep her in shape while her owner's away," he says, leaning in at the stall door. "Do you think you could help me with her?"

I let my pitchfork rest against the floor. "If you show me what to do."

"Of course. Come find me when you're done, and we'll take her out together."

The mare is a docile chestnut who would much rather spend the afternoon in her stall than tacked up with a rider atop her. It's only after much prodding that she finally heaves a weary sigh and pushes herself into a trot. I can't help loving her.

"You'll need to take her out every day for the next few weeks," Joa says as I lead her back to her stall.

"That's fine," I say, stroking her neck.

He laughs as he takes his leave. "We'll make a hostler out of you yet."

I watch the chestnut cross her stall to her grain bin, tail swishing. What a wonderful life that would be, here among my friends and the horses, never having to deal with Corbé again. I lean against the rough wood of the stall door. If only there were not Valka to consider, or the Lady, or the despair in Kestrin's eyes.

That evening, Violet walks into my room, rolls up my sleeping mat without a word, and carries it to the room she shares with Sage.

"Good," Sage says as Violet deposits it on the floor. "It'll be nice having you here."

"But—"

"Not a word from you," Violet says, shaking a finger at me.

I laugh and help her straighten the blanket.

"You'll sleep well," she promises. "You'll see."

She is wrong. I listen to my friends' even breathing, their faint shifts and—from Violet—the occasional endearing dream-induced giggle, and a strange peace steals over me. I lie wide awake, facing them, and think of their lives, of Tarkit and his mother, of all the people I have seen in the city. While sleep does not come until deep in the night, in the morning I am not quite as exhausted as I have been.

My days begin to fall into a new rhythm, strange and different because at each turn, Falada is gone, but slowly his absence becomes normal. It is a normality that grieves me at unexpected moments, but there is no fighting it. In the mornings, Corbé and I clean out the goose barn. Afterward, I walk out to the plains, pausing within the city gates to look up at Falada's head. Sometimes, I tell him about my morning, but mostly I stand in silence, staring up at a string of prayer flags that has fallen down to drape over his neck in a parody of a spring garland. His head remains always still and unspeaking. I wonder if I imagined his voice that first visit.

On the days when I prefer noise to quiet, I wander the bigger streets of the city, staff in hand. As Tarkit taught me, I steer clear of entering quiet streets or walking near groups of men, wary really of anything that might put me at risk of being attacked or snatched. But I cannot help my interest in the city itself, in its inhabitants: the men and women and children, each with their own stories. So many lives, so much need and hope and laughter mixed in together. Only near the palace, where the wealthy merchants and the best artisans and guild workers live, do I catch the scent of affluence in the air. Regardless of how far I wander, by late afternoon, I return to muck out my assigned stalls and exercise the old chestnut mare.

But as I work, or wander the streets, or sit with my friends in the common room, words echo in my ears, memories teasing the corners of my vision as if they are the future. I see the prince standing alone in Melkior's courtyard. I see him in his rooms, offering what protection he can, feel his touch on my palm. Or, much worse, I remember him facing the Lady, fear in his eyes. I keep the note that came with my cloak in my pocket, and in quiet moments, I slip my hand in to touch it and wonder if he will ever be able to truly escape the Lady. Everywhere I go, I carry him with me in the warmth of my cloak and the comfort of my gloves.

And each night I lie awake, listening to Sage and Violet, filling myself with the warmth of their nearness, their regard, before drifting off to sleep.

One afternoon, as I pick out the hooves of the chestnut, a soldier comes to a stop beside me. I look up, the memory of the quad that came for Falada twisting through me, but it is only Matsin en Korto. I glance at him askance. The dinner Kestrin spoke of when we parted is still a week away; even if he hasn't accepted the refusal I gave at the time, there should be no reason for him to send Matsin to me now. Unless he has changed tactics.

"Come to the palace tonight as you are dressed," Matsin says. "I will meet you at the gates at sundown."

Will he? What does Kestrin want, then? And why specify that I not dress up? But Matsin does not wait for a response, turning and walking on. Kestrin is not risking my refusal, this invitation a command rather than a question.

I watch Matsin depart in silence. For the first time, it occurs to me that he is Kestrin's man, first and foremost, his loyalty complete. Kestrin sent him to Adania for me, to keep me safe until I could be delivered to the palace. It is precisely the opposite of what I feared then—an effort by Kestrin to assure my safety to the best of his abilities while I suspected him and his father of considering me dispensable. However grim Kestrin's future might be with the Lady hunting him, I no longer believe he intended to give me up to save himself.

At the temple, I sit against the wall, wrapped loosely in my cloak. The weather has begun to warm up. Melting snow trickles off roofs, runs in rivulets down the roads, and churns the alleys to mud beneath the daily onslaught of wagon wheels, horses' hooves, and people's boots.

If the weather holds, within a week Corbé and I will take the geese out to pasture again. The thought makes my stomach clench, for Falada will not be there to protect me. But I will keep my staff with me, and a sharp eye on Corbé, and I will not let him catch me again. And Ash and Oak's promise will protect me as well.

I shift, listening for voices from the street. I have not seen Tarkit since the day I spent with him. I wonder if he has started his apprenticeship, and how his mother fares. I pick at the dirt beneath my fingernails, and my thoughts turn back to Kestrin's summons. Does he intend for me to dress up when I arrive there? Or does he only wish for a private audience with me? I turn Matsin's words over in my mind, trying to ferret out what Kestrin has planned.

I am still worrying at it as I make my way back to the stables.

"Thorn! Thorn!" a voice cries. I startle, twisting to spot Torto running up to me. A handful of children trail after him. "Lakmino says that you aren't really from the mountains. Is it true?"

"In a way. I lived over the mountains in—"

"Then you *are* the new princess's serving girl!" Torto crows, the gap in his teeth peeking at me.

"No," I say sharply. "I was never her servant."

The children stare at me.

"I only traveled with her," I clarify, trying to soften my tone.

"You speak Menay really well," says one of the other children. "The princess is terrible. I know because my aunt works in the palace and she heard her."

"Well, there's no one to translate for me in the stables, is there? I had to learn Menay."

"No," Torto agrees. "But if you aren't her servant, what are you?"

"I told you that on the first day," I say, trying not to sound so vexed. "I'm the goose girl. I serve the king, just like the rest of you."

"But shouldn't you serve the princess first?" asks Gira, one of the girls. "After all, he's our king, not yours."

"He gave me a job and a place to stay when I didn't have either. I think I'll stick with him."

Torto nods. "I'd do that too."

"Did you used to live at court?" pipes up one of the other children.

"Yes."

"What's it like?"

"Yeah, what'd you eat there?"

"Did you have a lot of dresses?" Gira asks, wide-eyed.

"Did you have a horse?" Torto asks.

"One question at a time," I say, laughing. "Walk with me and I'll answer what I can before we get to the stables."

"Did you have a horse?" Torto asks again, grabbing my hand and pulling me past the other children.

"I did." Though I dare not attempt to speak his name for fear of the choker still wrapped tight around my neck. Still, I can easily describe what Acorn looked like, and how often I rode him, and where I went, and also—upon request—what I wore while riding him, which leads directly to the question of how many dresses I had.

I leave the children at the edge of the road, promising to tell them more another day, and make my way up to my old room to rummage through Valka's trunks. Whatever Kestrin's orders, appearing before him with mud on my hem and stains spread across my skirts is out of the question. Unfortunately, most of my simpler outfits are work-stained by now, having stood in whenever the outfit Violet gave me required washing. And I don't dare go so far as to wear formal clothes; there is cleaning myself up and then there is disregarding the prince's orders directly. In the end, it is just a question of choosing the least-creased of my traveling outfits, brushing the straw out of my hair, and scrubbing my hands and face with water.

As promised, Matsin meets me at the palace gates. He leads me in a side entrance, past inner courtyards I do not recognize, then through a maze of wood-paneled hallways. Finally, he opens a small door set into a corner of a hallway. We enter an unused storage room, at the back of which stands a second door. Matsin ushers me through this door into a narrow corridor lit only by a lamp hanging from the wall. He holds a finger up to his lips, then lifts down the lamp. His eyes are dark in the lamplight, his features still, uncompromising. We pass four doors before we reach one that Matsin opens. Again, he touches his finger to his lips before gesturing for me to enter.

The room contains only a small table and chair with a meal laid out, and a spare chair facing the opposite wall. Light falls through the top half of the wall, creating an eerie twilight. I cross the room to the wall, looking down through the back of an elaborate wooden carving into a formal dining room illuminated by luminae stones. The table below is set for dinner. A single servant makes a last adjustment to a place setting and departs, his footsteps echoing up to me.

My room acts almost as a balcony, the carving providing spaces just wide enough to view the dining room clearly. I hear a faint snick and turn to find Matsin gone, the door closed. I wait, my eyes adjusting to the half-light left in the absence of his lamp. When I no longer hear Matsin's boots, I walk back to the door and gently try the handle. The door does not give.

I may as well enjoy the meal that has been provided for me, I decide, and step over to the table laden with platters. A carpet rolled out beneath the table mutes the scrape of my chair, just as a tablecloth silences the dishes. The first platter I uncover holds a trio of meat pies. I stare at them a long moment before I remove the remaining covers and sit down to eat.

It does not take me long to finish, anxiety having stolen my appetite. I push myself up and go to sit in the chair overlooking the still-silent dining room. My room is clearly meant for secretly observing the diners below; I can only assume Kestrin wishes me to watch what plays out over dinner. Whatever happens, I can only hope he will not force my return to the palace tonight. I clasp my hands in my lap and wait, wishing I could trust Kestrin's intentions, wishing I could have dared to ignore his orders.

Within a few minutes, I hear the faint sounds of people approaching.

Through a set of double doors, Kestrin leads Valka in on his arm, escorting her to the top of the table. Behind them follows a set of young couples, lords and ladies, walking sedately to their own places in a carefully orchestrated play of hierarchy. At least one of the women I have met before: she is one of Valka's attendants, who let me into her bedchamber after she had gone in to sleep. I doubt if they ever admitted the deed.

As the servants enter with the first course, the conversation starts up, Valka commanding the table's attention. Her grasp of Menay is limited, but a translator stands behind her chair, his clear, carrying voice cutting through the room as easily as Valka's more strident, authoritative tones. I cannot imagine this voice having been mine. It is as foreign to me as the Menaiyan language once was.

I listen with growing trepidation as Valka gives a snide critique of her afternoon spent with a lady not present, the other ladies tittering in response. Kestrin adds little to the conversation. Seated with his back to me as he is, I cannot even read his expression.

Valka moves on to a discussion of the plans for a ball the following week, and oh! What plans for the wedding! All present agree it will be a truly festive event, the palace swept up in banquet after banquet, ball after ball, and not quite two months left to finish planning it.

I stare blindly down at the room. Surely it is not as soon as that? But a quick calculation tells me what I have so happily forgotten: there are only seven weeks left till the royal wedding. Seven weeks until Valka will do what she needs to get rid of me, and not many more after that before she will betray Kestrin to the Lady. How can there be so very little time left?

"And even the street children shall have something!"

I blink, focus again on the diners below, Valka's voice still ringing in my ears as the translator repeats her meaning.

"You are so greathearted, zayyida," one of the ladies coos.

"With such a joyous event, even the common people should have the chance to join in the festivities," Valka affirms.

"What is it you intend to give the street children?" the man seated beside Valka asks. With a jolt I recognize Kestrin's cousin, Garrin.

"Oh, some treats for them—what is it we've said, verayn?"

"Apple cakes," Kestrin says. I cannot quite place his tone.

"How perfectly wonderful," cries another lady. "They'll love you for the rest of your life!"

"It's the least we can do," Valka demurs.

I stare at her. They are both right, of course. I have already seen Tarkit's and Torto's excitement over food, and can only imagine their ecstasy at having such a precious, unexpected treat as an apple cake. They would remember it well. And, considering the opulence of what must be a normal dinner here before me, apple cakes are indeed the very smallest thing that might be given. They would hardly make a dent in the royal treasury, providing only a temporary relief to the pinched, perpetually hungry faces of the street children, and yet would guarantee their love.

I stand, my boots scraping soundlessly on the carpet as I go to the door, even though I know I cannot leave. The handle turns in my hand, but the door remains locked. I lean against it, feeling a knot growing in my chest. I want to get out, get away, stop my ears from hearing any more. My own words echo back to me, spoken earlier today: *He gave me a job and a place to stay when I didn't have either. I think I'll stick with him.* And Torto's words: *I'd do that too.*

I slide down until I am crouched on the floor, my cheek and shoulder pressed against the smooth wood of the door. I think of Falada's words in one of our first conversations, his surmise that I had been chosen to marry the prince because they could trust me, because I would grant them my unswerving loyalty in return for their kindness. Truly I would have been speechless with gratitude to find protection, a shelter at long last, however easy it might have been for the royal family to grant it.

And for what a small price might the loyalties of the poor also be commanded—the price, I think, of providing just enough? I do not know where the tears come from, why they burn my cheeks or why my sobs seem stuck in my throat. I pull up my cloak, bunch it in front of my face to muffle the sound, and weep.

CHAPTER
27

The sounds of the servants clearing off below have nearly died away by the time I hear the faint tap of boots in the outer hallway. The lock clicks and Matsin pushes open the door, his face half lit by the lamp he carries. I rise from my chair and follow him back down the secret hall. I have scrubbed my face with water from the pitcher, and smoothed my cloak, and can now only hope all evidence of my tears has been erased.

When we reach the outer hallway I stop and turn to Matsin. If he is so much Kestrin's man, then surely he knows more than he allows himself to show me. "Why did the prince ask you to bring me here?" I ask.

He pauses, his gaze on the corridor ahead, and then he turns his head slowly to study me. "He asked me once what Veria Valka was like, if she could ever make a goose girl. I told him it would take a lady who dances through the kitchen with the scullery maids and hugs her hostler in farewell to accept such a fall with dignity and grace. Veria Valka was not such a woman."

"You—" I begin to say, and cut myself off before the chain around my neck tightens. I should not be shocked. Hadn't the Menaiyan quads attached to me had a fortnight to observe my character before we ever started traveling? Of course they would have seen a difference. I only assumed that they would not consider what it meant.

"Yes," Matsin says, his voice quiet. "So I beg you to speak with our prince, and meet with him."

"I come as he bids me."

Matsin's lips form a grim line. "I wish it were more than that."

I shrug, glancing down the hall as if to move us along. "Perhaps it is best this way."

Matsin begins to walk again, taking my hint. As we reach our destination, yet another carved door in a hall that looks only vaguely familiar, he says, "I do not believe that, veriana. I hope you do not truly either."

Kestrin rises from his seat as I enter, a fire crackling cheerfully in the grate. It is the same small sitting room where I wrote a letter to my mother, dictated by the prince. Just the sight of the room, the two armchairs where we sat, brings back the knife-sharp fear of that interview.

I drop into a curtsy, face downturned.

Kestrin bows to me as the door clicks shut behind Matsin. "Veriana."

"Zayyid," I say, straightening.

"I hope you have enjoyed your evening."

Enjoyed it? I lift my gaze to his, let my anger burn through my fear. "Tell me, zayyid, what do you hope to gain from this little game of yours?"

His eyes narrow slightly. "I wish you to know my betrothed as I do."

"I already know the princess, and you know that I do." I can feel the faint pressure of the choker against my throat. Whatever happens, I do not want to draw the Lady's attention to this conversation. Though perhaps she is already listening. There is no way to know, but I neither want to choke before Kestrin nor bring down the Lady's wrath tonight. I must tread carefully.

"Perhaps I sought to remind you," Kestrin says, as if I could forget what Valka is.

"To what end?"

He shrugs, opening his palms toward me. "Veria," he says, then stops. "Veria, what can I offer you?"

I look directly into his forest-shadow eyes. "Apple cakes."

He stares. I turn and move to the door.

"Veria, wait," he calls after me, rising.

"Good evening, zayyid."

"*Wait*." His voice reverberates with authority. I turn back to him, shoulders bowed, aware that I am a servant again, that I must obey his orders, that whatever power I might have I have only because he has granted it to me. I wish that I could hate him for it.

His features stiffen and he looks away. "Do what you will."

I hesitate, watching the fall of shadows on his face.

"Get out, then," he snarls, starting toward me. "Flee back to your geese and forget I called you here."

I watch as he advances on me, the way his eyes seem almost

black now—but it's not anger I see there. It's something else tearing at him, dark and ugly. But for once, I do not fear it. I do not think it will turn on me.

He stops a bare hand span before me. "That's what you want, isn't it? To get away from the court? Then run away, Thorn. I won't stop you anymore."

"If I truly wanted that, I should have left Tarinon by now."

He takes a heavy breath and lets it out slowly. "You told me once that you could not find a way to leave, nor a place to go."

"I have found a way since," I tell him, thinking of Red Hawk.

Kestrin waits, the line of his shoulders tense, as if he fears what I might say.

I smile tiredly. "I still do not have a place to go. I suppose it could be arranged, but you understand as well as I that I cannot leave quite yet."

"You are waiting."

"I must." How I wish I could forget all this! "Why don't you send her back?" I ask abruptly. "You know what she is. Why continue?" Why must it be about my decision to leave the court, and not his own to keep a viper by his side?

He looks down, then back up at me, his gaze strangely earnest. "If I send her away, will the woman who leaves this palace be the same one who reaches Adania?"

Perhaps not. Perhaps Valka would regain her body, and it would be me returned to a family that despises me. But that is something for me to manage, not Kestrin. "That concerns you more than preserving yourself from betrayal?" I ask, my voice echoing my doubt. I can feel the choker pressing against my throat, but it doesn't tighten. Not when I haven't made a specific reference to Valka.

His gaze wavers. "There is still a little time."

Seven weeks, to be exact. "And at the last moment, what then, zayyid?"

He shakes his head in frustration. "I don't know."

I blink at him, taken aback by how young his voice sounds.

He rubs a hand over his mouth. "What did you mean by 'apple cakes'?"

I shrug. "The princess intends to win the love of the common folk with apple cakes. You would offer me similar items of little worth to yourself in order to win my loyalty, wouldn't you?"

He regards me silently and I flush, realizing that I wear the cloak he gave me.

"It is your friendship I seek," he says.

"You do not seek it as a friend; you seek it as a prince seeks the loyalty of a subject. The trouble is this: I will not sell my loyalty or my friendship."

"I see." He steps back, his eyes holding mine. "Then how is your friendship to be won?"

"I can hardly explain it to you, zayyid. Suffice it to say that, while I might find experiences like tonight's highly educational, I neither respect nor admire anyone the more for it." I unclasp the cloak's brooch and slip the heavy fabric off my shoulders.

"You have now seen two very different dinners. Surely, in comparing them, you see how—company matters."

"I never doubted it. I appreciate the illustration, but it was hardly necessary."

"Then what is necessary, veria? What do you suggest I do?"

I wince. "I don't know, zayyid."

I walk to the armchair I sat in once before, aware of his gaze following me. I fold my cloak over its back, then lean against it, staring at my hands. "Suppose I returned to the court. What would that accomplish?"

"There would be the small matter of justice to be carried out," he says softly, as if afraid his voice might banish my words.

Justice. Against Valka, of course. But that isn't really what I want.

I shake my head. "I have seen enough here already to think little of my case for justice. There are other greater injustices that deserve your attention first. Is there no other reason?"

"You cannot be serious. We discuss treason—"

"Is that all?" I repeat sharply.

He crosses the distance to the armchairs and leans against the other one so that he can watch my face. "A traitor once is a traitor always, veria," he says.

"And a man warned is a man prepared."

"You have not considered the implications."

"I have. I believe you have greater concerns than the woman you are to marry—especially when you can still choose to break off your betrothal. Tell me, what would my return accomplish, beyond the justice you spoke of?"

"You could see to far more than apple cakes. You may address whatever injustices in this kingdom concern you." Kestrin's smile is that of a predator, of a hound scenting blood. How quickly he has understood me.

"An interesting proposition, zayyid, but I doubt such a future."

"Why?"

"Because I doubt the surety of your future, and that of your family." I shouldn't have spoken such a truth—I know it the moment the words leave my lips, but it's too late now. They hang between us, as brutal as anything my mother ever said to me.

He lowers his face, turning away, his features icing over.

"Forgive me," I say softly.

He shifts, his eyes coming to rest on me, his expression uncertain. He doesn't know what to make of me, of my apology. And I don't want it to take me in another direction, one where he holds the upper hand any more than he has always held it.

I clear my throat. "You are offering me apple cakes, zayyid. You would tempt me with an offer of justice for your people rather than striving for such ends yourself."

"Indeed. I perceive quite clearly why you prefer your work to the court."

"Then help me to understand why I should return. I see only lies, artifice, and . . . danger here."

"There is very little else to speak of." Kestrin leans against the armchair, resting his elbows on its back. A few strands of hair have slipped free of their tie, falling like a tracery of shadows over his brow. He looks weary, tired past bearing. The firelight casts a waning warmth on his features that makes me think of the last flush of life on the face of a dying man.

"Isn't there?" I ask, almost pleading.

"If you are not tempted by power, wealth, rank, or an offer of flawed protection, or by a personal concern for justice to be carried out for yourself"—he looks up and catches my gaze— "then what else is there?"

Surely there is more to life here—to *him*—than that? But if he cannot see his way to it, then certainly he cannot offer it to me. "That is not an answer I can give you, zayyid."

"No," he agrees, still watching me. "No, you can't." He steps back, smiles wryly. "I will never look at apple cakes the same again, veriana."

I arrange my face into a semblance of a smile. "See that you don't. And if you can think of a way to win loyalty without the use of apple cakes . . ."

"I do not think I know how. I have been too long at court."

"Perhaps you should come to work with the geese," I suggest lightly. "They may be temporarily won by treats, but their regard is as easily lost. It is a good lesson for us all."

"Perhaps I will visit you."

"I will look forward to watching their reception of you," I reply, knowing full well that is one sight I will never see. "It is late now, zayyid, and I must work at dawn. If I have your leave?" I walk toward the door.

"Your cloak, veria." Kestrin gestures to where it hangs over the chair back.

I shake my head. "It is not mine; I should not have accepted it in the first place."

He grimaces. "It is not an apple cake, if that is what you mean."

"Isn't it?"

"You were cold. I saw you once from afar while out riding; I could see the way the wind cut you. And I saw again how cold you were the day your horse died." He lifts the cloak from the chair and brings it to me. "Take this, veria. If you do not want it for yourself, then do what you will with it. Only do not return it to me."

I accept the cloak awkwardly. "As you wish."

"Hardly." He steps past me and opens the door. "Go in peace, veriana."

I dip my head and slip out in silence.

Matsin waits in the hall, his expression inscrutable. I follow him through the mazelike corridors toward the little courtyard and the carriage he tells me waits there. As we turn down another hallway, my eyes catch on the ornate mirror on the opposite wall. It is a gorgeous thing, long and shimmery, framed by silver and gold metalwork. My reflection shows pale, my dress a white shroud, my hair and eyes dark as the night—

I jerk to a stop, my eyes riveted on the mirror. My heartbeat thunders in my ears. But no, the face looking back at me now is the one I've come to accept: chapped lips, sun-touched skin, unruly red hair.

"Veria?"

I stare at the mirror, searching for the reflection I saw a moment ago. The Lady. But even if I do not see her now, I know she is watching me. How much of this is the game she wished to see unfold between Kestrin and me? Have I played right into her hands?

Matsin looks from me to the mirror. "Is something wrong, veria?"

I shake my head and start forward again on shaky legs. "It's nothing. Let us go on."

CHAPTER
28

The next morning dawns with a soft exhalation of warmth. The air outside brings heady whiffs of green with it, and around the corners of the goose barn, tiny purple flowers poke their heads above the earth. The geese honk eagerly, scrambling over each other in the rush to leave their winter prison, the ganders barely bothering to peck at me in their excitement.

I am amazed at how quickly my morning's work goes. Even with Corbé up in the pasture watching the geese instead of helping me, I am done within the hour. Without the geese underfoot, scronking and obstinately standing their ground, I suppose it should not have surprised me at all. Finished, I exercise the chestnut and then leave for the goose pasture.

At the gates, I pause beneath Falada's head, weathered and gray with damp. I mean only to whisper his name, as I have so many times before, but then I find myself coming to a stop. "I spoke to the prince," I say into the echoing quiet of the gates. It's an understatement, of course.

"The wedding is seven weeks away. He knows, Falada. He knows exactly what happened, but he hasn't called it off. He wants me to choose. And I don't . . . I don't want to marry him, to live at court, to spend the rest of my life fearing the Lady. I don't know what to do."

As faintly as a leaf dropping from a tree, I hear the word *princess*. But that is all.

The afternoon passes quietly, with far more time than I would like to reflect on my conversation with Kestrin, the knowledge that the Lady is still watching, and how Valka goes on playing at princess while Kestrin calls her traitor and speaks of bringing her to justice. I am grateful enough to rise and help drive the geese back to the barn.

A page waits for me beside the barn. He shifts from foot to foot, arms crossed and nose raised away from the stench of livestock. "Zayyida Alyrra wishes to see you this evening, kelari," he tells me as I shut the gate behind Corbé. "I'm to escort you up."

"Very well." I should have thought of a plan for handling Valka, for what I would say in this next interview that I knew would come, but I have no plan. I will not agree to write her a letter, can no longer support her in her ruse, but I do not know how to manage her beyond that. There is nothing to be done now but to think on it as I follow the page up to the palace, my staff beating a steady tap-tap as I walk.

Valka sits in a chair in her outer room, waiting for me, her attendants nowhere to be seen. She is dressed and groomed beautifully, her hair braided and coiled into a work of art, her jade tunic and gold skirts stiff with embroidery.

"A ball tonight?" I ask as the page departs, knowing full well that by virtue of our current ranks, she should be the first to speak.

Her nostrils flare, but then she smiles. "Jealous?"

"Hardly. What do you want?"

"One final letter from you."

"You know my answer."

"Every person has a price."

"Do you think you know mine?" I think for only a moment of Kestrin and of apple cakes.

"For all your apparent zeal for servitude, you must prefer a better position. I will grant you a place on one of my mountain estates. You will have a yearly stipend and may live the life of a lady. But you must write the letter tonight."

"My mother has written again, hasn't she? You're hoping to send a letter to catch her on the road here, to allay her concerns."

"She has written," Valka agrees, her expression shuttered. I do not trust the very stillness of regard. "The response must be written tonight."

"I do not believe your offer."

"You will have to trust me."

I laugh softly. "Have you forgotten why you were exiled from our hall? Because you cared nothing for the life of a servant. I do not think that has changed now that you are princess."

Her mouth twists, her eyes glittering with hatred. "Me? You blame me for what *you* did? What is a servant? That little rat is probably dead by now anyhow: they die like flies. And you—you betrayed me, made me the disgrace of the hall so that I had to leave." She snaps her jaw shut, glaring at me.

"It's still all about that, isn't it? You wanted your revenge. Is that what you like about sending me to live on a mountain estate you stole from me? That I will have gone into exile as you did? But that won't be enough for you. You want more; you've always wanted more. You wanted my brother, didn't you?"

"I would have been queen," she hisses. "And now I will be. It's your own fault you've been turned into a servant."

"And servants die like flies, don't they? You won't be happy until I'm dead."

She takes a deep breath. "I would not mourn your death. But I will grant you this one chance to have a better life than you deserve."

"You are the one with a better life than you deserve."

"I would have married your brother but for you! If you cared so much, you could have gotten the girl free later—but you had to betray me before everyone. In front of the servants!"

"I've regretted that, Valka, much as I have regretted that you blamed her that day. If you hadn't made a public show of her supposed guilt, I wouldn't have had to make a show of yours."

"Damn her! She was a servant. A nothing."

"Just as I am."

Valka bites her lip, her chest heaving. "What is your answer?"

"I will not write the letter for the price you named."

"Oh? And is there a price at which you will write it?"

Is there? If only Kestrin would call off the wedding. Or Valka would. The thought—the possibilities it offers—brings me up short. If Valka agrees to walk away from this, break off the engagement and depart of her own accord, then there will be a way to grant us each some chance of a way forward: Valka on her mountain estate, I among the hostlers, and Kestrin . . .

"Are you incapable of thinking through even that much?" Valka demands. "What is your price, girl?"

I meet her gaze stonily. It is a gamble, but the details can be worked out if only she'll agree. "You cannot carry this ruse off, Valka. My mother will know you to be an impostor, if not at once, then at some point during the wedding. Can't you see that?"

"I see your desperation," Valka says with a small sneer. "I've already made this court mine. You won't have it back. Your price, girl."

"My price is this: take up your own terms. Live out your life as a nameless lady on a mountain estate, and I will ensure you are not hunted down and executed for your betrayal."

My words sink into the room.

She sits silently, vibrating with the force of her ire, and then she nods once, an acknowledgment that has nothing to do with agreement. "So be it. You've made your choice. I hope you are willing to abide by it."

"I am certainly willing to live by it." The words are bitter on my tongue, however true they may be.

"You know you have chosen to betray me."

"Hardly."

"I am princess now and you—"

Fury fills my chest, coursing through me like liquid fire. "You will *never* be princess, Valka. You will always and only be an impostor. Do not think you won't be found out. This is your one chance to walk away unscathed."

"Wretch!" she cries, surging to her feet. "Do you dare to threaten me? Do you think I fear you? Have you forgotten who made you what you are?"

"Whether I die a servant or a queen, I will always be my father's daughter, and so a princess," I say tightly. "As for who made me what I am—that was the Lady. You are only a tool in her hands, and she will drop you for a better one whenever she pleases. Don't think she'll keep you safe."

Valka draws herself up. "I know how to deal with her far better than you do, *princess*. I hope you will take comfort in your remembered royalty when I am done with you."

"And what will you take comfort in when you are found out, Valka? The gallows? The executioner's smile? *You cannot carry this off.*"

She smiles poisonously. "I already have."

For a long moment, we glare at each other, the silence between us deafening. Then I dip my head. "I cannot imagine we have anything left to say to each other."

"No," she agrees.

I let myself out without another word. It is only as I reach the stairs that I realize I am trembling, whether from anger or fear I cannot say. I clench my hands around my staff and close my eyes, breathing deeply. Then I straighten my back and take the stairs down.

CHAPTER
29

I remain on edge for days, waiting for Valka to decide her next move. And yet each day closes as the one before. Either Valka has decided to find some other way to win my compliance, or she has not yet chosen an appropriate punishment. Or, perhaps, Kestrin has blocked her machinations, though that may only mean it will take her a little longer to reach me.

On the fourth morning after our interview, I sit watching my feathery charges in the pasture. They raise their heads, quieting even the friendly chuckling and mumbling that is their talk. I glance around but see nothing amiss. Corbé sits farther down the field; nothing else moves. The geese, while alert, do not seem frightened. I stand up, casting my gaze around the pasture, past the low stone walls.

And then I feel it: a faint brush against my face, a rippling of the grasses around me, the sudden lone whisper of the newly leafed branches above me, while the other trees remain silent.

"Wind?" I whisper, hardly daring to believe.

The Wind whips a circle around me, flapping my skirts against my legs and scaring off the sparrows in the tree above me.

"Wind! You've found me!"

The Wind slows, breathing gently. *Alyrra.*

I close my eyes, listen to the familiar touch of its voice.

"How did you recognize me?"

The Wind does not answer, instead settling down to ruffle the grasses. I sit with my back against the oak once more.

"Old friend," I say quietly. "I thought I lost you. I went to say farewell to you before I left Adania, but you didn't come to the dell that day. I never imagined you'd find your way here. It's a long journey and I—am not the same."

Different, the Wind agrees.

Tears spill down my cheeks and I laugh as I wipe them away. "I don't know why I'm crying. I'm so happy you're here."

Here, the Wind echoes, and I rest my head against the tree, smiling so hard my face hurts.

I carry the coming of the Wind with me all day. Although it did not stay long, the very fact of its presence, its recognition of me, has brought me both a desperate homesickness and a feverish excitement. For the first time in months, I can remember clearly the dell where I used to meet the Wind, the forest paths. I think of Jilna's laugh, the warmth of the kitchen, the cool sanctuary of our hall's little temple. Again and again I come back to this simple fact: the Wind saw through the enchantments and found me. It is a gift as unexpected as it is wonderful.

"You're happy today," Sage says when I join her and Rowan in the common room before dinner.

"I am," I agree. I know I cannot tell them of the Wind, so I say instead, "Joa gave me a pair of younger mares to work with before I go out to the pasture." The lovely old chestnut's owner returned a few days ago and has taken up their daily rides once more.

"Did he?" Rowan looks up with a grin, his hands paused as he wipes down the table. "He must have plans for you."

"He keeps saying he'll make me into a hostler," I say, amused.

"I wouldn't go telling that to anyone else; there're some as will be jealous," Sage warns me. "Corbé's been hoping to be made a hostler himself for a year or two now."

I hesitate, my eyes dropping. He will be furious, and while he hasn't moved against me since Oak and Ash cornered him, I'm certain I don't want him angry with me now.

"Corbé has a mean streak in him. I wouldn't trust him with a horse," Rowan says, filling the silence I should have spoken into. "It'll be good to get you away from working with him."

Sage nods her agreement. "I'd rather you were here too."

"Why wouldn't Joa trust him with a horse?" I ask.

"No one cares if their roasted goose had a mean temper," Rowan explains. "Corbé keeps them alive and well, and that's good enough for the kitchens. But horses will get cold-backed if their hostler's rough. You can lose a good horse to a bad hostler, and that's not something Joa would want to explain up at the palace. Just look at that dratted black of Filadon's—all these months Violet's been working with her, and she's still likely to nip. I'd wager a year's pay she was mistreated before he bought her."

"She was?" I ask, taken aback. I'd always assumed Moon-flower mean-tempered; it didn't occur to me to wonder why.

"It's likely," Sage agrees, and offers me a smile. "Anyway, we'll teach you whatever else you need to know. You've already got the basics."

What would it be like to work with Sage and Rowan and all from now on? I imagine exchanging Corbé's black looks for Violet's laughter and I can't help smiling. This is the life I want, surrounded by friends, my hands rough from the work I do, all of it honest and true. And I am so close to calling it my own.

"Sage," Oak says from the doorway, brow furrowed. "Is Violet back yet?"

Sage blinks. "I assumed so—she has those bay colts to ground train before dinner."

"Back from where?" I ask.

"We've another sick horse," Rowan explains. "It needs a poultice and we're out of the herbs to make it." He glances back at Oak. "But the apothecary's only up West Road and over two streets. She ought to have gotten back by now."

"I don't think she has," Oak says, running a hand over his head.

"What's wrong?" Ash asks, coming up behind Oak in the hallway.

"I'm just walking out to meet Violet. She's running a little late. You all start dinner and we'll join in when we get back."

Ash frowns and glances down the hall to gauge the light still falling through the stable doors. "You want me to come?"

"No, it's still light out and they're all busy roads she would have taken. She's probably almost here anyhow. I'll be back with her before you know it." Oak departs with a wave.

"I thought you were going to the apothecary's, not Violet," Ash says to Rowan as he joins us.

"I had to finish with Zeluar," Rowan says. "You know that horse won't work with anyone else. She told me she had plenty of time to run over, and not to be silly. I didn't think . . ." He hesitates, stops.

"She's fine," Sage says. "There's not much danger in broad daylight on busy streets."

I know that, I remind myself, trying to quell the rising sense of panic in my chest. I've gone walking often enough, careful of my surroundings and the time of day, but still, I've been perfectly safe. Perhaps Violet just met an old friend, paused to catch up, and lost track of time. There's no real reason to worry yet. Is there?

Dinner is quiet and awkward, the conversation stilted as evening deepens and neither Oak nor Violet return.

Finished, we continue to sit there, as if by refusing to leave the table, we could assure that Violet returns before dinner is over.

"I should have gone," Rowan says into the quiet. "Zeluar could have waited."

"Hush," Sage says firmly. "Violet knows to be careful. The busy streets are safe enough."

Only, Violet hasn't returned yet.

I clasp my hands, rub one thumb against the other, an old fidget I haven't quite left behind.

Then I lift my head at the faint creak of the stable door opening. A moment later, we hear Oak's voice calling from the hall.

"Yes? You found her?" Ash asks, leaping up from the bench and darting out, Rowan right behind him.

"She isn't here," Oak says as Sage and I follow the boys into the hall. It isn't a question, though from his voice I know he had half hoped for it. He slows as he nears us, worry written in the lines of his face. "The apothecary said she came by an hour ago, maybe more. I didn't see her anywhere along the way."

"We'll look again," Ash says, his voice hard and rough. "You just went by West Road?"

"Yes."

I wrap my arms across my chest, listening to the sound of fear in my friends' voices. Where is Violet? She's usually so dependable. I don't believe she'd allow herself to be distracted this long from returning. It's past dinner now. The boys are right: something has happened to her.

"Rowan, you go back by West Road again, in case I somehow missed her. I'll check the way there past the Dancing Goat; Ash, you search the side streets between the two," Oak continues.

"What about us?" I ask, standing beside Sage.

"Stay here and wait," Oak says. "We don't want either of you hurt, and someone has to watch the stable. If Violet gets home without us, you'll be here to greet her." He turns to Sage. "If she comes back on her own, just keep her here. We'll come back to check."

Sage nods, and then the men are gone, striding down the hall. We return to the common room.

I gather the plates and stack them on the counter, cover the pot with a square of cloth, and then stand uncertainly in the middle of the room. "What do you think happened?"

Sage shakes her head. "She's too old—she shouldn't have been snatched. There are other dangers. But I . . . I don't know."

I go to the door to peer out. Snatched or attacked? Enslaved or assaulted? My skin crawls. I cannot imagine one being better than the other. Perhaps she just twisted her ankle and has stopped along the way. Perhaps.

Or perhaps this is my fault. Perhaps this is the punishment Valka has chosen—to lash out at one of my friends when she was vulnerable. The thought burns through me. I think I might wretch, my stomach twisting. *No.* It can't have been Valka. She would have hinted at it first, as she did with Falada. She would have made me fear her actions first. Wouldn't she?

I can't stay here any longer, can't just *wait* for someone to find Violet. "What about the guards?" I ask abruptly, turning to Sage. "Won't they help search for her?"

Sage hesitates. "They don't help, not usually."

"We're right here by the gates. We can at least ask. Perhaps they even know something—or saw something."

"All right," Sage says, glancing once around the room, as if there were someone else to tell. "Let's ask."

The city gates are brightly lit by torches, the shadows deeper closer to the stables than out on the road. We walk right up to the nearest members of the quad stationed this side of the gate.

"Something wrong?" the taller of the two asks.

"Our friend has gone missing," I say without preamble. "She works in the royal stables. She was supposed to be back over an hour ago. We're worried something's happened to her."

"What's that to do with us?" the second soldier asks. "She's likely just gone off somewhere to get away from you tracking her every movement."

"She didn't run away, and she's not avoiding us either," Sage says, anger warming her voice. "She's very dependable. She was bringing herbs back for a poultice for a sick horse. She'd never leave an animal to suffer needlessly."

No, I think grimly, that's the reason she went in Rowan's stead—so the horse wouldn't have to wait any longer than necessary.

"I'm sorry, kelari," the first soldier says with a staying glance at his comrade. "Hopefully she'll be back shortly. We can't leave our posts here."

"Is there someone who *can* help?" I demand.

He sighs. "Young women staying out late isn't the jurisdiction of the guards. You're sure she doesn't have a—friend, somewhere? Perhaps a lover?"

"No," Sage says. "Not like that."

"Maybe you just don't think it's like that," the second soldier says with a smirk.

"We *know* it's not like that," I snarl. "Come on, Sage. Let's go." I grab her wrist and tug her around, back up West Road the short distance to the turn-in to the stables. Fury vibrates through me. Violet is missing, and the soldiers will do nothing to help. Even though I've been told this from the first, by every person who has ever mentioned the guards, experiencing their casual disregard makes my blood roar.

I pause at the turn-in to the stables, looking up the road, as if I might see Violet walking toward us through the gloom.

"We tried," Sage says tiredly, and I realize she is trying to comfort me. I don't want comfort. I want Violet back safely. I want someone to—*oh*. I know exactly who to go to. "Sage?"

"Yes?"

"There's someone we can ask for help, but you'll have to come with me now that it's dark. Will you?"

"Who?" she asks.

I hesitate, and Tarkit's words come back to me: "A friend of a friend."

She stares.

"Please, Sage. I know they'll help, but I have to get there."

"If they'll help," she says, and then we are well-nigh running up West Road. I make only one wrong turn, but catch myself within a block. We hold tightly to each other's hands, glancing continually over our shoulders, down alleys. Twice men call out to us from doorways or the corners of streets, but we hurry past, and they do not follow.

Inside Artemian's building, the staircase is dark, and we have to feel our way up to the door. I rap twice on it, then step back, waiting. We listen as footsteps approach the door.

"Who knocks?" The voice is sharp, hard, reminding me forcibly of the night I saved Red Hawk. Only this time, I know the words.

"Thorn," I say. "I need help."

The door opens, a flood of lamplight brightening the hallway. Artemian holds his sword at the ready as he did that night, but then he lowers it and steps back.

"Come in, veria."

Sage and I step into the room. I do not wait for him to close the door before I speak. "Violet—one of the hostlers from our stable—she didn't come home tonight. We think something's happened. The men have gone out looking for her. I thought you might be able to help."

Artemian frowns. "Where was she going?"

"To the apothecary on Relin Road," Sage says, and describes the location, and the different routes Violet might have taken to get there. "She made it there, but never came home again. Her brothers are searching them all, but we're worried. She's never stayed out like this, and she wouldn't delay bringing home the herbs she went for. The apothecary said she left . . . nearly two hours ago now. It's only a twenty-minute walk."

"Not good," he says. "We'll look for her."

Artemian insists on escorting us back to the stables. We describe Violet and what she was wearing when she left, Artemian nodding and asking the occasional terse question. At the stable, Sage checks the common room while I run up to our rooms to make sure neither Violet nor the boys have returned, but no one's there. Artemian leaves at once, telling us he will send us a message within an hour.

Sage and I return to the common room. It is late now, though not nearly as late as the night Falada and I met Red Hawk. We stand a moment together, and then Sage walks over to the bin by the counter and picks out two pieces of tack to mend, a saddle whose stitching is coming out for her to repair and an old horse blanket with an unraveling hem for me. We work silently, every stitch we sew a half-breathed prayer. I cannot search the streets for Violet. I've done all I can, and it does not feel nearly enough.

Rowan lets himself into the stable an hour later. We drop our mending, hurrying to the door to see who has arrived. He has little news, and stays only to drink a cup of water.

"We met some other men. Friends of yours." He nods to me. "They've been going through the taverns and inns, and have helped us search the alleys. One of them told me to come back and let you know we're still looking. I'm going back out to keep on."

"You bring her back, you hear?" Sage's voice is rough with worry. "Don't any of you come back without her."

"We'll find her," Rowan promises. He strides down the hall, his shoulders bowed with exhaustion but his pace still fast, still hurried by hope and fear.

CHAPTER

30

They return near dawn. We hear the tread of boots first, and then Oak's voice calling to us as we burst from the common room to meet them. Behind him trail his brothers, as well as hostlers from the first stable.

"Quickly," Oak cries. "We need a place to lay her down!"

Relief crashes through me—even if Violet is hurt, we've found her. She'll be all right now. Sage and I hurry back into the common room, drag the table and bench to the side, shove away the stray stools. I pull out one of the boys' sleeping mats, and then the men pour in, Oak kneeling as he lays Violet down. I catch only a glimpse of a hand, bruised and spattered with blood.

No. She's supposed to be okay now—

Beside me, Sage makes a faint sound, like that of a small animal crying, and stumbles into me. I stagger under her weight, crashing against the table as I wrap my arms around her, and then Ash is there, his face pale, taking Sage from me and carrying her out of the room to lay her down in the hall where the other hostlers wait.

"Your friends are sending a healer," Oak says to me, his voice trembling. He has not stood up, has not moved from Violet's side. I clench my teeth and kneel next to him, forcing myself to look at her.

They have wrapped Violet in a dark cloak. Only her face, one hand, and her bare feet are visible. Her face is swollen past recognition, dark with blood and bruises, her lips split and bleeding. Her hand is likewise swollen and discolored, her fingers not quite jointed right. There are marks near her wrist that I know to be bruises from a tight hold, or perhaps ropes. Blood has clotted on her feet, but I cannot tell if she is wounded there or if the blood has only run and dried there from another injury.

I cannot breathe, cannot find the air to fill my lungs. I turn my face away and see Rowan standing beside Oak, and behind him, returned from the hall, Ash. Their faces are sallow beneath the bronze of their skin, their eyes dead with shock and horror.

"She must be washed." It takes me a moment to recognize the voice that spoke as my own.

Oak turns toward me, waiting.

I stumble on. "The healer will need to look at her wounds. We should wash her."

"What do you need?" Oak asks.

I swallow hard. Must it be me? But who else is there? "Water—and strips of cloth."

Oak and Ash go at once, half running to fetch water, to find cloth that can be used, grateful to have something to do. But Rowan still stands, swaying, staring at his sister.

"Rowan," I call. "Rowan?"

He looks up slowly.

"When Sage wakes up, she'll need you. Go stay with her. Go on. She's in the hall."

He leaves, his shoulder knocking against the doorframe.

Ash brings me the cloth, and Oak the water, and I send them out to join Rowan.

I do not want to touch Violet—do not want to hurt her, or wake her, or see what else has been done to her. But she needs this, and if Sage cannot, then I must, as gently as I can. I dip the cloth into the water and work slowly, wiping away the blood from her face, then her hand and feet, not wanting to push back the cloak.

I cannot see clearly and I have to pause often to rub my sleeve across my face. Where is the healer? Why is he taking so long?

Gritting my teeth, I move back the cloak to reveal the rest of her arm, and after wiping this clean, I move on. When I am done, the water is dark red. I pull the cloak back over Violet, my teeth chattering, and stand up. The room sways around me, darkness chasing the edges of my vision. I back up until I hit the table behind me. I breathe slowly, staring straight ahead, but it will not matter where I look; I will still see the violence that has been done to her. It is so much worse than anything I have suffered. I do not know now how to help her.

"Here!" Ash cries from the hall.

"The healer is here," Oak calls in to me, and then a man hurries into the room, followed by Oak and his brothers and Sage, gray-faced but conscious. "Thorn was washing her—Violet hasn't woken yet."

"I see," the healer says.

"Oh, Violet," Sage whispers, leaning into Ash. He holds her as gently as if she were his own mother.

The healer sets down his bag of supplies. "Go out, all of you, except the girl who washed her."

Oak hesitates, and the man looks up at him sharply. "Go on. I'll take care of your sister."

"I'm staying here," Sage says.

The healer shakes his head, firm but gentle. "No. Stay outside till I call you in."

Sage opens her mouth to argue but Oak touches her shoulder. "Do what he says. He'll help her."

Sage closes her jaw with a click, turns, and stumbles from the room, the others following in her wake.

The healer peels back Violet's cloak. "What did you do, then?"

I avert my eyes, though I have already seen everything. "I washed her. That's all. I tried not to move her."

He nods and continues his inspection.

I sit down on a nearby stool. I look down at my hands, but there is blood dried beneath my fingernails and in the ridges of my palm. I look up quickly, focusing on the lamp, my chest aching.

"She's cold," the healer observes as he rummages in his bag. "Was she left out all night?"

"I don't know." How did I not notice how cold she was? But my own hands are too cool, horror numbing my senses. Still, I should have noticed, gotten her more blankets at least—

"I'm going to stitch up her cuts. That's about all I can do," the healer says. "You'll need to keep her warm, feed her broth, and give her some time to heal."

I push myself to my feet clumsily, as if my body were a distant thing. "I—I think her fingers are broken."

"And a few of her ribs," he agrees. "I'll do what I can."

"Is she going to be all right?" My voice sounds cool and calm and as far away as the ocean. But I can't let the numbness take me, not now, not when Violet needs me.

"I don't know," the healer says without looking up.

No. He's not supposed to say that. He's supposed to help Violet, undo this violence. Somehow. I hear a faint mewl and clench my jaw shut against the sound, swipe the tears from my face with a damp sleeve.

"I'll try," the healer says. "That's all I can do."

I nod and go to the door. "She needs blankets."

Oak barrels down the hall to the staircase, followed by Ash. They pound up to our rooms, returning within moments with all the blankets we have, piling them into my hands.

I wait for them to step back before I reenter the common room, using my body to shield their view. I fold the blankets over Violet, leaving uncovered only the spot where the healer works. Then I sit down opposite him, one hand resting gently against Violet's arm, and talk to her quietly, telling her that her family is near, that the healer is checking her.

He works systematically, lifting the blankets to check each part of her before moving on. He bandages her hand, then says, "I'm going to roll her on her side to check her back. It will hurt her, and she might wake. I want you to stay in front of her and help her balance. Don't let her roll onto her stomach."

He slides his hands beneath her and lifts. I join him, helping to turn her as gently as I can. She moans once, a long, low sound that fades to nothing. The healer works quickly, wiping her back clean and inspecting her carefully.

"All right. Roll her back."

I ease her down, grateful that I did not have to look, grateful that there was nothing requiring the healer's stitching.

"She's still cold," the healer says. "I want you to sleep next to her, under the same blanket. Don't touch her much or you'll hurt her. Just try to keep her warm. If you have to go out, warm stones by a fire and wrap them in the blankets. In fact, keep the stones there regardless."

He stands up, resting his hands on his waist and stretching out his back. "I've seen worse, but not much. The cold isn't good for her. You'll have to be careful."

"Kel?" Oak asks tentatively from the doorway.

"Aye. I was telling the girl here what to do." The healer takes his bag and joins the hostlers in the hall.

I can hear them speaking, but the words are far away, garbled. Exhaustion and horror weigh down my limbs. There is light now from the doorway, and I think it must be full day, but I cannot quite imagine that the sun was rising while I sat here with Violet. I listen to her breath. It is so faint and slow that I begin to worry, between breaths, that it will cease.

Boots enter the room. I look up to see Sage, and behind her Oak, Ash, and Rowan.

Sage crouches beside me, reaches out a hand to touch Violet and then stops short. "We should lie down beside her," she says finally.

I nod and lie down on one side of Violet while Sage slides under the blankets on her other side. The men glance at each other uncertainly.

"Oak, you bring in the warming stones when Joa sends them," Sage says.

He nods and departs, but his brothers still stand there.

"Go rest," she finally tells them. "We'll call you when she wakes up."

They nod, but it is still some time before they turn and trudge out to lie down just beside the door. But, from their shifting and the occasional soft word, I know that they, like me, cannot sleep. Eventually, I turn on my side to watch the rise and fall of the blankets with each breath Violet takes, and wait for her to wake.

She does not. By midmorning, her skin burns and her breath rasps in her throat. She moans when Sage wipes her forehead with a damp cloth, but her eyelids remain closed. We take shifts sitting with her so that we can each see to our work.

By the time I reach the barn, Corbé has already taken the geese out. I clean quickly, throwing myself into my work so I might return that much sooner to the common room. I leave only to help Corbé drive the geese back in.

Sage and I take turns feeding Violet, spooning a thin broth Joa had sent down from the palace kitchens. We prop up her head gently, afraid to move her, and empty a single spoon at a time in her mouth, praying she will swallow. We cannot tell, at the end, whether she has drunk any at all, or whether it has all run back out the corners of her mouth.

"Was it snatchers?" I ask finally as we sit together, Sage and I by Violet's side, and Oak sitting on the bench, his head bent and his massive shoulders slumped. I cannot avoid asking any longer, and it is something I need to know—*must* know, if Valka has had a hand in this. Just the thought closes up my throat again. No one has said anything, though, about Violet's attackers, and I don't know why.

"No." Oak looks up, the shadows beneath his eyes darkened almost to bruises. "Snatchers don't do this. Or at least, if they do, they don't leave their victims behind in a back alley when they're done."

Sage stares down at Violet's bruised face. "The women and children who come back to us escape of their own accord. They find a way to free themselves. This—this wasn't snatchers."

Please, I think, looking down at the still face of my friend, please let this not be because of me, because of Valka. *Please*, I beg, *please get better.*

The healer returns at sunset, sending the men into the hall while he checks Violet. Sage and I remain, watching. It is the first time that Sage sees the full extent of the damage done to Violet. When I glance at her, I think she has aged ten years. She sits with her jaw clenched, lips pressed together, her eyes dry.

"The fever's high, and these cuts don't look good," the healer says, pointing to the stitches he put in the night before. He hands Sage a pouch. "Make an infusion of these herbs. Give it to her every few hours, mixed with the broth."

"Is there anything else?" Sage asks.

"Rub ash into her cuts to prevent rot. Beyond that, there's nothing we can do."

At night, Sage and I lie silently beside Violet. The men sleep on the hard-packed earth just outside the door, quiet but for the faint rustle of blankets as they shift.

"I can't sleep," Sage says.

"I know."

"She'll wake soon, won't she?"

I press my eyes shut and a vision of the common room flashes before me: our hands all busy with small repairs, Sage shaking her head at some joke of Rowan's, and Violet with lamplight shining against her sable hair, her laughter ringing out as she pauses from tugging her needle through tough leather. I have no answer for Sage, no promise that I can be sure won't be broken.

"Will you sing one of your songs?" Sage asks, breaking the silence. "That you sing when you work?"

I open my eyes to look toward her, past Violet's unmoving form.

"I don't know any in Menay."

"I know. Sing them in your language. Violet always liked the sound of them."

And so I sing quietly into the night, picking an old love ballad from home. I sing until my voice is hoarse and I can hear Sage's even breathing just past Violet's harsh, rasping breaths.

CHAPTER

31

The following afternoon, Oak and Ash go to the palace to petition for justice. They return in the evening, coming to sit beside Violet, silent and grim-faced.

"Well, what did you expect?" Sage asks, her voice hard.

"We don't know who did it," Rowan says.

"It won't be that difficult to find out," Ash snaps. "And we will. God have mercy on those—" He clicks his jaw shut, glancing toward me. "We know where Thorn's friends found her. The types of men who do this like to boast. The king's men could find out if they cared to."

"They don't," Sage says with finality. "But they will care if we take justice into our own hands."

I look down at Violet, the purple bruises across her jaw, her lips still swollen and scabbed. How can the law do so little? Anger claws at my chest.

"We're not going to let those men go on thinking they can do this to other girls," Oak says, his deep voice hoarse and gravelly.

"Justice is not men beating each other up," Sage says quietly. "Justice is teaching men that there is a law and, if they don't abide by it, there is an established punishment."

"If the king won't uphold the law—" Ash snarls.

"Did you ask him?" Sage cuts in. "Or was it some idiot captain?"

I look up sharply and wait. Though even a captain should have helped.

Oak grimaces. "It was a captain. We couldn't hope to see the king himself; you know that."

"I'll try," I say, my voice raw and harsh. They look at me uncertainly. "Someone might listen to me."

"Aye," Sage says after a moment. "If the king doesn't, perhaps your other friends will."

"Justice?" Oak asks, raising an eyebrow.

"Thieves' justice or king's justice, so long as it's a known law, I don't care." Sage reaches out to smooth the blanket over Violet.

"Agreed," I say, though I cannot believe that Kestrin will not see to this if I tell him of it. He could not allow such an injustice to pass without even the simplest of investigations. And then I am not certain that Red Hawk will help me. If I go back to him, I may easily put myself in his debt. Far better to ask Kestrin.

So, that evening, Rowan and Ash walk with me up West Road to the palace. All the long way up the road, I try to figure out how I will find Kestrin. Always before, it was a chance meeting or an arrangement through one of his men. I realize now that I don't know how to contact him. Rowan and Ash leave me just below the gates, promising to wait until I return.

I continue on, through the gates and around the main hall. I find a side door, and from there wend my way to the royal wing. Hopefully, Kestrin will be in his apartments when I knock. More likely, though, he'll be dining somewhere. A prince does not sit alone in his apartments of an evening.

At my knock, a man I have never seen opens Kestrin's door. He looks me over with growing disdain. "Yes?"

"I wish to speak with the prince," I say. Instead of sounding commanding, my voice has the weakness of a plea.

"Ah. The prince . . . does not take petitioners in his apartments. How did you get here?"

"I think he will see me, if you would ask him."

"Indeed." The man's voice is laden with contempt. "But he is not here."

I bite my lip. I don't want to demand entrance, nor do I want to go back and tell Rowan and Ash that I didn't even manage to see Kestrin.

"Who is it?" a second voice calls.

"A serving girl," the man before me replies. "Wants to see Zayyid Kestrin."

"A serving girl? Is it—" The second man peers around the door, and his face lights with comprehension. I recognize him easily as one of the two servers from my dinner at Melkior's. It seems Kestrin was very careful not to involve anyone in that evening whom he didn't trust.

"She seems to think the *prince* will see her," the first man says, as if sharing a joke.

The second man dips his head to me. "He will. Come in, veri-ana. The prince is at dinner, but we'll let him know you're waiting."

I smile as graciously as I can, stepping in as the first man gapes at me. The second introduces himself as Finnar and seats me in the inner sitting room. I can hear him softly berating his companion once they close the door.

A full hour slips by, the men discreetly passing through the room once or twice. Finally, I hear the door open in the outer room, followed by lowered voices. A moment later, Kestrin enters and pulls the door shut behind him.

"Veriana," he says, bowing to my curtsy.

I forge ahead before he can ask any questions. "I'm sorry to come like this, zayyid, but I didn't know how else to find you. I have something to speak to you about."

"I should have made an arrangement." He grins and gestures for me to sit. "I never imagined you would want to speak to me of your own accord."

I give a pained smile. "You might have heard that Violet—a hostler from the royal stables—was attacked two nights ago?"

He sobers at once. "I have. A very unfortunate incident."

Incident? I make myself ignore the word and go on. "Her brothers came here today to ask for justice. They believe the men who attacked her can be found. They were turned away."

Kestrin frowns. "Who did they speak to?"

"Second Captain Elann."

"On what grounds were they turned away?"

"That the attackers could not be found. We know where she was left, zayyid. It would only be a matter of looking for witnesses, listening to the men in the taverns."

Kestrin runs a hand through his hair. "I don't know Elann, but my expectation is he knows what he is doing. I will look into the matter myself and see if anything further can be done. I can't make any promise, though, Thorn. It's a terrible situation."

"Yes," I agree. A cold anger has begun to grow in me, so that I think my bones have turned to steel, or that my voice will flash silver when I speak. It is all I can do to hold my anger in check.

"How is the girl doing?"

I meet his gaze. "She's dying."

He stares, and I know in that moment that what I have said is true: that Violet is slipping away with each breath, and I am no longer sure she will be able to come back to us.

"Has a healer-mage seen her?" Kestrin asks.

"A *wha*—no. Just a regular healer." I've *heard* of healer-mages, as one hears of far-off wonders, but it never occurred to me that there might be one here. But this isn't Adania, and why wouldn't at least one of the Circle of Mages be a healer? Only, not even Sage has mentioned one, so perhaps they are not easily gotten for those who are not noble.

"I'll send our court healer-mage as soon as possible."

"Thank you, zayyid," I say, and find that I mean it, that the fire in my breast has already burned down, leaving me only bone-weary and deeply grateful.

"As for discovering her attackers, I will find out what Elann says, what the guards know."

I look at him curiously. "The guards know nothing. We asked them to help us search when she went missing, and they refused."

"They *refused*?"

"We had to ask . . . others in the city to help us search."

"Why would the guards refuse?" Kestrin demands.

"The hostlers said they always refuse; I've heard the same from everyone who's mentioned searching for those who disappear. The guards don't care. When Sage and I asked them, they said they could not leave their post, that there was no one who would do it, and that Violet had likely run off with a lover."

Kestrin tilts his head, the angles of his cheekbones sharp in the lamplight. "I was not aware of the guard denying their aid. You're sure this is common?"

"Yes."

His eyes move away, focusing on some distant point. Then he shakes himself. "I'll see what I can find out about all of this, veriana. And I'll send Mage Berrila as soon as I'm able."

I nod.

"Is there anything else I can help with?"

Valka, I think, meeting his gaze. He could stop her—but he's leaving that for me. Perhaps he'll do something at the wedding, but that may still be too late. And, regardless, I don't know if she was behind Violet's assailants or not, nor will Kestrin know. No, to find that out, I'll need to visit Valka herself. "That's all," I tell him.

"Do you require an escort?"

"No, my friends are waiting. Thank you—for seeing me tonight."

"No," he says, looking distinctly gratified. "Thank you for coming to me."

I curtsy and let myself out. In the hallway, I stand a moment, looking at Valka's door. Then I walk over to it and knock. It is the distantly polite attendant who answers. She ushers me in, then slips away to inform Valka of my arrival. A moment later, I am led in to meet Valka in her inner sitting room, while her attendants are all sent out.

"Well, well, well," Valka says, eyeing me with amusement. "Have you reconsidered your decision?"

"Is there a reason why I would?" I ask softly.

"Have you a brain?" she demands, rolling her eyes. "I can destroy you, idiot. And I will. Do you think you can come back to me, pleading for mercy, and I'll grant you clemency? Write for me now, and I'll leave you alive to find a new place to shovel filth. You won't get a better place from me now."

She didn't do it. The realization leaves me nearly breathless with relief. If she had, she would be citing Violet's attack now, taunting me with it. But she doesn't even know about it to use it against me.

"I understand," I tell her.

She eyes me narrowly. "Why are you smiling?"

I shrug, using that moment to find an answer she might believe, one that could have been true had I not come here about Violet. "You still think you can do this, don't you? I didn't come here to beg clemency, I came to see if *you* had reconsidered. You haven't."

"Nor will I."

"Very well," I reply, and having nothing left to say to her, depart.

Rowan and Ash wait in the shadow of the first building past the palace gates, barely visible in the dark. I tell them what Kestrin has promised: to look into what can be done, and to send a healer-mage.

"Mage Berrila?" Ash echoes, his voice soft with surprise. "If anyone can help Violet, she can. But she only—she never treats common folk."

"Hopefully she'll make an exception for the prince," I say.

The men throw me the occasional unreadable glance as we continue on to the stables, but they ask no questions.

When we step into the common room, my gaze darts toward Violet. For the space of a heartbeat, I forget myself in the sudden, unfounded hope she will be somehow recovered, sitting up with a mug of warm milk in her hands, bruised and exhausted but awake. But no, she lies as I left her, her face flushed with fever.

I go to sit beside her, and leave Rowan and Ash to share what news I have with Sage and Oak.

Mage Berrila ni Cairlin arrives at dawn. She is built large, taller even than Oak, with broad shoulders from which her mages' robes drape elegantly, accentuating the grace with which she moves. She carries only a large brocade bag, no doubt containing what medicinals she might require.

Sage and Oak meet Berrila in the hallway and escort her into the common room. The rest of us are already gathered, though we move back, beside the table, that she might have room to inspect Violet.

"All the men outside," she says briskly, and turns to look at Violet. For a long moment she says nothing, her back to us, and then she glances up again. "I said *out.*"

Rowan nearly trips over Ash in his haste.

Sage and I ask no questions, other to inquire, once, if we can help. Berrila waves us off and uncovers Violet to assess her. She is gently efficient, her hands pausing only once or twice as she inspects Violet.

Violet's bruises have begun to fade, but her fever rages on. Now she moans softly, turning her head, shifting her body at the healer-mage's touch. Her stomach is bloated, tender to the touch. Berrila lays her hand so gently on Violet's belly, her expression one of fierce concentration. Then she moves on, as grim-faced as when she began.

One of Violet's cuts has festered beneath the healer's stitching, despite the ash we have rubbed into it. It weeps drops of pus, discolored a murky gray by the ash, the skin around it streaked red. The others, at least, look better.

"I'll do what I can," Berrila says, turning Violet's face and gently opening her mouth to inspect her teeth. At least there is no damage there.

"She'll get better, right?" Sage asks, voice wavering.

"True healing is in the hands of God," Berrila says gruffly. "Now let me work."

Sage and I exchange a single, frightened glance. *She doesn't know.* Berrila is not taking any responsibility, nor proffering any false hope. I reach out and grasp Sage's hand as we watch Berrila work.

For a long time, the mage simply sits, both hands placed on Violet's belly, eyes closed. The sapphire ring on her finger glitters in the dim light, the only sign that her magic is at work. Perhaps she is easing the pain in a way only her magic can, or perhaps she is treating some problem we cannot see. When she finally moves her hands away, there's no outward sign of any change, but Violet seems to lie a little quieter. Berrila then turns her attention to

Violet's hands, unwrapping them from their splints and cupping them in her own. As we watch, the fingers realign perfectly, bones shifting as the magic closes up the breaks. Then she turns to treating each cut, her magic sealing the wounds from within. With light fingers, Berrila picks away the stitching left behind, pushed back out of Violet's skin by the healing magic.

Finally, Berrila addresses the remaining bruises, gently touching each. The swelling seems faintly reduced when she is done.

"Continue what you've been doing to help her," Berrila finally says, pushing herself to her feet. "Except for the ash. You won't need that anymore."

She provides Sage with a pair of fine cotton pouches from her bag: herbs to steep for Violet, to replace the ones we've been using.

"I'll check back on her daily."

"Is there anything else we can do?" Sage asks.

Berrila shakes her head, her shoulders slightly bowed. The healing she has performed has exhausted her. "I'm afraid not," she says. "If you have faith, then pray for her. That's all."

The next day brings little true improvement, nor the day after that. Violet's fever has slightly diminished, her bruises are fading away much faster than normal, much of the swelling nearly gone. But her stomach remains bloated and tender to the touch, and she does not wake. Each time Berrila comes, she leaves looking as grim as she did her first visit.

After cleaning the goose barn, I sit by Violet while Sage and the men ready horses to be sent to the palace. With the weather warming up, the palace folk have begun afternoon excursions, and their needs must be met. I sing to Violet, wiping her face with a cool cloth.

Four days, Violet has lain here. Four agonizing, unending days, her body weaker each day, her eyes closed. Four days I have sung to her, sat by her, prayed for her to wake. By the time Sage comes in, I do not have any song left in me.

"Joa says some guards came by to question him last night," Sage says as I rise from my cushion beside Violet.

"They did?"

"Aye. He told them he wasn't with the searchers, and that they ought to talk to the boys about where she was found."

"Did they?" I ask, but I already know the answer.

Sage grimaces. "No. But they did want to know what she was wearing and if she had a lover."

It is all I can do not to curse, not to slam my fists into the wooden walls. Kestrin is trying, I know he is, but these guards don't care. They don't want to know, and they'd rather pin the fault on Violet than find the men who did this to her. Kestrin might be able to change how these things are handled in the future, but I want justice *now*. I want these men stopped. Somehow.

"It's all right to hit something," Sage says. "Bales of hay won't hurt your hands."

I blink at her and she shrugs. "Maybe I will," I say, and halfway mean it. I look down at Violet, who cannot express her rage, or sorrow, or pain. *Goddamn those men.*

I turn to Sage. "I'm going to the temple."

"It's on West Road?"

"Yes, just a few paces off, still within sight of the road."

"Take your staff and be back before dark."

"I will," I promise.

At the temple, I pray for Violet. Eventually, I lie down on my side, exhausted by the worry and horror of the last few days, the seething anger as each day slips by without bringing Violet's attackers to justice. The longer they remain at large, the harder it will be to find them. I do not fault Kestrin, but I know that I cannot wait for the king's justice.

It is time to seek justice another way.

I walk quickly, leaving the temple behind for now-familiar connecting streets. I knock three times on Artemian's door before accepting that he is not there. Crouching in the darkened hallway, my nose filled with the rank smell of damp and sweat, I open up my braid, make the thinnest of plaits, and use my teeth to snap it free. I loop this around the doorknob and make my way back to the stables, wondering just how much Red Hawk will do in payment of his debt, and whether he will accept recompense from me for what goes beyond that.

I wake in the middle of the night. Something is wrong, something is missing: the room is too quiet. I sit up with a jerk, throwing off my blanket, and Sage wakes with a gasp.

"Violet," I say, reaching out. Her skin is cold.

"No," Sage whispers. "Oh no."

Violet is dead.

CHAPTER
32

Oak and Ash depart at sunrise, shovels over their shoulders. Sage and I bathe Violet one last time. We bring down her spare tunic and skirt from our room and gently dress her. It is the same set I gave her in return for the gift she made me of her own clothes. My hands seem to function of their own accord, helping Sage to wrap Violet in a sheet and tie it closed. I cannot quite fathom how what we are doing can be real.

Joa pulls up in a wagon, the bed softened with a layer of straw, and he and Rowan carry Violet out. The hostlers from the first stables join us, and with them the now-haggard face of Massenso. We ride beside Violet, Joa directing the horse out of the city gates and down West Road, turning north at the crossroads, following a route I have not taken before.

Ash and Oak are still digging when we arrive. They switch off with Rowan and Massenso, taking turns until the grave is deep enough. When the work is done, her brothers lower Violet into the grave. There is no Speaker here to lead the prayers, and no one seems to expect one.

We stand beside the grave while Oak, in a hoarse and broken voice, recites the Final Blessings, and then we each toss a handful of earth into the grave. The dirt patters down on the white shroud, hardly audible among the rustling of so many people, and yet it echoes in my mind. Even after the men have filled the grave, I can still hear those first small handfuls of earth falling down upon Violet. There is no arguing with such a sound, no denying it.

Together with Sage, Violet's brothers walk across the road to the field. They return each with a single rock that they set at the head of the grave. The whole of the graveyard is filled with these graves: small piles of rock, grave after grave of men, women, and children, all the same in death.

Joa drives us back to the stables, the wagon wheels rattling over the uneven road. It hardly seems possible that we are home by midmorning. The hostlers move away in small groups, their steps and voices slow.

My body feels heavy now, so that it is an effort to climb down from the wagon, to take one step and then another. I walk away from the stables, away from Sage and the men, and habit carries me to the goose barn. I stop at the inner gate and stare in at the empty space, the trampled straw and scattering of droppings.

I let myself in, fetch a rake, and set to work. The raking and shoveling steadies me; it is work my body knows, and requires no thought on my part. Once I am done, I walk back to the stables, but I cannot bring myself to enter. I cannot yet look at Oak or Sage and see their grief written on their faces. It is too fresh.

"Thorn?" a small voice calls. I turn toward it. Torto peeks around the corner of the stable, lips parted in his signature gap-toothed grin. "Thorn? Come here!"

I trudge over to him. Behind him, Fen watches a pair of sparrows pecking through the dirt.

"We're not supposed to be here," Torto explains in a whisper. "Children aren't allowed. But I'm supposed to find you and tell you to go to the Curious Cat. I can explain how to get there."

"Thank you." My voice sounds strange to me, as if it comes from someone who stands just behind me.

"Are you all right?"

As I look down at Torto, and at Fen standing silent beside him, the tears finally come to my eyes. "My friend—was attacked," I explain. "We found her, but she died this morning."

Torto stares up at me. It is Fen who pushes past him to hug me tightly, his skinny arms wrapping around my waist. I kneel down and embrace him, and then Torto is hugging me as well, patting me on the back as my sobs break free. I wish that I could protect them, protect us all, from harm.

While the children wait, I fetch my staff once more, and then we walk to West Road together.

"We have to go," Torto says as we start up the road.

"How is Tarkit?" I ask, holding on to their company a moment longer.

"He's good. He's apprenticed to that baker now, and when there's burnt bread, all the boys at the bakery split it. Once he even had some extra he gave us."

"Say hello to him from me."

"I will," Torto says. "You're sure you're all right?"

"I'm fine." I smooth his hair with my hand, offer them both a final smile, and continue on, listening as Torto and Fen scuff their way down an alley.

Torto's directions serve me well. The Curious Cat, unlike the inn where I met Red Hawk, is a large establishment, the hallway and stairs wide and well-lit by windows open to the spring air. The proprietress takes one look at me and sends me upstairs. I knock on the second door on the right, and at once a voice calls for me to enter.

The room holds just a bed and two chairs set by the window. I squint, looking toward the window, and make out a figure seated in one of the chairs. The man nods to me, so I walk over and sit in the companion chair, watching him. It is Red Hawk himself.

"I did not expect to meet you again," I say.

He tilts his head as if equally surprised. "I am sorry about your friend. I heard this morning that she died."

"Yes." I look away from him, back toward the door.

"Is that why you wished to see us?"

"That's why," I admit, and stop again.

The silence stretches between us. Violet is dead. There is no bringing her back, no undoing what was done.

Red Hawk leans forward. "Veria, I would not have come to meet you myself if I did not believe there is more you wish to speak of than this. Tell me what you came to ask."

I stare at him, taken aback at the gentleness in his voice. I cannot tell from the shadows touching his face whether it is a true kindness or a calculated one, but I find I do not particularly care.

"I want to understand justice in this land. The men who hurt—who killed Violet can be found. Ash and Oak both believe it; they say that the men will talk, will boast, and that there will be witnesses. Yet the guards do nothing. They don't *want* to know."

Red Hawk smiles, but it is a slow, sad thing. "I told you before: you are very idealistic."

"This is about justice."

"Justice for the poor?" He laughs, sitting back. "There is justice for the rich here, and justice for the powerful. But for the rest of us, there is very little of anything."

I know it, and the knowing hurts. I lift my chin, meet his gaze. "Sage told me that there are two laws here: the king's law and the thieves' law. If the king's law only serves the rich, what of the thieves' law?"

His gaze sharpens, and I know he understands me, but he says only, "It is what we make of it."

"Which is what, exactly?"

"It is primarily only for thieves. It is somewhat less harsh than the king's law, and then again somewhat harsher."

"I don't understand."

Red Hawk gestures with his hand, as if he held something weighty in his palm. "Here is an example. If one thief steals from his brother, the first question asked is why."

"Isn't stealing what thieves do?"

"Aye, but between thieves there is a code of honor. We do not encroach on each other's territory, nor steal from each other. If a man steals out of need, because his family is hungry or the like, he is forgiven. But if he steals only to enrich himself, then the first time he is flogged. The second time, his hand is cut off so that he cannot steal again. By the king's law, the common thief is flogged, regardless of why he steals or how often."

"By the king's law, then, you are not a common thief."

"No," he says, amusement warming his voice. "The uncommon thief is subject to special treatment."

"And what of men who do . . . what was done to Violet?"

"By the king's law, those found guilty of rape and murder are hanged."

I have to hold myself still, for it is the first time I have heard anyone name the crimes committed against her. My voice cracks as I ask, "And under your thieves' law?"

"These are crimes that cannot be excused to necessity, so we are in agreement with the king's law: a public hanging. But before that, the men would be flogged that their punishment not go too easily with them."

"It is very similar."

"Yes. Am I to guess that you wish Violet's attackers brought to justice?"

I meet his gaze. "I do. But I don't know what I will owe you."

"The accounting is not quite clear, but I doubt it is very much," he says with a mock frown.

"I helped you one night, your men helped me another. You helped us find Violet. Now I am asking something in addition."

"When a thief tries to grant you a favor, don't protest it, veria. It is far too rare an occurrence to be disregarded."

I rub my cheeks and then pause, holding my head still, as if I might hold in the terror of the last few days, might somehow keep myself from breaking apart at the kindness of his words.

"You are not well," Red Hawk says.

I shake my head, dropping my hands to my lap. "I am fine."

"You have not seen a death like this before."

"No," I agree. "And I would not have believed that the only help to be had would be from those who evade the law, not those who swear to uphold it."

"I am sworn to my own law."

I did not mean to insult him. "You are. For that I am grateful."

He shifts, still watching me. "We can find Violet's killers and bring them to justice. It is hardly an impossible task."

"What will I owe you then?"

He taps his fingers against the armrest. "Tell me, veria, what is the price of justice in your land?"

I watch his fingers, thinking of Valka, of that day long ago and the sapphire brooch. "Justice in my land is very similar to the king's law here—it is to be had for the rich and held against the poor. True justice"—I glance up to meet his eyes—"that would be priceless, I expect."

His lips twitch, and I wonder if he has held back a smile, and what that smile would mean.

"Priceless," he echoes. "Can you offer me something equally priceless in return?"

"I have very little to offer—only what I brought with me in my trunks from home. That is all," I say humbly. He said the debt would be small, but what is it that he wants?

"There is more to you than just your belongings; what else can you offer?"

My mouth goes suddenly dry. I cannot look away from him. I am aware in an awful, sickening way that we are in a bedroom. "I—I can't," I stumble.

"Veria." He reaches out and touches my sleeve lightly.

I flinch away from him, then catch myself. Stupid to show fear, stupid to—

"Veria," he says softly. "Do not look at me so. Have I ever given you reason to fear me?"

Relief courses through me, and with it, shame. "I am sorry," I whisper, looking down to shield my face from his gaze.

"You feel for Violet because you too have been hurt before."

"I—no, not like Violet. I wasn't hurt like her. I was just—it was nothing."

"Nothing?"

I close my eyes. I have never voiced such things before, have never admitted to anyone what my brother did. It did not matter if others knew or not; there was a safety in not speaking it aloud, not admitting it to myself. Silence was a protection from some of the reality of it, and the idea of letting those words out now— they stick in my throat as if the Lady's choker held them there.

"It is all right," Red Hawk says softly. "You will survive the speaking of it."

I nod, take another breath, and speak. "My brother used to beat me. H-he would threaten me." The words sound strange to me, hanging in the air. Smaller than I expected. "It is nothing— when you consider what was done to Violet, to others here," I gasp into the silence. "A few bruises, a cut or two, that's all."

I open my mouth and find that I cannot go on, that the words have robbed me of my breath. I cover my face with my hands, bending down, my back hunched. Hidden, my breath rasps back into me in a broken, strangled sob. I do not want Red Hawk to hear me, so I hold my breath, shaking, refusing to breathe again until I must.

"Thorn," he says in the same soothing tone hostlers use with a frightened colt. But still I cannot look up.

He rises, moves away. He will leave now; he will look down on me for my weakness when so many others have carried burdens heavier than mine.

"Here," he says, walking back to me. "Drink this." He holds out a tin cup.

I take it from him in surprise.

He does not speak again until I lower the cup, stare down into the water left at the bottom. "I knew the night you first helped me that you were a strong woman at heart. I did not realize the depth of your courage until now."

I laugh, an ugly, harsh sound. "Courage? I am worse than the lowest coward. I've allowed—you don't know the things I haven't done, because I was afraid of what would happen to me." I press my hand to my mouth as if I might take back the truth of my words.

"As a thief," Red Hawk says, "I've found that acting when you are afraid is the greatest sign of courage there is."

"But I haven't acted. I've just let things go on because I was afraid. Because I didn't want to act."

"Ah," he says. "So, that night when you helped me through the depths of this city and delivered me to a safety that threatened you, you who are afraid of the brutality of men—that night is an example of when you refused to act for fear of what might happen to you?"

"Falada was there," I whisper.

"Your horse could have protected you from the soldiers?"

"No," I admit. "But he stayed with us, and carried me home."

"It is easier to be strong when you have a friend supporting you," Red Hawk agrees. "But that does not change the fact that you chose to act, and so saved my life."

"That was an exception," I tell him bitterly. "All these months here, I have been hiding from the one thing I fear the most. The one duty I must face."

"I expect, when you are called upon to do it, you will rise to the occasion very well. You are made of stronger stuff than most."

His faith in me reminds me forcibly of Falada, of the great Horse's certainty that I could overcome my weaknesses. In the silence between us, I hear Falada's voice once more, asking the questions I least want to answer. The questions I most need to face. *Can you live with the choices you are making now? Or will they end up destroying you?*

I know now the decision I must make, know that I can no longer deny what I must do. I cannot leave Valka as my successor; having been born to power, it is my responsibility to see it handled well by me, by those who come after me. I cannot leave her as princess, just as I cannot leave more girls to be attacked on the streets, the guards all uncaring and the law nothing but a farce—or more children stolen from their families. It seems an impossible duty, and one I will not survive long in performing, but it must be done.

Red Hawk must see some of my struggle in my eyes, because he grins and says, "I did not get this far by making mistakes. You must trust yourself a little more."

I smile wanly. "I will try." It is a promise, to him, to myself. I will do this thing. But I can at least give myself this much: a return on my own terms, at a time of my choosing.

"As for the question of justice, I will see to it that the attackers are found and punished. In return—" He pauses, watching me. "In return, I want something from you that, I fear, cannot be traded. It makes for a difficult bargain."

"What is it?"

"I should like your friendship and trust."

I stare at him, my mind flicking to Kestrin and his apple cakes, but the tenor of this is different. There is more truth between Red Hawk and me.

"Don't feel the need to answer at once," he says dryly.

"Why would such things matter to you?"

He raises an eyebrow. "Perhaps you underestimate yourself."

I do not answer.

"I know," he continues, "that such things cannot be bought. So I want from you only an offer of friendship, an attempt at trust."

"That is all?" I ask.

He nods.

I sit back, thinking. The friendship and trust of a goose girl is one thing, but that of a princess may be an entirely different thing. And then I wonder if Red Hawk might not be one of the best friends I could have as a princess, and if I, in turn, might be able to help him as well. Except that a princess cannot uphold a thief. I bite my lip. I am not there yet.

"I will try," I tell him. "And I will not betray the trust you have given me, now or in the future."

"Of course," he says. "Friends do not betray each other."

CHAPTER 33

Sage sits at the common room table, her back hunched, her face in her hands. I pause on the threshold, then retreat into the hall. But how can I leave her alone when I know the choking emptiness I feel over Violet's death? How much deeper must her grief be? I make myself enter and move quietly to the counter. Sage lifts her head, watching with dull eyes as I fill a cup of water and bring it to her. She takes it without a word, sets it on the table untouched. Her hair is matted together, the braid hardly discernible anymore. This woman is nothing, *nothing* like the Sage I know.

I fetch a comb from the cabinet, stand behind her, and work through the knots in her hair lock by lock. She rests her chin on her hands, and I watch the tension slowly go out of her shoulders. When I am done and her hair rests in a braid down her back once more, I kiss the top of her head and turn away.

She catches my hand and brings it to her cheek. For a long

moment we stay like that: her cheek, the palm of my hand, the damp of tears in between.

Once I finish in the goose barn, I return to the stables to look for her. At my call, Sage turns toward me and leans on her pitchfork, the stall only half mucked. There are circles under her eyes, and I know from the restless sounds of her shifting on her mat next to mine last night that she has not slept well.

I swallow to ease the dryness of my throat. "I wanted to tell you something—you and the boys."

"What's that?" Oak asks, stepping out of a stall two doors down. Like Sage, he is exhausted, his eyes sunken and his face sallow.

"I spoke to a friend yesterday about finding those men," I say awkwardly. "He's going to look for them."

Sage straightens. "Good. I hope they string them up and leave them to rot."

"Sage!" Oak says, turning toward her in surprise.

She dismisses his surprise with a single flick of her hand. "But Thorn . . . these friends of yours, will you owe them something for this?"

"Not really. It's evening things out," I say, which is not precisely true, but close enough. "I helped one of them, you see, when I didn't know who they were. Saved his life."

A faint smile flickers over her lips, there and then gone. "I wondered how you knew them. You're sure you won't owe them?"

"It's fine," I say.

"Good, then," she says, and goes back to mucking her stall.

Oak presses his lips together, as if there are words he does not know if he should speak. I wait, but he returns to his work in silence. He will leave for their family's farm in a few days' time to bear the news of Violet's loss to their parents. I hope that he might also have news of the attackers' punishment to take with him.

I am grateful for the walk to the goose pasture, the solitude. My grief is a quiet thing, wrapped so tightly around me that sometimes I cannot hear properly, my breath coming in strained gasps. Here in the fields it eases a little. I fill my cup with water from the stream and sit beneath the shade of a tree. The geese are spread about the pasture, snapping up grass and tasty bugs, or dipping into the water. It is as if nothing has happened, as if the pasture exists out of time and none of the violence or illness I have seen can touch it. There is a wordless sort of hope in this field that bears me up.

The royal wedding is a month and a half away, and I know my decision. I must make this choice for myself, for Violet and Fen, for Tarkit and Torto and all the other street children I have come to know. I must do it for Kestrin, who is only doing what he can, and cannot protect himself or me. I must do it because it must be done.

But at least for these next few days, while my friends are still reeling from Violet's death and her murderers yet walk free, at least for these days I will stay where I am. To walk away from Sage and the boys would be a cruelty I cannot visit on them. Kestrin will be all right a little longer.

In the late afternoon I lean back in the shade of a tree and doze. I wake with a start, but when I look up I realize it is only the geese passing near me; Corbé still sits by his tree across the pasture. I can feel his gaze on me, though, and I stand up, leaning on my staff as I return to the stream for a drink.

The Wind comes to visit, a faint puff of warmth that hints of summer. I follow the wall down a few paces as I speak to it, my hand drifting over the stones. "You should go home," I say. "The dell is a better home for you than these empty fields."

Stay, the Wind argues.

"There's something I have to do, something I've been avoiding. I don't think it will go well." Not with the Lady involved. "Even if it does, I won't be coming out with the geese anymore."

The Wind spins a circle around me. *Wait*, it suggests.

"You can wait, if you wish," I tell it. "I still have a few more days."

Ash sprints up to the goose barn as I rake up a new day's worth of goose droppings. "Thorn! Come quickly!"

I drop my rake and run to him, an unreasoning panic flashing through me. "What is it? What's happened?"

"They said—we heard," he gasps, catching hold of my hand and pulling me after him as he begins to run again. "The men were caught—they're at Hanging Square."

Relief lightens my step. We race together around the stables. *Hanging Square.* I truly did not believe Kestrin would see this through—that he *could*—but he has. I should not have doubted him.

Ahead of us, Sage runs, her boots flashing beneath her skirts, Rowan and Oak keeping pace beside her. We pound after them, people turning to watch our flight through the streets.

The square is filled to overflowing, people jostling each other for a view of the central gallows. I can just make out a body—no, two—swaying from their ropes beneath the main beam. I skid to a stop, pull my hand from Ash's, and bend over, digging my fingers into my side. He waits next to me, panting and stretching up on his toes to look over the heads of the crowd. I stare at the cobblestones, not wanting to look up now that I am here.

"It's already over," Ash tells me.

"That's right," says the man next to him. "We saw them go up—real fast and hard they did it, and then they were off. It was Red Hawk's men, so they wouldn't be waiting for the king's men to get here. But they made some proclamation afore they did it."

Red Hawk and not Kestrin, even if it is Hanging Square. I take a slow, steadying breath. Either way, justice has been served.

"Aye." A woman glances back at us. "I heard it myself. They said the girl was an innocent, and the men raped and murdered her, and it was a shame the king couldn't do nothing for it, so Red Hawk figured he'd help him."

"I'd like to see that old dog Melkior's face when he hears that," the man says, flashing a yellow-toothed smile.

"Who was the girl they hurt?" asks a man who has come up behind us.

Before Ash can answer, the woman does. "She wasn't anybody. Just some poor girl got caught out on the streets and the men thought they'd have their way with her. Didn't think Red Hawk'd get involved, did they?"

"Come on," Ash whispers to me. "I want to get closer."

I follow him through the crowd, keeping my head down, but when we reach the gallows I have to look up. The bodies twist slowly in the faint breeze, ropes creaking. Their hands are tied before them and their shirts have been stripped off to reveal welts crisscrossing their backs. I swallow down bile, wanting to turn away, *but this is what I asked for.*

I stare at the bodies until I have memorized each detail. The first man was barely older than Ash, with long black hair that sticks to the raw skin of his back. His mouth gapes open, eyes protruding, dark and unseeing. His arms are roped with muscles, long and sinewy. The other man was shorter, his feet barely reaching farther than his friend's knees. A dark beard covers his face, and his stomach hangs over his belt in fleshy rolls. The welts in his back have cut into the fat, leaving trails of blood that stain the back of his trousers. His hands are large and meaty; where his friend had muscle, this man had weight.

When I turn away, I think of Violet. I think of her terror as these men caught her. I think of her trying to fight them, of their bound hands binding her, of their limp, booted feet slamming into her ribs, crushing her hands. I see her again as I first did when the healer uncovered her; see her lying broken and used in the corner of an alley. I stagger to the side and Ash reaches out to steady me.

"This is your doing," he says, his voice a bright, fierce thing. "You've brought them to justice. There are women and children who will go free this month because you've made such men afraid of punishment. Put your head up, Thorn."

I force myself to meet his gaze.

"This is justice. Don't be afraid to look at it." He smiles as I look at him. "It may not be pretty, but sometimes justice has to be hard to keep the rest of us straight and safe."

I nod, but I am not sure of what I have done, or even if I am glad of these deaths. It is street justice that I have brought about, without court or judge, and without surety that any other rapist or murderer will be held to account. I watch the bodies slowly twist at the ends of their ropes. No, I *am* glad they are dead, but I want more than this. I want safety for the women of this city, and I want justice that is more than a favor granted, a debt repaid, a ploy to mock the king.

Beside me, Ash exhales slowly. The tension in his shoulder eases as he stares up at the gallows.

I look away from the bodies, and note for the first time the arrow stuck into the support beam of the gallows. A string dangles from its shaft, three feathers threaded to the end of it. They are the long, bright feathers of a red-tailed hawk.

A commotion erupts at the far end of the square, tearing my attention away from the gallows—shouts, and the sound of orders being barked. Ash catches hold of my hand. "That'll be the king's men. They'll cut down the bodies and question everyone they can. Hurry."

I follow him as he threads through the crowd, his hand tight in mine. We take the back alleys, slowing to a walk as soon as we have left the square behind. Ash matches his steps to mine, letting me take my time; I am still slightly off balance from what I have wrought.

At the stables, Ash leads me to the common room. "You'd better sit and have a bit of water," he tells me. "You're a touch too pale."

I take the water from him gratefully, sitting on the bench to drink.

Ash takes a cup himself, sits on a stool, and leans back to rest his head against the wall.

"Ash?" Oak's voice carries down the hall.

Ash leaps up and goes to the door. "In here."

Oak, Sage, and Rowan join us in the common room. Sage comes to sit next to me, wraps her arm around my shoulders, and squeezes.

"Our miracle worker," she says. Though her voice is not happy, some of the weight of the last week has lifted from it.

Rowan comes up to me, drops to his knees, and catches hold of my hand. "Veria Thorn."

"Rowan, what are you doing?" I try to pull my hand back.

"Veria," he says with all the seriousness and gallantry of youth, still hanging on to my hand. "I swear to protect you as if you were my sister, so long as I live."

"And I," Ash says from his stool. Oak echoes him a moment later.

When I glance at Ash, I find his regard bright and sharp as a gemstone. Oak smiles at me, a kind, gentle look, and then glances down at his hands.

Rowan stands up and claims the end of the bench. "That's all."

"You've done a good thing, Thorn," Sage says. "It's been a long time since folks saw something like this; mayhap there're other Violets that will be safe because of you. I know our Violet would be glad of that."

For all the horror of the hanging, I know Sage is right. It still unsettles me, though. I push myself to my feet. "I have to get back to the geese."

Ash nods. "I hear you won't be with them much longer."

I stare at him—how could any of them possibly know?

"What's that?" Sage asks.

"Joa spoke with the folks at the palace. Thorn'll be working with us as a hostler as soon as they find another goose girl to take her place."

Rowan lets out his breath in a whistle that easily covers the sound of my own breathy laugh of relief. Of course they don't know who I am, but I will have to tell them—at least that I must return to the palace, even if the choker will not allow me more.

Soon, I promise myself. Now that Violet's attackers have been punished, I shouldn't wait much longer. But I would like a day or two more as a goose girl, a few more evenings spent sitting together with my friends. Violet's death still feels too fresh, too grievous. I cannot walk away from them just yet, with her loss only half mourned, an ache within me that must be only an echo of the grief her family feels.

Ash nods at me. "You've jumped rank, you know. There's a few others that have been waiting for the stables longer than you've been here at all."

I shake my head, make myself answer as if I might truly have the chance of this life before me. "I don't want to upset anyone."

"Don't worry," Ash says, grinning. "No one's going to bother you while we're around."

"And we all know the best person gets the job here," Rowan says.

I look down at my hands. A fortnight ago, my heart would have leapt at this news. "I'd better get back to the goose barn," I repeat, standing up. "I've still got to work those mares afterward."

CHAPTER
34

I finish mucking out the barn and set off for the goose pasture only a little later than usual. It is strange to think that I was gone for less than an hour. I feel as though the day should have stopped, cut short with the lives of the criminals. How could something so momentous take so short a gasp of breath to happen?

I slow as I reach the city gates, looking up to Falada's head. It has darkened with grime, his mane stiff and matted, but beyond that there is no change, no sign of rot or life. I pause underneath, looking up.

"Falada," I call.

His head remains still, a thing nailed to the wall and not my friend at all. Looking up at him, though, I can still hear the remembered timbre of his voice, echoing within the stone of the gates. He always believed in me, in the choices I would make, and now that I am ready to make them, it is him I want to tell, him I want to speak my decision aloud to first, him I want to share with. I find the words gathering in my chest, until they are a weight I must release. I know my reasons now: there is Kestrin to protect, there are the snatchers to stop, there are criminals like those who attacked Violet, there is a whole city of children who go hungry every day. All of them I am responsible to, and I cannot fail them any longer.

If only it were as simple as taking back my role, sending Valka away before she's tried for treason. But there is still the Lady to contend with, the Lady with her death-still eyes, waiting and waiting for the betrayal she planted to bear fruit. There is only so much I can do to stop her—and sending Valka away will only push the Lady to set new events into motion. But I cannot control that. And, as Falada would say, no one has asked me to. I must take each step of this path as I can, and hope for the best.

"I'm going to find a way," I say now. "You were right, my friend."

The head hangs still above me. I let my breath out slowly and look down, take a step.

"Princess."

I twist, staring up at Falada. He meets my gaze, his eyes open and seeing, bright with life.

"Princess," he says again, and the word is the warm embrace of a friend.

Behind me, I hear a half-swallowed cry. I spin around to see a guard standing at the mouth of the gate, staring up at Falada, seeing him just as I do. The guard drops his gaze to me, his bronzed skin nearly as pale as my own. Dead creatures cannot speak. There is no magic I have heard of that allows it, and I know from the fear in the guard's eyes that he knows of no explanation either.

For a long moment, we stare at each other, then I turn my back and hurry through the gates, holding tight to my staff. I listen for the guard, for footsteps or a voice calling after me, but there is nothing. When I look back, the gate lies empty.

At the goose pasture, I drop down onto the grass, my staff beside me, my legs tired. The geese are scattered as usual, Corbé seated at the other end of the stream. He glances once from me to the geese and does not look back again.

The Wind comes visiting in the late afternoon. I stroll through the grass in its company, watching the geese.

"I know what I need to do," I tell the Wind.

It tugs at my skirt, as if it could hurry me along the path I have chosen.

"Tomorrow," I say, thinking of what that would mean: facing Kestrin, and then also exposing Valka. And, in the end, it would mean leaving Sage, Oak, Ash, and Rowan, which will be the hardest of all. I will speak with them in the morning, I decide, and go on from there.

"It would be so much easier to just let Joa make me into a hostler," I say to the Wind, trying to smile.

"You're no hostler," a voice growls behind me.

I whirl around to find Corbé glaring at me from a few paces away. I take a quick step back.

"I heard the talk this morning," he tells me, matching my step. "You're not going to be a hostler before me."

"I haven't agreed to it," I stammer, backing away further.

He keeps walking toward me, his eyes glinting in the

afternoon light. "You think you can come in here with your rank and walk all over the rest of us?"

"No, I don't!" I cry, sickeningly aware that I have left my staff by the tree, that Corbé is taller and stronger, and no doubt faster, than I am.

"You won't," Corbé agrees, and he smiles. It is an ugly smile, a smile of knowing and hatred and jealousy all mixed together. "You've made someone angry up at the palace, but you know that, don't you?"

I shake my head, my breath rattling in my chest. Valka. He means Valka.

"I've a promise that I can do what I like with you, and there won't be any price to pay. What do you think of that, girl?"

"It's not true!"

"But it is," he purrs. "The princess herself rode out this morning to tell me so. She really must hate you."

"Kestrin would punish you. She can't protect you from Kestrin—or Melkior."

"What would such men care for a servant like you?" Corbé sneers, and though he is wrong, it does not matter. What matters is that he believes this, believes that the law will not stoop to protect a servant. And if I were any other servant, he would be right.

"Red Hawk just hanged the men who attacked Violet," I nearly shout, stumbling away from Corbé as he continues to walk toward me, swinging his staff along. "He'll come after you too if you hurt me!"

"He won't," Corbé says. "You're lying, but even if he did catch Violet's friends, he won't care anything for a foreigner."

I run. I hear Corbé laugh behind me, but I do not look,

concentrating only on the possibility of getting away. I hear the thud of his boots gaining on me, hear him grunt, and then his staff knocks into my ribs. I stumble, pain lancing through me. His staff slams into my legs and sends me sprawling. I struggle to my knees, my hands scrabbling in the dirt for a rock, for anything to use against him. Before I can rise, his boot comes down hard on the small of my back. My hands fly out from under me and my cheek slams into the ground. I hold still, trying to breathe through the pain in my back. With my face sideways, I can see the geese waddling away from us in alarm. The breeze gusts, whipping around them and ruffling their feathers.

"Wind," I whisper. It's already here, gathering itself from a few breaths of air to a gale, these gusts a promise to me of the strength it will bring to bear.

"What was that?" Corbé winds his fingers into the roots of my braid, twisting my head around, his weight still pressing into my back. My mouth arcs in a grimace of pain.

"Don't do this," I whimper. Pain leaches the color from my vision, but I can still see his face, see the way the breeze lifts a lock of his hair.

"This is only the beginning," he promises, and the breeze gusts again, stronger now, whipping his hair around.

"It's coming for you," I say to slow him, until the Wind can reach us.

Corbé looks up, scanning the pasture, confusion touching his brow. As if from afar, a soft whistling grows, building into a howling gale that rips over the stream, lifting water and rocks with it as it approaches. The geese erupt in a flurry of feathers and tumble toward us, honking frantically.

Corbé swears and drops his grip on me, his eyes wide as a wall of debris and wind bears down on us. I curl into a ball, folding my arms over my face. The Wind passes over me so gently it merely fans my back. Then it slams into Corbé.

He screams in terror, arms over his head as stones and twigs flay his skin, tearing through his clothes. The Wind shrieks as if in response. I press my hands to my ears, shaking.

RUN. The word echoes in my mind. The force of it pushes me to my knees and then, staggering, to my feet.

I do not turn to see where Corbé is, whether he has fallen or fled. I take one step forward, and then another, and then I am running, stumbling over the rocks of the streambed and clambering over the low stone wall and on through the grasses.

I do not know how long I run, or where. My eyes blur until I cannot see and I lose my balance, one foot tripping over the other, spilling me to the ground. I lie sprawled on the grass, gasping for breath. It is a time before I realize that I am sobbing, that I cannot catch my breath because I am weeping.

In my mind, I see Corbé's face above me still, his features twisted by the blackness of his emotion, and there is my brother sneering down at me, his eyes holding the promise of pain in them, and there is Violet laid out on the floor, cold and unmoving, her face marred by dark bruises, and Falada hanging above me, a severed head, fur dank and blackened by soot. I wrap my arms around myself and cry until my fear and guilt have spent themselves and I am left shivering on the ground, chilled despite the warmth of the day.

Finally, I sit up. Pain shoots through my back and side. I press my hands against my ribs. My palms leave red smudges on my tunic; when I look at them they are scraped raw. I stare at them for a few heartbeats before I recall flaying them against the rocky ground as Corbé pinned me down.

I stagger to my feet, my legs weak beneath me. I have only to walk home, I think, seeing Oak and Ash and Rowan in my mind's eye. They will keep me safe from Corbé until I can return to the palace, and then he will never be able to touch me again.

The wind whips past me and I follow it, turning my face as it raises the dust of the plains into a swirling pillar. I realize with a jolt that this is not my Wind, for there is nothing familiar to it, not the way it gathers, not the snapping cold of its touch. As the swirling pillar grows darker, funneling into a small vortex, I step back once, and then again.

Out of the darkness at its center steps the Lady.

I stare at her, hearing the rasping of breath in my lungs, loud now that the wind has gone. Faintly, I hear a drumming *thuh-thump, thuh-thump*, and I wonder if it is my heart, the pulse of my fear.

Not like this. It is almost a prayer. *I am not ready*.

"I had not planned on coming just yet," the Lady says, as if she can read my thoughts on my face. Her voice is the whisper of leaves in the fall. "But perhaps I will enjoy it more this way." She smiles, an empty curl of her lips that sends me back two more steps.

"Look there," she says, tilting her head. "See who your friend the Wind really is, the one who comes to rescue you."

I turn slowly, not wanting to look.

Kestrin pounds toward us on a horse, the court clothes he wears at odds with the way he rides like a warrior into battle, poised and ready, his hair caught up in a tight knot, his mouth a grim slash across his face.

Kestrin? The Wind? *My* Wind?

"Did you not guess, even now?" the Lady asks as I shake my head, unable to look away. "It is how I knew you would be his undoing. He has visited you far too often to pretend not to care for you."

I shake my head again, my tongue cleaving to the roof of my mouth, even as I understand. This is the reason the king came for me, the reason my mother could not guess at. It is how Kestrin knew my life at home well enough to recognize Valka as an impostor, and how the Wind found me again, in another land. Because all along it has been him.

Kestrin swings down before his horse has stumbled to a stop before us. I cannot read the expression in his eyes. I am trembling again, disbelief bleeding to a certainty that shakes me to my core, because this I did not imagine of Kestrin: that he has been my friend when I did not know him at all, that he sought me out of *care*.

Now he spares me only one quick glance, his eyes flicking over me, and then he turns to the Lady. "Whatever hold you have on her, release it."

"Come now, my prince, what is she to you? A mere goose girl . . ." The Lady laughs, a poisonous sound that leaves me light-headed. "Why, who would even notice if she disappeared?"

Her eyes turn to me; they are the empty sockets of a skull. She gestures once, lazily, and the chain jerks so tight around my throat I think my neck will snap. My knees give out with the force of it. I fall, catching myself on my hands, the burn of my already raw palms barely registering. I raise a hand and claw at my throat, but I cannot touch the chain.

"Stop!" Kestrin is beside me now, his fingers brushing my throat, but even his magic cannot break the choker's hold.

"Does it not amuse you? Surely you enjoy seeing a princess at your feet?" the Lady asks, her voice faintly quizzical, as if I were not choking to death before her. "You descend from a line that takes pleasure in such things."

Black dots dance before my vision. I feel myself slipping, hands no longer able to support me, but Kestrin is there, lowering me gently to the ground. *At least I will not die alone.*

"*Alyrra.*" Kestrin's hands are at my throat, but no matter how he tries, he cannot touch the spell there.

"You haven't much time if you want to help her."

"Damn you," he whispers. "What do you want?"

"You."

Darkness closes in, dragging me down.

Dimly, I hear the prince say, "Very well."

CHAPTER
35

The plains have taken on the rosy hue of early evening. The grass waves gently beneath a light breeze. Some distance away, a black horse grazes. A bee buzzes past my shoulder on its way back to its hive, pausing a moment to investigate me. Soon, the plains will turn gray, then be lost to darkness. I cannot remember if there will be a moon tonight to light my path to the city.

What I do remember is the terrifying coldness of the Lady's face, and the sound of Kestrin's voice as he gave himself up. All this time I thought it would be Valka who would betray him. But Valka was only one pathway to gaining the prince; the Lady also baited her trap with me. So, in the end, it is I who have become the weapon of his destruction.

I sit up slowly, my bruised back so tender it drives the other minor aches and pains from my mind. I breathe through my mouth and wait for the pain to ebb. It takes me a long time to stand, for my legs will not answer to me as they should. They are soft, and when I finally manage to rise, my knees knock against each other. I wonder if I have become an old woman, lying unconscious through the passing of the years. But when I look at my hands, I see the same young, work-roughened hands of the goose girl I am, the palms dark with dried blood.

I make my way slowly toward the horse. I must return to the city, even though so much is lost. I must get back to the stables, somehow tell the king what has happened, and . . . I do not know what will follow that. I doubt the king will forgive me.

The horse Kestrin rode turns its head as I near, its ears laid back and eyes glinting, the white marking on its forehead fairly glowing in the half-light.

"Moonflower," I whisper, recognizing the black. My throat is raw, and the single word fires pain through it, making my eyes water.

She snorts, sidling away.

When I reach for the reins, she jerks back and then turns to trot away.

"Moonflower, no!" I cry, trying to follow, but my foot catches on a tangle of grass roots and I tumble to the ground. I huddle there, my breath shuddering through me.

I'll have to walk all the long way back to the city. I'll have to walk, and yet somehow I cannot quite make myself get my feet back under me. A whimper breaks from my mouth—stupid, useless sound. I need to get up, not lie here moaning.

A horse's hoof appears two paces from my face. I stare, holding myself perfectly still. Moonflower lowers her nose and huffs at me, a breath of warm air against the back of my neck.

"Moonflower," I say again, softly, barely daring to believe.

She raises her head, eyeing me warily, but she's here, come back for me.

I sit up slowly, then push myself to my feet, and still she waits. This time, when I reach for the reins, she lets me catch them. As I struggle into the saddle clumsily, Moonflower turns her head to watch with clear disapproval, but she does not move until I touch my heels to her sides.

"I love you," I tell her.

Her ears swivel, listening, as we start for the city.

We reach the gates without mishap. I do not raise my eyes to Falada, cannot imagine speaking to him now, when I have finally and truly betrayed Kestrin.

"That's her!" a man's voice cries as we pass through to the other side.

"Halt," a second voice commands.

Moonflower's ears flick toward the voices, but she keeps walking. Four soldiers surround us, their swords drawn. Moonflower snorts and steps around the man before her.

"Stop your horse," the soldier orders, reaching up to catch the bridle. Not a soldier—it's Captain Sarkor.

"Easy," I croak.

Moonflower swings her head up, her ears laid back. She snaps her teeth at Sarkor, making him step back, and then leaps into a gallop, nearly throwing me.

The soldiers shout, racing after us.

"Stop!" I gasp, but Moonflower is having none of it.

With the bit between her teeth, she carries me to what she

has always known as safety. The stable door stands closed, and for a terrifying moment I think we will crash into it; then she pivots and kicks through the door.

I slide onto her neck, clutching at the pommel, then nearly fall off as she whirls around and charges into the stable.

"Stop," I plead, and she, having arrived where she wished, obeys.

I manage a wobbly dismount, grateful when hands close around my elbows to support me.

"What's happened, Thorn?" Joa's face comes into focus.

I shake my head, watching as Moonflower spins and bugles a challenge to the soldiers as they sprint through the broken doorway. They stumble to a halt. Around us, the other horses neigh and snort, and from one stall comes an answering bugle, the horse within kicking at its walls.

"Here," Joa says, and another set of hands catches me. Joa stalks toward the soldiers, Captain Sarkor at their head. "Exactly what do you think you're doing chasing down my hostlers, spooking my horses, and causing damage to my stables?"

"The girl's wanted by the king," Sarkor says, the planes of his face taut.

"If the king wanted her, he would have sent for her through the stables, where she works. He wouldn't have sent soldiers to waylay her after she found Lord Filadon's mare that ran away, and managed to bring the creature back. Managed to do so, despite the fact that *you* have clearly convinced it you're going to attack."

I blink. *He's lying*, I think muzzily. *Moonflower didn't run away. I did.*

"We've orders to arrest the girl," Sarkor repeats, ☐ step forward, then another. "You'd best turn her over to us. She'll stand trial in the morning."

Moonflower snorts a warning at him, eyes edged in white.

"Can you hold Moonflower?" Joa asks me, clearly worried she'll break loose.

I nod, take an unsteady step away from the hostler who supports me. "Easy," I whisper, holding out my hand. Moonflower lets her breath out in a huff, sweet mare that she is, and lets me grasp the reins.

"The girl's been training as a hostler," Joa tells Sarkor. "She's done no wrong that we know of."

Sarkor shrugs. "There are witnesses who've made claims against her. You can go up to the palace and argue it if you like, but if you keep her here you'll be joining her in the morning."

For a long moment, Joa holds Sarkor's gaze. Then he dips his head. "All right." He turns to me. "See if Moonflower will let you hand her reins over."

I pass the reins to a waiting hostler. Moonflower stamps her hoof in irritation, but that's all.

I look up at Sarkor and the familiar faces of the soldiers beyond him. They're from the city gates; clear among their faces is the guard who heard Falada speak. But the king sent Sarkor for me, which means he knows something—that Kestrin is missing, or that the Lady has taken him, or that I am not what I seem, or perhaps only that the story of Falada speaking deserves at least a little of his attention. I'll be going to see the king. The rest of this—this talk of charges and trial—must be the excuse he is using to have me brought up, to make me feel at his mercy.

...ith you," Joa says, taking my arm. I lean on ... toward Sarkor. I don't think I could run if I tried.

...icks," Sarkor says tersely. It's the first time he's ...ed me directly since we gained the stable, but he's already t...ing to lead the way out, the remaining soldiers falling in around us. He doesn't want to look at me.

Joa waits until we've gained West Road to speak, his voice low. "Corbé came back hours early today, without the flock and gibbering all sorts of nonsense. I took half the hostlers out with me, including Ash and Oak, and we found the geese spread across three pastures, their feathers everywhere.

"I expect Ash and Oak would have killed Corbé if I'd let them. As it is, they're still out on the plains looking for you, along with a good number of my hostlers. This is the second time you've disappeared out there. Last time a rider from the hunt found you and brought you back. We weren't sure what we'd find this time." He swallows. "After what happened to Violet . . ."

I glance up at him. The moonlight softens the planes of his face, his eyes kind and veiled with concern. I return my gaze to the road, to Sarkor's back, straight and unyielding in front of us, remembering the day Sage asked me what had happened in the pasture. And another day, a lifetime ago, when Sarkor intervened between me and my brother in the hallways of my home.

I will tell Joa about Corbé, and I will do it where Sarkor might hear as well. But not here, in the road, with the tramp of boots to muffle our words. And then I will face the king and perhaps—perhaps there will be some way to help Kestrin. There *must* be.

We reach the palace in silence, follow the soldiers through a maze of hallways to a guardroom, and through this to a short hall lined with empty holding cells.

"We'll lock her up for the night and she'll stand trial in the morning," Sarkor tells Joa, his eyes refusing to meet mine.

Lock her up? Is this not a ruse, then? What charges could anyone— The truth slaps me in the face, a realization so unexpected I nearly stumble. This must be Valka's final vengeance: for me to be publicly humiliated as a criminal and then punished, just exactly what I served her.

"At the courthouse?" Joa asks as I stand there staring.

"No, here in the palace, on the king's orders. She came with Zayyida Alyrra, so her sentence will be of interest to her."

It certainly will. Does Valka have the king so tightly in her grasp, though? Or has Kestrin shared his discovery of my identity with his father? But if Kestrin had, then I wouldn't be here, in the bowels of the palace, being locked away for the night. My fingers tighten convulsively on Joa's arm.

He glances down at me, but at least he does not offer any false comforts.

Sarkor unlocks one of the cells and opens the door. Joa guides me in and lowers me to the floor.

I look past him, to Sarkor. The lantern light shows me nothing but the hard planes of his face. I do not know anymore how much I can trust him, just what I should let him hear. But perhaps, just perhaps, he stepped in to stop my brother by choice as well as on the king's orders. I do not know if I can survive the trial awaiting me, but at least I can make sure Corbé's actions are not ignored.

"Joa," I say, my voice rasping, and he kneels beside me to see my face. "Today in the pasture, Corbé attacked me."

Joa stiffens. I cannot see Sarkor past him, but I know from the absolute silence in the hall that he is listening.

"He hit me with his staff and knocked me down. I barely got away from him. He wasn't afraid of being caught, or punished. He said—that he had been promised safety. That he could do what he wished."

"Did he?" Joa asks, his voice steel-edged. "And who is his protection?"

I stare at the darkness gathered in the corner of the room. To name the princess, when I have no way to argue my case except through Joa, could endanger me further, for she has all the power right now. "That I can only tell the king," I say. "And there is more I would tell him, if he would meet with me." A whole world more, and he will know what I mean from our first conversation here in the palace, when he offered me a post and a listening ear, should I ever wish to speak of Valka.

"I'll go to Steward Helántor. He'll get me an audience with the king for you," Joa says. "It will be all right."

I nod, knowing what justice is in this land.

CHAPTER
36

C aptain Sarkor unlocks the door late the following morning. I heave myself up clumsily, half numb from the cold of the stones, my body still aching from Corbé's attack.

Sarkor meets my gaze for only a moment, then steps back to hold the door.

"Captain," I say, my voice rasping. I have not had anything to eat or drink since I left the goose pasture. "Do you know if Joa—if he delivered my message to the king?"

A silence spreads between us as Sarkor looks down the hall, then slowly turns his gaze on me. His eyes are dark and steady, and there is a regret in them I did not expect to see. "I believe he did," he says.

"Where are you taking me now?"

"To your hearing."

I dip my head and step out, my stomach heavy as stone. Does the king understand Kestrin's absence for what it is now? Has he found some way to help him? And why wouldn't he respond to my plea—at least grant me a chance to speak with him?

In the hall, Sarkor's quad flanks me and escorts me up to a hearing room. We reach it far too soon. It is a simple space with only a table and three chairs standing at the end, and two rows of benches facing them with an aisle up the middle. In the space between benches and table, to the right, a large fireplace fills the wall.

I walk to the center of the room and curtsy to the judges seated at the table, the stained, threadbare folds of my skirt swishing around me. With a jolt, I recognize Lord Filadon, seated on the right. He watches me somberly, no hint of friendship or even recognition in his eyes.

Beside him sits a man in a sky-blue robe, an emblem embroidered over each breast—overlapping indigo triangles bounded by a circle, the symbol of a Speaker. He is of middle age, with a potbelly and thick, hammy hands that rest on the table.

The man on the left, a captain of some sort, frowns as he studies me. He is of slighter build, with heavy brows, a well-trimmed mustache, and an arrogant mouth. By his hand sit a ceramic pitcher and cup. I have to force myself not to look at them.

"Goose girl Thorn," the captain says.

"Yes, kel."

He looks me over as if he might decide my fate based on the state of my clothes. "Do you know why you've been called before us today?"

I dip my head meekly. Language may be a weapon, but much depends on who has the power in the room. "I would hear the charges, kel, if I may."

He clears his throat. "You have been charged with using ungoverned magical abilities to attack others, converse with dead animals, and bewitch unbroken horses. How do you plead?"

I lick my lips, tasting blood where they have cracked. "Innocent, kel."

"There are witnesses," the captain says mildly. He sits back, resting his elbows on his armrests, as if he has finished with this business already, but his eyes are reasoning eyes.

"May I hear them?"

"We heard them earlier today."

It is all I can do to meet his gaze steadily, fury warring with frustration in my breast. "May I hear what the witnesses told you?"

He ticks them off on his fingers. "First, both a soldier and your fellow goose boy have heard the head of a horse hung at the West Road Gate answer you when you address it."

Nonsense. Corbé was never around when Falada spoke. More than that, Falada's head speaking should point to the Horse's own magical nature, not anything to do with me—but these men know nothing of Horses, and I will not be the one to betray that truth to them. Not when Falada was willing to die to protect it.

"Second, you used an undeclared magical talent to tame and ride that same horse, that would not answer to any man."

"Who is the witness there?" I ask, unable to help myself.

"The goose boy, though I expect that any of the hostlers in the king's stables would answer for it."

"And the third charge?" I ask, properly outraged by now. Never mind that I *had* ridden Falada—Corbé certainly never saw us.

"That you called the wind to attack the goose boy and scatter the flocks."

"Witnessed also by the goose boy?"

"Do you charge him with lying?" he asks, and I know from the very quietness of his question that this will damn me in his eyes.

I tamp down on my anger and answer as mildly as I can. "No, kel. I am sure he reported what he understood as truth."

"Was his understanding flawed?"

"It must be," I say, smiling wanly, "for I am innocent."

"What is your proof?"

I spread my hands before me. "The white horse could be saddled by our hostler from home. The trouble was that he was trained to answer to a single hostler and a single rider. Deprived of that, he had to be won over. I spent weeks with him before he began to forget his training; he allowed me to ride him only once. I used no magic on the horse. Kel Joa himself told me of horses trained this way from the south. In fact, there is another such horse in the stables now."

"A neat explanation," the Speaker says, breaking his silence and any hope I entertained that he might be open to considering my innocence. "Now explain how a dead horse spoke to you."

I shake my head. "Perhaps the sound was that of the wind whistling through the gates, kel. Or my own voice—I spoke to the head as a man might speak to the portrait of his dead father. How could it answer?"

"It answered," the captain says sharply.

"What did it say?"

The men regard me silently. I wonder if they understand that they have become witnesses to my identity—that Falada's words, naming me "princess," should lead them to another truth. But I can see in their faces that it isn't a truth they want to consider. It is much easier for them to dismiss this one aspect of the testimony out of hand than to wonder if there is more to a story they clearly have no interest in. Only Filadon might care, but he watches me quietly, his expression one of faint interest.

The Speaker clears his throat. "These are both lesser charges, kelari. Perhaps, as a foreigner, you do not understand the gravity of the first charge. You attacked a man through magical means— flayed his skin using the wind as a weapon. A mage living in Menaiya *must* be sworn to the king and trained by our Circle before they may practice magic. You have done neither. What's more, an act of magical violence is a grave offense, punishable by death. Will you claim innocence here too?"

"I do not command the wind, kel," I say steadily.

The captain smiles. "The evidence stands against you. A great wind came through your goose pasture, scattering the flock, battering your fellow goose boy, and stripping the leaves from the trees. You yourself escaped unharmed. It is damning evidence." He sits back in his chair, comfortable in his certainty of the truth.

To explain the Wind, to even hint at its source, would be to betray Kestrin and his father even further. I doubt that the royal family could be taken to trial, but I do not doubt that such a revelation would weaken the king's power over his land and shift the balance of power toward the Circle of Mages. They are already jockeying to name an heir and so take over the throne—*expecting* the royal family to die rather than working to protect them. I will not grant them any more power than they already have.

"I have no explanation for you," I tell the men before me.

The Speaker leans forward. "Then you admit to commanding the wind?"

"No. I have no control over the wind."

"Do you admit that it came at your call?"

"It came to the pasture," I say. "I cannot say how, or who sent it." I look to Filadon, who has not yet spoken, and who should know precisely who sent the wind. He only looks back at me in silence.

"But it seems to me," I continue, "that much of this case is a question of Kel Corbé's word against mine. I would beg your patience in learning more."

A satisfied, cat-with-the-cream smile curves the captain's mouth. "Ah, but we have here a letter from Zayyida Alyrra in which she describes her own knowledge of your penchant for lying in the most egregious ways. So, if we are to trust anyone's words, it cannot be yours."

I stiffen, but all the fury in the world will not make this man listen, nor change what Valka has written in her letter.

"I believe you are guilty as charged," he says, his tone almost sorrowful. Almost, but not quite.

"I concur," the Speaker says. He frowns as he looks at me. What sort of Speaker—a person of faith and principle, trained to uphold what is right—condemns a woman for magecraft without even testing her for a talent?

"I do not command the wind," I repeat, my voice deepening with anger.

"How did it come to you, then?"

"I cannot explain it, but I have no talent of my own."

"Oh, certainly."

This is what the shining bastion upon the river stands for, this is who holds in his hands the hope I saw in my young friends' faces: knowledge and schooling and freedom from want. How deeply they have been betrayed, by sovereigns who have no knowledge of what their soldiers stand for and scholars who cannot be bothered to ascertain innocence. I drop my gaze to the table, that the Speaker not see the rage glittering in my eyes.

He glances to his left. "Well, Verin Filadon, we are decided. What is your verdict?"

Filadon studies me, the corners of his mouth tipped down. "I think the lady requires some time to consider her predicament. Perhaps she will find a way to offer us a more convincing explanation. As she says, it is still primarily just one man's word against her own. Let us take our lunch and leave her here to consider her fate. When we return, I will hear her and give my verdict."

What more does he want me to say? He cannot wish me to spill out Kestrin's secrets before his fellow judges.

The captain shakes his head as he pushes back his chair. "I see no value in delaying the inevitable, but it will be as you wish, verayn."

"Indeed." Filadon follows the men, but he walks slowly, and by the time they reach the door, he has only just reached me. He pauses. "Will you not speak the truth, veria?"

He stands a full head taller than me, but his bearing is kind, reminding me of Oak when he used to speak to Violet.

Still, I shake my head. He knows who sent the wind. What could he possibly want me to say to the other judges? He seems no different in this moment than the Speaker who decided my fate before I ever opened my mouth.

He sighs, and his eyes wander from me to the small fire burning in the massive hearth. "Your sentence has not yet been passed. If you will speak the truth, you may escape with a lighter punishment. Or none at all."

"The truth is not mine to share, verayn." Anger makes my words snap through the room.

"Whose is it, then?"

Surely he is not as dull as all that? "You know that as well as I."

He hesitates. "Speak the truth, then, to this room. Perhaps you will find a way to defend yourself without betraying a confidence."

"If you know, then how can you not defend me?" I demand.

"It is not for me to defend," he says. "Only to judge. Find a way to give me something to judge. Warm yourself by the fire, tell your story to the hearthstones, until you know what to tell me."

I nod, caught between fury and despair.

He walks silently to the door.

"Verayn?" I ask abruptly.

"Yes?"

"How is it you keep such a mean-tempered horse?"

The question catches him off guard and he laughs. "Moonflower isn't friendly, is she? If I sell her, I expect her new master would take her on a short trip to the knacker."

"I see."

There is a game afoot here, though I cannot tell its purpose. But a man with that much kindness in him would not condemn me to die for protecting his prince. He wants a story from me. I must decide only what I can give him.

Filadon considers me a moment longer, gestures to the fireplace, and then he is gone. I wait, weighing the quiet, and when I am sure that the guards will not come to collect me, I hurry to the judges' table and pour myself a cup of water. I drink it down in three gulps, then pour myself another one, which I sip more slowly.

My eyes flick to the fireplace. Filadon's advice echoes in my ears. He must know my story, or some part of it, himself. He knows Kestrin is the Wind. Does he not know why Kestrin protected me?

I watch the dancing flames. The other judges will not hear any claims against Corbé, that much is also clear. Death, they had said. What will happen to Valka if I die? If the skin I wear is damaged, will it return to her bruised and raw, or healed? Or not at all?

I approach the fire slowly and kneel before the grate. The weather is warm enough now that the fire built here is only a small one, but I am still cold from my night in the holding cell, and this warmth is a welcome one. But what can I say? I swallow, make myself speak to the flames. "I am no mage, have no minor talent I'm hiding."

The flames do not answer, crackling softly to themselves.

I close my eyes, leaning my face forward into the heat. "Let us consider the charges. Falada's head speaks to me, calling me princess. He, a gift to the princess, allows only me to ride him." I pause, the choker a definite pressure against my throat. Even alone here, I cannot approach closer to the truth than that.

"Second," I continue, "the wind protects me when I am attacked; that same wind that befriended me at home, that found me again in this new land, and that followed me when I fled to the plains yesterday. The wind is not me, nor do I control it," I grind out to the flickering flames. "The wind is Kestrin. Even if he is lost now, I will not betray his secrets to the Circle."

I close my eyes. Perhaps I can convince the judges to have me tested for the talent they claim I have. Filadon *must* agree to that.

Something scrapes against stone, a sound rising up from the fireplace itself. My eyes snap open, but there is only the grate, the logs burning steadily. I stand, my gaze running frantically over the fireplace, the intricate brickwork: there are gaps between the bricks, and over the mantel a stone carving spreads, flowing down either side of the hearth, some portions standing forth, others recessed, exactly, I realize, like the wooden carving behind which I hid and listened to Valka speak of apple cakes.

"No." I step back.

Tell your story to the hearthstones.

I shake my head. "Who listens?" I spin on my heel and scan the room before coming back to the fireplace. "*Who listens?*"

The door swings open and the king strides into the room.

I stare at him, unmoving.

He comes to a stop a pace away and studies me, his face emotionless. In the darkness of his eyes I can see him sifting through the ramifications of what I told the fire.

"Finish your story."

Behind him, Filadon steps into the room, shutting the door with a click.

"Tarin," I say, striving to find my balance. *Your Majesty.* Like the judges, he has addressed me in Menay.

"What happened on the plains?" he demands.

I swallow, studying him. But he has every right to know what happened to his son. "The prince came to find me, riding Verin Filadon's horse. As he came, so did your enemy."

"Who is that?"

"She is—not human. I told you of her once before, in Adania. She wears always a long dress and a gemstone on her finger. She comes from a fall of moonlight, or flowing water, or in the form of a snow-white owl." Or a breath of dust in the air.

His features tighten. "And in this meeting yesterday, what happened?"

"She offered him a choice, tarin. My life or his."

The king makes no motion. I concentrate on my breathing, meeting his gaze, knowing that I cannot show doubt or fear now.

He turns to Filadon abruptly. "Ride out with Sarkor and the royal quads. See if Midael the Cormorant will accompany you. Comb the plains west of here. Find Kestrin's trail and follow it."

"Tarin," Filadon says, bowing. He leaves at once.

The king looks back at me. "For your sake, let us hope you are not lying, veria. Else the fate you will suffer will be much worse than a hanging."

I dip my head.

As he turns his back and departs, my hands begin to tremble.

It takes most of my concentration to keep them still. I am alone for the space of a few breaths, and then the guards push open the door.

"Veria," one of them calls. "You'll come with us."

I wonder what the king ordered, where I will be taken. He must have spoken to them or they would not have called me "lady."

They escort me to a small guest room, lock the door behind me, and remain on guard in the hallway. I pull the curtains back from the window. The view is of the palace wall, and, three stories below, the road that runs between. I pull one of the chairs to the window and sit, grateful for the thin rectangle of sunlight that falls on the floor, lighting the room.

Looking out, I think of Kestrin, willing to give himself over to the Lady for me. *Why?* Was it guilt? Or did he truly care for me?

I cannot count all the times I have spoken to the Wind, shared my secrets and taken comfort from its presence. All that time it was Kestrin. It hardly seems possible. And yet it is true, and it is how the Lady finally won her game. I *was* her pawn, and Kestrin is lost, and now the king will decide my fate, knowing I brought about his son's downfall.

I drop my face into my hands. I can only try, I tell myself. And if I fail, at least Falada will be there to greet me in the end.

CHAPTER
37

"I'm to ready you for dinner."

I look up in surprise to find a serving girl regarding me coolly from the doorway. She strides to the bed and drops a bundle of clothing on the covers, then looks to me. I cross to the bed and tug open the bundle. The skirt and tunic she has brought are well made though simple—something a high-placed servant might wear. That will be the king's decision, then.

"Very well," I say, my voice strangely calm to my ears.

The girl helps me dress, hustling me out of my work clothes. She startles when she sees the dark purple bruises on my leg and side from Corbé's staff, but she is well-trained enough not to speak. Still, I am glad to hide myself from her eyes again. The clothes are clean and crisp, and in them I can hold my head high and my chin firm, and act as though the king believes my story, that the clothes he sent befit a princess and not a maid. That there will not be a price much worse than a hanging to pay.

The girl gestures for me to sit and sets to work on my hair. Her hands are firm and impersonal as she pulls the brush through the knots and tangles. A small pile of straw and grass bits grows on the table beside us. By the time she can run the brush through my hair smoothly, the shadows are deepening outside. She winds my hair into a bun at the back of my neck and hurriedly departs, murmuring apologies to the guards outside my door.

I return to my seat and wiggle my feet out of my new slippers. They pinch my toes, but I doubt it will matter. I won't be wearing them more than a day or two. At least if I am to die, I won't look a complete disgrace. Mother would be pleased.

My guards escort me to dinner barely a quarter of an hour later. The dining room is elegant, decorated with fine mosaics and lit by luminae stones set in wall sconces, as well as an elaborate chandelier suspended above the central table. The guests are already seated; they turn to watch me as a page ushers me to my seat at the end of the table. At my right sits Filadon, his wife across from him, and across from me a lord I do not know. The foot of the table has no place setting, for which I am grateful. When I glance up to the top of the table, I meet first the king's eyes, and then Valka's. Her face is pale, her lips pressed together in ill-concealed fury. Across from her, I can just make out Verin Garrin, leaning forward to speak to her. She turns toward him and a smile flashes across her face as she replies.

Filadon greets me quietly. I cannot tell from his voice, from the faint smile and nod, whether he found anything in his search of the plains. I dare not ask him here. He keeps up an animated conversation with the nobles seated on his other side through most of the meal, while his wife engages the man across from me.

She is young, with a quiet smile and pleasant demeanor. Between them, I am left to enjoy my meal in silence.

My morning's hunger and thirst have long been allayed by the trays of food that were sent up from the kitchens to my room. Now I find I have no appetite for the delicacies before me. I take little and eat even less, instead listening as best I can to the snatches of conversation I catch from farther up the table. But the guests are strangely silent about Kestrin's absence. Perhaps they are versed in the sudden deaths of their royalty. Perhaps they know better than to ask. I don't think the king has admitted the truth yet—and if he had been successful in reaching Kestrin, I wouldn't be here now, not like this.

I look back to my plate. I've done this all wrong, waited too long thinking I had until the wedding to act. Now Kestrin is gone, and the king sits at dinner as if nothing were to be done about him, and Valka is still princess. I cannot swallow another bite.

As the last course is cleared, the king turns to Valka. "I have an interesting question for you, my dear. Would you mind my asking it?" He speaks in our language, but at his nod, the interpreter standing at Valka's elbow translates his question to Menay, capturing the full attention of the table.

Valka smiles. "Of course not, Your Majesty."

"There is a story that accompanies it, and the story is simply this: a princess and her companion were traveling one day on their way to some unknown land. During the journey, the companion displeased her mistress; furthermore, upon their arrival in that land she went to great lengths to turn all who were there against her lady. She brought false charges against the princess, and sought to undermine her authority. She even claimed to be the princess herself. My question is this: What punishment would such a woman deserve?"

He leans back in his chair, smiling amiably at Valka. I realize that I am shaking.

Valka glances down the table to me as the translator speaks, and in that look I see a terrible fate. Then she turns and meets the king's gaze. She answers him slowly, savoring each word. "Such a woman deserves no more than to be placed in a barrel that has been pounded through with nails and be dragged behind a brace of horses until she is dead."

The horror of it takes a moment to sink in. "No," I whisper.

Filadon turns toward me, but the rest do not hear me, focused on the translator. I watch the king, willing him to refuse this sentence. My brother's words echo through me, foretelling the death Kestrin would mete out to me. The cruelty and power of the family I would marry into.

"That is the punishment you decree?" the king asks, as if she might rethink it.

"Yes," Valka says firmly.

"Very well. You have chosen your own death. Take her away."

At the king's words, a pair of guards step forward from the back of the room. As alarm spreads across Valka's features, a sickening relief floods through me, leaving me light-headed. *Her*—Valka. It is Valka who will die, not me.

The guards grasp her arms and raise her from her seat. "Your Majesty!" she cries. "What can you mean by this? I am Princess Alyrra!"

"On the contrary, lady, you are not."

"I am! That girl is nothing, a servant—a filthy, wretched liar—"

The guards drag her from the room, still screaming protests, leaving behind a stunned silence. The king, at its center, seems utterly unconcerned.

It is Melkior who speaks next, looking down the long table at me with an expression of dawning realization. "Tarin, if that was the impostor, who is the true princess?"

The king nods once, meeting my gaze. "Veria Thoreena."

Every person at the table turns to stare at me.

If I look at them, I will lose what little composure I have. Instead, I hold the king's gaze and say, "Tarin, the sentence that was chosen is far too brutal a death. I would ask that you ease it."

Even as I speak my plea, I remember the king's words to me this morning, the words that have haunted me all evening: *the fate you will suffer will be much worse than a hanging.*

"The sentence chosen was for you. It is only just to visit it upon the traitor herself."

"Tarin," I say, but I cannot find the words to make my argument.

He shakes his head. This is Valka's payment for betraying Kestrin. "Let it be, veriana."

One of the ladies seated at the table leans forward. "But how could this happen? How was it not found out?"

The king has not yet looked away from me. Now, instead of answering the lady, he says, "Verin Filadon, Zayyida Alyrra has been through much today. Will you help her back to her rooms?" He stands as he speaks, forcing all those present to rise as well.

Filadon's hand comes under my elbow, urging me up. "Come," he murmurs.

I let him lead me out, aware that no one makes any move to follow us.

In the hallway, I pause, bewildered. My quad is gone. And Valka will die a terrible death. And no one has spoken of Kestrin—not one word. "I don't remember the way," I say.

"It's all right," Filadon says. "The king wants you closer to the royal wing. I will take you there."

I walk with him silently, gathering my thoughts. As we reach a stairwell, I glance back. "The rest have not left."

Filadon's voice is utterly neutral as he says, "The king will have to answer a few questions. He deemed it best that you not be there."

The words rub against me like flint against steel. "Why?"

"I believe he does not want them to question you until he has spoken with you."

"There are too many secrets to keep," I say wearily.

"There are, zayyida."

I wince, the title jarring against my ears. I want to tell him to call me Thorn. Instead I ask, "Verayn, did you find any sign of the prince?"

Filadon's face stills. "We found his tracks easily enough, and yours leading back. The prince's end where they meet yours."

"Yes." I swallow. "I know you have the family's trust. If you know—if you are that closely in their confidence—then you will know how Kestrin can be helped."

"There is nothing to be done," Filadon says, his expression bleak. "She will never let him go. He went of his own volition; he cannot fight her now."

400

My stomach gives a lurch. He cannot die. Not like this. Not for *me*. "But surely there must be some way," I plead. "Have you not spoken with the mages—or—" I shake my head, at a loss. They cannot just give up like this, not when they have so much power, so much they *can* do.

Filadon stops before a door, releasing my hand to open it. "She has taken the whole family, one by one. If there were a way, we would have found it. I am sorry, zayyida."

I shake my head again and step into the room, and still I can hear Kestrin giving his life away, the quiet resignation in his voice as he said, "Very well." He knew in that moment, better than I understood, that there would be no returning. All these last months came down to a single truth: I would be the tool for his betrayal one way or the other. And he accepted it.

CHAPTER
38

I lie awake in the great bed, listening to the silence that hangs in the suite of rooms. I miss the sounds of horses shifting and snorting nearby, of Sage's occasional snore and Violet's sweet laughter. They are lost to me now. Violet is gone, and though I might visit the stables again, I will never again be the goose girl, able to share an evening in the common room or listen to Sage drift to sleep beside me. No, I am princess now.

So, inevitably, my thoughts turn to Kestrin, who visited me in the guise of the Wind since we were both young. Kestrin, who promised me a protection I did not believe he could provide, if only I would return to the court; who came to my aid in the goose pasture, knowing as he must have that the Lady would take his help as a sign of his concern for me and use it against him.

She knew all along. She was only waiting for him to recognize the cost of his friendship. And, as with Falada, he had chosen death rather than betrayal.

But this time there is something I can do.

I stand up and go to the window, throwing open the shutters. Moonlight streams down. I close my eyes, breathe in its cool wash, the night breeze. "Lady," I call. "Lady."

I wait, listening to the faint sounds of the palace, voices drifting to me from far away. Nothing else stirs.

I step back from the window, wondering if I am wrong. The moonlight flows steady and true, unmoving. Surely she is still watching, waiting. "*Lady*," I call with all my strength and heart and mind. "*I would speak with you.*"

In the stream of pale rays, something flickers and strengthens.

"Lady," I whisper.

She looks as I remember her from that first night, her face white as bone, her dress shining as if it were itself woven of light.

"What have you done with Kestrin?" I ask.

She holds her hand out to me in silence, palm upturned.

I study her features. In the corners of her mouth, the tilt of her face, there is a deep and dreadful weariness. I take her hand.

The moonlight flashes once, bright and yet painless, and then we stand together on a gravel walk of a darkened garden.

"Where are we?"

"My gardens." Here, the Lady wears clothes as any mortal might, a simple white gown with white-embroidered bodice and flowing sleeves. Her dark hair has been braided back tightly.

"And the prince?"

"He is here. Come, I will show you."

I follow her down the walk into a small square. At the center stands a statue of a man, the stone shining a bright white. "This is the first of my collection," she tells me.

The man must have once been quite powerful, but by the time the likeness was made, his massive shoulders had slumped in defeat and his once-strong features wasted into a haggard, desperate mask. He wears the traditional Menaiyan armor of metal and leather, and at his side hangs a sword in its scabbard.

"He was your prince's great-grandsire. What do you think?"

I study the face and my breath catches in my throat: every detail stands out exactly, each eyelash casting its own soft shadow. "This—this was truly him?"

"Of course. Do you think I would put up a statue of such a man? No, it is he, exactly as he came to me. Do you not like him? I think he cuts a fine figure."

"You've turned him to stone," I say stupidly, staring at the frozen features. "Why?"

"Come along, princess. There is more for you to see." The Lady starts forward once more, toward the next gate.

I stay where I am. "How could you do such a thing to someone—to anyone?"

She turns back to me, her eyes glittering with anger. "Do you truly wish to know?"

"Yes."

"Then I will show you." The Lady reaches up and catches my face in her hands, and the world drops away.

A band of soldiers drag a prisoner through the brush to the clearing where a mounted rider waits just before me. They throw the prisoner down and step back, eyes on their leader.

"Well done." The rider swings down from his horse, his

leather and iron armor glinting in the sunlight, and kicks the prone figure onto her back.

A woman, I realize, staring in shock. She is Fae, her eyes bright and dangerous, but bound around her throat is a choker set with a black stone, and though I've never seen one like it before, I know what it is: an amulet that steals her magic from her, making her no different than a human woman as she faces these soldiers.

A child begins to shriek somewhere behind me, but I cannot turn my head to see who it is.

The rider pulls off his helmet, tossing it to one of the soldiers. His features leap out at me—the high brow, the cheekbones, the warm brown skin. He grasps the captive's clothes in one gauntleted fist, dragging her up.

The child's wails turn to a high keening.

The woman's face is battered and scratched, but as she looks up at her captor her features twist and she spits.

The rider laughs, a hearty, booming sound that fills the clearing, and then he drags the woman to a tree, shoving her up against it.

I look around frantically, but the soldiers all watch with lazy amusement. I cannot find my voice to scream for help.

With a sickening *thunk*, the rider thrusts his dagger through the prisoner's palm, pinning her hand above her head. She cries out, a hoarse sound, and then with a gasp she snaps her jaw shut. Tears spill from her eyes and trickle down her cheeks. She looks toward me and smiles an empty reassurance.

I am screaming silently, mindlessly, unable to look away as the rider impales her right hand beside her left. He steps back, considering his handiwork. Then, with the same genial laugh, he draws his sword and slits her belly open.

If I could move, if I could breathe, I would be sick with horror. But the child whose eyes I look through remains watching through her sobs, and so I cannot even turn away.

The rider sheathes his sword and returns to his horse. Mounted, he watches the writhing agony of the woman until her hands tear themselves free of the daggers and she collapses on the ground. She twitches a few times, her body shuddering, the tattered remnants of her hands pressed against the gaping wound of her belly. Then she lies still in a spreading pool of blood.

The man turns his horse toward me. I can hear the clump of the horse's hooves in the rich earth, can hear it through the gasping keen of the child. He looks down at me, his lips curling back in contempt. His booted foot lifts from the stirrup and snaps out, slamming into the child's face and sending me reeling back. The child's weeping abruptly stops.

"The prisoner was my mother," the Lady says, dropping her hands from my face.

I shiver uncontrollably, my teeth chattering as my stomach roils.

"I woke up alone with her body—they left me to tell my people what had become of her. She was one of our leaders, a great general, but she was betrayed. They caught me, you see, and used me as bait to catch her."

I close my eyes, shaking my head. As if I might deny this, might rattle these images free. Over and over I see the daggers impaling the calloused palms, the shine of the sword slicing through the woman's stomach.

"I swore I would kill him, destroy his line, for what he did."

"He was...," I say hoarsely, and a deep shudder runs through me. Dark hair, eyes the rich brown of earth ...

"Your Kestrin's great-grandsire. Now do you understand?"

The Lady does not wait for my answer but walks to a wrought iron gate set between two high hedges. I stumble after her, the garden a nightmare of moonlight and shadow around us. "Lady," I call, trying to regain my footing. My focus.

"Little princess."

"That was—not the prince. Why do you punish him for his ancestor's cruelty?"

"I swore to end his line."

"But if Kestrin himself has never harmed anyone, then to kill him for something he has no control over—"

"It is in his blood."

"But, Lady," I say, unable to find an argument she will hear. I know she is wrong—she *must* be wrong.

"Enough. Here, then, is your prince."

The garden shifts, whirling soundlessly to resettle in a different pattern. I find myself in another square surrounded by high hedges, but at the center, the stone figure does not stand. Instead, he kneels, leaning back on his feet to look ahead. One hand is curled into a tight fist pressed against his leg, the other reaches out in front of him, curving around the air as if resting on it.

The sight of him sends ice through my veins. I cannot bear to look at his face. Instead, I turn to the Lady. "He is dead."

"No," she says. "I have banished him deep within himself. It will take a few more days for his soul to tear itself away. But you cannot help him now; you have not the power."

"And will you kill the king? And Garrin as well?"

"They are the last," she says, her voice bereft of emotion, and I think suddenly of my brother in his worst moments, when he was nothing but calculated violence, every other feeling gone from him.

I raise my chin, so cold it is a wonder my bones don't shatter, and look the Lady in the eye. "Then you are just like him. You are just like the monster who killed your mother."

She stiffens. "You do not know of what you speak."

"I do—you showed him to me, and I've seen you as well. You take as much pleasure in their deaths as he did in your mother's."

She takes a step toward me.

"You are willing to kill innocents to have your way," I continue. "You allowed Falada to be killed. You would have killed me through Valka. And now she will die because of the games you played. For what? So you can avenge yourself against the man you already destroyed years ago?"

"You go too far, princess."

"No, Lady. You do. You kill people who have never wronged you, destroying them as ruthlessly as your mother was killed. You've had your revenge on the man who did it and now you've become him."

"You do not know of what you speak," she repeats, and I can see the shimmer of power in the air around her.

"Then show me otherwise, Lady."

For a moment that lasts a small eternity, she stares at me,

expressionless. And then she laughs, the sound a rippling of water over stones, her anger transforming to scorn. "What would you have me do, girl? Free him?"

"Give him the chance to win his freedom and your forgiveness."

"I think not. You have certainly learned to speak since we first met, but you are still naive. You have seen what is in his blood. If you do not understand, it is not my concern to teach you."

But I *have* seen Kestrin—both his fury, carefully restrained, and his unexpected kindnesses.

"Test him," I suggest, half wildly. There must be *some* way to convince her. "If what you believe is true, he will succumb to his blood. But if he passes, then he must be innocent of the taint."

"Test him?" the Lady echoes, her voice the ringing of steel on stone.

I swallow hard, gazing back into her deathless eyes.

"Fair enough," she says. "There will be three tests. If he passes them, he is free."

"And if he fails?"

"Then he remains mine, and you will be dead by his hands."

I do not let myself falter. "Very well."

CHAPTER 39

The earth opens wide its maw and swallows me, sharp teeth piercing the air as I fall into darkness. I stifle a scream, stumble back blindly as reality shifts around me. My shoulder slams against something hard—and dry. Wherever I am, it is dry as dust. I take a shaky breath and lean against the surface beside me, waiting for my balance to return and my eyes to adjust to the darkness.

Slowly I begin to take in my surroundings. All around me, stone teeth hover, glistening in the dark. Unmoving. With a rush of relief I realize that the "teeth" are those of a cave roof, hanging down around me. Smaller stalagmites rise up from the ground to meet them. My relief bursts from me in a single soft huff of laughter.

"Who's there?" a voice calls, the words loud and jarring.

I look up to see Kestrin standing at one end of the cave,

his figure just visible between the hanging teeth, a fall of light behind him. It must be daylight wherever we are.

"Who's there?" he repeats. "I have found no living thing in this land till now, but I heard you move. Show yourself." His voice echoes in the cave and raises goose bumps on my arms. He shifts, and in that movement, I see a fear I am all too familiar with.

I take a step toward him, my clothes rustling in the quiet. Surprised, I glance down, for I wore a night shift when I spoke to the Lady. Now I wear a white dress.

Kestrin recognizes it even as I do. "Sorceress," he says, his voice harsh with emotion. "I'll not be taunted by you here." He raises his hand, his mouth moving.

I throw myself to the side as his fingers flick toward me. The sickening memory of how hopelessly I tried to avoid Corbé's staff flashes through my mind. The power of Kestrin's spell only brushes me, but it is enough to slam me against the wall. The cave teeth crash down. They splinter into pieces on impact, raising a small cloud of dust. I take two breaths, my arm over my mouth to guard against the dust, then put my hand up and pull a strand of hair free of my braid: it is darker than night, the same ebony hue as the Lady's.

"Are you still here?" he calls, stepping farther in to scan the cave.

If I stay still, it is possible he will not find me. But then I will have failed—for the test is not if I can escape from him, but if he can control the taint the Lady claims runs in his blood. It is he who will have to let me go, regardless of who I appear to be to him.

I stand up in one fluid motion. "Kestrin."

He spins toward me.

"Hold your spells."

"Why? Because I cannot touch you with them? I know that." His eyes burn in the faint light.

"No, it is because you can. I have no magic here."

He laughs, a low, feral sound. "Don't you? In this place of your making? What a fool you must think me."

"I am as much a prisoner here as you. The difference is only that you still have your powers."

He walks toward me until he is only a pace away. Even in the dark, I can see the haggard set of his features, the dark stubble on his cheeks. "If you cannot use magic, then how will you defend yourself from this?"

His hand darts out and grasps my wrist.

Pain runs up my arm like wildfire, scorching my veins. I cry out, staggering back against the wall as I rip my hand from his grip.

He stands perfectly still.

I bring my hand to my chest. The edges of my vision are bleached white, but I cannot afford to give in to the pain now. Instead, I straighten and meet his gaze, holding out my hand to him. My wrist is blackened where he held it, bits of skin flaking off like ash.

"I have no defense here."

"What game do you play?" he asks, and I do not trust the very softness of his voice. He does not believe me because the Lady would not speak to him so.

"Look at it, princeling. Had I any power, do you think you could have touched me? This is no game."

"Then how did you come here, to this wasteland? Why would you come unarmed? You knew I would kill you for what you did to my mother."

I dare not even swallow. I must become the Lady now to win against Kestrin, become her even as I persuade him not to kill me. She would never fear him. I force a laugh. "We were never good at answering each other's questions, prince. As for your threat, you are not *quite* a murderer." I smile. "Yet."

"Yet," he agrees, and with one quick step he is before me, his hand reaching for my neck.

Without thinking, I catch his hand with my good one. When he freezes, I bring it down slowly, turning it palm up.

"Well done, Kestrin. Kill me and you will become me. You are a quick learner."

He pulls his hand away.

I think of the Lady and the vision she shared with me. "My mother was murdered too."

His head jerks to the side as if I had slapped him.

"Did you not think I had a mother? It was a man with your face who killed her. I thought to avenge her death when I killed him. I sought vengeance when I took your grandfather, and when I forced you to come to me. Hatred grows, Kestrin."

"My hatred will die with you."

"But it won't. If you find a way back, you will kill Valka, the impostor princess."

"It will end there," he says roughly, but he is listening now, despite himself, his hands clenched at his sides.

"It won't. You will kill Alyrra as well."

"No," he says, but I hear a slight tremor in his voice.

413

"Yes," I say, feeling the truth of it like a weight in my belly. "Doesn't she know your greatest weakness? Hasn't she betrayed you twice already? Having killed two, it is easy enough to kill a third, especially when there are no consequences."

He backs away from me.

"Murder makes one cold." I do not see him anymore; instead I see the Lady's face when she came to my room, weary and empty. "It takes away your soul, piece by piece. It turns your heart to stone. Is that what you want?"

"I would not kill her," he says, his voice that of a young boy.

"But you would, Kestrin," I say gently.

"It was I who betrayed her into your hands, not the other way around."

"Can you be sure? Didn't she know who I was by then, what would happen to you?"

He shakes his head, a sort of helpless desperation in his eyes.

"Once you start killing, Kestrin, everyone becomes your enemy."

"What do you want from me?" he cries.

My eyes wander to the shattered rock on the cave floor. I am still lost in my role, embodying the Lady. "Perhaps I want you to kill me. That would be a victory of sorts, because it would be an end."

"You will get nothing from me," he whispers.

A smile touches my lips. "That is a good sort of revenge in its own way, Kestrin. At least no one will die for it."

"May you rot in hell, sorceress." He leaves me, striding away. But as he turns out of the cave he begins to run, his boots thudding against the ground as he flees.

I sag back against the wall, trembling. The earth reaches up and pulls me to its breast, sending sparks of pain shooting through my vision.

"You are more talented than I would have credited," the Lady says as the garden flows into existence around us.

I catch my balance and squint at her through the bright light, then look down at my hand. My shift is gray with dust, as is my arm, but for the charred ring where Kestrin held me. The pain of it is a constant buzz, the burrowing of white-hot needles into my flesh. I look up quickly, fighting a wave of dizziness. "You turned me to stone."

"Had he killed you, your body would have remained stone. As it is, you have only lost a dusting of yourself."

"Then how—how has my wrist been burned?" I ask.

"The wounds of the spirit are borne out upon the body," she says, as if stating the obvious. She turns from me. "Come. I will allow you a rest before the second test."

I follow the Lady up the path to the wrought iron gate, each step sending pain jolting through my wrist. When she swings it open for me, I enter not another garden, but a large apartment.

"You will find all you need here," she tells me, and closes the door, leaving me alone with my fears and the ring of charred skin about my wrist.

CHAPTER
40

C ome morning, I follow the Lady wordlessly back to the square where the statue of Kestrin waits. The pain of my wrist jars through me with every step. Last night, I cooled the burning for a time by applying a cream from a small pot I found on the table beside the bed. But the relief was temporary, and the pain burrowed into me through the night, a live thing eating at me. Now I try not to look at the charred skin or my flesh showing red and raw beneath the burns. I lower myself to the ground before Kestrin so that I will be sitting when I return from the next test. If I return.

"Tell me," the Lady says. "How did you speak of murder when you know nothing of it?"

"I know something. I know that the men who killed Violet had no concern for her and feared no punishment. They would have done it again." I trace the Lady's delicate features with my eyes, following the fine cheekbones, the line of her jaw, the empty eyes. "I tried to become you, Lady—or what I thought it must be like to be you—because Kestrin had to believe I was you."

The Lady gestures toward me, the gemstone on her finger flashing. "The second test, then."

The light shimmers and spins around me, taking away the garden and setting me down in a strange, rocky valley cut into high cliff walls. As far as I can see, the valley continues in both directions, the cliffs riddled with caves carved out by wind and rockfalls. Here, in the belly of the valley, rock formations rise up, uneven and rippled, as if formed by the currents of an ancient river long dried up.

I stand and begin walking, knowing that I will meet Kestrin. A shadow flickers at the edge of my vision. I pivot, but see only a pillar-like rock that stands like a giant sentinel some distance away. I hesitate, watching.

Kestrin will not hide from me, nor will he attack me on sight again. The Lady will have set a different kind of test this time. But what is the test? Nothing moves in the valley. Perhaps the shadow was just my imagination. I start forward again. Kestrin himself said that nothing lives in this land.

I hear a faint sound behind me and whirl around. A beast streaks toward me, its mouth open to reveal wickedly sharp teeth, its head large and flat, legs hardly more than a blur. For one surreal moment I watch it coming and then I flee, sprinting through the maze of rocks. Its roar echoes through the valley, bouncing off the cliffs as it chases me. Desperately, I scan the valley, the cliffs—surely there must be a way out?

My side cramps with pain as I weave between rocks. I can hear the creature behind me, closing the distance. I cannot outrun it. But perhaps I can trick it, hide from it somehow. I follow the turn of a larger rock formation, double back, then race toward a great slab of boulder rising at an angle from the earth. I scrabble up, throw myself down flat against its top, and hope against hope.

The beast passes below me, hurtling around the boulder to follow my path. Does it hunt by sight or smell? Can it tell it has lost my trail? I push myself to my knees, my breath sobbing in my lungs, and scan the land below for the beast. I do not see it.

I sit back, raising my gaze, and see Kestrin instead.

He stands at the mouth of a cave, and as I look at him, his eyes meet mine. Of course. He must have witnessed the whole chase, seen the creature come after me. Watched.

"Kestrin," I whisper, staring at him.

Something scrapes against stone behind me. I know with a knowing that turns me cold, but I look anyway to see the beast hurl itself up the boulder, its claws cutting into the stone. And then it is upon me. I duck to the side and throw my hands out to shove it away. Its teeth snap shut by my ear, and I smell its breath, the stench of rot and death. My fingers close on its shaggy coat and I push, trying to overbalance it and send it off the end of the boulder. But its claws dig into the soft stone and it twists to lunge for me again. My hands find its neck, and I am able to keep its teeth from me, but now it is above me and it claws my arm, snarling.

Desperately, I twist away and fall, bouncing off the boulder to land on the ground. Above me, the beast roars again. I push myself forward, my hands searching for something—anything. My fingers close around a rock, and I turn as the beast leaps down.

It snarls again, facing me, and I know this time I cannot escape. I hold the rock tightly, as if it might protect me, but it is round and dull, composed of a soft, crumbling stone. The creature leaps forward, an impossibly long jump, so that even as I stumble back, its paws slam into my chest, claws piercing my flesh. I fall backward, flailing at the creature with my rock, my hand.

Something hisses. The beast is ripped off me, thrown back against the boulder. It roars, struggling to its feet, eyes still intent on me. Again, I hear a faint hiss, and watch as the beast is lifted and tossed back, its legs pinwheeling through the air. This time when it rises, it flees.

I let out my breath in a soft, whimpering sigh, and lie still, hoping that the world will fade around me, that the Lady will take me back. I think perhaps she does, for the light has become too bright, and I am cold.

"Get up," a voice says from behind me.

I squeeze my eyes shut but I know he will not leave.

"Get up, sorceress."

I push myself up with my good arm, only it is no longer quite good. There is blood on it, and when I look down at my chest, I see splotches of red through the cloth, the stain spreading as I watch. Pain washes through me with each breath. But Kestrin is behind me, waiting, so I stagger to my feet and turn to face him.

His eyes widen slightly, and his jaw snaps shut on the words he meant to speak. After a breath, he turns and starts back toward his cave.

"Kestrin," I say, knowing now that I cannot let him go. There is too much blood. "Don't leave me."

He stops.

I take a step toward him, then another. With each movement, I struggle to remain above the swirling tide of pain pulsing through me.

"I should have let it kill you," he says. He turns as I reach him, his eyes flat, pitiless.

"Why didn't you?"

"Why didn't you scream?" he counters. "You knew I was there."

"I needed my breath." It is hard for me to keep my chin up, but when I let it sag I see the red on my dress.

"Now you have it." He begins to walk again, his pace too fast for me to match.

A dry breeze whispers through the canyon. I feel myself swaying with it, the rush of pain through my body. "Kestrin."

He swings around to glare at me. "You brought this on yourself, sorceress. You made this wasteland. Do not ask me for pity now."

"No, Kestrin," I say. "I did not make this place. It is of your own making."

"I would never dream such a place."

"It is your heart."

My legs feel like stone. When I try to step toward him, I find they are too heavy to lift. I fall, but the fall is long and sweet, and I hardly feel the ground come up to meet me.

I wake to twilight, a steady burning in my arm and wrist, and a pain that slumbers in my chest. I stare at the stone roof overhead, my breathing shallow. I cannot quite seem to remember things rightly. Who am I just now? Thorn or Alyrra? I turn my head to the side, my thoughts muddled, to see Kestrin.

He sits watching me, his back against the opposite cave wall. I cannot read his expression.

"You really don't have your magic here, do you?" he says into the quiet. "I thought perhaps you were playing a game—forcing me to do things, making me hate you or hate myself all the more for not being able to kill you. But these past hours you have lain here defenseless as a child. You would have bled to death out there if that beast did not return to finish you first."

"Yes," I agree, remembering. I twitch one hand toward my chest, think better of it as pain flares through my arm. Kestrin has bandaged it with strips of cloth. More cloth wraps over the wounds in my chest.

"That is all you can say? 'Yes'? You have no explanation?"

I sigh, my eyes resting on his dark form. "Why did you bring me here and close my wounds? Why not let me die outside?"

"I had no choice," he snarls.

"Neither did I."

He leaps to his feet, glaring down at me. "You speak in riddles. Do not toy with me."

The Lady. I must speak as if I were her. "Riddles are all I have left, prince. I can give you nothing more."

"Give me my freedom," he says tightly.

I wonder how much those words cost him, his pride. "You know I cannot."

He walks to the mouth of the cave and looks out. "What did you do to Alyrra?"

I stare at his back.

He turns to glare at me. "What did you do to her?"

"Nothing. I left her there."

"Then the impostor you put in her place is still in the palace."

"Alyrra has her position once more. Your father learned the truth of her identity. The impostor will be executed."

"So she at least is free."

"Free?" I echo. I would laugh but for the pain that sears my chest with each breath.

Kestrin's hand goes to the curved dagger at his belt, but he says nothing in response.

"There are different types of freedom. She will blame herself for losing you. She was afraid to help you, to take back her position, until it was too late. She will always carry that with her."

"It is not a heavy burden," he says. "She hardly knew me. She will forget in time."

How is it possible that even now, when his life is all but lost, Kestrin is thinking of me? But I know how, for he is my Wind, and all these weeks and months he has only been trying to find and protect me, however flawed his effort. How deeply I have misjudged him. I will never forget him, but if that is what he needs to believe, I can at least grant him that. As much as the Lady would. "Perhaps."

"You say this land is of my making—that it is my *heart*."

She banished him to the deepest part of himself. What is that but his heart? "Yes."

"Then to escape, I must break out of myself."

I watch him mutely.

He crosses the ground to kneel beside me. "Tell me how to escape."

Pressing my palms into the ground, I push myself up until I am sitting with my back against the cave wall.

"Tell me," he repeats.

"I cannot tell you what I do not know."

"You know. You have come and gone easily enough." His hand tightens on the hilt of his dagger.

"I can't explain." I need to get away before he breaks. Each sentence brings him closer to violence and I do not know how to stop him when I must be the Lady as well.

"Try," he says tersely.

"I cannot."

"Enough." He slides the dagger free of its sheath, moving so fast I have only enough time to jerk back before the cold blade presses hard against my skin. "You killed my mother, you've slain my family for generations, and now you are killing me. Do you think I can't see for myself what will happen to me in this waste-land?"

"That is your choice," I whisper.

"I have no choice!"

"There is always a choice." It was Falada who taught me that.

The blade slides against my skin, and I feel a faint tingle where the skin parts beneath its pressure. "I will kill you for what you've done."

"All I've done is offer you a choice, Kestrin. It was your choice to trade your life for Alyrra's. Just as what you do now will be your choice as well."

His hand closes on the front of my dress, scraping against the wounds there. He hauls me to my feet and pins my back to the wall as I struggle to breathe again. "Indeed. Here's a choice for you then, sorceress. Admit you are a murderess."

"Is this your justice?" I catch hold of his wrist with my hands, but I have not the strength to force the blade away.

He draws his lips back from his teeth and brings the butt of the dagger down, slamming the metal hilt into my chest.

Somewhere behind me, a child cries out, keening softly, but it is not me—my teeth are clenched against the pain. My legs give out beneath me and darkness eats at the edges of my vision, but I cannot fall because he holds me up, holds me tight against the wall, with nowhere to run.

"Admit you are a murderess and I'll give you an easy death."

The words float down around me like the first downy snow-flakes of winter. I stare at the dark, stained cloth of Kestrin's tunic and the keening of the child teases the edge of my hearing. Two men hang from a gibbet, turning in slow circles, ropes creaking. The woman tears her hands free of the daggers and presses their ragged remains against the pain in her belly, the emptiness. Valka smirks as the soldiers catch hold of the serving girl and search her for a brooch she never stole.

Kestrin's hand finds my braid and jerks my head back, forcing me to meet his gaze. "Say it."

"If you will say it with me." The words are thick and slow on my tongue, but they are not what Kestrin expects.

His hand tightens on my braid and yanks my head back further, making white pain streak across my vision. "Damn you."

His grip on the dagger shifts. As it cuts into the skin of my neck, I inhale sharply and he jerks it away, pausing. His rage shimmers in the air around him, but he will not kill me by magic.

The death he will give me will be that of cold iron, a slow and brutal death. The dagger he holds is dark with blood now, dripping as it did when it pinned the Lady's mother to the tree. Dark as my mother's blood . . . three scarlet drops on a white kerchief. *This alliance hinges on you.*

I raise my eyes from the dark blade to his face. *I am the Lady who has lost her soul.* I straighten my back and let the pain run through me as a tide does, flowing and ebbing. *I am the princess who has lost her self. I am the goose girl who has lost her way.* I meet his gaze, holding the darkness there with all I have within me. *I am the child who can scream no more.*

In this moment I stand for all I am, and have been, and have known, every whisper of pain and memory of fear. I am all this, and I will stand strong and fight.

"Put away the dagger, Kestrin."

He braces his feet, as if expecting me to attack.

"Put it away," I repeat.

He holds the dagger in a death grip.

I reach up and cover his hand with mine, curling my fingers around the hilt with his.

He drops my braid, freeing me, and tries to pull away, but I only tighten my grip, matching his step back.

"Decide," I tell him. "Either kill me without attempting to torture a confession out of me, without this farce of justice, or put away your dagger."

"Justice is not a farce." He steps back again and twists his hand out of mine.

"It is in your land, princeling. Ask the people. They go to thieves for protection and justice while your guards sit by and your courts condemn the innocent. Do not pretend to justice here, where you have neither evidence nor judge."

"I do not need more evidence. You killed my mother."

I hold still, watching him. I wonder what it was that the Lady did to his mother, how she died.

"You can't deny that she is dead," Kestrin says, as if my silence had questioned him. "I know what you are."

I laugh, a sweet trip of sound that leaves Kestrin stunned, staring. "You cannot guess what I am, Kestrin. You do not know the least of my story, just as you could not imagine me as a child with a mother, could not imagine me without my magic."

"You twist meanings with your words." He raises the dagger, the tip wavering over my heart. "You killed my mother. That is all I need to know." He steps forward, his dagger touches my breast, and there he stops.

"Just as I have killed you," I agree quietly. I can feel him trembling through to the tip of the dagger, his breath ragged and unsteady. "If you want to kill me, Kestrin, if you want to watch me die by your blade, this is your chance. I am unarmed, I have no magical defense, and I am weak. But do not pretend to justice. What you do now will only and ever be murder."

The dagger falls to the ground with a dull clatter.

I wait, swaying slightly, watching Kestrin. Is it over? He raises his hand to his face, passes it over his eyes.

"I wish that you were dead," he says, his voice hoarse and grating. "There is nothing here to allow for justice. Nothing at all."

His eyes are dark, but it is no longer anger that burns in his face. Instead, despair loosens his skin, leaves his eyes red-rimmed and empty. He turns and makes his way to the mouth of the cave, one hand on the cave wall for support.

"Do not seek me out again, sorceress." His words fall like small stones into a pond, disappearing even as they are heard. As he passes from my sight, the cave closes in on me and twists around to spit me out into the gardens.

CHAPTER
41

Night has fallen, the moon filling the garden square with silvery light.

The Lady stands before me. "Come," she says.

I push myself to my feet, staggering upright because I must. The garden whirls around me again, though this is no magic. It is the same tide of pain I've endured all evening, grown stronger. Dust falls in sheets from my shift, from my shoulders and hair. I follow the Lady to my room, keeping my eyes on the white of her dress so that I will not falter. My shift clings to me, growing wet and heavy as I walk, each step a battle I might yet lose.

I pitch forward onto the bed, unable to lower myself, and have to bite my lip to keep from crying aloud. And then the Lady's hand helps me onto my back. I close my eyes and wait for her to leave, but she does not.

Instead, I feel her push up my sleeve and wipe my arm with a damp cloth. Then she opens my shift and cleans the wounds on my chest. Her touch is firm, neither gentle nor hurtful. I suck in my breath and stare at the ceiling as she presses the cloth firmly against my gouged flesh, wipes the blood from the shallow cut on my neck.

When she moves away, I turn my head to inspect my wounds. A long gash runs down my right arm, still seeping blood. Had Kestrin not bound it, I likely would have bled to death. The cuts on my chest are less deep, showing the print of the thing's claws: two sets of punctures, each an array of four holes, ripped slightly open as the beast landed on me. They cannot be stitched shut, dug as they are into my flesh.

The Lady returns and sits beside me, her hands clasped lightly in her lap. She studies my arm in silence, then raises her gaze to my own. I wait as a trickle of blood slowly drips down from the gash. She exhales softly and sets her hand upon my arm, her fingers cool, but the magic they release is warm and gentle and numbing, pushing back the pain to a faint hum. Her magic flows just beneath my skin, mingles with the blood in my veins, and comes together at the gash. I hold my breath as it presses the cut closed, sealing it more finely than any surgeon's stitches. I stare at the wound, now nothing more than a line across my skin, its once-rough edges smoothed down.

The Lady winds a bandage around my arm, then moves on to bandage my chest.

"Why are you doing this?"

Her hands rest on the bedsheet. When she speaks, her voice is thoughtful. "You interest me."

"Interest you?"

The Lady smiles faintly. "Yes." She stands up and brushes

out her skirts in a gesture so common to all women that I am left stunned. But I should not be. She is not just a sorceress following a bloody oath.

"Wait," I call after her. "I don't understand."

She pauses at the foot of my bed, looking down at me. "It is a side effect of using your mother's spell to gain power over you," she says.

"The kerchief—the drops of blood," I whisper.

"Yes."

"You used my strength to bind me." The remembered press of the choker makes my skin crawl.

"Only the strength you gained from her, which is to say, the strength of your silence." The Lady waits, watching me expectantly.

The power of silence was perhaps the only thing I learned from my family, and it has taken me months to learn to find strength in breaking my silence. But that's not why the Lady is helping me now. I am almost too tired to try to work it out, but this conversation is a rare thing, and I dare not waste it. I must focus.

There were three drops of blood: strength, knowledge . . . and love. I shake my head. "You cannot have allowed her love to touch you."

"No," she agrees. "That was easy enough to evade—as simply cast as the spell was. But I accepted her knowledge through the blood, and so thought I knew you from her. I do not. I know only one aspect of you, and even after watching you these months, you still surprise me."

I squeeze my eyes shut, open them again. It doesn't astonish me that my mother hardly knew me. But the Lady's words still shed no light on her actions.

"I don't understand," I say softly. "*Why* do you help me?"

"When you speak to Kestrin, I hear both your voice and mine."

"Yes," I murmur.

"How is that?"

She looks to me like and yet unlike my first vision of her, and I find myself speaking dreamily. "When I looked into your eyes for the first time, I thought I saw my death there. I think I still do. But I also see your pain now."

Something flickers in her face, but I cannot say whether it is an emotion winging past or only a weakness of my sight. She nods, a single dip of her head that carries a weight of meaning I cannot parse, and departs, taking the light with her.

The Lady returns with the morning and escorts me once more to the square. Despite the rest I've had, I am exhausted. The Lady's magic has worn off and my wounds ache when I am still and flare with pain at every movement.

I sit down facing the stone prince and look up at the Lady. "When you send me this time, will my cuts remain bandaged?"

"Yes." The Lady pauses. "If you wish to return to Tarinon, you may. I will not force you to this last test." She glances toward me, her face a perfect mask. "The first two have weakened you."

"Would you release the prince?"

"No."

"Then why do you ask?"

The Lady purses her lips, watching me. A breeze wanders through the garden, touching a wisp of hair that has escaped her braid. "I do not like to send you to your death," she admits.

"Hasn't he proved himself yet?" I ask. "He saw his greatest enemy unarmed and let her go. He saw her attacked and defended her. He saw her wounded and helped her. What more could you want?"

She looks away from me to Kestrin's statue, kneeling before us. "I want him dead," she confesses.

"Then you are what you accuse him of. Let him go, Lady."

"Why do you fight for him?"

Even when Kestrin played his games with me, he stopped short of ever hurting me. In the pity I glimpsed in his eyes before he found me out, there had also been regret. "I know he will not fail your tests."

"He has been very close often enough."

"He has." The pain of the cut at the base of my neck, the great dark bruise on my chest, bear silent witness to that.

"You did not doubt him last night?" she asks, bemused. She knows that I did, if only for a moment.

"I knew if I could make him pause long enough to think, he would not kill me. I do not doubt the power of his anger and hatred, but I believe there is good in him that is stronger." I close my eyes. "I do not know what your third test will be, Lady. I have tried to imagine it, and I think the only way he would fail is if he reached that pitch of helplessness and rage I saw in him last night, and then was called upon to save me rather than let me go. I think perhaps he would let me die, tricking himself for those few moments into believing he did no wrong. But I do not doubt he would regret it, even if he never learns who I am. That is the only test left which he might fail."

I open my eyes, meet her gaze. "Which of us has not made mistakes when faced with more than we can handle?"

"Go back, child," the Lady says with surprising gentleness.

"I am not a child to be sent home, Lady. I will not go without the prince."

Her hands flick over her skirts, then come to a rest clasped together in front of her.

I wait, not daring to speak, for some things require quiet to come into being.

"He is yours," she says, her voice heavy with weariness. "I will return him to the plains."

"What of the third test?" I whisper.

"You are right," she says simply. "So let us both watch him."

Let us— "No," I say roughly. I shake my head as if I could deny her words, because I *have* been watching Kestrin. I have only ever expected the worst from him, and so watched for that and not seen the rest of what he has done, or struggled with. "He has passed your tests. Let him go free. There is no need for watching, and I will not do it."

Her lips curl in cool amusement. "No, I don't suppose you would. Very well."

Relief rushes through me, but still I ask, "And then?"

She raises an eyebrow in an eloquent, arched question.

"What of the rest of the Family?"

Her gaze grows deep and dangerous as the night. "What of them?"

"They are as innocent as Kestrin."

"You know what your king has planned for Valka."

"I know." I look down to the gravel walk. "They say it is justice: she has been found a traitor and passed her own sentence." I swallow hard. "It is the law that a traitor must die, Lady. And it was you who made her into that traitor, made her so convincing that the king would not have suspected her. No doubt, one by one, she would have given them over to you as she could. For that, she cannot hope for forgiveness . . . it is justice, but a cruel and ugly justice. I wish that it were tempered by mercy, that she might have an easy death."

I think of the Lady herself, her mother's death. Perhaps, had the woman been cleanly executed, far from the eyes of her child, the Lady would not have become who she is. Though she *has* made each of her decisions in her own time, chosen each death she has brought about with her eyes wide open. Planned each murder. She should never have been made to watch her mother die, but that does not excuse her actions.

The Lady tilts her head in a fair imitation of curiosity. "Do you argue for the lives of men who cloak cruelty in the guise of justice?"

"Lady, you condemn them without fair trial. You saw the taint in Kestrin, but when he was put to the test, he passed."

"What trial shall I set them, princess? Will you put yourself into my hands to pose them their tests?" She raises her hand quickly. "Do not offer. I am sending you home because in this case you are right, and I do not want you dead because I wish Kestrin dead."

She holds out her hand. "Come."

I push myself to my feet and clasp her hand in mine, ignoring the pain of my wounds. "What if I should need to speak with you again?" As I will if she has not given up her vengeance against the king, or Garrin.

"Call me by my name and I will come."

The gardens melt away, the hedges rise up into walls, and the Lady stands in my bedroom in the palace, illuminated by a fall of morning light through shattered shutters.

"Your name," I echo.

"Sarait."

I let go of her hand and she fades into the sunlight.

CHAPTER
42

Berrila ni Cairlin tends to me silently during her daily visits, her face still and stern, accented only by a small line running deep between her eyebrows. She asks no questions I cannot answer, and gives me only a cream for my burns and a strict admonishment to watch my wounds for purulence. Her magic can do no more than the Lady's did; only time can bring what healing must come now.

After the Lady returned me to my room, I made my way out into the hallway, accosting a passing servant with a message for the king. The servant had run for all that he could not have understood it: *Look for the Wind on the plains.* It was only when I returned to my room and caught my image reflected in a mirror, my shift dark and stiff with dried blood, that I realized the reason for his haste. And so, the healer-mage, and the chance to stay quietly in my rooms a little while.

My attendants move about me quietly, gauge my silence, my

pain, and share the rumors of the palace. So I know that shortly after my return, the prince was found walking over the plains toward the city, haggard and thin. I know that before Kestrin's return, the Circle of Mages demanded that the king appoint a new heir, only to have to eat their words. And I know that Valka is imprisoned in a holding cell awaiting her execution, which will be carried out once I am well enough to ride out with the royal party to watch it.

Perhaps it is this that keeps me in my room.

Finally, though, I make myself get up and change. My attendants assist me quietly, watching me carefully. I recognize Jasmine, who questioned me and sent me in to Valka while she slept, and Zaria, who laughed with her about it. The third is Mina; she I still have no sense of. She is just as quiet and distantly polite as ever; I do not yet know her mind.

Once I am dressed, I send them out and return to sit on the bed, wishing again for the little room in the stable I shared with Sage with its three small sleeping mats, side by side, and the wooden pegs on the wall to hold all we need. The sheer volume of my new belongings oppresses me: the huge, empty bed; the veritable forest of chairs and tables cluttering each room. The wardrobe is filled with the clothes Valka brought with her in her trunks, brought from my room in the stables and unpacked without a word, so that it was done before I knew what was intended.

I will change these things, but not in this moment. There will be time enough for a new wardrobe, for rearranging the furniture in straight lines and clean curves so that I can think clearly again.

I glance around from my perch on the bed and notice a small inlaid wooden box on the bedside table. It is new, placed there sometime in the last day by one of my attendants. I open it, then dump the contents into my palm: a thin silver chain looped through an oval pendant bearing a delicately carved rose. I close my fingers over the pendant and chain, holding them tightly. Kestrin watched me very closely indeed. I wonder if Joa sent the pendant directly to him, or if Kestrin dispatched someone to buy it back from the knacker afterward.

"Zayyida?" Mina stands in the doorway.

"Yes?" I ask, watching her.

Though she stands straight, she somehow still manages to fade into her surroundings. Perhaps it is the way her face tilts down, how even when she reaches to pick something up, her manner is confident yet unassuming, perfectly adapted to rendering her invisible.

"Will you dine in company tonight?" she asks, as one of my attendants has asked every night since I returned.

I glance down at my closed fist. Kestrin deserves more from me than the cowardice and anxiety that have already kept me in my room too long. "Yes."

As I step into the gathering room before the doors to the dining room are opened, I realize just how alone I am. My attendants, who walked half a step behind me all the way here, have fallen back farther. The room is half filled with nobles, exquisitely dressed, and all of them engaged in their daily dance of manners and status. The quiet flow of conversation falters as first one lord and then another lady notices my entrance, and then it fails altogether.

I want nothing more than to step away, to retreat from this

room of men and women who are assessing me, deciding in these next moments just how much respect they should accord me. Instead, I look over the room with a slight smile and dip my head as if I greeted them all.

The king steps forward from where he converses with a pair of lords. "Zayyida Alyrra."

I curtsy to him, and at his gesture, move to join him. As I approach, the men he speaks with turn their faces to me, and in their eyes I see the same velvet depths I thought only the Lady's eyes could hold, though here there is warmth. *Fae.* It is all I can do to keep my expression easy, a faint smile on my lips as I reach them.

"Allow me to introduce the permanent ambassador from Chariksen, Verin Stonemane," the king says, gesturing first to the Fae lord beside him. Stonemane offers me a bow, one hand going to his breast. His skin is paler than mine, his hair as dark as anyone else's here. He is tall and lithe, graceful as a hunting cat.

"I am honored," he says.

"The honor is mine."

"And with him, a mage of great renown in their land, Adept Midael, called the Cormorant."

Where Stonemane is pale, this mage is dark, his skin the deep brown of forest earth, his hair braided into long ropes that fall down his back, gems and silver rings glittering from them. He holds out his hand, a gesture simultaneously welcoming and authoritative.

I set my fingers in his without thinking.

His mouth moves, forming words I cannot catch, his eyes holding me, pinning me where I stand. How did I imagine there was nothing of the hunter in him? I cannot move, caught perfectly in a web of his devising. My skin shivers over my body as magic flows through me. At my throat a line tightens, crawling beneath my skin, curling around the Lady's choker. I stare at him, a smile frozen on my lips. His gaze sharpens, cutting through what defenses I have, as if he can see all that binds me.

And then he releases my hand and steps back, dipping his head toward me.

What did he do?

The king is saying something now, about how pleased the Family is to have the ambassador establish a permanent residence here. I can feel both the Fae lords watching me. They were called here to help against the Lady—I remember Ash saying as much. Whatever the Cormorant did, he was likely only testing the Lady's hold on me. I will have to trust that much for now, and see what I can find out later.

"Ah, there is Kestrin," the king says, breaking me from my thoughts.

I turn, following his gaze. The prince scans the room as he enters. I know from the way he finds me at once, the way his eyes fasten on the bandage at my wrist, that the Lady explained the whole of his ordeal to him.

He crosses the room with barely a nod to the other guests. These few days' rest have helped him, easing the tension and exhaustion from his features, but his face is eerily gaunt, as if his youth has been bled away, leaving a faint gray tinge to his skin. He offers me a smile, his eyes strangely alight. "Father," he says in greeting. "Zayyida, I am glad to see you well."

I smile and curtsy prettily to his bow. "And I you, zayyid."

"Verin Stonemane, Adept Midael, I trust you have found all well here." There is a harsh note to his voice, a rasp of anger that tells me Kestrin is not pleased with our meeting.

"Indeed," Midael says softly, his gaze moving to me. "Very well."

I raise my brows, as if bemused, and look back to Kestrin. I don't know what game the Cormorant plays, but I will not allow him the satisfaction of seeing me frightened.

"Let us go in," the king says, gesturing for the servants to open the doors to the dining room.

Kestrin offers me his arm, and I find myself taking it. It is a strange play we put on, as if we had barely met at all, and then only at court.

At dinner I sit below the king, Kestrin across from me and Melkior at my side. Thankfully, the Fae lords sit further down the table, Verin Garrin beside them. When he catches my gaze, he holds it a moment, gauging my reaction before bowing from the neck. That will be another relationship I will have to navigate carefully.

I look up as I turn back, and see a wide band of wood carving where the walls meet the ceiling. Kestrin catches my speculative look and smiles guiltily.

The king asks me only a few questions, but they are questions of some substance and I take my time answering them: What have I learned of his city while living outside the palace? Was I treated well? Would I be averse to keeping the wedding for when it is set in roughly a month's time?

The rest of the evening I maintain a friendly discussion with Melkior, asking after his family and revisiting the topics first mentioned at his dinner. I am careful not to mention Red Hawk or Violet. It is too soon, just yet, to venture there.

When we rise to leave, Kestrin offers me his arm, circling the table to escort me out after his father. As we leave the gathering room, he waves away our attendants. I eye him curiously, but make no argument as we leave them behind.

He leads me to a marble square with a fountain playing at its center. I drop my hand from his arm as we approach it, and take a seat on a stone bench. Kestrin sits beside me, watching me covertly. I do not speak, engrossed in the play of moonlight on water.

"Veriana," Kestrin says softly. "Are you well?"

It is a strange question, for it has none of the court in it, though it should. "We are both here, are we not?" I ask.

"It has been three days."

"Yes." Three days in which my arm healed enough to no longer require a sling, and my chest wounds closed enough so that each breath brings only a whisper of pain.

I wonder how long it took for Kestrin to recover. Perhaps his wounds were deeper, being cut into his soul and not his body. In the moonlight, his face still has the look of stone upon it. Only his hair, smooth and shining, softens his aspect.

"Are you truly the Wind?" I ask, though I know the answer.

"Yes." He runs his hands through his hair. "I used to plan how I would tell you, what I would do. Stupid." The word is laden with contempt.

"Childish," I amend tactlessly, but he only laughs. Looking at him, I remember how I worried over the betrothal, how even my mother could not understand it. Now I have some idea, and yet I still find myself asking, "Why did you wish to marry me?"

"Can you ask?"

I do not answer.

Kestrin bites his lip, then speaks. "When I first found you, I was a novice testing my abilities and you were a child in the forest hiding from your brother. I could not help returning to check on you, and with my father's tutelage I learned to send words on the Wind to you. I waited for your stories; I wished to get you away from your brother; and more than any of that, I wished I might see you with my own eyes." He clasps his hands together. "When it came time for me to seek a wife, I knew it would be you."

"I did not know what you were." It is a small betrayal. There are so many other, greater things between us, yet this seems the deepest.

"I know. I am sorry."

I trace the embroidered design along the hem of my tunic, my finger running over the perfect stitches. "You have heard Valka's sentence?"

"I have."

I wait, but he says no more. "Is that how all traitors die?"

"Traditionally, a traitor is hanged until dead. Their body is left for the crows to pick and the rain to rot for a month before being thrown into a ditch and forgotten."

"Then why must she be tortured to death?"

Kestrin rubs his chin. "I believe that Red Hawk saw your friend's attackers executed, did he not?"

"Yes," I admit.

"Was that your doing?"

I consider him carefully, weigh the risks. "It was."

"I thought as much." He hesitates. "I was trying, you know."

"I know," I confess. "But the guards who came to investigate didn't even speak to the men who found her. The longer they took, the more likely the men would not be found. And . . . I realized too late how Red Hawk would use their deaths to mock the king's law. I am sorry."

He shakes his head. "Your friend died. I cannot blame you for taking the steps you did. But, speaking of justice, consider that the men were flogged before they were hanged. Why did you agree to their 'torture' before their deaths?"

I try to swallow, but my mouth has gone dry. "I didn't," I begin, and then stop.

Kestrin watches me keenly.

I hear Red Hawk's voice discussing the flogging: *that their punishment not go too easily with them.* I had not paused to consider this addition to the punishment. They had caused physical harm, and I wished it all back upon them. There had been nothing of mercy in the justice I had sought. "I did not think," I whisper.

"They were made an example of to deter others from their path. This is much the same. The greater the offense, the greater the punishment."

"No," I say. "Even what the thieves did—it was their justice. Every man in this city knows the punishment the thieves exact for such a crime. It is the same for all. What you would do to Valka goes beyond the punishment for treason. It will only haunt the rest of us."

"Valka's deeds will die with her."

"Her memory will remain. Those who liked her will

remember not just that she died, but that she was made to suffer. That will create hatred in their hearts where there was none before."

Kestrin sighs. "My father—"

"Is the law," I supply. "But is his decision just?"

"I will speak to him on your behalf," Kestrin says. "Perhaps I will succeed where you have not yet."

I look at him curiously—I believe he may, for it was him his father most wished to protect, but I did not expect Kestrin to admit such a thing, even if only by implication.

"My father said you spoke against Valka's punishment at once," he says carefully.

"I don't know what justice really is," I tell him. "But I am trying to get right what I can. The death she chose lies beyond all law. Her thoughts were cruel, and the power that carries out such a sentence would be equally cruel."

"I will speak to him," Kestrin assures me.

"There is one other thing," I say slowly.

He waits, watching me.

"Are you sure that when you execute her, she will be the one to die?"

For a long moment, Kestrin stares at me. Then he says, his voice strained, "Tell me exactly how the spell was cast upon you. Describe what happened."

I gaze at him, the invisible line of the choker pressing gently against my throat. I should have asked the Lady to remove it when I had the chance, but I did not think of it. I won't call her back now to ask.

His eyes narrow. "You cannot."

"Did you think I could?"

He lets out a soft, self-deprecating laugh. "No. I know better than that. Tell me this, then, if you can: When she cast her spell, did you find yourself suddenly moved to Valka's body?"

I shake my head, not daring to use my voice.

"So you remained in the same body, but its appearance changed?"

I nod, the choker tightening so that I must breathe slowly, shallowly.

Kestrin sits back slowly. "Then it will be all right. She exchanged your skins, not your actual bodies—or your souls. When Valka dies, the spell may even come undone, returning your old appearance to you. I will speak with the Cormorant about it; if I am not mistaken, he took the earliest opportunity to study you."

That he did, but I don't allow myself to be distracted now. "What if the skin I am to wear again is destroyed?" I ask.

Kestrin goes still.

"What then?"

He drops his chin, staring down at the tiles. "I will speak to my father," he says again, his voice firm. And this time I believe the king will hear him.

I look down to my calloused hands, the chapped skin still not quite smooth despite the lotions my attendants have pressed on me. Will the switch be as simple as that? Will I suddenly regain my old scars, a skin gone soft when I am now accustomed to hard work?

Loss eats at me. Perhaps I should not have spoken—would the king have spared Valka's life if taking it endangered me? Or is a kinder death all that I should be fighting for, that justice might be done?

I slide my fingers beneath the embroidered cuff of my sleeve and pick at the bandage around my wrist, fraying the cloth with my fingers.

Kestrin does not speak again.

Finally, I look up at him. "It's late," I say into the quiet.

"Your wrist—what happened—it's the same," he stumbles, his eyes anguished.

It isn't a question. He knows the truth as well as I, however difficult it may be to accept, but I answer anyway, "Yes."

His hands curl into fists and he crosses his arms quickly, as if to hide his fists, though his anger is directed toward himself now. I know the look, know the way he trains his breath, and I am sorry for him. This will remain between us the rest of our lives: a legacy of hidden identities and shadow truths and violence left to us by the Lady.

"Can you—is there any way you can forgive me?" he asks.

Forgive him? "No," I say tightly. "No, I won't forgive you, Kestrin, because you did nothing wrong."

He stares at me. "How can you say that? I hurt you. The evidence is right there."

"Yes, you hurt me," I allow. "But you thought me the Lady. You were still her prisoner, Kestrin, still expecting to die, to be murdered, as your mother was. You were fighting back, however you could, with words, with deeds, and there is no fault in that. Not on you, not on anyone who must defend themselves."

I understand that now, about his actions as well as my own. I might wish that I hadn't taken such vicious pleasure in hitting

Corbé, but there is no place for regret in having actually defended myself. I would do it again, as Kestrin should as well.

"There is nothing for me to forgive," I say again, more gently. "I—I am the one who feared to trust you for far too long, who believed there could be no winning against the Lady."

"There *hasn't* been," Kestrin says, smiling crookedly. "And perhaps I am equally to blame for how I treated you when I first called you here to speak with me."

That is true enough.

"Can you be happy here?" he asks abruptly. He is looking away, at the fountain now, his eyes intent on the water.

I feel the strangest tingling sensation in my chest. I think that I might cry. "Does it matter?"

Still he does not look at me. "You can return home if you wish. You have been through enough to warrant breaking the betrothal without endangering our kingdoms' friendship."

"I told you once before, there is nothing for me there."

"You did."

"I have come to love your land and your people very much, verayn. I would not leave by choice." But I am grateful still that he has given me one nonetheless. It is a thing to be treasured.

He turns to me, a flicker of hope in his eye. "There is—would you walk with me, veriana? I would like to show you something."

I take his arm and follow him back into the maze of hallways.

"It is a little ways from here," Kestrin explains, and then falls silent.

We reach a part of the palace I have never seen before, moving through quiet corridors until we come to another set of wide doors leading into a square. But this square is unlike anything I have seen in Menaiya. There are no marble tiles, no mosaics, no elegant fountains. Here grows a wood.

I stand frozen on the threshold, gazing at the trees—pine and birch and oak and a few slender aspens. They are silvered in the moonlight, their leaves rustling in a faint breeze, filling the air with the scent of the forest: leaves, and beneath that, damp earth and moss.

I move forward in a dream, reaching out to touch the rough bark of a pine tree. A gravel path wanders off through the grove, curving into darkness. I want nothing more than to walk it, to lose sight of the palace even as I stand in the belly of it, surrounded once more by trees.

"Do you like it?" Kestrin asks from behind me.

I had forgotten him, had dropped his arm and walked forward without a thought. Now, with an embarrassed smile, I turn back to him. "It's lovely. Who planted it?"

"I did—or rather," he says with uncharacteristic humility, "the gardeners did. But I planned it. For you."

My hand rests against the tree. "This garden has been here some time. These trees aren't newly planted."

"I was very sure of myself," he says with a mocking smile. "At least it served one purpose. When I brought the impostor here, she glanced at it once, thought it quaint, and wished to go on to a lunch party."

"You knew."

"I knew she wasn't you. But I didn't know who she was, or who you were." He crosses to me. "I knew that, as happy as you might one day be here, you would still like a memory of home."

How close we are, I think, gazing at him, this man who is

both a shrewd politician and a fiercely protective friend. Here, among the trees he planted, I can finally understand that for all his strategies, he is fundamentally nothing like my brother. How close we are, and yet how far. He will not cross this final distance, will not or cannot. So I must.

I reach out and brush his arm with my fingertips. "I *am* home, Kestrin."

His hand reaches up to touch mine, and we clasp hands, awkwardly, uncertainly.

"It's strange." I smile sadly. "I trusted you completely, you know. When I followed after the sorceress. I knew you wouldn't kill me. You might rage, you might act like a bully—"

He swallows a laugh.

"But I knew you wouldn't kill me."

"I wouldn't have been so sure."

"You protected me and helped me."

His mouth twists.

"Remember that, Kestrin. I do."

"Do you remember also that you have seen the wasteland that is my heart? Could you marry such a man?"

I hesitate, trying to find the right words.

I must take too long, for he adds, "Could you ever come to love me?"

I respect him, I trust him, and I have come to think of him as more than just an ally, a friend. Perhaps love will flow from that.

"I don't know," I admit. "But I know that there is more to your heart than those places the Lady allowed you to wander. Look around." I gesture to the trees around us, the myriad sleeping creatures hidden in the grove. "This too is a part of your heart. How could it not be?"

"Do you believe that?"

I take a step forward, so that I am barely a hand span away from him, and rest my other hand on his chest, feeling the rise and fall of each breath. "I have no doubt of it," I say.

I cannot yet tell him I love him, because we need more time without games and deceit between us to find such love.

He looks at me wonderingly, and then, hesitantly, brings his other arm around me and draws me to him. We stand there together a long time, his cheek resting on the top of my head, my own against his chest.

I close my eyes and listen to the steady beating of his heart and the gentle rustle of leaves overhead.

CHAPTER

43

The day of Valka's execution dawns bright and gentle, the sun warming the tiled courtyards and bringing the scent of growing things on the breeze.

Kestrin meets me in the Receiving Hall. Our attendants and every noble in the great room shift to watch us. Kestrin bows, the corner of his mouth quirked, and I find a little of my tension easing. I take his arm, and we turn toward the main doors.

"It will get better," he murmurs. "They won't always stare so much."

But they'll always be watching. I have no doubt that is how this court works—observation and politicking at its sharpest.

"They'll have good reason to stare soon enough," I say. I mean it lightly, but my fingers tighten on his arm nonetheless.

Kestrin hesitates, looking out to the wide courtyard filled now with horses, then back at me. "I'll be there with you."

I smile, grateful for his words, even if some things must be gotten through on their own. I've brought Valka her death, as I promised her so many months ago, and now I must watch it be carried out.

In the courtyard, Sage leads a horse up to me. The mare is a gentle creature, Solace, who can be trusted to children and anxious beginners. I almost laugh. Whoever chose her for me wanted to make sure I didn't fall off. And they certainly didn't ask the hostlers what sort of horse I might be capable of riding.

Sage dips down in an awkward curtsy as we reach her. I ignore it, releasing Kestrin to wrap my good arm around her.

"Zayyida," she stammers.

"Sage," I whisper. "I'm still Thorn."

She embraces me then, and though her hold is gentle, she makes no move to release me until I step back myself.

The courtyard is filled with nobles and hostlers leading their charges, not a few of whom watch our exchange. Kestrin discreetly moves away to mount his own horse.

"How are the others?" I ask.

"Ash and Rowan are here, but I'm not sure they'll be able to get close." Sage turns the mare and holds the stirrup for me. "Oak may decide to stay on at their parents' farm."

I pat Solace's shoulder, my sleeve falling back to expose the bandage wrapped around my wrist.

Sage glances at me. "They said you were hurt after you came up here, when you disappeared those days."

"Just a few scratches," I say through gritted teeth, and heave myself up onto the horse. My arm shrieks its dissension at that.

Thankfully, Sage makes herself busy checking my stirrups and smoothing my skirts, and does not notice the set of my face until I have managed to rearrange it.

"And how is Joa?"

"Well enough," she says. "You've heard Corbé's gone? He lit out of here like a dog with its tail on fire as soon as the news of who you truly were reached the stables." Sage smiles humorlessly. "Mind you, that was after Ash and Rowan thrashed him again and Joa fired him."

"I hadn't heard."

"It would be foolish of him to stay after all he's done against you, wouldn't it? We were expecting you'd send someone after him."

I watch Solace's ears flick back to listen to us, the morning light catching in the soft, fuzzy hairs of her inner ear. "I suppose I should."

"Aye," Sage says. "A man that attacks a woman shouldn't be allowed off like that."

"I know," I say softly, thinking of Violet, and street justice, and how I do not yet know how to bring about a change in laws, and in how they are applied. "There's so much that needs doing," I tell Sage, my uncertainty bleeding into my voice.

"Start somewhere and keep going," she suggests practically.

I nod, wishing it were as easy as that. And perhaps it is. Perhaps I cannot fix everything in this moment—stop the snatchers, or keep the women of this city safe, or even protect my own people from a king such as my brother. But I can do this: start somewhere and keep going.

Sage reaches up and pats my hand hesitantly, as if unsure that she has the right to anymore. Kestrin walks his horse up next to us, dipping his chin to her.

"Zayyid," she murmurs, and with a curtsy hurries away.

"She's your friend from the stables," Kestrin observes.

"Sage," I agree.

"You miss them."

I readjust my grip on the reins. "I miss all of it," I admit. "But I've made my choices."

"You could ask them to join you here," he suggests, his voice pitched so that only I may hear. "Good friends are hard to come by. We could find them posts that would suit them."

"Perhaps," I say, wondering if Sage would come. I remember how tired she has been, how little her heart has been in her work since Violet's death. Perhaps she would welcome the change. I feel myself beginning to smile.

I turn to Kestrin with another question. "I was wondering, verayn, how my attendants were selected."

His eyes flick to the side, but both my attendants and his are waiting a few paces back, far enough that we might converse without their hearing. "They are the younger daughters of some of our lesser noble households."

"I know that," I say, amused. "I meant them in particular. As you said, good friends are hard to come by. I would like an attendant who does not have prior allegiances that are stronger than what she holds for me."

Kestrin meets my gaze. "That will take some doing."

"Of course. I wondered if you might help me with that."

He grins and dips his head.

We ride down in procession: an honor guard, the king, then

me and Kestrin, followed by Verin Garrin and the king's closest vassals, all of us flanked by more guards. I feel faintly foolish riding with so many eyes on me, with so many men surrounding me as if I were afraid of the people. I have never seen Kestrin ride through the city without a guard. I wonder now if I will ever again roam these streets with only a horse for company. It seems unlikely.

Valka has preceded us to Hanging Square. She stands at the center of the platform, a guard to either side of her, and it is all the soldiers in the square can do to keep control of the people. As I watch, a piece of rotten fruit flies through the air and splatters against the wood at Valka's feet.

She does not flinch, does not even look, her chin high and her eyes trained on an unseen spot in the middle distance. She wears the clothes I sent her, a simple skirt and tunic set. Her hands are bound before her, and her hair straggles free of its braid.

Looking at her, I see my own nightmares brought to life, for there I stand, despised and alone, awaiting my death at the hands of the royal family. Even though it is Valka and not me up there, my eyes bear witness to a different reality, one that I have brought about.

We come to a halt beside the platform, Solace stopping even though the reins hang slack.

The king holds up his hand. The crowd quiets in expectation, until all that can be heard is the faint shouting of a group of children.

"Veria Valka, you stand accused of high treason and attempted murder of a royal person. You have been found guilty. Have you any last words?"

Valka maintains a stony silence, her eyes finding mine. In her eyes, I see my own guilt, see the same betrayed, hateful look as that day, years ago, when I trumpeted her theft of the brooch to everyone. If only I had sought justice more kindly. If only Valka had chosen a better path for herself.

The king nods, and Valka is led to the gibbet, guided up onto the bench waiting below it. The executioner fits the rope around her neck, pulls her braid through it, and then steps back.

She does not take her eyes from me and so I do not see the king gesture, or the executioner step forward to kick away the bench. I see only the way her head snaps back, caught by the rope, the jolt as her body's fall is broken with the breaking of her neck.

A coldness slides beneath my skin and burns off my flesh. I watch her body swaying before me through a whirl of colorless cloud. Solace sidles nervously and swings her head around to watch me, the whites of her eyes showing.

The crowd backs away, voices murmuring, "The princess. Look at the princess."

I feel the change shudder through me, twisting my bones and squeezing the breath from my lungs. At my throat, the choker I have worn so many months surfaces and burns to ash, as if it had never been.

As I watch Valka's bent head, her hair writhes, the brown running to golden red, her clothes blown by an unknown wind, whipping around until they are no longer the tunic and skirt I sent her but the stiff, embroidered set gifted to me by the king.

As the wind calms, I turn my head to look out over the crowd. They stare at me in return, a sea of faces. At the very back, standing against a wall, I find Red Hawk. He meets my gaze and then he smiles, a kind, encouraging smile that has nothing of the death I have just caused in it. He bows slightly, his fingers over his heart, and then he steps to the side and is lost in the crowd.

"Veriana, are you well?"

I blink, surprised to find Kestrin beside me, his hand steadying mine on the reins. I don't recall him reaching out to help me.

"Veriana?" he repeats, his fingers squeezing mine once, gently, as if to bring me back to myself. "Are you well?"

"We are both still here," I say quietly, echoing the words I used only last night.

He releases my hand, the line of his shoulders easing, and sits back.

The king waits on his horse, observing us both narrowly. In truth, there's not a set of eyes in the whole square that doesn't seem trained on Kestrin and me.

I raise my voice over the growing murmur of the crowd, knowing I must give the king a reason to allow Valka's burial, and I will never have a better moment than now. "Tarin, Veria Valka was the daughter of a high vassal of my mother's realm. Though she betrayed her oath of fealty, her father has remained true. For his sake, I ask that you grant her a quick burial."

My words do not meet with the crowd's approval.

"Leave the traitor to rot," one man cries. And then they are all shouting their suggestions, their anger.

"Tarin," I repeat, my voice now only for our small party. "She has paid the price of her treachery. Do not make her actions cost my mother the queen more than they already have." It is the only argument he will understand, and so I use it. I cannot bear the thought of Valka's body abused and left unburied.

For a long moment, he considers me, his gaze shrewd. He understands me perfectly. "Is that your wish?" he asks.

"It is."

The king nods and gestures to Captain Sarkor behind us.

I turn Solace away so that I will not have to watch as Valka is cut down and carted off. I wonder where she will be buried, and before me flashes a vision of the graveyard where Violet now lies. Valka's grave will be just another grave there, just another small heap of stones in a field where all are nameless.

The ride back to the palace passes in a dream of quiet. Everywhere I look, I see people I have known these last months, these years of my life. They turn toward us, smiling, and in their eyes I see the lives of unborn children, the certain strength of the young, the lingering illnesses of the elderly.

In the palace courtyard I dismount awkwardly, patting Solace until Sage reaches us.

"You must be glad to have your old body back," she observes.

A few paces away, Kestrin pauses in the act of handing his horse's reins to a hostler, listening.

In truth, my body feels strange to me, like a half-remembered haunt, a childhood home. It has filled out, grown taller and softer while Valka cared for it. I miss the calluses on my palms.

"I rather like not having a burnt wrist anymore," I say lightly.

Sage laughs grimly, shaking her head as she leads Solace away.

As I turn my hand, though, I can feel the same raw pain beneath my new skin that I felt beneath the charred remains of my old one; and when I dismounted, my arm muscles cried out beneath the new seal of my skin. The damage has not been undone, only removed from sight. In that, there is much to be grateful for: without the scars between us, perhaps Kestrin and I might truly find a way to look at each other without guilt or pain.

"Veriana," Kestrin says, joining me. "Will you come in?"

I take his arm as I am expected to, turning with him toward the Great Hall with its doors thrown open. A stray breeze flits through the courtyard, wraps around me. I glance sharply at Kestrin as it lifts up a loose lock of my hair and then rushes toward the open doors.

He raises his eyebrows, the corner of his mouth quirked upward, a glimmer of mischief in his eyes.

I let my breath out in a quiet laugh, squeeze his arm beneath my hand.

Together, we walk up the steps to the Great Hall.

Questions for Discussion

1. Alyrra has been deeply betrayed by both her family and her peers, which influences her relationship with Kestrin. In what ways have you dealt with betrayal in your life? How has that impacted your relationships with others?

2. Over the course of the story, Alyrra learns to find strength in breaking her silence. What events or incidents do you think affected Alyrra the most in this regard? Is this something that you have struggled with?

3. What are the dynamics of power between Alyrra and Kestrin? Does the power shift over the course of the story? How would you characterize their relationship at the end of the book?

4. Consider our legal system in the context of mercy and justice. Where does it fall short or succeed? Is it applied equally or unequally across our society?

5. When Alyrra is put on trial, she faces a panel of judges who appear to have already decided against her. Have you ever faced a situation in which losing seemed inevitable? Looking back, what would you have done differently?

6. After the Lady's testing, Alyrra tells Kestrin she didn't know he was the Wind. She feels this to be the deepest betrayal of all. Why do you think it was the deepest for her? How would you feel in her situation?

TURN THE PAGE TO READ

THE BONE KNIFE

A SHORT STORY
FROM THE WORLD OF

THORN

The Bone Knife

INTISAR KHANANI

"We've a visitor," Niya says as I enter from the kitchen yard. She kneels before the low worktable at the center of the room, punching down the morning's dough, her arms daubed with flour and her hair wisping out of her braid. "I heard Baba answer the door a moment ago."

"I know. He's trouble." I cross the kitchen, debating how to handle the sort of trouble he is. With our mother gone to town and our father already busy with him, it falls to me as the eldest of my sisters to figure out what to do. "Did you make any of your specials?" I ask, taking a taste from the pot bubbling over the fire.

"Just the bread—who is he?" Niya turns toward me, pushing her hair back from her face and coating the stray locks in white.

"I don't know." I join her at the table and lean down to take a pinch of the dough. Underlying the gentle flavor of rosemary, I catch a hint of warm blue skies, wheat fields golden in the sunlight, swallows warbling. I have to hold back a sigh as the taste of

Niya's magic fades. "We'll make flatbread for lunch just in case he stays," I say. "He may not even be here long enough to eat."

She refuses to be distracted. "If you don't know who he is, why'd you say he was trouble?"

I hesitate, uncertain of so many things: what to tell her, how to protect her, exactly what I saw a handful of minutes earlier. Looking over the low mud-brick-and-adobe wall bounding the kitchen yard, I was slow to realize that the man walking down our drive, a journey bag slung over his shoulder, was not a man at all. The signs were there in the impenetrable obsidian of his eyes, the flawlessly sculpted features, the strange paleness of his skin. The paleness alone would have set him apart from the people of our land, but it was the exquisite grace of his movements, the ageless-ness of his face, that marked him as something *other*.

Leaning on the wall, watching him, I forgot myself: forgot that young women should beware of the Fair Folk; forgot that my sister with her life's secret was within; forgot, impossibly, my own unremarkable features, my deformed foot. Only as he neared the corner of the house did he glance at me, amusement in the tilt of his lips, as if to say, *Did you think I didn't see you?*

I turned my back on him, tossing a final handful of grain to the chickens, and then hurried indoors to my sister.

"Rae? What *is* it?" Niya watches me now expectantly.

"Well," I begin when an explosion comes through the hall door in the form of a gangly girl with flying hair, pointy elbows, and pounding boots.

"Rae!" cries this ball of energy. "Niya!"

"No need to shout," I say mildly. "We're right here." Our youngest sister skids to a stop, thumping into the table as she drops down beside it and sending the tin cup on the corner fly-ing. It clatters to the floor, spraying an arc of water across the worn stones. At least it wasn't milk.

"There's a faerie come to visit Baba!"

I guess I needn't worry about how to word my news now.

"A *faerie*?" Niya echoes, gray eyes widening as she turns to me. "Why didn't you tell me?"

"I told you he was trouble," I remind her. "And I was going to tell you what kind when Bean"—I glance at our little sister pointedly—"knocked over the water."

"Oh well," Bean says, reaching to scoop up the cup and return it to the table. "Some of us do get excited once in a while."

"But he might guess," Niya says, worried. "About me." *About her magic.*

"Which is why he'll eat my bread, not yours." Even though that's hardly a guarantee. I forge on, feigning confidence. "Bean, check the curry, would you? I thought I could just taste Niya's touch in it as well."

"He's magic," Bean says, walking over to the stove. "Do you think he'll be able to tell about Niya just by looking?"

"I don't know," I admit. The faerie has likely come from the king's city, and will know as well as any of us what a law-abiding citizen would do: report us to the Circle of Mages for secretly harboring a magical talent—one that should have been sent to them when it surfaced, to be properly trained and sworn into the service of the king. Niya has turned a shade paler. If she were discovered, she would be taken from us, and we would be punished. I touch her shoulder, though I have little comfort to offer. "There's no saying what faeries can tell just from sight, what with those eyes of theirs. Keep out of his way unless Mama thinks it's okay." Which she won't, if I know our mother at all.

Niya rests her hands against the worktable, palms down as if steadying herself. "We've never had a faerie visit before," she whispers.

I've never even heard of a faerie passing through our town. It's never been a problem to hide Niya's talent from the average visitor, and we've had many to our horse farm. But a faerie . . .

"First time for everything," Bean points out cheerfully. "Might even be the first time I don't burn lunch, if he's lucky."

"Bean, would you *please* try to be helpful?"

"Okay, all right," she grouses at me. "What do you want me to cook?"

"Something edible." At her hurt look, I relent. "How about your potato and garlic dill dish? It's quite good." And she typically manages to not burn it.

She rolls up her sleeves with a grin. "I can do that."

The dish, as I had hoped, turns out well, as does my flatbread, though neither could ever vie with Niya's work. Our faerie visitor does indeed stay for lunch, and then returns to inspecting our horses with Baba, apparently having come to buy from us. Since we do not want to draw attention to Niya, Mama and the rest of us take our lunch in the kitchen.

As always, Bean and I spend the afternoon training horses. We take our colts to the back pasture, far past the stables and out of the way of Baba and the faerie. As we lead the colts out, I can feel the faerie's glance, taking in Bean's quick light step and my own slight limp. With my clubfoot, I walk on the side of my foot. While it is hardly painful, the movement is pronounced just enough for anyone to guess at my deformity, even with my feet hidden by the grasses and my long skirt. Now I gaze forcefully ahead, ignoring the faerie's regard. Bean's current reclamation project, Hop, a three-legged calico, follows along behind us, mewling, until Bean takes pity and picks up the dratted cat, carrying her with us to the pasture.

"She can get along perfectly fine," I tell Bean. "You're just spoiling the creature."

"So?" Bean asks, scratching the little cat's throat. It stretches its neck rapturously and purrs fit to burst.

We focus on groundwork with the colts, switching off between them until both they and Bean have had enough. Hop sleeps in the sun and then prowls the longer grasses beyond the fence before finally making her way back to the stables by herself, clearly put out by our long stay. When we return the colts to their usual field by the stable, I see Bean looking around curiously. I too can hear the faint sound of voices.

"They're in the practice ring," I tell her. I can just see the edge of the ring past the stable. "They must be trying out some of the horses."

"Baba might need help," Bean says, shifting from foot to foot, her eyes trained on the ring's fence.

"Mama will want our help making dinner. And," I point out sweetly, "you said you were tired."

Bean gives me a black look but follows me to the house. She does get her wish to see more of the faerie, though, for he has decided to stay the night with us. We had set out lunch while the men were out and cleaned up after they'd left. Dinner, though, will have to be more formal. By rights, as eldest daughter of the house, I should serve them. But Mama gently suggests that Bean do the serving, and I understand at once. With my limp, I would be an obtrusive presence. Bean, for all her excitement, knows how to slip in and refill glasses, serve dishes, and remove empty platters without drawing notice. I force a smile, pretending not to mind, and it is a sign of Mama's own guilty conscience that she quickly changes the subject.

"How many horses will he buy?" Niya asks Mama as we sit around the kitchen table eating the last of the potatoes. It irked her to stay hidden all day, knowing nothing of the faerie's review of the horses.

"And how did he hear about us?" I poke at my potatoes. They are significantly better than Bean usually makes them, but I am not hungry.

"He wants five or six, and he hasn't said much of anything about himself," Mama says. "Though I've barely had a chance to speak with him or your father."

"Five or six!" Niya and Bean exchange an awed glance.

"Best make sure he doesn't pay with faerie gold," I warn Mama.

She chuckles. "If your father isn't wise enough to beware of that, he deserves to lose them."

"We've some of the best horses in the south," Niya says in answer to my first question. "I expect he heard of us and came to see himself. I'm sure he'll deal honestly."

I have been to Spring Fair with Baba to sell our horses; ours *are* among the finest, though not necessarily the very best, in all of southern Menaiya. It is possible Niya is right. I bite my lip, wondering why I am so suspicious of him.

"Why would a rich faerie come walking through the dust and the heat?" I ask no one in particular.

Mama casts me a quieting glance.

It doesn't occur to me until much later, as I make my rounds assuring all the doors and windows are barred against the night, that the faerie might notice the strangeness of our absence, the careful withdrawal of the women from his presence. That he might find it curious enough to inquire about.

I pull the shutters closed in the dining room and draw the curtains to hide them, grateful that the men have finally retired for the night. But as I turn back to the room, I realize I am not alone. The faerie stands in the doorway, watching me. I start with surprise, and at his slight smile, I make an awkward curtsy.

"Can I help you, kel—" I stumble to a stop, realizing belatedly that I never learned his name.

"Genno Stonemane," he supplies, his voice lilting, deep, and sweet. I find myself pressing my back against the wall. Whatever is the miserable fellow doing down here? And why does he have to be so lovely? At least Niya is safe in our bedchamber.

"Kel Stonemane," I amend. "May I help you?"

"I have noticed something curious. I thought you might explain it to me." He steps into the room. In the candlelight I can see that he has had a chance to wash the dust from his face and hair; the result is an exquisite and frightening beauty. His hair shines darkly, falling smoothly over his shoulders, setting off the luminescence of his skin, the midnight shadows of his eyes. I drop my gaze to the low table, grateful for its presence between us.

"I am not very good with explanations," I say, lifting my

candle from the table in the hopes of escaping him. "Perhaps my father can help you?"

"Not unless he does the sewing in the house," Stonemane says.

"The sewing?"

"Those are lovely curtains behind you," he remarks genially, walking toward me. I retreat to the other side of the window, my turned foot making every movement doubly awkward. He smiles as he reaches me, the space between us made up now of only two narrow panels of embroidered cotton. "Did you sew them yourself?"

"No," I answer gladly.

"Ah, then it was your younger sister who served us dinner."

"No, I'm afraid not." Nor was it my mother, and since there's no way for him—

"Of course. Then it was the third sister, the one who has stayed hidden." I take a quick step back—how could he know about Niya? His teeth glint in the candlelight. "She has a fine way with stitches. Just here"—he reaches out a long-fingered hand to tap a flower—"she has caught the scent of a spring day when the daffodils first turn their heads to the sun, and here"—his fingers follow a tracery of blue—"flows the warmth of a late summer breeze."

We are caught. I know it from the smile that plays over his lips, from the very words he uses to describe Niya's work. I see it all in the blink of an eye: Baba and Mama imprisoned, Bean whipped in the stocks, and Niya—taken. My hand shakes so that I spill beeswax over my knuckles. The fire-hot bite of the wax jolts me back to myself. I straighten my back, glaring at him. "Kel Stonemane, your imagination is quite exceptional. I am sure Mama will be pleased to hear your compliments; she purchased the curtains last year at the fair. Now, if you have no more pressing questions, I must be about my work. Good evening."

I turn and stump around the table, dreadfully aware of my uneven pace and his eyes boring into my back.

"Kelari Amraeya," he says as I reach the door. It is neither a command nor a question, and I find myself glancing over my shoulder. I can only just make out his form beside the curtains, for the light of my candle cannot reach him where he stands. "A host and their guest share an equal burden. Give your sister my regards."

I turn away and hurry up the stairs. *An equal burden*, he said. Is it some sort of Fae saying? A host shelters their guest—does he mean that he in turn will shelter our secrets?

The door to my parents' room is closed, the space beneath it dark. I stand a long moment before it, considering what I should tell them, what Stonemane might mean, what they can actually do. But they can do no more than I, only hope that Stonemane will leave without betraying our secret. Better to let them rest.

I continue down the hall to the bedchamber I share with my sisters, bolting the door behind me. They are already changed and settled beneath the blankets on the quilted sleeping mat we share. I set my candle on a low table and change into my shift, my hands faltering. *He will not betray us*, I tell myself. *He sent her his greetings—he can't mean to report us to the Circle for hiding Niya's talent. It is only a small talent.*

Somewhat steadier, I slide under the covers. Niya, stuck in the middle for the night, scoots over, shoving Bean into the corner to make space for me.

"Whozzat?" Bean asks groggily before falling back to sleep.

Niya huddles against me. I think her asleep until she says, "I heard your voice before you came up." I close my eyes. I do not want to tell her. "Was it him?"

"Yes," I whisper.

"What did he say?"

"He just had some question or the other." I pretend a yawn. "I'll tell you in the morning, all right?"

She relaxes beside me. "Okay."

I fall asleep praying the dawn will take Genno Stonemane and leave Niya as safe as ever.

I had not thought, as I drifted off to sleep, that my prayer was all that bad. And, at cock's crow, when I clump downstairs to the kitchen to start breakfast, there is every sign that Stonemane remains our guest regardless of my secret wishes. So I set about the business of breakfast, starting the dough to rise and then going out to the henhouse to collect eggs.

As I make my way back, six lovely, warm eggs nestled in the pouch I make of my apron, I glance over the low kitchen wall to the road expecting to see our stable hands walking in from their homes. Instead, a mob of townspeople march down the road, hardly a stone's throw from our house. They are all of them men, their faces grim and, if I am not mistaken, angry, and on their shoulders ride the tools of their respective trades: hoes and axes and smooth wooden staffs.

I drop the eggs and run as fast as my turned foot will take me, barreling through the kitchen and down the short hall to the front door. I shove the bolt home just in time. On the other side of the door, a fist hammers against the wood and a chorus of voices rises up, shouting for my father. I turn back to see Stonemane at the top of the steps.

"I must close the back door," I tell him. "Please fetch my father." Thankfully, he does not argue but turns back toward the rooms. I return to the kitchen, barring the back door and closing up the shutters as well. The rest of the windows on the ground level remain barred from the night; we will be safe now till Baba can calm the townspeople.

As I reach the hallway again, I hear Baba and Stonemane descending the stairs.

"If it is me they want, I will be happy to show them what a faerie is," Stonemane says, his voice amused.

"I'll not have it," Baba says, his deep baritone gruff with anger. "No guest of mine will be threatened—certainly not by my own neighbors!"

As Baba takes the final steps, he spots me. "Rae, my dear, you're all right?" I nod. He looks back toward the door, which rattles beneath a hammering fist. "Would you accompany Verin Stonemane to the business room upstairs?"

I glance at the faerie, astonished. He's a *lord*?

His eyes flash with annoyance. "I see no need to hide. I am not afraid of these fellows with their sticks."

"Some of them carry iron," Baba points out. The battering on the door has increased, and now I hear voices coming from farther along the wall as a group of men begin to make their way around, pounding on the shutters. Suppose they break in? We cannot stand about arguing in the hallway until they do.

"Please, verayn," I say, taking a step forward. "If the townspeople see you, they will know we shelter magic here." *When we should not.* I leave the last words unspoken, but he knows them as well as I, and knows that I speak of Niya. Only let me have judged his intentions last night correctly.

Baba stares at me, and then Stonemane nods. "I understand," he says quietly, and turns back up the stairs. I hurry after him. The moment we are out of sight, Baba throws the door open.

"What is the meaning of this outrage?" he roars, his voice reverberating through the walls. A deafening silence follows. I try not to smile, knowing it's too soon to judge whether Baba has actually cowed the men. Silently, I push open the door to Baba's business room, ushering in the faerie.

"You'll be able to see from the window," I tell him. He goes to peer down through the deep-set window, staying in the shadow of the wall. I watch from across the room, my back against the door. I can hear my father's voice again, berating the men for their rudeness.

"We heard there was one of the Fair Folk sheltering here," a voice says; I recognize it as old Bemain's, the swarthy, heavyset blacksmith of Sheltershorn.

"Aye," says another man. "My boy Goran says he saw the faerie walk right up here."

"Saw him?" Baba scoffs. "Walk? Is that Goran that I took into my stables because he couldn't make a living anywhere else? That lackadaisical fool of a boy is telling tales about his master's house affairs?"

"Well, now, kel," comes the stumbling reply. "The boy just told what he saw. And you went and gave him the afternoon off, you did. Seemed right strange to me."

"If a faerie were to come to my home," Baba says steadily, "do you think he would come walking or riding? A faerie? And if he *were* to come, do you think he might be coming from Tarinon—from our king's city and with our king's protection? Which would make your turning up on my doorstep with your *axes* a bit like high treason, wouldn't it? Turning on the king's own guest!"

The men sputter in confusion, and then Jako the tanner's voice rises up. "We didn't mean any rudeness, nor certainly any treason, but I spent the whole of last night setting by my girls' bed worried they'd be snatched up by the Fair Folk."

"You'd have been wiser to take your sleep," Baba says, not unkindly. "I've three of my own girls to worry about. Do you think I'd endanger them?"

I feel Stonemane flash me a glance. I turn and slip out, careful not to look at him. All of the upstairs rooms open onto a seating area at the top of the stairs. Now I find Mama standing at the head of the stairs, one hand on the smooth adobe wall, listening intently.

"Mama," I call softly.

She whirls around. "Rae! Where is everyone?"

"Verin Stonemane's inside. Will you stay with him? I'll just see if the noise has woken Bean and Niya."

Mama breathes a sigh of relief. "Aye, go check on them."

As I push open our door, I nearly knock Bean over.

"Hey!" she cries, stumbling back and dropping her boot. Niya, dressed as well, stands by the shuttered window, her face pale as she strains to hear the exchange below.

I close the door. "Sorry, Bean." She grunts as she shoves her foot into her boot. "Where do you think you're going?"

"Baba might need help."

I close my eyes. Dear hotheaded Bean. "Perhaps Niya needs our help more than Baba."

"Niya? She's fine up here." Bean straightens, her skirts swishing around her boots and her eyes sparkling with excitement.

"You aren't going down, Bean. Baba is sending the men away, and he doesn't need to worry about us showing up along the way."

"They aren't leaving," Niya says from the window.

"See?" Bean crows. "I need to go down."

"No," Niya says, shaking her head. "You don't understand. They're too ashamed to demand anything further of Baba, but they still think the faerie's here. They're going to watch the roads for him."

I cross the room to her, peering down through a crack in the shutters. The men are already halfway down the drive. "Can you hear them?"

"The breeze carries their words."

I can't hear a sound, but I nod anyway.

Bean makes a little moue of frustration. "They're gone?"

"Far gone," I confirm.

"But he's still in danger," Niya says matter-of-factly.

I turn back to consider her in the half-light. She is tall and slim, her black hair caught back in her typical braid, locks falling loose from all sides, her unusual gray eyes—a gift from our grandfather—bright in the darkness. From the steady light in her eyes and the set of her face, I know we are thinking the same thing. I suppose Bean must get it from us. I let my breath out with a sigh as she says, "Perhaps we can help him slip out."

"He was here to buy horses," Bean says. "I doubt he'll leave without them."

"You're as good with horses as any faerie," I tell her. "You can ride out and picket them on the plains for him. The men won't stop you. Then he can slip out on his own and fetch them without attracting any attention."

"They'll stop him," Niya observes. "They'll be watching for him, not just horses."

"Let's see what Baba says," I suggest. At least he will know better how to keep Bean out of trouble. And Niya. I pause, holding the door shut, and glance critically at Bean. She'd served Stonemane dinner. "You didn't tell us he was a lord."

"I did!"

"She told me," Niya says. "You came up so late, though—Bean was asleep and"—her complexion gains a faint rose undertone—"I forgot."

"Never mind." I open the door, intending to catch Baba as he comes up the stairs. Just as Niya steps out after me, Stonemane comes out of the business room.

He smiles his faerie smile and bows to us. "Ladies."

Mama, exiting the business room behind Stonemane, jerks to a halt, her eyes finding Niya's.

"Verin Stonemane," I say, my voice dry. "You will remember my sister, Kelari Samayna." Bean bobs her head beside me. "And this is our middle sister, Kelari Niyagara." Niya gives a small curtsy. I can almost feel her trembling behind me—as much as she wishes Stonemane safe, she hadn't intended to let him see her. I would like very much to march over and give Stonemane a good hard shake and a shove out the door.

"I am honored," he says, his voice sweet as honey.

I glare at him. "We were just seeking our father."

The corners of his eyes crinkle with amusement. "As was I."

Baba reaches the top of the steps just then, his face flushed and his eyes still glittering. "I'll have that lout Goran whipped for this," he mutters under his breath, though I know better than to believe him.

"With your permission," Stonemane says, "I do believe he spoke truth."

Baba throws up his hands. "Forget the boy. He's caused enough trouble. At least the men are gone."

"They're watching the road," Niya says, her voice barely carrying the distance.

"So they are," Stonemane agrees.

Baba looks ready to burst. "They're *what*?"

"It's no trouble," Bean says quickly, stepping forward. "If Verin Stonemane has chosen his horses, I can take them out and picket them down by Empty River. No one will stop me. Then—"

"Pah," Stonemane laughs. "There's no need for that." He turns to my father. "I'll take my leave of you and your family. The horses we discussed yesterday will do just fine."

Mama purses her lips. "And what of the men on the road?"

Stonemane spreads his hands. "They've lost a night's sleep over me. I will be happy to grant them a week's sleep in return."

Baba runs his hand over his hair. "Well, now," he says uncertainly, and I realize in that moment that he doesn't know how to cope with Stonemane, that the townspeople might very well have the Faerie Sleep put on them—a sleep they won't forget or forgive. They will come after us, and someone, somehow, will discover Niya, a week from now, or a month, or a year. Better to risk helping Stonemane than that.

"We'd rather not make such a scene," I say coldly. Stonemane turns back to me, catching my gaze before I can look away. His eyes are as deep and endless as the mountain wells, a faint ripple of light upon their surface all that keeps me from falling into them. "Bean will take the horses out," I stumble on, fighting the pull of his damnable faerie eyes. *An equal burden*, that is what we need. "And Niya can hide you in her stitches."

I hear Niya suck in her breath, but I cannot look away from him.

"Can she?" he asks softly. "And how will I reach the horses if I am stitched into hiding?"

"I can carry you," I say, barely hearing myself, caught in the velvet darkness of his gaze. "No one ever looks at me."

"I see," he says, and turns his gaze to Niya. I take a gasping breath of air, my sight rushing back to me. "Can you do such a trick, kelari? With your stitches?"

"I have done it once or twice before," Niya admits, her voice feather-soft.

"With a live creature?"

I feel Bean give a little jerk and glance at her. She is fighting a smile, staring steadfastly at the floor. Of course—she is thinking of Baba's prize nanny goat. I have to bite back my own smile at the memory. Niya, perhaps thinking the same thoughts, answers much more confidently, "Yes, verayn. And it was fine."

Stonemane turns to our father. "I'll do as you wish. I would not endanger your family; the choice is yours."

Baba wets his lips, glancing toward us, his gaze lingering on Niya. Never has a stranger known her secret before, but

Stonemane knew it last night, whether Baba realizes it or not. There is no further danger in the Fae lord seeing the truth of it again today. Or at least, I hope not.

"I would suggest," Mama says gently, "that we have our breakfast and consider the matter at greater length. Since we are quite safe here, there is no reason for anyone to go rushing off."

"True enough, kelari," Stonemane says with a slight bow. "And I would be grateful to start my journey with a meal."

The men return to Baba's business room to finish their accounting for the horses. The rest of us troop down to the kitchen.

"I broke the eggs," I confess as I unbar the kitchen door for the second time this morning. "I dropped them when I saw the men coming."

"No matter," Mama says. "We've five left from yesterday. Niya, would you punch down the dough Rae started? And think a warm thought while you're at it."

Niya obliges, singing under her breath as she dumps the bread out of its bowl. Mama starts a pot of spiced oats on the stove and Bean begins peeling potatoes, poor girl. It seems potatoes are the only things she's comfortable with.

"Now, Rae," Mama says, stirring the pot, "what exactly do you think you're about with this plan of yours?"

I set a skillet over the cooking fire to warm, before getting to work on the eggs. "He knew about Niya already—he figured it out last night, without ever seeing her. If she helps him now, he'll be duty-bound to help her in return, keep her secret."

"I see," Mama says. She takes a long slow breath, looks back at me. "But her stitches?"

"I think it's best no one else sees the faerie," I argue. "If word gets out that he was here, and Baba sent the villagers off assuring them there was no danger, that would mean a bit of grumbling but nothing too bad. But if Stonemane has his way, he'll play a trick on them, lay the Faerie Sleep on them, and then there'll be real trouble."

"What do they think they can do?" Bean asks. "I mean, they know he's a faerie. What makes them think they can catch him?"

"People are stupid," Niya says, as if this explains it all.

"Or just afraid," Mama says, her voice calm. "And they know they can use iron as a weapon against him. So."

Bean snorts with disgust, and for once I have to agree with her.

Mama turns to me and asks, "Do you really think it wise to take him out to the plains yourself, stitched up in a bit of cloth?"

"I could take him out," Bean points out. "There's no need for you to go all that way—I'll be with the horses."

"No," Mama and I say together. Mama winces, glancing at me, but I keep my gaze on Bean.

"If anyone follows you, we don't want them to see you let Stonemane out. Better that I carry him and you simply leave the horses. No one will stay to watch horses graze." I turn to Mama. "The men watching the road would never expect it of me. You or Baba could try, but Baba they would watch, and since you don't wander about half as much as I do, even you they would take note of. If I'm walking, they won't expect me to go as far as the horses."

"I don't like it," Mama says, and I know that whatever her reservations, she will agree to the plan.

I dump the eggs out onto a platter. "Neither do I," I tell her. "I trust him as much as I would a dog with a bone. But it's the best way out that I can see."

Niya returns the dough to its bowl to rise again. "I could stitch something into your sash for you," she suggests. "As a protection."

"Like what?"

"The skillet," Bean suggests with a wicked smile. "You could do some damage with that."

Niya grins. "All you'd have to do is break the knot to get it out."

"Girls," Mama says warningly. "If we're trying to help Verin Stonemane escape unscathed, knocking him over the head with an iron skillet is not likely to help."

We look at each other and burst out laughing.

After breakfast, Stonemane fetches his journey bag and joins us in the front sitting room. He wears his traveling clothes again, though they are stiff and clean now. I study them covertly; we have not done the wash since he arrived. Did he wash them out in a bucket in his room, or merely wave his fingers and shoot sparks from his eyes?

He sits on the floor, his bag over his shoulder, and looks to Niya. The rest of us are seated around the room, Bean rocking back and forth on the edge of her chair in excitement. Niya holds my sash in her hands now, needle and thread in her lap.

"Are you ready, verayn?" she asks.

He dips his head. "I thank you all for your hospitality."

"I am sorry for this trouble," Baba says.

"So you have said," he agrees. "But it is not of your making. Kelari"—he nods at Niya—"do your work."

She does. In five simple stitches, she sews a small circle on my sash. She pauses as her needle begins the final stitch. Stonemane waits, his eyes on her fingers. I glance between them, my eyes alighting on Stonemane just as Niya pulls the needle through with a single, confident tug. Stonemane snaps out of existence; one moment sitting before me and then, between one blink and the next, disappearing so completely I can almost believe he had never been there at all.

Bean gives a little shout of glee and jumps up. "Oh, you're *good*!"

Niya smiles as she knots the thread and breaks off the extra. She looks relaxed, the tension slipping from her shoulders. It had not occurred to me that holding her magic might be so difficult, or that having an opportunity as significant as this to use it would be a welcome reprieve rather than exhausting. She winks at Bean now. "Let's hope he's comfortable in there."

"The goat never complained," I tell her comfortingly, taking my sash back and binding it around my waist. It feels no different than it did this morning; it seems strange to imagine that the stitches themselves hold a faerie within them.

"What goat?" Baba asks.

"Nothing," we chorus together.

He regards us with fatherly suspicion. Mama just shakes her head, though even she doesn't know.

"It's just an old joke," Bean says a little too brightly.

Baba huffs softly. "There are some things I suppose I'm better off not knowing."

Mama stands up, brushing out her skirts. "Bean, you'd best head off at once if you're going to take the horses the long way round. Rae, let's get you a spot of food packed so you don't come back starved."

We leave the room together, Niya catching hold of my hand. Her eyes dance with excitement. In the kitchen, Mama finishes packing a rucksack with bread, cheese, a few bits of dried, seasoned meat, and a water flask while Niya fetches my walking stick. We had packed food for Stonemane as well, which he slipped into his travel bag. Now I lace on my leather shoes, ruminating on the wonders of his bag—it clearly holds more than its small size suggests. Perhaps it also washes clothes.

Bean manages to leave a scant few minutes before me, riding out of the stable yard with five horses on a lead rope behind her. They are some of our best—Diamond and Harefoot and Storm among them. How very odd that he came to us walking when he had wealth enough to buy them. Storm alone, with her long legs and sculpted nose, with her frothing dark mane and the speed of the wind, must have cost him thrice as much as a regular riding horse. Baba would not have parted with her for less.

I take the back path leading out of the kitchen yard, walking down through the pastures. I see no one till I reach the old wagon road that borders our land. Bemain the blacksmith sits with Ferin the wheelwright, each gazing down opposite ends of the road. I raise my hand in greeting, and Bemain returns the courtesy. He says something and Ferin turns to watch my progress across the road, the walking stick swinging in time with my bad foot. Ferin snorts, and even though they are a good thirty paces down the road, I hear him say, "What, the cripple? She's nothing to worry about."

I set my features and keep walking, pretending their words did not carry to me. By midafternoon I reach Empty River. It is, as its name suggests, a great empty riverbed carved into the sandstone ground. Here, it is hardly deeper than a man stands tall, though farther into the plains I have heard it runs deeper than some mountains rise high. I follow it to where the horses are picketed in an ash grove, happily grazing on the sweet spring grass. Sitting down beneath the shade of a tree, I lay my staff on the ground and turn the end of my sash over in my hand.

I need only break the knot and the spell will be undone. Yet I hesitate. He is one of the Fair Folk, to be dealt with respectfully, but—how much can he be trusted? Mama was afraid to leave him alone with Bean. I run my hand over the sash, then clench my fingers to keep them from shaking. I am different. I am, after all, the cripple. I take the knot between my fingernails and with one swift yank, snap it.

Genno Stonemane sits before me, utterly at ease, his journey bag beside him. His eyes run over me, and then he tilts his head to survey the horses. I push myself up, taking my staff with me, and brush the dust from my skirts.

"Empty River is there," I say, nodding toward the sunken riverbed. "If you follow it south one day's ride, you'll come to Kharite Road. It runs east–west, all the way to Lirelei, if you wish to reach the sea. If you stay on Khariti Road heading east another league, you will come to Gurail Road, which runs north to Tarinon." West of us rise the mountains, sharp and clear, hardly a morning's journey. But I doubt the faerie will be going there. That way lies only the uninhabited forests and the long, winding road to the lesser kingdoms beyond the mountains.

"Thank you," he says. He stands fluidly, the essence of grace. I wonder if all faeries are as perniciously lovely as him, or if it is his particular gift. "Do you go back at once?"

"I must," I say, keeping my eyes on the horses. I can feel his gaze again, coming to rest on my face. "It is a good walk, and I wish to be home by nightfall."

"Are you afraid of the land around your home at night?" His voice is warm, amused.

"It is not fear," I reply coldly, "but practicality. It is harder for me to walk when I cannot see where I step. The new moon will not cast enough light for human eyes."

"The ever-practical Rae," he says agreeably. I glance at him, surprised that he would use my nickname so easily, without permission. I should not have looked, for he was waiting to catch my gaze. "Tell me, why would your parents let you walk here on your weak foot, when your sister might easily have carried me as she rode? Why didn't she wait for you here?"

In the afternoon light I realize that his eyes are not all black, but the deepest brown fringing a night-dark center. There is a warmth there that blackness cannot hold, like a forest in darkest night, the trees still friendly company. "Bean is pretty," I say, my voice no more than a whisper.

"Ah," he says softly, and turns back to the horses. I clutch my staff, leaning heavily on it, grateful for his attention elsewhere. I know I should leave now, that he will let me walk away without another word, but there is an unbearable bitterness on my tongue. I watch as he moves among the horses, greeting each with a cupped hand, checking their hooves to ensure they are ready to travel.

When he is done, he crosses back to fetch his journey bag. "I suggested it," I say suddenly.

He frowns slightly. "I recall."

"They weren't happy."

"Yet here you are. Suppose that I have now what I wished from your father: five of the finest horses in Menaiya and his daughter's company."

His words surprise a laugh from me. "The horses are lovely, but I'm afraid you've gotten the raw end of the deal when it comes to me. Better luck next time."

I start away, my staff swinging out as I begin the trek back home. Faster than I've seen any man move, I find him a bare pace in front of me. I lurch to a halt.

"I make my own luck," he says, smiling. "I rather like what I have just now."

"Verin Stonemane," I say carefully, hoping the formality will keep him at bay. "I should not have stayed this long; the way back is not short and, as I told you, I would not walk at night. I wish you safe travels and prosperous arrivals." I breathe slowly, knowing that he plays with me, that I have nothing truly to fear. Do I?

"You're a hard woman, Kelari Amraeya," he says quietly. "You should on occasion be kinder to yourself."

"I don't know what you mean."

"No," he agrees. "Before you go, I would repay my debt to your family."

"Debt? Do we not share an equal burden as host and guest?"

A smile flickers across his lips, there and gone. "The burden is somewhat skewed. You have risked more than I think you realize to deliver me here. I do not allow myself to remain in debt when I can help it." He pauses, his eyes wandering past me as he considers his words. "For your sister of the gray eyes, I offer this: there are many different paths to working magic. She has found one, and the mages of this land would have taught her another. Tell her, among the Fae, the highest magic is that of understanding patterns."

I nod, storing away his words. His eyes return to me, dark and, despite their human aspect, utterly foreign. He swings his journey bag around and delves into it. "For your sister who loves animals," he says, and brings forth a stone no bigger than the pad of my thumb, carved in the shape of a stocky little horse. I hold my hand out silently, and he drops the tiny statue in it. For a heartbeat, it feels as though the stone moves, as though what I hold in my hand is a living creature. But it is only a little figurine, and I drop it into my skirt pocket with some relief.

"And this," he says, "is for the cripple."

He holds his hand out to me, his fingers curled around the mottled wooden hilt of an old bone knife. I stumble back, staring at him, at his perfect face, smooth and unsmiling. I had not thought his words could hurt me so.

"I do not require your thanks," I say, my voice uneven. I want only to get away now, to have nothing more to do with faeries and their hellish eyes that see everything.

"My debt must be repaid," he says. "And you walk so easily into danger, you may need a knife."

"I absolve you of your debt," I say, my voice shaking. "Safe travels, verayn." He lets me pass him. I walk as quickly as I can, my staff meeting the ground with purposeful thunks. I dare not look back.

"Prosperous arrivals," he says, the wind bearing me his words. I jerk my chin down, careful not to raise my hand to wipe away my tears. I do not look back until the path has wound away from Empty River and turned north toward home. By then the copse has sunk into the gently rolling land.

I reach home just past sunset, a faint pinkish-blue light still lurking in the west. Our house has never looked so welcoming before. I pause a moment at the edge of the kitchen yard, my eyes running over the adobe walls. The timbers that support the roof extend through the walls, throwing a row of shadows over the smooth earthen sides. Lamplight falls through the kitchen doorway, creating a golden path across the yard. I have only to step onto that path and be returned to my family.

And then I do not have to take a step at all.

"You're back!" Bean shouts, bursting forth from the doorway. She crosses the yard at a dead run and very nearly knocks us both down with the force of her hug.

"Of course. Did you think I was running away?"

"He was *faerie*," she cries. "I should have stayed and waited for you."

"Rae?" Niya calls from the lamp-lit doorway, and then there are three of us nearly falling over. "I kept thinking I should have sewn you a skillet," she gasps, her arms tight around my neck. "Or—or *something*."

"Don't be silly," I scold her, hugging her back just as tightly. "What would a faerie want with me?"

"He rather seemed to like you," Bean says diffidently. "He listened to what you said."

"Ha," I say, remembering our last exchange. "He listened because I gave him a plan."

"I dunno," she says, unconvinced.

I laugh. "Did you see him, Bean? Then imagine their women.

We must look like little old hens next to them." I take my sisters' hands and lead them toward the kitchen. "What would they want with the likes of us?"

"I suppose we look different to them as well," Niya says thoughtfully. "Perhaps they think their own folk look a little too everyday in contrast."

"Oh, Niya."

Bean, not as concerned with the unknown as what happened, asks, "What did he say? When you let him out?"

"Not much."

Niya glances at me nervously. "Did he look okay?"

"None the worse for wear," I assure her, and then glance up to see Mama in the doorway, her hands fisted in her apron.

"Rae."

I reach her, smiling, but she doesn't smile back, only holds out a hand to me. I take it and find myself folded in a fierce hug. Inside, Baba climbs to his feet slowly, standing before the low kitchen table as if lost. He looks suddenly, inexplicably, like an old man.

"I was going to come looking for you," he says, his voice rough, "if you didn't get back soon. Don't you ever let me allow you to do such a thing again."

"Yes, Baba."

At which point Mama, strangely silent till now, launches into a full-fledged rebuke of all involved, including herself, and ends with a clear directive to my father to never invite another faerie into the house.

"Ah, but love, he's taken some of our best horses. I'm sure he'll show them off; and we can't very well treat faeries rudely if they do come to our doorstep. An angry faerie is more trouble than a wildfire."

"Oh, brilliant," Mama says. "Are we going to stitch them all into sashes?"

Later that night, as I am getting ready for bed, Niya comes up to our room. "There was something in your bag," she says. "It must be what Verin Stonemane gave you."

"What?" I look up. The gifts for my sisters I passed on to them, the words for Niya exciting general interest, and the stone horse amusement. I had not looked for anything in the little rucksack, leaving the empty water flask and cheesecloth at the bottom of it. I certainly had not noticed anything else in it when I'd reached in for the flask or a bite of food to munch during my walk back.

"Let's see," Bean says, coming up beside us.

"This," Niya says, and hands me a slim object, a little longer than my hand. It is a bone knife the like of which I have never seen before, the handle inlaid with mother-of-pearl and onyx, the ivory blade sharp as steel, its center carved in a flowing, rippling design of curves and flourishes.

"He had an odd idea of gifts," Bean remarks. "Little stone horses and chipped kitchen knives—it's not even metal."

"I doubt he'd carry iron," Niya points out.

"No," I agree, turning the knife over in my hand. The knife I hold is a work of time and art, a precious thing. It is hardly a chipped kitchen knife—and yet, Bean's description matches what I first saw on the plains, what Stonemane offered me in the palm of his hand.

"You didn't accept it when he tried to give it to you, did you?" Niya observes, watching me. I shake my head, wondering that even she cannot see it for what it is. "That's a faerie for you."

Bean grins. "That ought to teach you. I wish I could do that little trick."

"I'm glad you can't. I wish he couldn't either."

"I wish you wouldn't hate him so for my sake," Niya says, moving away to change out of her tunic and skirt. "He turned out to be quite all right."

I lay the bone knife on the floor beside our sleeping mat and slide into bed. "I don't hate him," I say. I think of him, his lips shaping the word *cripple*, and I find myself hating my turned foot, my deformed ankle and stilted gait. And there it is in truth: I disliked him because of his own beauty, because of his grace and elegance and perfection of form, none of which I can ever hope to attain.

"I don't think he liked you the way Bean thinks he does," Niya continues, pulling on her night shift. "But I think he found you the most interesting of us three. Even if I could sew him up in a circle."

Bean climbs into her corner, nestling into the blankets. "And even if I didn't burn the potatoes."

I smother a laugh as Niya blows out the candle, crawling in between us. "He was a clever one," she says, yawning. Bean just snorts. She was not particularly impressed with his gift to her. Mama offered to string the horse on a cord for her as a pendant, and Bean halfheartedly agreed. I suspect that Mama knows as well as I that there is more to the little horse than we can see. I expect Bean will discover its secret in time.

Lying awake now, I think of Stonemane's words before he gave his debt payments. *You should on occasion be kinder to yourself.* The bone knife glows a faint white in the darkness of the room. He picked his gifts well for one who had met us each only briefly. I reach out a hand to touch it, finding the hilt cool and smooth. It was my own thoughts and arguments he turned back to me, calling me by the name I have accepted as my own and branded myself with. A word that cuts deep as bone.

I wonder if it is a word I can cut out of myself, a word I can learn to forget. Perhaps he spoke truly, and I should offer myself some little kindnesses. Perhaps his knife is meant as a token to keep with me, to help me look past my poor clubfoot. And, I think with a smile, something to take with me the next time I walk blindly into danger.

"Warm nights," Niya murmurs, rolling over and taking the sheet with her. Bean grunts in return.

"Pleasant dreams," I whisper back, grateful for the dark of the room and the love of my sisters.

If you enjoyed this story, look for Rae's further adventures in *The Theft of Sunlight*, coming in 2021.

ACKNOWLEDGMENTS

When I first published *Thorn* back in 2012, my acknowledgments were a whopping one paragraph long. I was new to publishing, it was an indie release, and there were just a few incredible people who helped me get that far. Now, with *Thorn*'s re-release from HarperTeen slotted for 2020, I have *so many* people to thank. It is a wonderful thing to realize what a community has come together around sharing Alyrra's story.

First off, to all the readers and reviewers and bloggers who gave *Thorn* wings as an indie release, and to all of you who are reading it and supporting it now, I can only say this: a book is nothing without its readers. Thank you, so much, for allowing me to share *Thorn* with you.

Alyrra would never have found her new home with Harper-Teen had she not first met my agent, Emmanuelle Morgen. I am so grateful to you, Emmanuelle, for reaching out to me after coming across *Thorn* on your own, for believing so deeply in the story you read, and for working to help *Thorn* reach so many more readers. And for always having my back. You're quite frankly amazing.

Many thanks to Emilia Rhodes, for being so intrigued by Emmanuelle's excitement at signing me as to buy your own copy of *Thorn*, fall in love with it, and become my acquiring editor at HarperTeen. Heartfelt gratitude goes to my now-editor, Alice Jerman, for taking on *Thorn* when the chance arose and for helping to take it to a whole new level. I'm also deeply grateful to my editorial director, Erica Sussman, for approving a full new pass with Alice to make sure we got the story right. And to all the other wonderful folks at Harper who have helped make this book a success, from Clare Vaughn, to my awesome marketing team, to all the people whom I've never met who've helped *Thorn* along on its way—thank you all. I couldn't ask for a better team.

Much gratitude to Jenny Zemanek for creating *Thorn*'s final indie cover in all its beauty and licensing her illustrations to Harper so that Thorn could re-release with the same gorgeous signature images on a lovely new background. Your work is pure magic.

I should probably mention about now that *Thorn* underwent a colossal number of drafts (sixteen?!) over nearly seventeen years. There were many, many beta readers who helped out along the way. I owe great thanks to my early beta readers: my mom, my brother, writing circle cronies Nat Kutcher and Janelle White, Rima Dabdoub, and of course my husband, who valiantly read multiple drafts of *Thorn*. I am also deeply indebted to Shy Eager, Charlotte Michel, Anne Hillman, and author-friends A. C. Spahn and W. R. Gingell for your insight and feedback, and to Laurel Garver for your amazing eye to detail. I owe you folks All The Chocolate. If I have left anyone's name off, please forgive me.

As many of you who follow me on Facebook know, naming is the bane of my writerly existence. Thank you to Kellie Marie Smith for Sage's name, and to Shy Eager for Midael's, and Sierra van Winkle for Acorn's. Many thanks to LaLa Caniff for the final forms of "veria" and "verin" and Jacque Lopour for "tarin" and "tarina." I am also grateful to my Facebook author page fans for all your brainstorming that helped me to finally settle on Moonflower's name.

A heartfelt thanks to my friends for your kindness and support, and especially to Stacy Crawford for book-related snack suggestions and a host of playdates for my girls that doubled as focused writing time for me. Those deadlines were a lot easier to meet with your support! Thanks also to Melissa Sasina, for night-time writing sessions when I most needed a little push to keep me going. Friends really do make all the difference.

To the Deer Park and Blue Ash branches of the Public Library of Cincinnati and Hamilton County . . . what can I say? So much of this book was revised beneath your roofs while my girls were at school. Here are to public spaces free to use, to a "writing office" surrounded by books, and to a staff who are straight up fabulous. Libraries are literally the best.

I am, as always, grateful to my family: Mummy, Abba, Anas, Ahmed, Bekah, and my two wonderful girls, Fatima and Khadija. Thank you for always supporting me, for helping me to get my writing time, and for bringing so much love and joy into my life.

Finally, as a person of faith, I am ultimately grateful to God—for granting me the love of writing, a way to share my stories, and the support I need to keep going.

Intisar Khanani

Intisar Khanani grew up a nomad and world traveller. Born in Wisconsin, she has lived in five different US states as well as in Jeddah on the coast of the Red Sea. She currently resides in Cincinnati, Ohio, with her husband and two young daughters. Prior to publishing her novels, Intisar worked as a public health consultant on projects relating to infant mortality and minority health, which was as close as she could get to saving the world. Now she focuses her time on her two passions: raising her family and writing fantasy.

Find out more at booksbyintisar.com or on Twitter, Facebook or Instagram: booksbyintisar

Thank you for choosing a Hot Key book.

If you want to know more about our authors and what we publish, you can find us online.

You can start at our website

www.hotkeybooks.com

And you can also find us on:

We hope to see you soon!